*They found shelter in a warm embrace,
and love in a tender kiss...*

Love Is Welcome Here

"Luke, wait!" Rebecca flew across the room and out the door to the porch. Before he could go down the steps, she grabbed his upper arm. He halted immediately, his muscles tightening at her touch. She marveled at the power she felt in his arm and let her fingers tarry there. Tension radiated from him, an unexpected heat that warmed her from head to toe.

"I don't stay where I'm not wanted." Luke glanced down at her hand, expecting her to remove it. Instead, the pressure of her fingers increased, holding him captive with a delicate strength. The scent of wild roses curled around him, invoking images of flower-garnished prairies, summer sunshine, and blushed skin.

"I want you to stay . . . please."

He had to touch her. Luke lifted his hand, skimming the calloused edge of his thumb back and forth across her bottom lip. She gasped softly at the gentle, unexpected touch and closed her eyes . . .

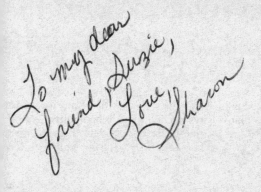

To my dear
friend Suzie,
Love Sharon

COUNTRY KISS

SHARON HARLOW

DIAMOND BOOKS, NEW YORK

This book is a Diamond original edition, and has never been previously published.

COUNTRY KISS

A Diamond Book/published by arrangement with the author

PRINTING HISTORY
Diamond edition/February 1993

All rights reserved.
Copyright © 1993 by Sharon Gillenwater.
Cover appliqué illustration by Kathy Lengyel.
This book may not be reproduced in whole or
in part, by mimeograph or any other means, without
permission. For information address:
The Berkley Publishing Group,
200 Madison Avenue, New York, New York 10016.

ISBN: 1-55773-852-1

Diamond Books are published by The Berkley Publishing Group,
200 Madison Avenue, New York, New York 10016.
The name "DIAMOND" and its logo are trademarks
belonging to Charter Communications, Inc.

PRINTED IN THE UNITED STATES OF AMERICA

10 9 8 7 6 5 4 3 2 1

*To Uncle Walter and Aunt Marie,
and Uncle Bruce and Aunt Zanata. Thank you
for your love over the years, for your
kindness and words of wisdom, and for a
lot of just plain fun.*

*And to Charlotte, dear friend and very
special person. Thank you for sharing your
memories of Grinnell.*

I would like to sincerely thank Ms. Lorna Caulkins, Director of the Stewart Library in Grinnell, Iowa, for her assistance in obtaining background information for this book. The early histories of Poweshiek County were a tremendous help, as were the early business directory listings and the April and May 1882 newspaper ads. The newspaper articles written the week after the tornado were invaluable. I hope I've done your history and your community justice.

∞

Chapter 1

Central Iowa
Mid-April, 1882

"OH, NO! NOT again!" Rebecca Stephens stopped in the hall doorway and stared at the empty kitchen windowsill, one hand holding her new spring bonnet on the top of her head, the other holding a long hatpin poised in midair. "I'll catch that thief yet," she muttered. Jabbing the hatpin into place, she dashed out the back door to the long wooden porch.

Her gaze quickly scanned the yard, from her partially planted garden, past the buggy and horse waiting beside the back steps, to the large red barn, and back to the kitchen window. Nothing seemed out of the ordinary. No footprints marked the path of the intruder; the new spring grass hid any sign of his steps. If he had only come a few days before, the mud left from last week's rain might have shown his direction.

"I hope he didn't get into the other things." She hurried across the porch and down the steps to the buggy. To her relief the items for the church bake sale, four pies and three cakes, had not been touched.

"Two pies in one week." She shook her head, now more curious than angry at the disappearance of her baked goods.

In the eight years she had lived on the farm, the only things that had ever been stolen were some apples and an occasional melon swiped by the neighbor boys on their way to the creek. She knew the boys were not responsible this time because they were still in school. She did not bother to search the grounds. He was probably clear down at the creek by now, and there was no sense in chasing after him.

"Well, at least my thief has good taste." She smiled ruefully, knowing pride was not a worthy trait. Yet, there were two facets of her life in which she allowed herself a little vanity—her cooking and her quilts. Both had taken top honors at the county fair the past three years.

She breathed deeply of the fresh spring air, thankful for the warmth of the sun on her face. It would be a pleasant day to sit outside her father's store and sell pies and cakes. Faint honking drew her gaze upward to a formation of wild geese flying high overhead on their way north. A flock of ducks followed, dropping lower and lower as they approached the large pond on the Neeley farm next to hers. More than a hundred birds landed on the pond, amid a great quacking and fluttering of wings.

"Uncle Wylie and I made it through another winter, Anthony," Rebecca said softly, touching the silver locket that hung about her neck. "He says we should have another good year." Turning abruptly, she buried her grief and loneliness before it had a chance to fully surface. "I'd better hurry, or they'll start the sale without me," she said briskly, talking to no one but herself and the sparrows chattering noisily nearby.

Her steps slowed as she neared the back door, and a smile lit her face. Instead of hanging on its normal nail, the wire egg basket sat conspicuously beside the door, holding the previous day's contributions from her hens. Busy with her baking, gathering the eggs was a chore she had left undone. "Thank you, Mr. Thief."

Rebecca picked up the basket and took it into the kitchen, deciding that "thief" was the wrong title for the person who had taken her pies. It seemed their visitor always repaid them in some way. The first time, he had milked the cow before the hired hand, Jackson, got to the barn. Although he had gathered the eggs this time, from the number in the basket he had helped himself to half a dozen or so. She did not begrudge him the food. There was more than enough to share.

She supposed she should be frightened that someone might be lurking around the farm, and when she looked at it strictly from a safety standpoint, it did bother her. Jackson was out in the field most of the time now, as was Ted Smith, who also worked for them. Jackson lived at the farm so he was there nights, but much of the time during the day, she was alone.

Her uncle Wylie was often in the fields with the men or in town. Even when he was at home, Wylie could not defend her except with a gun. Crippled from a fever when he was a young man, her sixty-year-old uncle was confined to a wheelchair. She knew how to shoot every gun in the house, but when it came right down to it, Rebecca doubted if she would ever be able to pull the trigger against another person.

Jackson and Wylie had first thought the man was sleeping in the barn since the nights were still cold, but they had never found any evidence to support the belief. Neither could they catch him, although Jackson had gone out to the barn in the middle of the night a couple of times. That led to the supposition that their unknown visitor was probably sleeping in the barn across the road at what was now the Northcutt place. Although the land had been leased out, no one had lived there in over four years. The house had been locked up until yesterday, but the barn had been easy access for anyone passing through.

Rebecca placed the basket on the table and checked her appearance in a small mirror that hung by the door. In her earlier haste, the rose pink bonnet had been pinned on crooked. She eyed the cluster of pale pink feathers lying horizontally between the crown and wide brim. The hat was a little jaunty for a widow, but she decided it looked fine. After all, she was only twenty-seven, not yet past her prime.

The remaining box on the kitchen table contained a meal for their new neighbor across the road, Luke Northcutt. Rebecca had not met him but intended to stop by on her way to town and welcome him to the community. She picked up a warm, off-white wool shawl from the back of a kitchen chair and draped it across her shoulders and over her arms. Carrying the box out to the buggy, she placed it in the boot and climbed in.

Her gown was made of rose pink cashmere accented with pale pink embroidery. The silk foundation skirt was covered in front by a draped embroidered apron that was gathered to the back to form a pouf and free-falling drapery. The bodice fit snugly, the pointed waist and bosom adorned with more of the pale embroidery. The neckline came up to the base of her throat and was trimmed with a small collar.

After arranging her skirt carefully to avoid creases and the pies on the floorboard beside her, she picked up the reins and clucked gently to the horse. "Come on, Cinnamon, we have a busy day ahead of us." Rebecca guided the horse and buggy carefully onto the drive, going slowly so the boxes of food would not slide. The lane ran almost a hundred yards along one border of her property before it intersected with the county road.

Some fifty yards down the road toward town, she turned into the Northcutt lane and scanned the field. As expected, her neighbor was already at work, guiding his team as the two draft horses pulled the spring tooth harrow over the broken ground. The powerful horses, one gray and one black, were not quite as large as two-thousand-pound purebred Percherons, but their size and build indicated their lineage was not far removed from the pure blood of one of the French stallions.

The team drew the harrow easily along the ground, making the process look as simple as running a comb through a woman's hair. It broke up the dirt clods and pulled up any remaining grass and weeds, leaving the soil soft, fine, and tangle free.

"Well, he didn't waste any time getting to his crops," she murmured in approval. Rebecca did not stop at the house but passed through the open gate at the edge of the field. She drove along beside the barbed wire fence and parked at the end of the row to wait for him. Wylie had made their neighbor's acquaintance the day before when he was moving in. He had reported that Luke Northcutt was single and seemed nice enough, although his manner was a little gruff.

Rebecca did not normally go about introducing herself to single gentlemen, but since this particular man was their nearest neighbor, she felt no qualms about it. She always made an effort to be on friendly terms with those who lived nearby and saw no reason to treat Mr. Northcutt any differently.

She watched him as he approached, maneuvering his team with an ease of control that spoke of strength and experience. He was not as tall and slim as her Anthony had been, but then few men were. Although he was sitting down, she estimated Mr. Northcutt would be almost a six-footer. His faded, dark gray, wool shirt stretched across wide shoulders, emphasizing his stocky build. As he drew nearer, Rebecca remembered her uncle's description of their neighbor and wondered if the frown darkening his face was his normal expression, or if it was a direct result of her visit.

Anticipation brought a sparkle to her eye. By nature she was warm and caring. She seldom met a person she did not like, and nothing gave her more delight than bringing a smile to the face of someone who so obviously needed it.

Luke Northcutt eyed the finely dressed woman waiting in his field, his frown deepening into a scowl. *Thunderation*! *Two women in one morning. Am I going to be badgered by every old maid and widow woman in Poweshiek County?* He decided that Iowa women set great store by how much land a man owned. Luke was thirty-three years old and until the day before, when he had officially become a property owner, he had not been considered particularly good husband material.

Well, at least this one doesn't look like a crow, he admitted as he got close enough to see her face. She was not the most beautiful woman he had ever seen, but she was more than pretty enough for a man to enjoy looking. His gaze skimmed her face and the honey blond curls tucked up beneath her bonnet, then flicked down her body and back up again. Although she appeared to be slightly below average height, her figure was on the curvy side—not at all like that skinny Mrs. Davis who had stopped by at eight o'clock that morning. He wondered if this woman would gush and carry on like the crow had.

Luke felt a little twinge of guilt. He knew he should not think so unkindly of Mrs. Davis. After all she had left him a vinegar pie. It was his least favorite dessert, but a pie was a pie and the woman meant well.

Stopping the team near her buggy, he held onto the reins as he climbed down from the harrow and walked around in front of the horses. He knew if he left the reins free and dangling, the animals might decide the day's work was done and head for the barn. Already two weeks behind with the planting, he did not have time to chase a runaway team—or to shoot the breeze. The sooner word got around that he was not interested in the ladies, the fewer interruptions he would have. He intended to send this woman back to town with a message for her man-hungry cohorts.

Then she smiled. Her whole face lit up, her cheeks blossoming a delicate shade of pink, her gray-green eyes sparkling like an ocean tidal pool kissed by the morning sun. Luke felt the effects of that smile all the way down to his toes. It was warm and genuine, as if she were actually happy to see him—almost as if she were greeting a friend. Luke had never had a real friend, especially not a female one. He didn't know how to react.

He pulled off his hat and nodded curtly. "Ma'am."

As he ran his fingers through his black hair, brushing it back off his forehead, Rebecca absently noted that he could use a trim. He had not bothered to shave that morning, but the shadow of his beard over the tanned, weathered texture of his skin was strangely appealing. He was no longer scowling, but the deep lines between his dark brows indicated it was an expression he used often. There were no laugh lines around his lips, and Rebecca instinctively knew that the crinkles at the corners of his sky-blue eyes came from squinting at the sun, not from smiles.

She was determined to make him smile.

"Good morning. I'm Rebecca Stephens." She waved a graceful hand toward her farm. "Uncle Wylie and I are your nearest neighbors."

He was taken by surprise. Wylie Montrose had said he lived with his widowed niece, but Luke had not expected her to be so young. "Luke Northcutt. Pleased to meet you, ma'am."

From his clipped reply, Rebecca wasn't really sure that he was. She forged on anyway, enjoying the challenge. "Uncle Wylie and I are having some of the neighbors over to dinner Sunday. We thought it would be nice if you could come, too. It would give you an opportunity to meet them." His frown came back. "Just the Ferguson and Jones families." She pointed to the farms on either side of his. "And Winston Neeley. He lives west of us."

"I'm behind. I need to work on Sunday." He expected to see her lips purse in disapproval. Most folks didn't hold to working on the Lord's day.

Rebecca wondered if his deep, gravelly voice always sounded so gruff, or if he worked at it. She also wondered if he could sing. They could always use another bass in the church choir. She suspected he thought she would chastise him about working on Sunday, or at least about not going to church. Personally, she felt he would benefit far more from the church service, a good meal, and fellowship with his neighbors than he would by working so hard, but she wasn't about to tell him so.

And she knew about farming. Every step—plowing, harrowing, planting, cultivating, harvesting first one crop then another—all had to be done at the right time. Otherwise the harvest would be small or nonexistent. He had more than enough acreage to keep one man busy, especially when he had to tend to all the other chores himself.

She smiled again. "You've made quite a bit of progress already. Did you start yesterday?"

He nodded and glanced at his team to avoid looking at her. The horses were munching on the grass and weeds in the strip between the broken ground and the fence. "Yesterday afternoon. I'm fortunate the tenant plowed last fall before he quit farming. The land is easier than any I've worked. No rocks, except down by the creek."

She looked out across the fields and sighed in contentment. "It is good land, the best in the country, in fact. I love the feel of Iowa soil." Her gaze moved back to him, and she saw that her remark had surprised him. Rebecca laughed. "I'm not always dressed up to go to town, Mr. Northcutt. I have an orchard and a half-acre garden near the house. I enjoy sifting the rich, dark soil through my fingers and picturing all the vegetables and fruit I'll be putting up." She grinned. "But do you know what I do first?"

He felt the corners of his lips lift ever so slightly. That mischievous grin was even harder to resist than her smile. "No ma'am, I wouldn't have any idea." He put his wide-brimmed hat on to shade his eyes from the sun. She did not seem to mind.

"I kneel in the middle of a furrow and plunge my hand and arm down in the dirt as far as it will go, clear up to my shoulder."

"Straight down?" He couldn't imagine this delicate woman getting her hands dirty, much less burying her arm in the soil.

"Well, no, at an angle, but I know I could go farther if my arm was longer. You should try it, Mr. Northcutt. There is just something wonderful about feeling how deep that rich soil runs. It keeps the hope and dreams alive."

Luke briefly pondered her words. He had his dream, one hundred and twenty acres of prime Iowa farmland, but a man always needed to keep hope alive. His mind flickered back in time to the years when there had been no dream, or any hope, either. After a moment he realized she had paused to give him a chance to respond and then had started speaking again.

"You could spare a few hours on Sunday afternoon, couldn't you? Everyone needs a little rest and a good meal."

He studied her face. There was nothing flirtatious or coy in her expression. If she were man-hunting, she certainly did not act the part. He looked down, crushing a dirt clod in front of the buggy wheel with his scuffed boot.

Luke was a solitary man, more at ease with his own company and that of his horses than with humans. But even if a man did not want friends, he needed to be on good terms with his neighbors. When harvest time came, he would be expected to shoulder some of their work. In turn, they would help him bring in his crop. He figured it would be easier to meet them at her house than paying a call to each farm. He knew himself well enough to know he would put off paying those visits until it might be too late.

He slanted a glance up at her. "A good meal, huh?" *Now where in tarnation did that come from?*

"The best in the county." Her eyes twinkled as he frowned again and looked away. *Why, Mr. Northcutt, I do believe you just flirted with me.* She had the notion that he was as surprised by his question as she was. The spark of interest in his eyes had not been just for food, but she doubted that he was aware of it. For the first time in five years, Rebecca felt a little flutter of excitement. Without her realizing it her expression softened. "Please come, Mr. Northcutt."

At her quiet statement he thoughtfully met her gaze. It seemed as if she spoke to him with her eyes, telling him she understood that more than work kept him from accepting the invitation. He could tell she sensed that he would be uncomfortable, but he also knew that she would do everything she could to make the day pleasant. There was gentleness in her eyes and in the softness of her face—a warmth that drew him like a fluffy down quilt on a freezing winter night. He found he couldn't say no.

"All right. What time?"

"Oh, come about one o'clock. I should warn you that both the Fergusons and Joneses have several children so there will be a houseful." He nodded without comment, and she decided to change the subject.

"Someone took a peach pie off my windowsill this morning. I know it isn't any of the boys who live around here because they are still in school. They sometimes sneak apples from the orchard, but they've never taken anything from the house."

Luke's eyes narrowed as he wondered if she thought he had stolen the pie. It wouldn't be the first time he had been accused of such a thing.

"Well, if you come across an empty pie tin, send it my way."

I'll be hanged! She does think I took it! Luke's temper shot up. *You sure had me fooled, lady.*

Rebecca had glanced away and was completely unaware of his reaction. "Two pie tins, actually. One also disappeared four days ago. We haven't seen any sign of anyone around our place, so we thought he might be hiding in your barn at night."

Luke's anger disappeared in a whoosh. He had not realized he had been holding his breath until he released a heavy sigh. At the sound Rebecca looked back at him, a perplexed little frown marring her brow. "I'll keep my eyes open. No one wants a thief around," he said.

"I can't really consider him a thief. Both times, he has done something in repayment. The first time, he milked the cow and left the milk on the back porch. This morning he had gathered the eggs for me since I didn't get around to them last evening. I find myself thinking of him more as a visitor than a thief."

"I expect he has been sleeping in my barn. This morning the stalls were mucked out when I went out to tend the horses. I figured somebody had spent the night there and did some work as payment." It was something he had done more than once himself.

"A young man stayed here for over a month last year, but he was open about it. He worked for the farmers in this part of the county until he had enough money to move on."

"I'll look around in the barn for those pie tins."

"Thank you. By the way, I brought over a pot of soup for you. May I leave it in your kitchen?"

Luke shifted his weight, absently wiping a smudge from the side of her buggy with his hand. He was not used to people showing him kindness. "You didn't need to go to any trouble, Mrs. Stephens," he said without meeting her gaze.

"It was no trouble. I simply added a little more to the kettle. I'll be in town most of the day, so I made a dinner I could leave for Uncle Wylie and Jackson. It's our custom to take something over to a new neighbor. Settling in is hard enough without having to worry about cooking."

"Thank you, ma'am. I appreciate it." He stepped back from the buggy, hoping she would be on her way. Being near Rebecca Stephens had a strange effect on him. She wasn't like the women he had usually been around. They had been hard-working women, mostly farm wives with a passel of kids who hadn't had the time or the inclination to worry about how good they smelled or how nice they looked. She smelled good. And looked even better.

"How about a pie or cake? I have both." She glanced down at the boxes at her feet. When she looked up, she saw the question in his eyes. "I'm on my way to a church bake sale, but I would be happy to leave you some dessert. I always make extra anyway. There are gooseberry, peach, rhubarb, and apple pies; two chocolate cakes and a spice cake."

Any of them would have suited him just fine, but he reminded himself he already had a dessert at the house. After hearing his choices, he disliked the thought of vinegar pie even more. "No thank you, ma'am. Mrs. Davis brought over a pie this morning, so I've got enough sweets for a few days."

Rebecca's eyes began to twinkle and her lips lifted in a tiny smile. "Aggie Davis?"

"I think that was her name. Tall, skinny, with black hair." *And a beak that makes her look like a crow.* "I should have known Aggie would be out here," she murmured.

"Beg your pardon?"

"Nothing. Well . . . maybe I should warn you. Aggie's husband died a few years back. Since then, she's gone after every eligible man in three counties. She will probably be back."

Luke groaned and the frown settled on his face again. "If she's tryin' that hard, you'd think she would have won someone with her cooking by now."

"Aggie means well, but her cooking leaves something to be desired."

Like the rest of her. "How bad is it?"

"I don't like to speak ill of anyone, Mr. Northcutt."

He could tell she meant it. "How bad?"

"She might have gotten a new recipe, but in case she hasn't, take a small bite first. Now I must be on my way. I've taken up enough of your time, and if I don't hurry I'll be late for the sale." She picked up the reins and clucked to Cinnamon, deftly turning the buggy around as the horse moved. "See you Sunday at one o'clock," she called as she drove past him.

Wondering why he had ever thought she might be husband-hunting, Luke pulled off his hat and combed his fingers through his hair as she drove away. He glanced across the road at her farm, and jerked the hat down hard on his head. Her place was twice as big as his. All the farms were laid out in neat squares or rectangles, so it was easy to judge the size.

Her big, two-story white farmhouse gleamed in the morning sun. He doubted if she even cleaned it herself. A huge red barn stood a comfortable distance away, along with a toolshed, corn crib, and the other buildings necessary on a farm. But unlike the ramshackle structures he owned, Rebecca Stephens's place was in excellent condition. Even the hired hand had a separate, small house instead of living with the family as was customary. Everything about the farm and the woman spoke of prosperity.

A lady like her would never take a second look at a man like him. That suited him just fine. Luke was not interested in a wife or even a lover. Either one required some measure of affection and a certain degree of trust. He did not know anything about showing—or even feeling—affection. And he hadn't trusted anyone since he was two years old.

He led the team around in a tight half circle, bringing them to the start of the next section, before walking to his position near the back of the harrow. He stepped up onto the metal frame and eased down on the curved metal seat, settling his feet on the footrests. Tapping the horses with the reins, he started across the next stretch of field. Although he concentrated on keeping the animals and the harrow straight, thoughts of Rebecca Stephens and her visit teased his mind.

"Wild roses," he muttered, thinking of the sweet, delicate fragrance she wore. He had not realized how much he liked the scent. Now, every time he smelled a wild rose, he would be reminded of her. And from what he had been told, the blasted flowers grew all over Iowa.

Rebecca stopped by his front door and walked carefully up onto the porch. One step had part of a board missing and a corner of the porch sagged badly. The house needed a lot of work and a good coat of paint. She carried the pot of soup, a tin of corn bread, and a small crock of fresh butter through the empty front room and into the kitchen. Aggie's pie sat on the table. Rebecca leaned close and took a sniff. It smelled so strongly of vinegar that it made her eyes water.

"Oh, my. It's too bad you don't have anyone around to kiss, Mr. Northcutt, because that pie is going to make your lips pucker," she said with a quiet laugh. She glanced around. Like the front room, the kitchen had been well cleaned. The furniture was sparse and worn, probably secondhand. A table and two straight-backed chairs sat across from the single battered cupboard. A large, cushioned armchair, which sagged a bit to one side, was located near the kitchen stove. Rebecca thought it was sad that he had no woman to look after him and make a home for him.

"You need a friend, Luke. And I'm going to be one whether you want it or not." She returned to the buggy for a cake tin which held one of the chocolate cakes. She placed the cake on the table, wishing she could see his face when he bit into it. That rich delicacy always brought a smile to a man's face. With nothing further to do, she hurried on into Grinnell.

Luke quit early for dinner. Normally he would not have stopped until noon, but he had not had much breakfast. Besides being hungry, he was curious to see just how good a cook his neighbor was. One eyebrow rose when he saw the cake tin on the table, but he was glad she had left it just the same. A little frown touched his face when he thought of how she had gotten him to come to dinner on Sunday. *I bet she usually gets her way.* He carefully pulled off the lid on the tin to check the contents. *Chocolate cake.* His favorite. His frown turned into a smile.

He walked over and lifted the lid off the pot on the stove. His stomach growled as the fragrant aroma teased his nostrils. Picking up a big spoon, he stirred the soup to see what was in it. Big chunks of beef, potatoes, carrots, onions, dried beans, and tomatoes swirled around in a reddish brown stock. He dipped out a spoonful of the broth and meat and raised it to his lips. The liquid was perfectly flavored and still warm. The meat was so tender it practically melted in his mouth. His stomach rumbled again.

Luke did not bother to heat up the soup but quickly dished up a large bowlful. As he sat down at the table, he noticed another covered tin and a small crock sitting beside the cake. With a bite of meat and vegetables in his mouth he opened the tin while he chewed and took out a piece of corn bread. He took a bite as he lifted the crock lid. Smearing a thick layer of creamy butter on the corn bread, he set to his meal like a man half-starved.

Two servings of soup and four pieces of corn bread later, Luke decided he had better stop. Otherwise, all he would have for supper was corn bread and milk. That would be a tasty treat, but a bowl of soup would be much better.

He leaned back in his chair, full and contented. Eyeing the two desserts on the table, he decided he had room for a little more. The chair dropped back down on all four legs when he leaned forward and pushed aside a bit of the meringue on the pie. It looked like a normal vinegar pie, opaque and quivery. But the strong odor of vinegar hid any trace of the usual spicy scent.

"Could it be as bad as she thought it would be?" he wondered out loud, dipping his finger into the filling. He licked the swirl of custard from his finger and instantly choked. His eyes watered and his lips puckered. Jumping up from the table, he ran to the water bucket and gulped down a dipper of water . . . then another.

When he could catch his breath and move his lips, he spat out a few mild cuss words. "What in the devil did she do to that pie?"

Luke took another deep breath and wiped his eyes before collecting a plate and fork from a nearby shelf and going back to the table. Dropping down in the chair, he muttered, "Well, Miz Stephens, you were right about that one. Let's see what yours is like."

He cut a large wedge-shaped piece of the cake, carefully easing it out of the tin onto his plate. The two layers of yellow cake looked moist and light as a feather. The thick chocolate icing on the top and sides was dark, smooth, and creamy. In most respects, it looked like a typical chocolate cake. Slicing off a bite with his fork, he made a closer inspection. Between the layers was a filling of chocolate pudding. He lifted the bite to his mouth, his eyes drifting closed at the first taste. A little sound of satisfaction rose from his throat, and a smile of pure pleasure lit his face. "Yes, ma'am, Rebecca Stephens. You've got braggin' rights."

A picture of her twinkling eyes and smiling face flashed through his mind. Suddenly, he looked forward to dinner on Sunday—and it wasn't just because he was going to get the best meal in the county.

Chapter 2

REBECCA DREW HER buggy to a halt in front of Lansing Dry Goods, the store owned by her father and her brother, Eben. Her mother and another lady from the Congregational Church in Grinnell already had a long table set up on the sidewalk in front of the store. Several pies, cakes, and plates of cookies were spread on the white linen tablecloth. A bouquet of multicolored tulips and greenery purchased from Kelsey's Greenhouse made a pretty centerpiece.

Howard Lansing came over to the side of the buggy and helped her down. "Good morning, daughter." He dropped a kiss on her cheek as he set her on the ground.

"Good morning, Papa." Rebecca slid one arm around his waist and gave him a hug. "I see Mama has everything under control as usual."

Her father chuckled. "Trust Clara to fancy things up." He leaned down near her ear. "The table had a big stain in the middle and nothing would do but to cover it up." He straightened and grinned. "I have to admit the tablecloth and flowers are good merchandising. Your ladies' group should do a brisk business today."

He lifted a box from the buggy floorboard and fussed at Rebecca when she picked up another one from the boot. "Now, Becky, you let me get that. You don't need to be carrying anything so heavy."

"Are you saying my cakes are heavy, Papa?" Rebecca laughed as she carefully stepped up onto the sidewalk and set the box on one end of the table.

"Never, child. Light as a feather. It's the wooden box that's too heavy for a little thing like you."

Rebecca smiled indulgently and let him go back for the other box. It was an old theme. All the men in Rebecca's family were over six feet tall. Her mother, sister, and every female cousin were at least five feet eight. Grandmother Lansing had been barely five feet, and Rebecca took after her, reaching five feet three if she stretched and lifted her heels slightly. Even though she had proven herself as capable as anyone, her family still alternately pampered and teased her.

"Good morning, dear." Clara enveloped her daughter in a hug, then stood back at arm's length. "Aren't you a sight this morning! That color practically makes you glow. We're bound to sell out before noon."

Rebecca glanced down at the rose pink dress. "Well, I figured I'd wear something bright." She looked back up at her mother and grinned. "If you don't attract the customers' attention, you can't sell anything."

Clara rolled her eyes and smiled, helping her daughter take the baked goods out of the boxes. "You've been listening to your father. Don't get me wrong. I'm not complaining. It will be interesting to watch all the eligible men in town make a fuss over my daughter." She waggled a finger at Rebecca. "Don't let them simply come by and flirt. Make sure they buy something."

"Yes, Mama." Rebecca chatted with the other lady for a moment as one of the clerks came out of the store to take Cinnamon and the buggy down to Child and Son Livery Stable. Rebecca thanked him and followed her father into the store.

"Mornin', Shorty." Rebecca's oldest brother, Eben, smiled at her from behind the counter.

"Mornin'. You're looking chipper today."

"Toby's finally over his cold so Amanda and I got a good

night's sleep for the first time in a week. It's a good thing today is sunny and warm. She can turn the younger boys loose outside while Robert is in school. This morning Toby was pestering his mother with questions about everything from what makes sugar sticky to why dogs chase cats."

Rebecca smiled and nodded in understanding. Toby's favorite word of late was "Why?" Eben's boys—Toby, three; Jacob, five; and Robert, eight—were a handful for their mother. They were not bad boys, just bright and full of curiosity. What one of them didn't think of to get into, another one did.

"Will came by the house last night." Rebecca's father absently straightened a stack of sheets on the counter. "He got a job at the *Grinnell Herald*."

"As a reporter?" Rebecca's face shone with happiness. Her youngest brother would be a June graduate from Iowa College which was located in Grinnell. Since his first year at the school, he had worked on the college *News Letter*. He was currently the editor of the twelve-page monthly. Writing was his great love, with gathering the news a close second.

Howard nodded. "He starts part-time today and will go to full-time when he graduates in June. I've never seen that boy more excited."

"Well, he should be. He'll do a good job for them, too." She waited patiently while her father and brother dealt with a few customers. When the store was empty she said casually, "I met our new neighbor, Luke Northcutt, this morning."

"The one that bought the old Prescott place?"

"Yes."

"Single fellow?"

"Yes." A little smile touched Rebecca's lips. She knew what her father was going to say.

"He come calling already?"

"No, I called on him." As Howard leveled her a look, she laughed. "All done in innocence, Papa. I took a pot of soup to a new neighbor and invited him to Sunday dinner. He was already out in the field with the harrow. He's made a good start for just having moved in yesterday."

"What's he like?" asked Eben.

Rebecca thought a minute. "A big gruff bear." At her father's raised eyebrow she continued. "He was nice in a gruff way. I have the feeling he is used to being alone. It took a while to persuade him to come to dinner on Sunday."

"Maybe he has his reasons for not wanting to be around people. Not everyone is like you, little sister."

Rebecca shrugged. "I'm just being neighborly. Besides, he needs friends. Everyone does."

"Rebecca . . ." Her father's pause and the stern note in his voice told her she was going to get a lecture. "I know you mean well, dear, but be careful around this man until Wylie gets better acquainted with him. He is a stranger to these parts. No one knows anything about him. Even a neighbor can be dangerous if he is the wrong kind of man."

"Papa, I'm not a girl anymore," she chided gently.

Howard's face was sober. "No, Rebecca, you're a grown woman and a pretty, wealthy widow to boot. You're a prime candidate for someone looking to improve his lot quickly."

"Papa, I've been a widow for five years. I haven't been hoodwinked yet." She patted his arm.

"She's right, Pa. She's probably lost track of all the gentlemen callers she's sent packing."

"Besides, Uncle Wylie has met him and likes him well enough. He thought it was a good idea to invite him to dinner Sunday. All our closest neighbors will be there."

"Even Winston Neeley?" Eben's eyes twinkled.

"Yes, even Winston. I couldn't very well invite the others without inviting Winston, too."

"Wish I was a little mouse so I could watch what happens when he meets this Northcutt fellow. Poor old Winston is liable to get jealous if you so much as smile at the man."

"Winston has no right to be jealous. He knows I'm not the least bit interested in him and never will be. He hasn't come calling for almost two years now."

"But that doesn't keep him from wishing it was different."

"He has his eye on my land much more than on me. And he's not going to get it." The man had been a thorn in her side ever since Anthony died. He had respected her first year of mourning then started coming by at least once a week to discuss marriage. He never actually courted her in the sense of trying to woo her. He simply stopped by, pointed out the advantages of uniting their two farms and waited for her to agree. For two years Winston seemed to think that if he asked her often enough, she would see the wisdom of his plan.

He was a big, rough, opinionated man with poor manners. The only day she could stand to be around him was on Sunday after he had his Saturday-night bath. The rest of the time, it didn't pay to stand downwind. Finally, one day she met him at the door with a shotgun in hand—unloaded, of course—and told him if he mentioned marriage one more time she was going to fill his hide full of buckshot. Winston had never seen Rebecca angry before and evidently it made quite an impression. He never mentioned marriage again.

"Winston is still liable to get his nose out of joint," said Howard. "He might get obnoxious."

"Luke could whip him," she answered without thinking. Her father raised his dark, expressive eyebrow again. To her surprise, Rebecca felt a blush warm her cheeks. She shrugged nonchalantly. "He's a big man and carries himself well. He looks like he could take care of himself in a fight." Her father had planted a little seed of concern, but she did not intend to let him know it. Luke Northcutt did not look like a man who would let another man insult him. *Or me.* The thought surprised her, making her wonder why she was so certain he would defend her.

"Whoa, Short-stuff. Seems to me you noticed a lot this morning. Do I detect a little interest here?" Although Eben smiled, he watched her closely. She had had numerous suitors over the last few years, but she had never shown any serious interest in any of them, including Ben Crowder, a local banker who was currently favoring her with his attentions.

Rebecca considered his question. In the few minutes

she had spent with Luke, she had felt stirrings she had not known since Anthony died. There had been no spine-tingling excitement, but he made her very aware of herself as a woman—and of him as a man. It was a good feeling.

She looked up at her brother and grinned, her eyes sparkling. "Maybe." Then without another word, she scurried from the store, leaving her father and brother gazing thoughtfully after her.

More women had dropped off their baked goods while she was in the store. When she stepped back out onto the walk, the table was loaded down. In only a few minutes, the customers started arriving. It was almost comical how the single men gravitated to Rebecca's end of the table while most of the women and married men did their business with the other ladies.

One of Rebecca's first customers was Ben Crowder. At thirty-five, Ben was every single woman's dream—and probably a few married women's, too. Handsome, with golden blond hair and hazel eyes, he was sinfully charming and one of the richest men in town. He owned railroad stock and was a partner in Grinnell Savings Bank, which was prosperous and growing. In addition, he had an interest in the Randolph Header Works, which made castings for headers and other machines. One of his pet projects was the fledgling Grinnell Electric Light Company and their plans to better illuminate the streets of the community. He could have his pick of any available woman in the county. It was clear to everyone that he wanted Rebecca Stephens.

"Good morning, Rebecca. You look lovely today."

The intimate way his glance flickered over her should have made her heart flutter. It didn't. Ben's diction was precise and cultured. He had a nice voice and sang tenor in the church choir, but Rebecca unconsciously compared his smooth tones with Luke's deep, rough voice—and found the latter more intriguing.

She gave herself a mental shake and smiled up at him. "Thank you. Are you in the market for something sweet?"

"Yes."

His gaze dropped to her lips, and Rebecca realized she had been unwittingly provocative. She leaned forward, pointing at the various delicacies on the table. "We have a large assortment. Do you prefer pie, cake, or cookies?"

"Anything you made . . . and your company for dinner at Chapin House."

Rebecca had expected the invitation since he had taken her out to eat several times for the noon meal when she was in town. She found that she did not want to go as much as she usually did. *This is nonsense,* she thought. *I always enjoy Ben's company.* She smiled brightly. "I'm sure I can get away for an hour or so." She pointed to a pie directly in front of her. "This one is gooseberry."

Ben smiled and leaned a little closer. "You remembered that I liked gooseberry."

"You like every kind of pie, Ben Crowder," she said with a laugh. "Now, hand over your money and be on your way. I have to help my other customers." She winked playfully at the young man standing behind him.

Surprise and annoyance flashed across Ben's face, but it was quickly replaced with a charming smile. "As you wish, my dear." He placed the money in her hand, three times as much as the price tag on the pie. When she closed her fingers around it, he covered her hand with his own. "Put the change in the coffer." To Rebecca's embarrassment, he made a great show of picking up her hand and kissing the back of it. "I'll see you at noon."

As he turned to go, he shot a dagger glance at the young man behind him, his proprietary warning clear.

"Whew! I think you just got me in hot water, Rebecca." John Davis shook his head and grinned at her. "I'll have to remember that move, though. That was pretty slick the way he kissed your hand."

"Well, don't do it in the middle of Main Street with half the town looking on." Rebecca tried to push her annoyance aside and smiled up at her brother Will's best friend. "I bet I know what you're after."

John's face and ears grew red. "Did Sally make anything?"

"Yes. That tin of shortbread cookies are hers. I'll be sure that she learns you bought them."

"Thanks." He handed her the correct change and picked up the cookies. He had not gone two steps before he stopped to fish out a cookie. He took a bite and flashed Rebecca a grin. "Now I know I'm in love."

If it only was so simple.

Rebecca turned her attention to the friendly folks inspecting the baked goods and soon her good humor was restored. They did a brisk business as fresh items continued to arrive all morning. No one worried about the return of the pans, tins, or plates. It was the custom for the purchasers to take the dishes to the church when they were done with them. The large stone building, which could easily seat the six hundred members as well as two hundred guests, was not hard to find.

During the occasional lull she had a chance to visit with her mother. She told her about meeting Luke and inviting him to dinner. Clara, too, advised caution, then promptly commanded her daughter to pay her a visit Monday morning and tell her all about Luke Northcutt.

Rebecca had the beginning of a headache when Ben picked her up for dinner. She was very aware of the speculative looks people gave them as they strolled down the street to the restaurant. With her hand curled around his forearm, he escorted her in a gentlemanly fashion and was at his charming best. For some strange reason, Rebecca found it irritating. During dinner, he carried the bulk of the conversation, which was unusual. One of the things she liked about Ben was that he cared about her ideas and opinions, and they often had lively discussions.

At the moment she didn't seem to have any ideas or opinions, at least not ones she particularly wanted to voice. She was still irritated by his actions at the bake sale. It was true he had held her hand and even kissed it last week when he came out to visit one evening. But he had made a spectacle of her in town, and she did not appreciate it. Rebecca's reputation was without blemish, and she wanted to keep it that way.

"I embarrassed you earlier." Ben studied her face intently as she nodded. "I'm sorry. It's just that when you winked at that kid . . . well, I was jealous. It's silly, I know, and I apologize." He reached across the table for her hand, but she drew it away before he could touch it. He settled back in his chair as irritation flickered across his face.

"Apology accepted." She toyed with her napkin, trying to understand her feelings. It was difficult to think when her head pounded like a bass drum.

"I'm buying the Snyder place."

Her gaze shot to his. The Snyder house was one of the largest and finest in town. It would easily house a large family, but mostly it was built for entertaining. She had always thought it was a bit elaborate. Yes, it's the type of house he would want, she realized. Something fancy. Something in town. "It's a big house. You'll get lost rambling around by yourself."

"I'm hoping I won't be by myself much longer." The look he gave her was warm and seductive. Although they were tucked away in a quiet corner of the restaurant, out of the view of most of the patrons, Rebecca's face turned red. "I haven't made a secret of the way I feel about you, darling," he said.

"No, you certainly haven't."

"Rebecca, I apologized."

She sighed. "I'm sorry, Ben, I know you did." She rubbed the back of her neck. "I'm afraid I'm not very good company right now. I have a splitting headache. I really think I should go home."

"Of course." He motioned to the waitress for the check. "I'm sorry you aren't feeling well. Why didn't you tell me sooner?"

"I didn't want to spoil our dinner." She looked at him ruefully. "But I guess I did that anyway."

"Don't worry about it." He collected the check from the waitress, paid their bill, and escorted Rebecca down the street toward her father's store. "Do you get these headaches often?"

Rebecca glanced at him sharply. His tone was casual, but

something in the inflection of his voice told her that he was not simply inquiring out of concern for her health. *Ah, Ben, now you realize I'm not perfect.* "Not often. I suspect it is from sitting out on the sidewalk. It was warm in the sun but underneath the awning the breeze was colder than I had anticipated. I'm sure I'll feel better after I rest a bit."

"Well, I hope it goes away soon." They stopped in front of Lansing Dry Goods. "May I come out tomorrow evening? We could play a game of chess or perhaps a game of dominoes with Wylie."

"Not this week, Ben. I'm having company for dinner Sunday, so I'll be wanting to get to bed early. Maybe next week."

"Very well. I'll see you at church." He tipped his hat and walked away. She could tell he had been itching to ask her who was coming for dinner and would have liked an invitation, too. As she went into the store to wait for the clerk to fetch Cinnamon and the buggy from the livery stable, she was suddenly anxious to get back to the farm. Grinnell was not as busy on a weekday as it would be on Saturday, but she still needed the kind of peace and quiet that came from being out in the country.

She thought of Ben Crowder and the busy life he led, of the fine big house he was buying. He was a city man through and through. He would not consider residing in the country; he had said as much several times. If she married him, she would have to give up living at the farm. He would be a good husband and an excellent provider. He was an interesting man, fun to be with, and could be tender and kind.

Love had brought fulfillment and joy to her first marriage, and she often thought that she could settle for nothing less. But at times, when loneliness crept out of its dark corner and threatened to overwhelm her, she wondered if a nice companionable marriage might be enough.

Chapter 3

FOR THE FIRST time in his life, Luke wished he had a white shirt and fancy collar. He had never owned any dress clothes. Ever since the money he earned had started going into his own pocket, he had saved every cent he could. It had taken more years than he cared to count, but he had finally achieved a lifelong dream—to be answerable to no man but himself.

He fastened the top button on his newest flannel work shirt and decided it did not look too bad. The material was soft so it did not hold a lot of wrinkles, and the bright blue stripes went nicely with his eyes.

He took one last look in the wall mirror and decided he could not do much else to improve his appearance. The mirror had been left in the house by the previous owner. It was about two feet tall and a foot wide. A long crack ran diagonally from the top right corner to the bottom left. It distorted the image, making the right side of Luke's face look as if it did not quite match the left.

Grimacing, he leaned a little closer to the mirror, checking the place on his cheek he had nicked shaving. It had quit bleeding, but had left a small scab. He straightened, wishing there had been time on Saturday to go to town for a haircut. The dark curls brushed his collar and kept falling down across his forehead. Normally he would not have cared, but today it made him more self-conscious.

Luke moved toward the door and plucked his hat from the peg on the wall. Looking at the dirt and sweat stains on his comfortable old felt hat, he hooked it back over the peg and stomped out the door. Thirty seconds later, he came back in, picked up a box containing Rebecca's dishes and left again. It was a pleasant, sunny day so he walked over to the Stephens farm instead of riding. By the time he got there, he was as nervous as a cat in a room full of rocking chairs.

When he walked up the steps, surrounded by four of the five dogs that had adopted Rebecca over the years, she opened the door. She had seen him coming up the drive even before the dogs barked at his arrival. She had been watching for him, hurrying to the entry whenever she got a chance, peeking out the window every few minutes for the past quarter hour.

He was not dressed in a Sunday suit, but she liked the way he looked. The color of his shirt intensified the blue of his eyes, making them striking. He still needed a haircut, but when Rebecca noticed the tiny cut on his cheek, she felt a little swell of tenderness. Meeting so many new people probably made him nervous.

He liked the way she looked, not as fancy or polished as the day before. She had been pretty all gussied up, but he was more comfortable with her this way. Her face was flushed from cooking, and her honey blond hair was caught up in a thick, loosely braided twist at the back of her head with a soft fringe of short, gently curled bangs across her forehead.

Her cotton print gown of pale lemon yellow reminded him of the yellow star grass he had spotted the day before in the pasture. He had the feeling that like the lone little plant, which had blossomed earlier than the rest of its clan, Rebecca wanted to hasten the unfolding of spring. A long, white, ruffled apron hid most of her skirt, and a dozen ruffles of tiny white lace going from her bosom to her throat drew his gaze back to her face.

He wondered if she had been watching for him.

"I was just passing by the window and saw you coming up the walkway," she said with a smile.

He felt a surprisingly sharp stab of disappointment. "I decided to walk since it was such a nice day."

For one of the few times in her life, Rebecca felt shy. She dropped her gaze and stepped back from the door so he could enter, telling herself not to be silly.

"I brought back your pot and things. Everything tasted real good." *Come on Northcutt, you can do better than that. Don't be so tongue-tied.* "I think that cake was the best thing I've ever eaten."

She accepted his compliment with a smile and gracious nod. "Thank you." Her eyes filled with mischief. "How was Aggie's pie?"

"Don't ask!" He grimaced. "I sure was glad you warned me about it. I took a tiny taste and almost choked to death. Did she poison her late husband by any chance?"

She laughed and shook her head. "No."

A tiny smile touched the corner of his lips, and Rebecca felt a little surge of triumph. "You can put the box in the kitchen. It's this way." She could easily have carried it herself, but she figured he would object—and she liked talking to him. She glanced down at the box and saw two pie tins sitting on top of the other things. "You found them!"

He set the box on the kitchen table and absently rubbed the back of his ear. "When I got up this morning, they were on my front porch, all washed and clean. I have the feeling the thief knew I was coming over here." He frowned, his expression thoughtful. "He must have overheard you and Wylie talking."

"Or perhaps Uncle Wylie and our hired hand, Jackson, discussed it outside where he could hear."

"I hope so. It's not good to have someone hanging around so close that they can hear your conversations, especially if you haven't seen them."

She nodded in agreement. "Well, I had better get back to my cooking. Uncle Wylie and Jackson are in the parlor. This way."

They left the kitchen, going back down the wide hall that connected it to the front of the house. She showed him into a room off the hallway, to the left of the front door.

Wylie and Jackson were in the middle of their proverbial checker game. She heard Luke's quiet but sharply indrawn breath when he realized Wylie was in a wheelchair. She glanced at him quickly, relieved to see that he instantly hid his shock before Wylie looked up from the checkerboard.

"Glad you could come, Luke." Wylie pushed his chair back from the game table and held out his hand.

Love welled up in her heart as she watched her beloved uncle's smiling face and his big hand reaching out to Luke. Wylie Montrose had reached out to people all his life, even after he was stricken down in his prime. When her father had gone off to fight for the Union, it had been Wylie who held them all together. Even though he couldn't walk, he had looked after the family farm, supervising the work from his buggy. He had looked after their hearts, too, holding frightened children on his lap, telling them stories until they fell asleep. His courage and ability in spite of his physical handicap had given his sister Clara the strength to go on without her man and the children the faith to believe that everything would be all right until Pa came home.

When Rebecca had lost her little son and husband within a few days of each other, Wylie had been there to take over the running of the farm. She had been shattered, without a reason to go on living. The farm could have fallen to ruin for all she cared, but he slowly helped her to see that keeping it in the fine condition in which Anthony had left it was a tribute to his memory. Many were the days and nights those big hands had held hers or stroked her hair in comfort while she knelt beside his chair and wept for her loss. She loved him as much as she loved her own father.

Luke accepted Wylie's offered handshake without his usual reserve. There was something symbolic in those clasped hands, both equally large and capable, and in Wylie's welcoming smile and the one Luke gave him in return. Oh, it was a beautiful smile! Rebecca's heart skipped a beat, and she wished he would bestow one on her, too. She had known a smile would change that rugged face into a thing of beauty.

Wylie sent a quick glance her way, and it struck her that he was doing more than greeting a new neighbor. It was as if he had sized up the man and decided that he was to be more than a friend. He was the one for her.

Startled, she looked at Luke, letting her gaze travel from his clean black hair, across those broad shoulders and arms, down his muscular back, hips, and powerful legs. She wondered how it would feel to have his arms around her, to have him draw her close in the night. Heart pounding, Rebecca quickly excused herself and raced into the kitchen.

Flustered, she picked up the lid on a graniteware pot to check the carrots and promptly burned her fingers. She released it with a small cry, and the mottled gray enameled lid crashed to the floor with a loud clang. Seconds later, Luke was at her side.

"Did you burn yourself?"

"A little." Her face was beet red, and she couldn't seem to catch a breath. Her fingers hurt like the devil.

"Let me see," he said gruffly. Luke picked up her hand and carefully turned it over, resting it in his palm.

She was amazed that such a large man could be so gentle.

"You'll have blisters." He kept her hand in his and splayed his other one across her back, urging her to walk over to the dry sink. "Come over here and put it in cool water."

"I'll just put some butter on it."

"Not yet. Cool it down first." He pumped the iron hand pump that was built into the wooden cabinet, splashing water into the dishpan that sat in the zinc-lined sink. Then he lowered her hand into the water. "Keep it there," he ordered, his gravelly voice going even deeper, sending shivers down her spine.

Rebecca felt like a schoolgirl. Her heart pounded like a runaway horse. The air that had been so fresh and clean only moments before seemed to weigh a ton. When he removed his hand from her back, she silently thanked him. His heat had touched her all the way through her clothes, even her corset. She looked down at the big hand loosely clasped around her wrist and felt infinitely fragile, overwhelmingly feminine. He could snap her bones with a twist of that powerful hand, yet he held her arm as if it were made of the finest, most delicate china.

Luke wondered if she could hear his heart pound. He took a deep breath, intending to clear his head, and filled his nostrils with the faint scent of wild roses. An image of Rebecca sprinkling pink rose petals over a tub of steaming bathwater came to mind. He quickly curbed his imagination before it went too far. He released her hand and stepped back. Being so close to her made him feel both protective and like a big, clumsy oaf.

"How long has your uncle been confined to the wheelchair?" he asked quietly.

"Twenty-five years. He had a slow fever when he was thirty-five that left him paralyzed."

"I didn't have any idea." Luke shook his head. "I never would have guessed from the way he handles the buggy."

"He is a very capable man." Rebecca withdrew her hand from the water. Interestingly, it did feel better. She wondered where he had learned that little trick. She smeared some butter on the blisters for good measure, then turned toward Luke, feeling more relaxed with some distance between them. "Thank you for not saying anything in front of him. He doesn't let on that it bothers him when people make a fuss, but it does."

Luke shrugged. "It would bother me if I were in his place." He picked up the lid and set it on the counter. He glanced around the room and through the open pantry door. He had never seen a kitchen so adequately equipped. Instead of the dasher churn he had used as a child, a metal and wood tabletop model with a hand crank sat on a pantry shelf. Next to it was a large Universal Mixer that looked like a kettle with a crank fastened over the top. He had seen one once in a general store and vaguely remembered it being advertised as capable of doing everything from whipping cream to kneading bread dough.

His gaze skimmed the room, taking in the milk safe, meat safe, pie safe—which evidently she only used after her pies had cooled, since one was sitting on the windowsill at the moment—and an icebox. *An icebox?* Usually that piece of equipment was reserved for town dwellers where ice could be delivered daily. He felt as out of place as a mule in a buggy harness. "Have you had any more missing pies?"

"No, but our visitor did the milking yesterday. He must be mighty fond of milk because the pail was only half full. If this keeps up, I'll have to get another cow just to make butter."

"He gathered the eggs at my place yesterday evening. I suspect he kept a few of them, too. Haven't really had the chickens around long enough to see how much they'll lay. He must be moving back and forth between the two barns."

"Or staying in the woods down by the creek. It looked like someone had taken some hay out of the barn yesterday morning. It's still awfully cold at night. I hate to think of anyone sleeping outside."

"Mrs. Stephens . . ." Luke paused, not sure how to express his concern.

"Please call me Rebecca. Everyone else around here does."

He nodded, a frown settling between his eyebrows. "Rebecca, are you sure you're safe around here? With the hired hands out in the field most of the day, and Jackson sleeping out in his house at night, and with Wylie like he is—now don't take me wrong. I don't mean to slight him. It's just that he would have a hard time protecting you if someone broke in and tried to harm you."

Warmth spread through Rebecca's heart. "Thank you for your concern, Luke." She smiled when he looked uncomfortable. "But I don't think we have anything to worry about. If our visitor had intended to steal anything of value or do us harm, he would have already done so. He wouldn't hang around to gather eggs or do the milking."

"You're right. Still, keep your eyes open." He pushed away from the counter. "I'd better get back to the parlor."

The other families and Winston Neeley arrived some fifteen minutes later. The Fergusons had three boys in their late teens and another one eleven years old. Artie and LuAnn Jones had a seventeen-year-old daughter, Ann Marie, and two younger children, a boy nine and a girl seven. From the moment they were in the same room, the oldest Ferguson boy, Tom, and Ann Marie made eyes at each other.

Rebecca sensed that Luke was uncomfortable. And to her shame, part of it was because she had set an ornate table. Since it was Sunday and they had guests, she had used her finest china and pure white damask tablecloth and napkins. Her family had not always been affluent, but she realized in dismay that she had grown so accustomed to having fine things that she had forgotten how intimidating fancy trappings could be.

But she gave her new neighbor credit. He handled himself well, quietly and surreptitiously observing the others at the table, and quickly learned not to follow Winston's example. When Winston stuffed his napkin in his shirt collar so that it hung over his broad chest and wide stomach, Luke looked relieved and shook out his snowy white linen, apparently intending to follow suit. LuAnn's quiet admonition to her son that the napkin belonged in his lap instantly changed the direction of Luke's movement.

She suspected that he was not at ease around people generally, and this type of situation was even worse. It was almost as if he were on display. As the new man in the circle of friends, he was the center of attention and the odd man out. Even Winston, for all his blunders, was an accepted part of the group. Whenever Luke glanced in her direction, she tried to tell him with her eyes and her smile that he was doing well, that they liked him.

Luke appreciated her kind, encouraging smiles, and her pretending not to notice the mistake he almost made with the napkin. He preferred to either be alone or in such a large group of people that he was swallowed up by the crowd. He had little experience making conversation around a dinner table. And he had never eaten from a bone china plate or been served coffee from a silver coffeepot. He had dined with smaller and larger groups but had seldom been included in the camaraderie. All his life, Luke had been on the outside looking in.

He knew he would get along with Ralph Ferguson. Both he and his wife, Hattie, were down-to-earth, friendly people. He suspected Winston could be as obnoxious as all get out, but for the moment he was nice enough. Anyway, Luke could handle him. Winston forgot himself and cussed a couple of times when the discussion drifted to politics, and right before dessert, he belched loudly, sending the younger children into fits of laughter. The adults, even the women, seemed to take it all in stride.

Artie and LuAnn Jones were cordial but reserved. He knew they were waiting to see what kind of neighbor—and man—he turned out to be. He didn't mind their coolness. In fact, he welcomed it. It was what he was used to, what he understood.

After dinner Tom and Ann Marie went for a walk, while the younger children raced outside to play tag. The men retired to the front porch to smoke or chew while the womenfolk cleaned up. The other two Ferguson boys joined the men. Since Luke was not fond of tobacco in any form, he made certain he sat upwind of the smokers and clear of the spitters' line of fire. They chatted about the planting, assuring Luke that though he had gotten a late start, he could get his timothy and clover in the ground and still have time to prepare the fields and plant corn. They offered Luke first choice of the calves and weanling pigs they would have for sale in the summer.

It was typical farm talk except for the deep thread of optimism running through the conversation. As the discussion continued, Luke was more convinced than ever that he had been right to settle down in Iowa. To hear his neighbors tell it, if a man worked hard and used his brains, he wouldn't go broke. There were some years of drought or flood, but seldom were there two bad years in a row. If a man was careful and put aside all that he could, he could survive the lean years, too.

Ralph slanted a knowing glance at Winston. "I saw Rebecca having lunch yesterday with that slick city feller."

"You mean Ben Crowder?" asked Artie, puffing on his pipe.

Ralph nodded sagely. "Looks to me like things are getting serious." He spat off the end of the porch. "You gonna try your luck again, Win?"

"Naw. A man can't compete against a smooth-talkin' rich feller like that."

So she has a serious suitor. A rich city slicker. Luke wondered why he felt like hitting something.

"Besides, Rebecca set me straight on the subject of matrimony a long time ago," said Winston. He scratched his stomach and spat a wad of tobacco at one of the dogs stretched out for an afternoon nap in the sunshine. His aim was a foot short. The dog raised its head and looked at Winston as if judging his ability to spit farther. After a moment's stare-down between dog and man, the floppy-eared animal dropped its head back to the soft grass and closed its eyes. Winston grinned and announced quietly, "I been thinkin' about hitchin' up with someone else."

"Who?" asked Ralph.

Everyone except Luke sat up a little straighter. He wondered who in their right mind would want to marry a man like Winston. Gazing out across the yard, he counted five dogs in various stages of afternoon rest. He figured Rebecca kept every one of them that came around.

"Aggie Davis."

He must have a death wish, thought Luke in amazement. The other men laughed as Artie voiced an opinion of a similar nature.

Winston cussed proficiently. "I know the woman can't cook." He leaned toward his cronies and said quietly, "But there are other benefits to havin' a wife, and I happen to know she's good at those. If you know what I mean."

"You been taking advantage of that gal, Winston?" asked Wylie, his voice thick with disapproval.

"Heck fire, no. She's as fine and upright as Rebecca, and I ain't sayin' nothin' agin her. I ran into her husband one night in Des Moines, and we found us a bottle. Once his tongue got loosened up a bit, he admitted she was a lousy cook but that she excelled—that's exactly what he said, excelled—in things that made a man not give a hang whether she burned the biscuits or not."

"Well, I'll be," murmured Ralph.

"A woman can always learn to cook," said Winston, leaving it unsaid that a woman did not always learn to like what went on in the marriage bed.

Nobody could think of anything to top Winston's statement, so they simply sat in silence. After a few minutes, Jackson announced solemnly that it was going to rain. It was the first time he had spoken since Luke arrived at the farm before dinner. Luke's gaze narrowed as he first looked at Jackson, then at the clear blue sky. When he glanced at the others, he found them nodding in agreement.

"How do you know?" he finally asked.

"Rheumatism."

Luke waited for Jackson to explain further, but the man simply took a long drag on his cigar and watched a flock of sandhill cranes fly high overhead. The birds flew northward in a long sweeping circle.

"By morning," Jackson intoned without moving a muscle.

Wylie chuckled at Luke's frown. "Jackson hurt his knee three or four years ago, and whenever a storm is heading our way, it acts up. He can practically pinpoint what time it will hit by how bad his knee hurts."

"Ain't ever been wrong," said Ralph.

"Well, in that case, I'd better be going. I need to get more work done if we're in for a storm." He stood, walking into the house. The women had cleaned the kitchen and settled in the parlor. Rebecca was sitting in her rocker, piecing a flower garden quilt while she visited. She looked up when Luke hesitantly stepped into the room. "I'm going to head on home now, Mrs. Stephens. Jackson says there's a storm coming."

"He's usually right." Rebecca put her needlework on the table beside her and rose, walking over to Luke's side.

"It was nice to meet you, ladies." He nodded to the women. "Thank you for the fine meal." He included all the women in his expression of gratitude since each one had brought a dish. "It must have been the best in the county." He flashed Rebecca a smile.

When her heart fluttered and filled with happiness, she thought she must be a foolish woman to be so thrilled. "I'll see you to the door."

Luke stared at her for a moment. Her eyes sparkled, and her face shone with pleasure. *If a compliment and a smile makes her look like that, I'll have to do both more often.* Then he called himself an idiot for thinking she really cared about what he thought.

When they reached the door, she said, "If you happen to see our visitor, please tell him I would be glad to give him a meal or two. Milk, eggs, and pie aren't a very nourishing diet."

Luke had seen the tramps' marks carved in the fence post where her lane connected with the county road. One sign, a simple circle with an "x" in the center, indicated a person could always get a meal at this house. He had learned about the mark when he was just a boy. Several times it and the fulfillment of its promise had been all that kept him from starvation.

"You never turn anyone away, do you?" he asked quietly, remembering the scrawled picture of a cat on her fence. It was the tramps' sign for kindhearted lady. Thinking of the ragtag collection of dogs in the yard, he knew she never turned anything away.

"No."

"You feed every tramp that comes by?"

"If they find their way to my door, I'll feed them."

"Oh, they'll find their way here without any trouble. They can tell you're good for a handout." His tone and expression were tinged with sarcasm.

"What do you mean?"

"There's a couple of marks down on the fence post by the road, probably put there by the first tramp who ever had a free meal here. They wouldn't mean much to most people, but anyone who's been roaming for a while will know a softhearted woman lives here and that they can get food."

How long did you roam, Luke? She felt a tug on her heart.

"And they always will, as long as I have a bite to share."

"Why?"

"The Bible tells us to feed the hungry."

"Even if they don't repay you with work?"

"It wouldn't be a gift of Christian love if I expected repayment."

His gaze narrowed and his voice dropped low and quiet. "And you believe in Christian love?"

"I believe in many kinds of love, Luke," she said with equal quietness. "The love of God and Jesus, the love of a husband and wife, the love of parents for their children . . ." She halted at the stark pain in his eyes.

"Then you're a fool, Rebecca, because it's all a lie." He turned abruptly and walked out the door, not giving her a chance to answer.

Chapter 4

"HE DOESN'T SMOKE or chew, and eats his vegetables."
Rebecca smiled. "In fact, he had two helpings of everything, including carrots and turnips." She paused, eyeing
the embroidery stitches in the elaborate parlor quilt she
and her mother were making. Luke had not taken second
helpings of anything until the other men did. Even then,
she had to invite him to take more. It was almost as if he
expected someone to reprimand him for eating too much.

And as hard as that man worked, he needed to eat. He
had gone to the field as soon as he left her place—she
had looked. When she had looked over at his place shortly
before dark, he was still at it. Jackson had been right about
the rain on Sunday night. It would have washed away most
of the timothy Luke had planted on Saturday if he had not
run the harrow over it Sunday afternoon and covered up the
seed. As it was, Wylie said he hadn't been able to get it all
covered and a couple of acres would have to be replanted.

"Is he as reticent as when you first met?"

"He shared in the conversation, although he seldom ini-
tiated the discussion. He may have opened up more when
he was out on the porch with the men."

Silent for a moment, Clara concentrated on a difficult
stitch in the panel she was piecing together. The Japanese

Fan quilt, made of silk, velvet, and satin, was little more than a thin throw destined to grace the back of the piano. It had no batting for warmth or actual quilting and was meant only to please the eye, not warm the body. Each section was made up of narrow, multicolored strips forming an open fan and was accented with intricate embroidery stitches. "Was his manner still gruff?"

"Not always." Rebecca looked down at the small blisters on the index and middle fingers of her left hand. "He can be quite gentle," she said softly.

Clara's needle halted as she glanced at her daughter. "Oh?"

"I burned my fingers right after he arrived, and he doctored them for me." As her mother's gaze settled on her hand, she knew what she was thinking. "Yes, I could have tended to them myself. I was reaching for the butter, but he insisted I soak them in cold water first. It took away much of the pain."

"It makes sense." Clara went back to her work but noticed that Rebecca's fingers were still idle. She said nothing, not certain if her daughter was thinking of Luke, or if her thoughts had traveled farther into the past. Rebecca's husband, Anthony, had been an unusually gentle man in regard to his wife. She had never heard Anthony speak an unkind or angry word to Rebecca. They had shared a very special love. Maybe too special, thought Clara. It would be hard to find another husband or another love to equal it.

"He has been so badly hurt that he doesn't believe in love," murmured Rebecca.

As Clara's head snapped up, she pricked her finger. "Ouch!" She sucked her fingertip for a second, then frowned slightly at her daughter. "How do you know?"

"He said it was a lie."

"You've seen the man twice, and you've already discussed love?"

"We were talking about tramps and Christian love and charity." Rebecca's cheeks turned pink. "I told him I believed in many kinds of love. I mentioned the most common ones—husband and wife, parents and children.

But he called me a fool and said it was all a lie. Mama, there was such pain in his eyes. It made me want to weep."

"Affection is not always returned, my dear. Perhaps he has been disappointed in love or even in marriage. Or maybe he was orphaned as a boy. It happened so much during the war."

"I wish I could help him some way." Rebecca's voice was sad and wistful at the same time.

Maybe Wylie's right, thought Clara. Her brother had stopped by earlier in the day to share his belief that a match was in the making and that he approved of it. Since she had never met Luke Northcutt, she was not so quick to accept the idea.

"He's not a stray puppy, Becky."

"I know that."

Clara was not surprised at her daughter's mild irritation. She probably would have reacted the same way. "All I'm saying, dear, is that it will take more than feeding him and being kind to him to bring him contentment."

"I could scratch behind his ears," Rebecca said with a grin.

Clara laughed at her oldest daughter's audacity. "And get more than you bargained for, if you're not careful."

That might be nice, thought Rebecca. A little tingle of excitement raced through her. She picked up her needlework and lowered her head to hide her face from her mother's sharp eyes.

"Have you seen Ben since Sunday? He made quite a point to sit with you at church." Clara returned to her embroidery.

"No. His father is ill, and he left for Chicago Sunday afternoon. He was late for church because he was packing for the trip."

"And he made sure he saw you so he could tell you he was leaving. That was thoughtful. How long does he expect to be gone?"

"Probably a couple of weeks. His father had a mild heart attack. The doctor has assured the family that he will be fine as long as he slows down a bit, but Ben wanted to make certain himself. He is very close to his father and felt his presence would help him to rest like he is supposed to."

"I assume you know he bought the Snyder house."

"He told me he was buying it."

"There's a lot of speculation going around as to who might share that home with him. Has he said anything to you?"

Nothing like being blunt, Mother. "He didn't propose, if that's what you mean." Rebecca did not like to keep things from her mother; she was her dearest friend. "But I think he has it in mind. He said he would come out to see me as soon as he got back. I have the feeling he won't be calling just to ask about the weather."

"And will you accept?"

Rebecca's fingers halted once again as she gazed across the room, seeing none of the ornate Victorian clutter that filled every nook and cranny. "I don't know." Could she be happy with Ben? She pictured his blond hair and handsome, smiling face, mentally tallying his many good points. Any woman with a lick of sense would jump at the chance to be his wife. Because she hesitated, she wasn't sure she had any sense at all.

Another image filled her mind—a man with hair as dark as night and eyes the color of the summer sky, a man whose creased brow bore the burdens of his life, and whose eyes revealed an abyss of pain. The memory stirred such powerful compassion in her heart that she almost gasped out loud. *He needs someone so much.*

Ben Crowder didn't need anybody. He might want her. He might even be halfway in love with her . . . but he didn't need her.

"You should marry again, Becky dear. It's been five years since Anthony and little Michael died. You're too young to live your life alone. Take your time and make your judgments carefully but don't wait until you are too old to have more children. There are plenty of men interested in you."

"But I'm not interested in any of them."

"Don't dismiss Ben too quickly. You might regret it later."

"Do you think I should marry him?" Rebecca knew her parents liked the man, but they had never attempted to sway her one way or the other with any of her suitors.

"If he is the one who can make you happy, I would be pleased to have him for a son-in-law. But the choice of your husband is up to you alone. You're the one who has to live with him day in and day out, cook his meals, wash his clothes, share his bed. We will welcome any man you choose because we know you will do so with care."

"Thank you, Mama." Rebecca was silent as she resumed the task at hand.

Clara deftly changed the subject, prattling on about Will's new job and some new drapery material at her husband's store. She knew her children well, respecting and appreciating the talents and personalities of each one. Of her five offspring, she worried the most about Rebecca. She was a very capable and intelligent young woman, steadfast in her beliefs, and compassionate from the very depths of her soul. That compassion had left more than a few sprinkles of gray in Clara's hair.

As a child, Rebecca had given away her school lunches so often to those of meager means that Clara took to sending extra so her own child would not go hungry. As an adult, hardly a week went by that she did not take an overflowing basket of food to someone who was sick or had fallen on hard times.

The girl had given away more clothes than Clara could remember and not always just her own. She smiled inwardly, remembering several times she had had to stop Rebecca from handing out Eben's outgrown clothes, firmly reminding her that there were other Lansing boys who could make good use of them.

Rebecca had learned to piece patchwork patterns when she was ten and to quilt by the time she was twelve. Her creations were seldom of silk and velvet, merely decorations for an affluent home. Her beautiful coverlets no longer came from the scrap bag but were made of the finest cotton material and filled with thick cotton batting. Even as a young woman dreaming of marriage, one out of every two quilts she made went into an old trunk she had dragged down from the attic. They were sent to orphanages, hospitals, old soldier's homes—to anyone who had a need. For the last several years, with her own linen presses well stocked, each new one she made was given away.

Clara worried that Rebecca would mistake compassion for love. It was one thing to want to bring happiness to someone—it would be another to spend a lifetime with a man who had no love to give. She sighed softly. There would be more prayers than normal winging their way heavenward in the days ahead.

Rebecca left her mother's around four, stopping by the Shirland Nursery to select two more apple trees and a plum tree for her orchard, and mulled over buying some evergreen shrubs for the side yard. Unable to decide which ones she liked best, she left that task for another time. After a stop at Kimball and Merrill in the Opera House Block for a new cane doormat, she dropped by her father's store for a brief visit and wound up taking home three pair of fancy striped hose and a piece of gingham plaid for a new everyday dress. The stockings were on sale at three pairs for twenty-five cents, but as usual, her father would not take her money for the hose or the fabric.

A beautiful Turkish rug caught her eye at Kimball and Merrill, and she spent the drive home mentally redecorating the parlor. Her thoughts of carpet and rearranging the furniture receded to a corner of her mind when she drove past Luke's place. Although it was near dusk, he was hard at work in the field.

He drifted through her thoughts for most of the evening and during the following days. On Tuesday, like every Tuesday for years, Ted Smith's wife, Ellen, came out from town to help with the wash. Usually Ellen also came on Wednesday to iron and Friday to clean the house. She had worked for Anthony before he married Rebecca, and he had insisted they keep her on a part-time basis. He had been well off enough to make Rebecca's workload lighter, and Ellen and Ted needed the money. Rebecca considered herself spoiled, but since she was not particularly fond of cleaning house, and doing the laundry was an all-day chore if she did it alone, she gladly paid for the help.

Besides her normal chores, Rebecca spent several hours almost every day that week and into the next working in her yard and garden. As her father and uncle had done before her, she faithfully followed the *Old Farmer's Almanac* for the proper time to plant. The onion sets, beets, carrots, parsnips, and peas had gone into the ground in March.

According to the *Almanac,* almost everything else was to be planted in April. Since potatoes were underground crops, they were planted during the dark of the moon, from the day after it was full until the day before it was new again. Thus, they had been planted very early in the month.

Plants, both vegetable and flowering, that bore their crop above the ground were to be planted in the light of the moon, between the day the moon was new until the day it was full. This meant that more than half of her garden, as well as most of her flowers, had to be planted within a fairly short time. Tomatoes, cucumbers, muskmelons, squash, and two rows of beans went in first, as well as the sweet peas and nasturtiums in her front yard.

No matter what the task, her future was not far from her mind. Even as she pondered the possibility of marriage to Ben, Luke shadowed her thoughts. She would suddenly remember his smile, the gentleness of his touch as he held her hand in the water, or the way he had unconsciously flirted with her the morning they met. She would hear his deep voice and see his frown and wonder what had made him so gruff. From her garden plot, she saw him diligently working in his fields day after day and her respect for him grew.

Swirled in with the other thoughts were memories of Anthony and the love they shared. She did not think of that love in the past tense, for she still cared for him as much as she ever did. No one could take his place. She was not sure there was room in her heart for another such love.

"Anthony, I'm so confused," she muttered as she walked out to the garden Thursday morning. Ben had been gone for a week and a half, and she was no more certain of her

feelings than when he had left. She touched the locket that
nestled against her heart beneath the bodice of her work
dress. "I know you would want me to remarry, but I can't
help feeling disloyal to you every time I think of Luke
or Ben."

Rebecca stopped at the edge of her garden and rested her
hands on her hips in disgust. She had spent over an hour
the day before tying up the lines for her pole beans. More
than half of the string was gone. As she glanced around, her
irritation dissolved. Every inch around the lacy green carrot
tops had been weeded. Checking closer, she found that all
of the tiny vegetables that had been planted in March had
been carefully weeded. The unwanted intruders had been
left in a wilted green pile at the end of a furrow.

She quickly looked around the small pile for footprints, but
the dirt had been brushed with a branch, blurring any sign the
mysterious gardener might have left. Rebecca walked down
the furrows, but they had been brushed, too. Here and there,
the branch had not been swept back and forth with quite as
much care, and the ground was compressed as if a person
had scooted along on his knees. The depression was vague,
but it appeared their visitor was not a heavy man.

"There!" She stopped suddenly, peering down at the footprint left in the soft dirt, and measured her shoe against it.
The indentation was less than an inch longer than her own,
and Rebecca had a small foot. "Well, Mr. Gardener, thank
you for pulling the weeds," she called loudly, just in case
he lingered near the barn or in the orchard. "I'd be happy to
hire you if you need the work." She turned around slowly,
her gaze scanning the farm yard, but no one stepped out of
hiding. "At least let me give you a good meal."

To her disappointment the visitor did not show himself.
She was still excited. Now, she knew a little more about
him. Not only could he tell a weed from a carrot top, but
he wasn't averse to hard work, either. And, he was not a
large man. At least he had small feet and was probably
thin. A tiny frown touched her brow. That really didn't
tell her much. He could be young, old, or somewhere in-
between.

"Oh, botheration." Rebecca stared at the garden for a minute. Suddenly, she didn't want to think about anything serious—not marriage, or living her life alone, or the needy soul lurking around her farm, or even raising a garden. She wanted to do something totally frivolous, something just for herself.

"I do believe I need to buy another ball of string." Grinning, she turned back toward the house with a spring in her step. "And a new rug for the parlor."

THAT AFTERNOON WYLIE ran into Luke at Barnes and Sons Blacksmith Shop. Charlie, one of Luke's work horses, had thrown a shoe. Wylie had stopped by to check on a plow which was being repaired. Luke waited outside the shop with Wylie while the smithie replaced the horseshoe.

"Looks like you're making progress in your fields. Did you get your hay sown?" asked Wylie.

Luke nodded and rested his hand on the side of the buggy. "Finished the timothy last week and put in the last of the clover on Tuesday." He glanced up at the dark, threatening clouds and frowned. "Hope I don't have to do it over."

"Feels like we might get a little snow." Wylie grinned at Luke. "Tired of your own cooking?"

Luke chuckled. "I'm always tired of my own cooking."

"Why don't you come over for supper tonight?"

"I wouldn't want to put Rebecca to any trouble." After calling her a fool and storming out of her house he doubted if she would let him in the door. If she did, she might throw the skillet at him.

"It's never any trouble for that little gal to hustle up more food, and I could use the company. Jackson hardly ever says anything except 'pass the biscuits,' and sometimes it seems like Becky and I run out of things to talk about. She's been kind of quiet the last week or so. Guess she's got a lot on her mind."

Luke glanced at him, his expression questioning.

"I 'spect that Crowder fellow is going to pop the question soon." Wylie watched Luke's face closely, noting the twitch in his jaw as his muscles tightened.

"From what I hear, he's a good catch."

"Maybe." Wylie's tone indicated he wasn't so sure.

A fierce scowl settled on Luke's face. "You think he might hurt Rebecca?"

Wylie hid his smile. *So you are interested.* "I don't think he'd ever lay a hand on her. And he'd provide a good home for her, there's no doubt."

"But?"

"But I don't think he can make her happy. It will be hard to follow a man like Anthony Stephens." Wylie paused. Luke's closed expression hid any emotion. "There was something real special between those two. Most folks count themselves lucky if they find love once in a lifetime. They're usually willing to settle for less the second time around."

"Is she looking for a husband?" The thought troubled Luke, and he didn't know why. It shouldn't matter if she were interested in Ben Crowder or anybody else. He had no intention of taking a wife, even if his thoughts and dreams had been plagued all week with laughing gray green eyes, honey blond curls, and the soft fragrance of roses.

Wylie shrugged. "She's lonely and has a lot of caring inside her. It just about destroyed that gal to have her husband and little boy die within two days of each other. I thought for a while she might lose her mind."

A sharp, burning pain shot through Luke's chest. His mother's words rang in his ears, words spoken as she wrapped her stillborn daughter's cold body for burial. He had tried to offer comfort, but his mother had merely shrugged. *Just one less mouth to feed. It's too bad all the other brats lived.*

Luke had been eleven at the time, moving from one farm job to another. He had walked five miles out of the way to take his hard-earned money to his pa. He arrived in time for the funeral—if it could be called a funeral. There was no preacher to say words over the babe because his pa had not wanted to trouble himself to go to town. His old man had expended little effort in digging the grave and got angry when Luke made him wait while he dug the hole deeper. Luke left the minute the child was buried, going south when he was supposed to go north. He walked away and never went back.

Wylie's sad eyes misted over. "Sometimes I still hear her crying in the night."

I believe in many kinds of love, Luke . . . the love of a husband and wife . . . of parents for their children . . . It wasn't fair for someone like Rebecca to lose her only child, and the man who could give her more. *She still grieves for them.* He wondered what it would be like to have someone care whether he lived or died.

"How did they die?"

"Pneumonia. We had an outbreak of influenza. Becky got it first. About the time she was out of danger, little Michael caught it. Anthony rode to town through a raging blizzard for the doctor. Two days later, he took sick. Practically everyone in the county was laid up, and the snow was over three feet deep. Some of the drifts reached the top of the windows."

"She was all alone?" asked Luke, his voice rough.

Wylie nodded. "Jackson had gone down to Texas for the winter to visit his kin. Our whole family and all the neighbors were sick. Eben lost his firstborn then, too. Winston Neeley lost both parents, and Hattie Ferguson and her boys almost died. There was no one to check on Rebecca and Anthony, even if they could have gotten through the snow."

Luke closed his eyes against the pain. *If this is compassion, Lord, I don't want it!*

"Becky could barely stand on two feet, but she did what she could for them. The boy went first." Wylie wiped a tear from his eye. "She wrapped him in his little quilt and a piece of oilcloth and buried him in the snow by the back porch. Anthony died two nights later. Her brother Tobias was able to get through to them the next morning."

Luke had trouble getting enough air. A pain, unlike any he had ever known, constricted his heart. To think of her facing their deaths alone was almost more than he could bear. Gentle, kind, Rebecca. *No, I won't care! It only brings pain! There's no such thing as love.*

Rebecca's face filled his mind, her eyes serene and her sweet countenance angelic as she quietly declared her belief in love.

Understanding, like the swift and sure thrust of a mighty sword, filled his soul. He was the one who believed a lie.

Chapter 5

"BETTER FRY UP a few more potatoes, Becky. I invited Luke to supper." Wylie rolled his wheelchair through the back door.

"No!" Rebecca whirled away from the cabinet where she was slicing salt pork, knife in hand. "I don't want him here . . ." Her voice trailed off as Luke followed Wylie into the kitchen. "Tonight," she added softly, looking at Luke's thunderous expression.

Throwing her a scathing glare, he did an about-face and stomped out the kitchen door.

"Luke, wait!" Rebecca tossed the knife on the counter and flew across the room and out the door to the porch. Before he could go down the steps, she grabbed his upper arm. He halted immediately, his muscles tightening at her touch. She marveled at the power she felt in his arm and let her fingers tarry there. Tension radiated from him, an unexpected heat that warmed her from head to toe. A delicious weakness stole over her, leaving her amazed and a little shaken.

"I don't stay where I'm not wanted." Luke glanced down at her hand, expecting her to remove it. Instead, the pressure of her fingers increased, holding him captive with a delicate strength. The scent of wild roses curled around him, invoking images of flower-garnished prairies, summer sunshine, and blushed skin.

"I want you to stay . . . please."

Her voice held a husky note that Luke had not heard
before, and he wondered if she was as affected by their
closeness and her touch as he was. "I don't want to put
you out," he said stubbornly, not looking at her.

"It's no trouble." She moved her hand away, her fingers
lingering on his arm for a heartbeat.

Luke drew a sharp breath. Had she intentionally caressed
his arm or was it an accident? His eyes narrowed as he
looked at her face. She quickly glanced away, not meeting
his gaze. Her cheeks were rosy, and she appeared flustered
and shy. *Rebecca, shy?* He found it hard to believe, yet when
she nervously plucked a bit of salt pork from her apron and
flicked it out on the grass, his heart skipped a beat. *I want
you to stay . . .*

He had to touch her. Luke lifted his hand, skimming the
callused edge of his thumb back and forth across her bottom
lip. She gasped softly at the gentle, unexpected touch and
closed her eyes. "Why didn't you want me here, Rebecca?"
he asked quietly, lowering his hand to his side.

Her eyelids fluttered open, and she looked up at him. "I'm
not exactly in any condition to receive company. My hair is
too damp to put up, and I'm wearing the oldest dress I own."
Her cheeks flooded with color once again, and she glanced
down, wiggling her bare toes. "I'm not even wearing any
shoes," she whispered.

Until that moment, he had paid little attention to how she
looked. He had been too mad to care. Now, as his gaze slid
over her, he understood what she meant. Her glistening,
honey blond hair fell around her in soft waves, the golden
tips of the long locks brushing her skirt well below her hips.
Her faded, light blue calico dress was made in the wrapper
style with a loose, comfortable bodice and full gathered
skirt. The edge of the small round collar lay at the base
of her throat, and a worn belt made of the same material
was tied around her waist. It was the kind of dress women
favored at home because it did not hamper their movements.
And it didn't require a corset.

Luke swallowed hard, focusing for a moment on the neatly trimmed toenails that peeked out from under her skirt. Slowly he brought his gaze back up to her face. He looked into her eyes, discovering that up close, flecks of blue, brown, and gold sprinkled the gray green.

He glanced at her hair, aching to bury his fingers in it. "You washed your hair today." His deep voice was like thunder rumbling off in the distance.

She nodded and smiled self-consciously. "I was playing in the dirt out in the field, and O. P. knocked me over."

"O. P.?" A faint smile touched his lips.

"Overgrown Puppy, the big black short-haired one. He doesn't realize he is full grown and should act like an adult. I was sitting in a furrow out in the field, sifting the dirt through my fingers when he jumped on me. By the time I could get up, I was so filthy I needed a bath and to wash my hair."

Pink rose petals floating on steaming water . . . flowing honey-colored hair glistening in the lamplight, shifting to reveal a glimpse of a creamy shoulder . . .

"No, you're not dressed for company." *But for a locked door and a long night of lovin'.* In a far corner of his mind, Luke wondered when he had begun to think of sex as making love. He curled his fingers into his palms to keep from touching her again. "But you look pretty anyway." *Beautiful.*

"I wasn't fishing for a compliment, Luke."

"I wouldn't have given you one if you were."

"Then I thank you." She stepped back. "Please stay for supper." When he nodded, she flashed him a beaming smile.

Wylie's voice came booming from inside the house. "What in tarnation?"

Rebecca rolled her eyes. "I forgot about the parlor." She turned away, hurrying back into the kitchen.

"What's wrong with it?" Luke slowly followed her, admiring the gentle sway of her hips.

"There's no furniture in it." She grinned at him over her shoulder. "You'll have to move a chair if you want to sit down."

They stepped out into the hallway. At the far end of it, Wylie craned his neck, trying to see into the parlor. Rebecca's rocking chair blocked his way into the room. "What have you been up to, gal?"

"I bought a new rug, Uncle." Rebecca hurried past him. Taking hold of the heavy walnut rocker, she began to drag it through the door into the parlor. Seconds later Luke's hand clamped down on her shoulder, firmly bringing her to a halt.

"Where do you want it?"

"Anywhere for now." She moved aside, admiring the way he effortlessly lifted the rocker and carried it into the room. He sat it near the small wood-burning stove.

Wylie let out a long, low whistle as he rolled his wheelchair through the doorway. "When did you decide to buy a new rug?"

"This morning." She cringed inwardly at Wylie's look of disbelief. "I saw it at Kimball and Merrill's on Monday. The more I thought about it, the more I decided I wanted it. The other one was looking a bit worn for parlor use. The carpet men carried it up to the spare bedroom for me."

To avoid his thoughtful gaze, she turned her attention to the rug. The broad center pattern was an oriental motif of cream, red, and gold. The first of the three borders framing it contained red, orange, gold, and cream flowers on a blue background. The next border, which was wider, had a light brown background with leaves in fall colors. The blue outer border matched the first one. "Do you like it?"

"Yep, it's pretty." A tiny smile touched his face. *Don't look like you're planning on moving to town anytime soon, Becky gal.* "Haul in a chair for yourself, Luke, and we'll visit a spell while Becky finishes supper."

It took a moment for Wylie's words to sink in. Luke was engrossed in watching Rebecca's bare feet. A smile tugged at his lips as her toes curled and uncurled in the thick, soft carpet. Every so often, she would slide one foot back and forth over the plush pile. He was positive she didn't even realize she was doing it. Now he understood why she was running around in bare feet on an April evening.

"Oh! The potatoes!" Rebecca sailed from the room, grumbling all the way down the hall about interruptions that made a woman burn dinner.

Wylie and Luke shared a grin before Luke removed his hat and coat and walked to the entryway. After hanging them on the ornate walnut hall tree, he wandered down the hall, taking a little side trip to more closely inspect the bathroom before looking for the rest of the furniture.

He had seen other bathrooms, of course, but this was the first one he had seen in a farmhouse. It was not completely modern because it did not have a sink; family members and guests alike still washed up before dinner at a washstand in the kitchen, using hot water from the cook stove.

The elliptically shaped porcelain-covered iron tub had a wooden rim around the top which served as a seat. Hot and cold water was piped to the tub with the hot water coming from a water heater sitting nearby. He held his hand near the tank. It was cold. He expected they only fired up the heater when someone wanted to take a bath.

A network of pulleys, ropes, and bars hanging from the ceiling over the tub and toilet gave testimony to the main reason the house had an indoor water closet and built-in bathtub. Although Luke was certain Rebecca used the facility, it had been built primarily for Wylie.

Luke found the rest of the parlor furniture crammed in the dining room. He paused to study the parlor suite. The sofa and chairs were made of walnut, with padded seats and backs upholstered in red plush velvet. Luke had an appreciation for fine craftsmanship. He stopped behind the gentleman's chair and ran his fingers along the smooth curved wooden frame, which was called a finger roll, from the padding on the arm up to the cluster of fruit carved in the crest.

One of his most valued possessions was a book of drawings and descriptions of different kinds of furniture. On his earlier visit, he had recognized the furniture in both the parlor and dining room as being Louis XV. It was a style that had reached the height of popularity some twenty years before. It struck Luke odd that Rebecca would have such a modern kitchen—and that fancy bathroom—and have such old-fashioned furniture in the rest of the house. He glanced over at the pictures sitting temporarily on the sideboard. Her husband had been quite a bit older, so he supposed the furniture had belonged to him.

He carried the gentleman's chair, which had closed arms and button tufting on the back, into the parlor. "This yours?"

Wylie nodded. "But I won't shift over to it until after dinner. Just set it over by the stove."

Luke brought in Rebecca's rocker next, then went back for an oval table. Like all the parlor tables, it was made of walnut and had a white marble top. The thick cabriole legs curved up to a base ornate with carvings of fruit and leaves. "Where do you want this?"

"Just put it by my chair. There's no telling where Becky's going to put things. Get yourself a chair and come sit a spell."

"I will. I'll bring a lamp, too. It'll be dark pretty quick."

When he went back toward the dining room, he saw Rebecca at the bottom of the stairs.

"I decided I'd better put my slippers on," she said.

"The kitchen floor doesn't feel as good as that carpet, does it?"

Rebecca blinked in surprise, then grinned at the twinkle in his eyes. Next to his smile, that sparkle was the nicest thing she had seen in a long time. "You caught me."

"Yes, ma'am. I bet you like to wiggle your toes in the sun-warmed dirt, too."

She nodded. "Guilty again. In late spring, it's so nice to feel the warmth after everything has thawed out. But in the summer, I'd much rather stick them in the creek."

He had cooled his feet in snow-fed streams in Montana, shallow trickles down in Texas, and mosquito-infested bayous in Louisiana. A lot of water—warm and cold, crystal clear and murky green—had flowed over the boy and then the man. But he couldn't remember the last time he had warmed his toes in the dirt. Sometime before manhood, he guessed. He still remembered the feeling though—it had been a small ritual for many a spring, drawing the last vestiges of cold from his bones and celebrating the survival of another winter. There had been few other celebrations in Luke's life.

He watched as she moved up the stairs, her long hair rippling with each step. He appreciated her ability to find pleasure in simple things. It was the only kind of pleasure he had ever known, and there had been little enough time for that. She reached the landing, glancing down at him when she turned. Simple things . . .

"Don't put up your hair," he commanded quietly.

Her eyes widened slightly, then grew tender as her expression softened, and she continued up the stairs.

Luke's heart slammed against the wall of his chest. What the devil was he doing? He had no right to issue such intimate orders, nor did he want that right. And he didn't want her looking at him with bone-melting tenderness, either. Tenderness only led to caring, and caring for a lady like her could rip out a man's heart and freeze his soul. Suddenly Luke realized he was scared. It would be much too easy to develop deep feelings for Rebecca Stephens. He wanted to run, but it would not do any good. The only place he could go was less than two hundred yards down the road. With a snarl at his foolishness, Luke turned away.

Rebecca wondered at Luke's silence during dinner. Since they were eating in the kitchen with their everyday pottery dishes, she had thought he would be more comfortable. Every time she glanced at him, he was watching her, but the minute their gazes connected, he looked away with a scowl. His black brows were almost touching by the end of the meal.

She told the men about finding the footprint in the garden and the missing string. When she asked Luke if he had seen any more signs of the visitor, he mumbled something about some missing wire, keeping his gaze directed toward his plate. Growing irritated that he could be so warm one minute and snarl like a wounded bear the next, Rebecca was a bit snippy when she asked if he had any idea what the man would use string and wire for. Luke merely shrugged.

"Goin' fishing," said Jackson, forking up a bite of thin, skillet-fried potatoes.

"You boys better check along the crick in the next day or two and see what you can find," said Wylie.

Both Jackson and Luke nodded, neither one looking up from their plates.

After supper, the men settled in the parlor, discussing crops and politics, while Rebecca did the dishes. It bothered Luke to have her working while they were sitting, but he told himself she was doing woman's work. That didn't make him feel any better, but he wasn't about to volunteer to help her. He figured Jackson and Wylie would have a good laugh at his expense if he did. Besides, he didn't want to be close enough to smell her special scent, or see the changing colors in her eyes, or watch the lamplight flicker across her hair. He forced himself to concentrate on what Wylie was saying, but with every faint rattle of dishes or pots and pans, his concentration wavered.

Rebecca was still miffed when she joined the men in the parlor. Luke stood when she entered the room, giving up her rocker so she could sit in it. Jackson immediately told Luke to take the side chair he had brought in earlier. The hired hand fetched a slat-backed, cane-bottomed chair from the kitchen table, saying it fit him better than her "company" chairs. He spoke more words in those two sentences than he had said all evening.

Moments after she sat down, Rebecca bounced back up again to look for her needlework basket. Everything was so piled up in the dining room that it took a few minutes to spot the basket sitting across the room on the sideboard. The sofa, two chairs, and three tables blocked her path.

After a brief hesitation, she kicked off her crocheted house slippers, gathered up her skirt in one hand, and climbed up onto the ladies' chair. Swaying slightly on the bouncy springs, she stepped over the short wooden arms onto the side chair. Again her feet sank in the thick cushion, then bounded back up again on the spring. She gathered her skirt up almost to her knees to keep from tripping on it.

Knowing Rebecca would need a table and lamp beside her chair, Luke went to the dining room after them. He halted in the doorway, the sight of shapely feminine legs stopping him cold. He watched in utter amazement as she stepped onto the sofa, traveling from one end to the other with bouncing steps and a giggle. She scooped up her basket and tucked it precariously under her arm. When she turned, she almost lost her balance. With a little squeak, she grabbed the tall back of the sofa, then straightened and saw him.

"Oh!" Even as she grinned, her cheeks turned pink. "My mother would kill me if she saw me walking on the furniture."

"I might help her." Luke shoved the first chair to the side, but it bumped into the dining room table. There was barely enough room for him to walk between the chair and a heavy parlor table.

"Humph." Rebecca made a face at him and gathered her skirt up in her free hand, lifting it more discreetly this time. "I'm not going to hurt the furniture by walking on it this once."

He tried to move the second chair but there was no place for it to go except out in the hall, and he didn't think she was going to give him time for that. "Hang the furniture."

"That might be hard," she said with a giggle. She started back down the couch, finding it more difficult to walk with both hands occupied. Near the end of the sofa, she lost her footing and pitched to her left.

Instantly, Luke stretched over the chair and caught her around the waist before she crashed into the marble-topped parlor tables. Fighting for balance himself in the tight space, he hauled her across the chair and hard against his chest as he took a step backward. Her sewing basket fell from her grasp, tumbling behind her onto the chair cushion.

He eased his way backward until there was room to turn around. He lowered her until her feet touched the floor, but when he felt her tremble, he wrapped his arms around her, keeping her pressed against him. It felt much too good. "It's a wonder you've lived this long," he said angrily.

"I'm a careful person." She looked up at him, a mulish glint in her eye.

"Thunderation, woman! You could have broken your neck."

She bit back a response and lowered her eyes, leaning her forehead against his chin. "You're right. It was silly." She raised her head again, meeting his gaze with twinkling eyes. "But it was fun." *And worth the fright to have you hold me like this.* A shiver danced over her skin. She had forgotten how nice it was to be held by a man.

He shook his head, his expression resigned. "Did I hurt you?"

She felt his deep voice rumble in his chest and realized with some surprise just how closely she was pressed up against him. *I should be ashamed,* she thought. But she wasn't. *He'll think I'm a loose woman.* She hoped not. "No, I'm fine now. It gave me a good scare, though." She pushed gently on his chest, and he immediately released her. "Thank you. I'm sure you saved me from a cracked head or at least a bad bruise."

"How did you plan to get the furniture back into the parlor?"

"The carpet men offered to come back tomorrow and move it for a fee, but since they had already broken one of my vases, I declined. I was going to ask the Ferguson boys to come over tomorrow night and move it. I'm sure they can use a little extra spending money. And I want to rearrange things, but I'm not quite sure how I want it."

"I'll ask Jackson to help me move it back tonight."

"Luke, you don't have to do that. You've both worked hard all day."

"Not all day. I had to go to town this afternoon and have Charlie's shoe replaced. I've got lots of energy left. I'll do most of the work." *If I don't wear myself out, I won't sleep a wink tonight.* "Besides, you're liable to need something else from the sideboard and risk your neck again. We'll move it now."

She shot him an irritated glance. She very well might need something, but his high-handed manner was annoying. Then it occurred to her that he was being dictatorial because he cared about her safety. True, he might have done the same for any woman, but she hoped his motivation ran deeper. He also might need to earn some money.

"Very well, but only if you'll let me pay you what I intended to pay the Ferguson boys."

He glared at her. "I don't want your money." Was that all she thought of him—that he wanted to help her just to make some money? He wondered if she thought he had embraced her for the same reason. "I'll do it for nothing, or I won't do it at all." He rested his hands on his hips, angrily awaiting her decision.

Oh, dear. She took one look at his hard face and snapping eyes and knew she had stirred up a hornet's nest. *Such pride.* It was hard to keep her hand away from his face, to keep from smoothing away his frown with a gentle touch. "Forgive me, Luke, I didn't mean to offend you. I would appreciate it very much if you moved the furniture back tonight. No payment . . . except for a peach pie. I have another one in the pie safe."

Luke knew Rebecca had an independent streak a mile wide. She probably always had been headstrong, but he suspected her self-reliance had grown since she lost her family. She was used to getting her way; that was certain. It was hard for her to receive help without giving something in return. She was used to doing for others, not having them do for her.

"Nobody in his right mind would turn down one of your pies," he said, relaxing his stance. "Now, where do you want these chairs?"

"I'm not certain. The sofa needs to be situated before I can decide."

"I'll set them in the hall for now." After moving them out of the way, he went to the parlor and asked Jackson to help. The hired hand merely nodded, his expression indicating he had expected to do the job all along. They moved the tables into the hall toward the kitchen, then carried the sofa into the parlor.

Rebecca followed, carrying a walnut lamp stand with a thin tripod base. Along with the other furniture in the house, it was a remnant of Anthony's first marriage. His first wife, Ollie, had been Rebecca's neighbor. Even though she had been twelve years older than Rebecca, they had been close friends. She had died when Rebecca was sixteen. Anthony was twenty years older than Rebecca, but when he came courting two years after Ollie's death, Rebecca was already halfway in love with him.

Most of the furnishings in the house, except some of the kitchen items, had belonged to Anthony when she married him. Although she liked much of the furniture, she had never particularly cared for the lamp stand. Because the top was wobbly, she had always been afraid to set a lamp on it. Instead she usually placed an inexpensive vase or figurine there. She had considered giving it away several times, but like the other things she had shared with Anthony, she could not quite bring herself to part with it.

Watching surreptitiously as Luke worked, she admired his strength and the way he moved. No effort was wasted. The six-foot sofa, with its red velvet upholstery and heavy walnut frame, matched the chairs. The three men from the carpet store had barely been able to move it. Jackson's grimace showed his effort, and he was breathing hard when they put it down at Rebecca's direction in front of a side window. Luke took two slow, deep breaths and was ready to go again. He hauled in two more side chairs while Jackson rested a few minutes.

She eyed the furniture arrangement, nibbling on her index fingernail and silently tapping her toe. "No, I don't like it. There isn't room for the table there. Let's try it over by the front window."

Luke shot Wylie an amused glance, and the old man chuckled.

"She'd be right at home in the army, wouldn't she, son."

Luke's gaze narrowed. No one had ever called him "son," not even his own father. It was not uncommon for older men to use the term when addressing younger men, but Luke had never heard Wylie use it with anyone else. He slanted a glance at him, but Wylie was busy laughing over Rebecca's wiggles as she tried to picture how the sofa would look sitting off center in front of the window.

They moved it to the spot indicated.

"A little to the left, please."

They lifted it again, careful not to slide it on the carpet, and moved it six inches to the left.

She nibbled on her thumbnail this time, wrinkles marring her brow. "No, that won't work." She sighed in exasperation. "It will have to be centered to look right. Move it to the right about a foot and a half." They obeyed her command, and her face brightened. "Yes, that's much better."

Luke leaned one hand against the back of the sofa. He was feeling a little tired. Poor Jackson looked about done in. Maybe he had been wrong to insist they move the furniture after all. He doubted if Jackson had idled away his time during the day.

A knock sounded at the door. "Oh, dear, who could be calling at this time of night?" Rebecca smoothed her hair and her dress and stepped out into the hallway.

Luke walked over to move the lamp stand and make room for another table, pausing to stretch his back. From where he stood, he had a good view of the front door. He picked up the lamp stand, intending to set it out of the way, but halted when Rebecca's expression caught his eye. A happy smile filled her face as she opened the door.

"Why, Ben! Welcome home."

Luke's gut twisted into a knot. He couldn't tear his eyes away from the cozy little scene in the entry. Ben Crowder stepped across the threshold, gently gripped Rebecca's upper arms, and dropped a kiss on her cheek. She blushed prettily as he whispered something in her ear.

A loud crack ricocheted around the room; the sound jerking Luke's gaze downward.

He had snapped the tiny table in two.

Chapter 6

REBECCA'S GAZE FLEW toward the parlor. A dull red spread across Luke's tanned face as he looked down at the lamp stand in his hands—the tripod base in one, the tabletop in the other. His jaw was clenched in anger.

She quickly shut the door as Ben removed his rain-speckled hat and coat. She reached for them, but he quietly told her that he would hang them up. Smiling her thanks, she hurried into the parlor as he hooked them on the elaborate hall tree beside the front door.

"I'm sorry, Rebecca. I'll replace it."

"There's no need, Luke. I've been looking for a reason to get rid of that table for years."

He leveled her a look that plainly said he did not believe her.

"It's always been unsteady. I never could put a lamp on it. Please don't worry about it." She took the pieces from him and leaned them against the wall.

"I'll replace it," Luke said firmly. He was so mad he wanted to hit something. *Of all the times to look like an idiot!*

Don't be so bullheaded! She felt like shaking him, then smiled when she realized how ridiculous that thought was. "If you wish," she said quietly, knowing she would only embarrass him further if she tried to dissuade him. When Ben stepped into the room, she asked, "Have you two met?" When both men shook their heads, she politely introduced them.

Neither man smiled as they shook hands. She noticed Ben flinch, but Luke did not seem to realize that he was squeezing excessively hard. She knew better. "How is your father?"

"Doing well, thank you." Ben dropped his hand to his side, trying to hide it when he flexed his fingers. "He has agreed to turn over more of the business to my older brothers and to take life a little slower. He and my mother are planning a trip to Europe in June. That will force him to rest." He glanced around the room. "You bought a new rug?"

"Yes, isn't it lovely?" Rebecca's beaming smile slowly faded beneath Ben's questioning look. She could almost hear him asking why she had bought a new rug if she was planning on moving to town. *Because I'm not.* Suddenly the answer to that part of her problem was very clear. She did not know if she would ever remarry, but she knew she could not become Ben Crowder's wife. She did not love him, and she did not think he loved her. She would settle for nothing less.

"Luke was helping Jackson move the furniture back in."

"I see," drawled Ben, a flicker of amusement touching his face. "Why don't I pitch in, too, and we'll have it done in no time." He glanced at Luke, his expression subtly indicating the farmer's presence was not wanted.

He smiled at Rebecca, his face a picture of innocence, but she had not missed the sarcasm in his voice, and the look he had given Luke. "That would be kind of you," she said coolly.

Luke and Ben spent the next fifteen minutes trying to outdo each other. Ben was quicker because he carried the lighter items such as the remaining side chair, walnut tilt-topped game table, and magazine rack. Luke carried in the ladies' chair that matched Wylie's armchair and the four marble-topped tables. When he hauled in her small parlor desk with two footstools perched on the top, Rebecca held her breath, waiting for something to get broken. If she hadn't been so annoyed at their boyish antics, she might have found the whole thing amusing. Wylie and Jackson were busting their buttons trying to keep from laughing out loud.

The last thing to be moved, other than the figurines and pictures that normally sat on it, was the large étagère. Like the other furniture, it was made of walnut with elaborately carved clusters of fruit for ornamentation. It was seven feet high, extremely heavy, and required both men to carry it. Even Luke strained beneath its weight.

Although Rebecca found she preferred to watch Luke, she kept her eye on Ben. She was afraid he would hurt something. He was slim, trim, and in reasonable shape for a man who spent his days in an office. But he was no match for Luke. Where the farmer lifted his side of the whatnot six inches off the floor, the banker's side barely cleared the carpet. With a grunt and grimace from both men the cabinet was finally set in place.

"Whew! Now I know why I prefer to make my living with brains and not brawn." Ben grinned good-naturedly at Luke and jerked his handkerchief from his pocket to wipe his brow.

Luke swiped his forehead on his sleeve. He nodded at Ben, a hint of grudging admiration in his ghost of a smile. "I'd rather pitch hay all day than move furniture."

"Thank you both. I appreciate everything you've done."

Ben glanced at the clock on the mantel. It was almost nine. "Rebecca, could I have a word with you in private?"

"Of course." She glanced nervously at Luke, then turned her gaze to Ben. "We can talk in the dining room." She excused herself and led the way down the hall, dreading the next few minutes. Rebecca had been ill at ease ever since Ben had arrived. She had welcomed him home, simply meaning that she was glad he had returned to town safely. But when he had leaned down and whispered that he looked forward to the time she would welcome him home with a real kiss, she knew he would be proposing before the evening was over.

Ben closed the dining room door behind them. He watched Rebecca move across the room, her fingers skimming over the frames of the pictures that had been left on the buffet. His gaze moved slowly down her flowing hair. It was the first time he had seen her when it was not pinned up. "Do you always dress so casually when Northcutt is around?"

Glancing sharply at him, she pressed her lips together to keep from making a retort. She understood his jealousy, but she did not like the accusation she heard in his voice. "Luke's visit was a surprise. Uncle Wylie invited him to supper," she said crisply. "I had washed my hair, and it was too damp to put up."

"It was dry when I arrived."

"Yes, it was, but by that time, it seemed silly to bother with pinning it up."

He crossed the room, smiling contritely. "I'm being a pain in the neck, aren't I?" He slid his arms around her, tangling his fingers in her hair.

"Yes, you are." Rebecca gave him a little smile. She liked Ben very much. It was unfortunate she didn't love him.

"You look so lovely with your hair down."

Rebecca had the distinct impression he had spoken those same words before—probably more than once.

"It makes a man think about things he shouldn't." He smiled at the soft blush that stole into her cheeks. "I don't want anyone else having those thoughts."

"Ben, I—" The gentle pressure of his fingertip against her lips stopped her.

"I know I don't yet have the right to imagine you in my bed, but I want that right, Rebecca." He brushed her cheek tenderly with his fingertips. "Will you marry me? Will you make me the proudest man in the county by being my beautiful bride?"

Oh, dear! This is going to be harder than I thought. She reminded herself that he had not spoken of love, only pride. Still, she did not like to disappoint or hurt anyone, least of all someone she cared about. She shook her head minutely. "Ben, I can't marry you."

"Why not?" he asked in surprise.

"Because I don't love you." She raised her gaze to his. "I admire you greatly, but too much of my past gets in the way. I could never love you as you deserve to be loved."

"Are you sure?" Passion darkened his eyes. He pulled her closer. "Can't I convince you differently?"

"No—" His lips covered hers, giving no chance for her intended polite, but firm refusal.

LUKE WAITED BARELY a minute after the dining room door closed to say his farewell to Wylie and Jackson, waving away the hired hand's offer to drive him home. He could not stand to stay in the house, knowing Crowder was sweet-talking Rebecca. He jerked his worn hat and faded coat from the hall tree and sent a scathing glance at the banker's expensive coat and derby. Luke stormed out the front door, only to be hit in the face by a blast of icy rain. He pulled his collar up to his chin and the hat down low on his forehead, preparing to step off the porch.

The dining room shared the front of the house with the parlor, although its doorway was farther down the hall. The light shining on the porch through the dining room window—and the shadow intertwined with it—drew him away from the steps. Heart pounding, Luke told himself to stay back, but he couldn't seem to heed his own warning. Hiding in the darkness, he peered through the window— and wished to God he hadn't.

Stifling a cry, he whirled away, gripping the porch post for support. The image of Crowder and Rebecca sharing a passionate kiss chilled his soul like a vengeful specter, vowing to torment him day and night.

Why do you care? She wants a marryin' man. Let her fancy man have her, he thought savagely. With a muted growl of rage, Luke plunged off the porch into the drenching blackness.

BEN HELD HER tightly against him, caressing the tense muscles in her back with gentle hands. Rebecca stood perfectly still, allowing his kiss but not encouraging it. Any desire she should have felt for him would have been quickly stirred by his ardent expertise. She felt nothing. She considered trying to push him away but did not want to make a scene. If Luke even thought he heard a protest, she figured he would come to her rescue whether she needed it or not. The idea of Ben sporting a broken jaw because of her was not at all appealing.

Soon, Ben drew back, searching her face intently. He released a long, heartfelt sigh. "I guess I can't convince you, can I?"

"No, Ben. I'm sorry." She looked up into his hurt-filled eyes and felt tears sting her own. "I wish it could be different, but I can't marry you knowing that I can't give you love. You deserve more than just companionship."

"I'd be happy with that."

"No, in time you would think differently. And so would I. You'll find a woman who can give you her whole heart. Any number of women in town, and probably Chicago, too, would jump at the chance to be your wife."

His hands tightened on her shoulders. "But I want you."

"I know." *But not for the right reason.* "You're a good man, Ben. I wish I didn't have to hurt you."

He dropped his hands to his side, attempting a smile. "Oh, I'll survive. I always have. Don't be surprised if you see me sporting a new lady on my arm in a few days." He turned away and walked toward the door, his face flushed with embarrassment. "I'm not getting any younger, you know."

"Search carefully, Ben. Look past her beauty to her heart. A plain face will become beautiful in your eyes if it shines with love."

He winced and glanced at Anthony's picture sitting on the sideboard. Anthony's face had not been the kind to turn a lady's head. "Was Anthony's face handsome to you, Rebecca?"

"There was none more beautiful."

Ben nodded and gripped the doorknob, then looked at her over his shoulder. "Tell me this, Rebecca. Did I lose out to a dead man or a live one?"

Her eyes widened in surprise and her cheeks paled. She

hesitated, considering his question, then shook her head. "I don't know."

His expression tightened with anger as he jerked open the door. "You're going to look like a fool."

Rebecca waited in the dining room until she heard the front door shut. She considered going directly upstairs but knew Wylie would be worried about her, so she squared her shoulders and marched down the hall. With Ben's last comment ringing in her ears, she dreaded seeing Luke. What would he think of the confusion that was bound to show in her face? And had he heard him?

When she stepped into the parlor, only Wylie was waiting. She didn't know whether to be happy or disappointed not to find Luke there.

"Jackson's in the kitchen, getting us another piece of pie. Luke went on home." He took her hand when she knelt beside his chair. "Are you all right, Becky gal?"

"Yes. I turned Ben down."

"I gathered as much."

"I don't love him." She looked up at her uncle, tears burning her eyes.

"I know, child. I've known it all along and was hoping you wouldn't make a mistake."

"But sometimes I'm so lonely," she whispered.

"I know that, too." He patted the back of her hand with his free one. "God has another man for you, one who will need you as much as you need him. The good Lord has a way of putting together those who need love and those who can give it. Just give Him time to do His job."

She nodded, swallowing back her tears. "Did Luke take his pie?"

"No." A tiny smile touched Wylie's time-worn face. "Pie was the last thing that man had on his mind."

"Do you think he was jealous of Ben?" *And do I want him to be?*

"No, I don't think so."

She felt a stab of disappointment.

Wylie chuckled. "I know so. When that door closed behind you two, he was mad enough to eat nails. He'll be mean as a grizzly for a while, but he'll settle down. You might want to avoid him for a day or two."

Rebecca gently tugged her hand free and rose. "Well, I can't very well drop by and tell him that I'm not going to get married, now can I?" she asked ruefully.

"No, I reckon not. Although I sometimes wonder if directness wouldn't cut through a lot of the misery people put themselves through."

"Well, if I were more certain of my own feelings, I might be a little more direct, but for now I guess he'll just have to be patient."

Wylie snorted with laughter. "Gal, that boy doesn't have enough patience to put in a thimble." He sobered quickly. "From what I've picked up when we were talking, Luke's been alone for a long time. There's a lot of hurt in the man, Becky. Hurt that's not going to heal with a smile and a few kind words. It's going to take time before he knows what he wants."

"That's just as well, Uncle Wylie, because it's going to take time to know what I want, too." She kissed him on the forehead and went upstairs to bed.

She lay awake, listening to the quiet sounds of Jackson helping Wylie change his clothes and get into bed. A few minutes later, the front door opened then eased shut as Jackson made his way to his home. Hours passed before sleep finally claimed her, and then it was fitful and fleeting. She woke up before daylight, exhausted.

Ellen came early Friday morning and bustled about doing her cleaning while Rebecca baked the bread she had mixed up and left to rise the evening before, dusted, and finished moving the pictures and what-nots back into the parlor. Ellen completed her work by two o'clock. Rebecca sent her on her way with three fresh loaves of bread and a plate of fried apricot pies. When she had the house all to herself, she decided to leave a loaf of bread and some of the hand-sized pasties on the windowsill.

She gathered up the basket with her quilting pieces, pulled her kitchen rocking chair with its comfortable cane back and seat over into the corner, and sat down to keep an eye on the window. She pieced the quilt diligently for a quarter hour before her mind strayed, and she lost interest in her task. Rebecca leaned her head against the back of the chair, listening to the sounds of spring.

A red cardinal glided to a stop in the maple tree outside the kitchen window, adding his sharp, clear whistle to the sweet song of the white-throated sparrow perched nearby. In the distance, a lark's melodious song reached to the heavens and mingled with the *bum-bum-boo* of the prairie chickens resonating across the pasture.

A warm breeze blew through the open windows, bringing with it the fresh, clean smell of the rich dirt, wet from last night's rain. She closed her eyes and stepped back through time to another spring, when life was full and her heart overflowed with happiness and love.

Her mind traveled the well-worn paths of memory, stopping to listen to a tiny tot's squeal of laughter and a deep masculine chuckle. She peeked past the curtain of time, looking through one window then another at scenes shared with her husband and little boy—the pride and tears on Anthony's face when he held his newborn child, the first of his flesh . . . his tender, awe-filled kiss as he thanked her for giving him a son . . . Michael's delight when he learned to walk and could explore the world on his own . . . her son's enchantment as he watched a butterfly . . . the funny face he made at his first taste of spinach—on and on her mind spun images so real she could hear the sounds and smell the fragrances.

The only thing she could not do was touch them. Setting aside her quilting, she gathered the memories to her heart and wandered into the parlor. Her fingers absently stroked the locket around her neck which contained curls of Anthony and Michael's hair.

She gazed at her husband's picture, at the thin, craggy face of the man who had won a place in her heart for all eternity. She felt his gentle touch across her cheek as if he stood beside her to wipe away her silent tears. The feeling of his arm around her shoulders was so real that she shuddered, her heart aching. Her loneliness had never been more poignant than in that moment.

When her gaze drifted to little Michael's portrait, a sob escaped her throat. She tried to remember him as he had been moments after the picture was taken, happy and giggling while his doting father made faces to make him laugh more. Instead, the vision of his peaceful but lifeless little body filled her mind, bringing her to her knees with a cry of pain.

Clutching her locket, Rebecca sobbed in grief and despair. The pain of their last days together shattered her heart anew as her relentless mind played out those desperate hours. Her only comfort was the joyful expression on Anthony's face as he neared heaven's gate. "I see Michael," he whispered. "He's waving. Ollie's with him . . . holding his hand." He curled his fingers around her hand with his last strength. "We'll meet you . . ." She kissed him, and he sighed peacefully as he passed from this world to the next.

Rebecca wept until the pain eased. As she wiped the tears from her eyes, a faint, out-of-place noise from outside the window captured her attention. "Self-pity is a waste of time, so just quit." Pushing to her feet, she hastily wiped her eyes on her apron and hurried to the window. At first she didn't see anything, then her gaze fell on the footprints beneath the window—footprints that were headed toward the kitchen.

Chapter 7

SHE DASHED DOWN the hall, careening through the doorway into the kitchen. The windowsill was empty. Running out the back door, she spied a young, towheaded boy making a beeline toward the creek. "Wait! I won't hurt you!"

The youngster did not slow his pace, even though he slipped in the mud and almost landed on his face a couple of times. Rebecca flew after him, calling until she was out of breath. She closed the distance between them, but the boy gradually stretched it out the farther they ran.

Luke stood at the edge of his cornfield estimating how many days it would be until the ground was dry enough to continue with the harrow and then plant. The rain, sometimes mixed with flurries of snow, had been slow and steady all night. It did not appear to have washed away any of the seed he had already planted, but he was still in a surly mood. He knew the cause, but he refused to acknowledge that the loss of Rebecca to Ben Crowder had put him in one of the blackest moods of his life.

A faint cry from across the road turned his attention to Rebecca's field. He caught a glimpse of a towheaded boy running along the creek that meandered through both farms, and Rebecca running after him. He figured the boy to be around ten or eleven, and boys that age did not travel by themselves if they could help it. She could be running head-on into trouble.

"Rebecca, stop!" he shouted. Placing his hands on the top log of the split-rail fence that separated his land from the road, he swung over it. He raced across the road and jumped over the fence on the other side in the same way. Cupping his hands around his mouth, he called again, "Rebecca, stop!"

She looked at him and slowed down, finally coming to a halt as he cut across the field. It was impossible to run in the plowed dirt. Luke sank almost up to his ankles with every step, the mud closing around his work boots like a trap. He realized too late that it would have been quicker to run along the grassy land beside the creek, even though the stream twisted and turned twenty times between his place and the little bend where Rebecca stood.

When he finally reached her, he was gasping for breath. She was also breathing hard, although she had had a few minutes' rest. "I saw him!"

He nodded. "Me, too." Resting his hands on his hips, he took several deep breaths and scanned the area, waiting until he had enough air to chew her out properly.

"He's just a boy. I put a loaf of bread and some fried pies in the windowsill. I intended to watch for him, but I was distracted. He made a little noise—slipped in the mud, I guess—and I heard him. I was after him like a shot," she said proudly. "Thought I might catch him, too, but he runs like a jack rabbit."

Luke slanted her a hard look. "Was Jackson or Ted around when you put the food in the window?"

"Uh, no." She looked sheepish.

"Rebecca . . ." He grabbed her hand and pulled her down the slope toward the creek, out of view of anyone who might pass by on the road or any neighbor who might be in the field.

"Well, I knew he wasn't very big."

"And how did you know that?" He glared at her.

She glared back. "By the size of the footprint I found in the garden yesterday. It was hardly any bigger than mine.

I told you about it last night."

"I didn't hear anything about a footprint."

"That's because you were too busy being grouchy during dinner."

He ignored her jab. "Some men have small feet. And even small men can be strong. Did it ever occur to you that he might hurt you?"

Remembering the sound she had heard outside the parlor window, she uncomfortably shifted her feet. The boy had been listening and perhaps watching. She swallowed hard. It could just as easily have been a man. "No." She raised her chin stubbornly. "If he was going to hurt me, he would have done it before now. Besides, he's just a boy."

"And you were chasing after him."

"Well, of course I was." She frowned and sighed in exasperation. "I wanted to stop him, to tell him he could have a warm bed and decent food."

"What if he's not alone?"

"What?" Rebecca blinked.

"Suppose someone else is hiding in the trees down by the creek? Someone other than a young boy." He stepped closer, towering over her, then leaned down until his nose was only a few inches from hers. He growled in his deepest voice, "What if there's a man down there, just waiting to get his dirty hands on a pretty little thing like you? What if he's big and mean and ugly? Do you think his kisses would be hot and sweet like Ben Crowder's?"

She was momentarily distracted from his tirade by the sarcasm when he mentioned Ben's kisses. *Oh, Lord, he saw Ben kiss me.*

Luke gripped her shoulders, his fingers digging into her flesh. "Would you like to have some tramp's slobbering lips cover yours, or feel his dirty hands on you? Don't think for a minute that he would touch you with a gentleman's passion, or that he'd stop with a kiss. He'd want it all with a woman like you, and he'd take it."

She shuddered and looked away, her face pale. "Luke, stop it! You're scaring me."

"Good! Maybe I'll scare some sense into you." He

straightened. "You've got no business down here by yourself, or tempting a man with fried pies." She looked up at him, remorse written all over her face. "Or with anything else," he muttered, losing himself in her beautiful, sad eyes. He noticed the dark smudges beneath them and the telltale red puffiness left by her tears. *Who made you cry?* He wondered if maybe Crowder had not proposed after all, or if they had had a fight.

The nervous movement of the tip of her tongue across her dry lips drew his gaze. He eased his grip and almost, just almost, brought his thumb up to caress her lip as he had done the night before. She had liked it. Lord help him, so had he.

"Aw, heck fire." He released her and stepped back before he pulled another man's woman into his arms and kissed her breathless. He felt like saying something a lot worse, but he didn't. Luke had never had much instruction regarding polite society, but he was enough of a gentleman not to cuss in front of a lady—at least not with full-fledged swear words.

"I'm sorry, Luke. I guess I didn't think." Rebecca's excitement over seeing the boy was short-lived. She was emotionally drained, and Luke's scold hurt worse than it should have. She looked down, unconsciously clasping her hands in front of her like a repentant schoolgirl, feeling every bit as contrite as her action appeared.

"Don't do that!" he said harshly.

She looked up at him in confusion.

"Don't hang your head in shame," he said in a gentler voice. She looked as if she might crumple any minute. He couldn't stand it. Wrapping his arms around her, he drew her firmly but gently against his broad chest. "Honey, don't ever do that—not because of me or anybody." *Lord, I swear I'll never shame her again.*

Rebecca rubbed her cheek against his faded blue flannel shirt, vaguely aware of the contrast between its worn softness and the hard body beneath it. Until that moment, she had not realized how desperately she needed to be comforted. And Luke was so good at it. One big hand held her against him, using just enough pressure to give her a feeling of security. The other hand roamed slowly and lightly up and down her back, occasionally making a little side trip up the nape of her neck so his fingers could brush against the thick braid pinned there.

She knew he had wanted to touch her hair; she had seen it in his eyes the night before. She snuggled a little closer, wishing her hair was still unpinned, and slipped her arms around his waist. Closing her eyes, Rebecca cherished the feelings his closeness gave her—the peace and refuge he brought to her weary soul, the stirring of womanly desire so long forgotten. She curled and uncurled her fingers against his back, smiling faintly as the hard muscles tensed even more beneath her touch. He smelled of hay, damp earth, and faintly of hard work—a potent mixture to Rebecca.

He had not shaved. When he had first walked up, she had noticed how the dark stubble made his face even more rugged. She felt a tiny pull as he bent his head close to hers and wisps of hair along her forehead caught in his beard. It was an intimate sensation and caused her heartbeat to jump. Luke's hand halted on her back, and she felt the answering staccato of his heart against her cheek.

Luke reluctantly raised his head and swallowed hard. He had been oblivious to time and place, lost in the feel of her, in the subtle fragrance of perfume and woman, and in her soft sighs. She raised her head, meeting his gaze. He searched her face and saw the beginning of passion in her eyes. All he had to do was bend his head. She would welcome his kiss.

Just like Ben Crowder. An angry snarl escaped him, and he released her so suddenly that she stumbled.

"Luke?" Rebecca caught his arm to keep from falling. The second she was steady, he jerked it away.

"Sorry, lady. I don't kiss another man's woman." His voice was harsh and filled with contempt. *Not even if she asks me to with her big, beautiful eyes.* "What would dear old Ben think if he found out?"

Rebecca gasped. Her face paled, then flooded with color.

"It wouldn't matter what Ben Crowder thought. He has no claim on me."

"You could have fooled me. He sure seemed to think so last night. Or do you let any man kiss you that wants to?"

Rebecca felt like slapping him. Only the flicker of hurt she saw in his eyes kept her from it. *He thinks I'm toying with him. Oh, Luke, do you think so little of yourself? Or of me?* She closed her eyes briefly and took a slow deep breath. When she opened them again, she met his angry gaze with directness and determination. "You're right about one thing. Ben did think he had a claim on me. He has been courting me. I was even considering marrying him, but last night I realized I couldn't."

Luke eyed her warily. "Why not?"

"Because I don't love him." She waited for him to call her a fool again.

Luke knew she expected him to say something about her foolish belief in love. He kept his mouth shut—on that score, at least. "Was this before or after you kissed him?" He could not quite keep the jealousy out of his voice.

"Before. I refused his offer of marriage. He thought maybe he could change my mind. His kiss took me by surprise." Her voice softened. She needed for him to understand. "Luke, I didn't push him away because I didn't want to hurt him any more, and I didn't want to make a scene. I felt nothing when he kissed me. He got the message without my being dramatic."

He looked away for a minute, then back at her. His eyes burned with his unspoken question: *What would you feel if I kissed you?*

She chuckled softly, then shyly lowered her eyes. "Certainly more than nothing," she murmured.

Startled, Luke laughed.

Rebecca thought she had never heard a more beautiful sound.

"Woman, I never know what to expect from you."

"Surprises are good for the mind," she said demurely. At his raised brow, she explained with a grin. "Keeps you on your toes."

"I ain't no ballerina." He smiled good-naturedly. "Come on, let's see if we can find any sign of the boy." He started walking along the creek bank. Rebecca followed, letting him look for the signs. She spent most of her time looking at him.

They found the remains of a small campfire. It had been built carefully and just as carefully put out. The thick, dead grass and shrubs hid any footprints, but the bones from several catfish lay in a pile beside the ashes.

"Looks like he's put your string and my wire to good use," said Luke. They looked around some more but figured the lad had put a lot of ground between him and them. He walked her back to the farmyard.

"Do you really think someone is with him?" she asked.

"Maybe. It's hard to tell from the number of catfish bones. A growing boy can get real hungry when it's been a long time between meals."

Did you get real hungry, Luke?

"He may be alone, but it's hard for a boy that age to be on his own." He looked out across the farmyard, remembering the loneliness and the fear. "Black nights and scary noises," he muttered.

The bleakness of his voice and expression pierced her heart. Without thinking she rested her hand on his arm. "Were you alone and frightened, Luke?"

"Sometimes." The shutters dropped into place, both in his eyes and his expression. Further discussion about it was forbidden.

She squeezed his arm. "How can I help him?" she asked, thinking not only of the boy they had seen earlier but also of the man standing beside her.

"We'll have to catch him. If he wasn't afraid, he would have come forward by now." He glanced at Rebecca's hand on his arm. She moved it back to her side. The boy was not the only one who was afraid. Some of the things that happened down by the creek were starting to bother Luke. He had been terrified when he saw her running across the field alone, so frightened for her safety that he tossed aside his pride and went after her. All his life, pride had been his shield. It had been battered and dented, but it had held steadfast. Now it contained a hairline crack.

Simply holding her had stirred her passion and given him the sweetest pleasure he had ever known. She had even wanted his kiss. To her the ultimate passion meant lovemaking, with a big emphasis on love . . . and to a fine, Christian lady like Rebecca, love and lovemaking meant marriage. Pure and simple. Marriage meant commitment . . . and being locked into a world of hurt when she grew tired of him and wished he wasn't around anymore.

He watched her chew on her fingernail and knew a plan was forming.

"We'll set a trap. One a hungry boy can't resist. Come to dinner Sunday. We'll fill both kitchen windows with all kinds of good things to eat and then keep watch for him. We can catch him before he cleans off the second window. And if we don't, then at least he'll have plenty of food."

"That's as good a plan as any. I've gone out to the barn several nights and haven't seen him. Of course, I always go before bedtime. Once I fall asleep, it takes an act of God to wake me up."

"Jackson has checked our barn, too. We've found indentations in the hay where he's slept, but that's all. He must be sharing his loot with these mangy mutts of mine. They never bark when he's around."

"That's an old trick." Luke looked down at the five dogs trotting up to greet them. The panting dogs had come running from the other field. "Looks like they've been on a rabbit hunt and missed out." He grinned. "Poor kid. No wonder he's hungry enough to steal things in broad daylight. Feeding these critters must take half of what he finds."

"You'll come over Sunday afternoon?"

Luke nodded. "Same time as before?"

"Yes. That will be fine. I won't ask anyone else. I don't want to scare him away."

"Well, I'd better get back to work." Luke turned to go, but stopped when Rebecca softly spoke his name.

"Thank you for coming to protect me, even if I didn't realize I might be in danger. I appreciate it."

He shifted uncomfortably. "Be more careful."

"I will."

He shifted again, looking at her eyes. They were still slightly puffy and red. "Rebecca, what made you cry?"

She looked away, her earlier heartache brushing her soul once more. Absently touching the locket, she ran her fingertips over it in a loving caress. "I was remembering other springs."

Pain slashed through Luke's heart. She had been thinking of her husband—that was why she had welcomed his arms around her. She had been vulnerable and needed comfort. It hadn't mattered who had given it. Now he understood why she didn't love Crowder and wouldn't marry him. She was still in love with her husband.

Yet, fool that he was, as he watched the grief and sadness reflected in her face, he knew he would do it all over again. Anger filled him at his stupidity. "I'm sorry for your loss, Rebecca," he said tightly, then turned abruptly and started down the lane.

He told himself it didn't matter. He didn't want to care for anyone, anyway. *You already do.*

"No," he muttered angrily. "She just stirs my blood. I just want to make love to her." *Love.* The word mocked him. Before he met Rebecca Stephens the slaking of a man's lust had never been *making love.*

His anger kept him going until he slammed the front door behind him and slumped down in his lopsided, almost comfortable chair. "I don't care for her," he cried between gritted teeth. But he knew he had begun to, in his own inadequate way.

Luke closed his eyes, suddenly exhausted. He had not slept all night, but sleep was still slow in coming. Loneliness and vulnerability overtook him. "I don't need anybody to love me," he mumbled.

It was a lie, and he knew it. He just never admitted it unless he was too tired or weak to fight. "Am I so bad?" His eyes burned as sleep slowly covered him with its comforting blanket. "Can't someone love me . . . just for a little while? Is that . . . too much to ask?"

He drifted off to sleep, dreaming of gray green eyes, a soft crooning voice, and gentle arms that held him, shielding him from the scary noises of the black night.

Chapter 8

THE DOG TROTTED down the lane with a disdainful dignity that would have made an aristocrat proud. He moved with a sense of purpose—as if he knew exactly where he was going and had every right to be there.

Eyeing the mongrel as it approached the back porch, Luke walked toward the house from the barn. He rotated first his right shoulder, then his left. Sleeping in the chair half the night had left a kink in his back and a snarl in his disposition. "Get out of here! Go on—git! I don't need another mouth to feed."

The dog stopped beside the house and stared at Luke until he was a few steps shy of kicking distance. Then, calm as a judge, the animal walked up the steps and plopped down on the weather-beaten boards of the porch. A long pink tongue curled from his open mouth, and his protruding ribs heaved with each panted breath.

Glaring, Luke halted at the bottom of the steps. The scruffy mutt had a regal manner, but it was the ugliest dog he had ever seen. The animal's long coat reminded him of a crazy-quilt pattern, a hodgepodge of black and brown with patches of dirty white thrown in here and there. The lower half of his body was caked with dried, black Iowa mud. About a third of his tail was gone, as was the tip of one sharply pointed ear. The other ear was intact but sported a long scabbed cut. Luke could not see any additional wounds at a glance, but the animal had plenty of battle scars. Luke knew instinctively that he usually won his fights.

"I don't take in strays." Luke rested his hands on his hips and scowled.

The dog raised up to a sitting position, wrinkled his face, and scratched vigorously beneath his chin.

"Go see the lady down the road. She's a sucker for sorrowful big brown eyes." When the critter shook his head, Luke didn't know if he was disagreeing with him, or if his ear itched. Amusement gently nudged at Luke's irritation.

Suddenly, the dog's ears sprang to attention. With keen eyes focused on the barn, he slowly eased to his feet and assumed a position vaguely resembling that of a pointer.

Luke glanced in the direction of the dog's gaze and laughed. "Those are chickens, you mangy mutt! You're the poorest excuse for a bird dog I've ever seen."

The animal broke from his position and walked down the porch steps. He stopped in front of Luke, sat down, and lifted one paw. Luke stared in amazement for a second, then bent down and shook the dog's muddy paw. "I guess I might as well be sociable. Looks like you're stayin' whether I agree or not."

When Luke walked across the porch to the back door, the dog followed him, his snubbed tail wagging. "Hold on, drifter. I don't mind you in the house, but your fleas and mud aren't welcome. I'll bring you some food, but you can't come in until after you have a bath." He grabbed a flea as it hopped across his hand and squished it between his thumbnails. "Looks like I'll need a bath, too. It's a good thing it's Saturday, you mangy mutt."

He grinned as he stepped through the doorway into a tiny room off the kitchen. Using an iron bootjack sitting beside the door, he pulled off his muddy boots. His damp socks, a pair of mud-caked pants, and dirty shirt quickly followed. Padding barefoot into the kitchen in his drawers and undershirt, Luke decided living alone in his own house had some definite advantages.

He added more wood to the embers in the kitchen stove, building up the fire to heat the water in the reservoir. After crumbling some bread and flavoring it with a little bacon grease, he carried the pan of food and a bowl of water out to the dog. The bread disappeared in seconds.

"You're going to eat me out of house and home," Luke grumbled as he looked down at the dog's still-hungry expression. The pooch sat up on his hind legs in a classic begging pose. Luke would have laughed at the blatant theatrics if the poor half-starved animal hadn't looked so pathetic. "All right, cut out the act. I'll get you something else."

He went into the house, returning to the porch a few minutes later with three thick ham sandwiches, a glass, and a crock of milk. He dropped one sandwich into the dog's pan. It vanished instantly. "These two are mine." Luke pointed to the plate of food he set on a washstand beside the door. "Leave them alone," he said sternly.

The dog obediently sat down and watched as Luke filled the pan with milk, then poured himself a glassful. Luke took his plate and sat down on the porch steps while the dog lapped up the milk. The back of the house was hidden from the road and secluded from the neighboring farms by a thicket of wild blackberries. A sugar maple tree grew in the yard, and another, along with two larger elm trees, stood farther out toward the blackberries. The new, tiny leaves on the maple allowed plenty of sunlight to shine down on the steps, warming the man and his companion with golden rays.

Luke ate one of the sandwiches and stretched his legs out in front of him, chuckling. It was probably sinful for a man to enjoy sitting outside in his underwear, but it sure felt good. For the first time in his life, he was master of his own house. There was enough space between him and his neighbors to allow him to sit in his yard naked if he wanted to. He laughed out loud at the thought.

The dog licked the last drop of milk from his chin and cast a questioning look in Luke's direction.

"I'm king of the castle, mutt. A contented man." Luke sighed as the smile faded. *Almost contented.* In the hollows of his heart was the bleakness he refused to acknowledge. It had escaped for a while the day before, but now the pain was back where it belonged, deeply hidden in the shadows of his soul.

"I think I'll call you Drifter. How does that sound?" He took the wagging of the dog's tail as a sign of approval. "Been called that before, huh? Yeah, me, too. But no more. I'm home." He peeked between the blackberry vines and trees at his land, then looked back at the dog. "You're home, too. For as long as you want. We'll be friends until you get the itch to move on."

He lifted his hand, thinking he might pet Drifter on the head but changed his mind before he touched him. It wouldn't do to get too attached. That would only make it hurt more when the mutt found some place he liked better.

Like Clancy did. Luke's tiny smile was bittersweet. *Clancy.* He had been twelve when he had latched on to that old hound. He'd never had a dog and thought it was the most grand thing in the world to have a pet of his own. They kept each other warm on cool spring nights and shared a swimming hole on hot summer days. Luke found a job harvesting corn that fall, and the farmer allowed the dog to stay, too.

Clancy proved to be a good hunter and taught the younger hounds a few tricks of the trade. When the harvest was finished, the dog had a home. Luke didn't. Old man Brown gave Clancy a choice—a warm, dry bed by the fire and the assurance of good food every day, or the love of a boy who had no place to lay his head.

The decision was not an easy one, even for an old vagabond like Clancy, who had picked up a lot of stray people in his day. The dog walked to the edge of the farmyard by Luke's side, but refusing guaranteed warmth for his rheumatic joints and a full belly in his old age was too much to ask. In the end, he gazed at Luke with sorrowful big brown eyes, licked his hand, and turned back to the house.

Luke did not beg his friend to come with him. He had never begged, not even as a child. He really didn't blame the dog. Clancy would not have survived the winter—Luke barely made it through himself. In a way, he thanked old man Brown for giving his tired companion a few more years of life. But he had never quite forgiven the man for providing a dog a home and turning away a boy.

A gentle tap on his leg brought his mind back to the present. Drifter settled his paw back on the porch and wistfully eyed Luke's other sandwich. "Okay, half." Luke held out one portion of the sandwich, and the dog grabbed it from his hand. "Watch the fingers! You don't have to be greedy. Nobody's going to steal it." Luke stood. "Now, stay put."

He went into the house but was back again moments later, hauling out the big round wooden tub that served as a washtub for clothes, man, and now dog. He carried out the things he would need—soap, towels, and several buckets of hot water, setting everything on the grass in the sunshine. All the while, Drifter lay on the porch with his head resting on his paws. Luke chuckled at the melancholy expression on the dog's face. "Believe me, I don't think I'm going to like this any more than you do."

Fifteen minutes later, Luke looked as if he'd been caught in a downpour. His black hair was slicked back from his forehead, water dripped from his nose onto his soaked gray undershirt, and his matching drawers were splotched with large, dark wet spots. He could have sworn the minute he plopped that dumb dog into the tub, a hundred fleas made their escape—right onto him. In desperation, Luke had dumped a bucket of water over himself and scrubbed a very uncooperative Drifter as fast as he could. When Luke lifted him from the tub, the dog shook as soon as all four feet touched the ground, drenching Luke anew.

Drifter moved farther out in the yard, carefully watching Luke. His wet coat clung to his skin-and-bones body, making him look like a starved, overgrown rat. He shook again, and little tufts of fur randomly sprang up across his back.

"I'll dry you off in a little bit." Luke grimaced as he pulled the long-sleeved undershirt off over his head and tossed it on the grass. He dumped the water out of the tub, pumped a fresh bucketful from the well and rinsed the tub. "Looks like I'd better bathe out here, too." He slapped his thigh, then scratched his head. Fleas were hopping all over him.

He quickly pumped several buckets of cold water and poured them into the tub. Drifter caught Luke's eye as the dog headed around the corner of the house. "Don't roll in the dirt!" he bellowed, scratching his hip. "Dang fleas are eatin' me up!" He cleared the six porch steps in two long strides. Moments later he returned from the kitchen carrying two buckets of hot water. He dumped them in the washtub and turned back toward the kitchen just as Drifter trotted around the house.

"Is Luke back here, doggy?"

Luke gasped as Rebecca's soft voice drifted around the corner of the house. Dropping the buckets—one on his toe— he hopped around on one foot and searched desperately for a place to hide, mumbling curses about stupid dogs and nosy women. Seconds before Rebecca stepped into view, he dove behind a pile of brush the former tenant had left for firewood.

Rebecca paused a moment to scratch Drifter behind the ears, then looked up, her gaze scanning the yard. "Luke? Are you out here?" She walked over to the washtub and looked around the yard again. Spotting a man's foot—with a very red big toe—peeking out from behind the thick pile of branches, she asked hesitantly, "Luke?"

"Yes?" came the muffled reply.

"What are you doing?" she asked softly.

"Scratching."

She giggled. "Why?"

"Because I itch."

"Oh." She heard a heavy sigh. Dry leaves rustled and a twig snapped. A minute later, Luke stood up, and Rebecca gasped softly, her eyes growing wide. "Oh, my . . ." she breathed.

He was hidden from the waist down, but she could see enough of the top edge of his drawers to know he was not wearing any pants. Above the underwear he was bare and glorious—thick rippling muscles and a chest covered with black, curling hair. Rebecca had seen a man's chest before; after all she had been married. But as much as she loved Anthony, his tall, lanky body was no comparison to Luke's stocky, muscular build. He crossed his arms across his chest, and she released a silent little sigh. *No wonder it felt so good for him to hold me.*

Hot color flooded her cheeks, and she quickly looked away. "Excuse me. I didn't expect you to be bathing in the back yard."

"I don't usually, but now I've got the dog's fleas. I didn't want to get too many in the house."

"I see." Her eyes strayed back to him. She watched in fascination as he unconsciously scratched his hairy chest with one hand and his firm stomach with the other.

"Do you want something, Rebecca?" he asked quietly.

Yes, but I can't have it. "Uh . . ." Her face burned as she quickly looked away again. "Please come over an hour later tomorrow." Her words came out in a rush. "Both Uncle Wylie and I have committee meetings right after church. They shouldn't take long, but I wouldn't want you to have to wait."

"I'll be there at two."

"Fine. Uh, I'll see you tomorrow." She spun on her heel and raced around the corner of the house. "I like your dog," she called, safely hidden from his view—and he from hers.

"Thank you. He's adopted me for a while."

Rebecca leaned against the side of the house, her gaze darting nervously across the field, as she tried to still her pounding heart and catch her breath. She knew she should leave, but she didn't want to. She felt young and foolish—and so very alive. "What's his name?"

"Drifter," he called.

She hesitated a minute, then did something totally out of character, something daring and even a little bit wicked. She peeked around the corner. "I like . . . his name." Her quick glance soaked up the sight of him before she ducked back behind the house. "Good-bye, Luke."

"Good-bye, Rebecca." Luke's voice reflected his bewilderment. He stepped out of his hiding place and picked up a towel from where he had dropped it earlier on the grass.

Holding it in front of him, he waited nervously to see if she would pop around the house again. When she did not return, he whistled softly. "I'll be . . ."

Thinking about Rebecca, Luke fetched another bucket of hot water from the kitchen and poured it into the tub. He stuck a finger in the water, barely noticing that it was only warm, and set the empty bucket down on the ground, well away from his foot. The dull ache in his toe was forgotten. So were the fleas. Rebecca's actions and obvious interest filled his mind. He unfastened one button in the waistband of his drawers but halted at the second when she suddenly flew around the corner.

Chapter 9

"LUKE NORTHCUTT, GET your pants on!" She raced across the yard and grabbed him by the upper arm, pulling him toward the back door.

"Rebecca! What are you doing?" Dumbfounded, he stared at her even as he allowed her to propel him up the steps to the porch.

"Get in that house and get your clothes on!"

He planted his feet firmly in one spot, and though she tugged on his arm, he didn't budge. "Why?" His eyes narrowed.

"Because Aggie Davis just turned down your lane!"

A slow twinkle filled his eyes and the corners of his lips lifted slightly. Luke shifted his position, bringing his free hand up to rest on the doorjamb beside her head. He wondered if she realized she still clutched his other arm. Leaning closer, he dropped his voice way down low. "Seems to me the best way to scare her off would be to show her how uncouth I am." His gaze flickered from her eyes to her lips and back to her eyes again. "It sure sent you packing." *But not soon enough.*

As his warm breath skimmed her face, Rebecca strove for sanity. There was no time for the feelings he stirred inside her—no time to watch a drop of water trickle down in front of his ear and slide down his neck, no time to relish the heat radiating from him, no time to listen to the intimate, sensual timbre of his voice as it wrapped around her like a caress.

"Luke, there will be a scandal if Aggie arrives to find you in your drawers and me here." Releasing his arm, she attempted to look serious and very prim.

He wasn't sure why he pushed it, why he teased her. Maybe it was the longing he had seen in her eyes a few minutes earlier—the longing she was trying so hard to disguise even now. "Then hide." He smiled—a slow, sexy, mischievous smile. "There's a pretty good brush pile out there by the washtub."

"Luke!" He shifted closer until his thigh pressed lightly against her leg. First she felt heat, then a coolness as the wet cloth of his drawers dampened her skirt. Her gaze settled on that teasing smile, on those lips so close to her own. *No time.* "You'll never get rid of her once she sees that magnificent chest of yours," she murmured.

Luke chuckled and eased away. "Magnificent, is it?"

Rebecca's face turned bright red. She had not realized she had spoken out loud. *This is getting out of hand.* She took a deep, steadying breath and said briskly, "Like Hercules. Now, kindly step aside, and I'll do what I can to stall her while you get dressed."

Luke gave her a cocky grin—the first he had ever bestowed upon a woman—and stepped to one side. "Yes, ma'am."

That grin was almost Rebecca's undoing. Gathering what was left of her wits, she hurried away, not daring to look back.

THAT EVENING AGGIE leaned her head against Winston's arm as the porch swing shifted lazily back and forth with a steady creak. The nights were still cool, and she welcomed the warmth of his big body next to hers and the comfort of his arm around her shoulders. The stars were beginning to twinkle in the heavens, and she delighted in each sparkling diamond. Until a few days before, she had never seen their beauty—not until Winston convinced her to get glasses.

"You look mighty nice tonight."

"Thank you. You're the second man who complimented me on my appearance today."

"Oh, yeah? Who was the other one?"

"Luke Northcutt."

"Where'd you see him?"

"I stopped by his place on my way out here."

"What for?"

She smiled up at him in the darkness. She could feel his sudden tenseness and wondered in amazement if he were jealous. "To pick up my pie tin. I had taken him one of those awful vinegar pies when he first moved in."

Winston relaxed and chuckled. "What did he say about it?"

"Oh, he thanked me and said he really enjoyed it. Poor man. I told him he was very kind, but that he didn't have to try to make me feel good. I explained about my poor eyesight and misreading the recipe and that I realize how awful it must have been with a cup of vinegar instead of a quarter cup.

"Part of the blame goes to Robert's mother since her writing looked like hen scratching. I usually remember whatever I read, so I never looked at the recipe more than once or twice. I don't like vinegar pie myself, and I never tasted it. It was Robert's favorite, so I figured most men would like it. Of course, he always made it himself. He did most of the cooking because I ruined everything."

"Now, Aggie, that's just because you couldn't see the recipes too good. That apple cake you brought tonight was as fine as any I've ever eat. You keep practicing, and you'll be taking home some ribbons next year at the fair." He squeezed her shoulder. "You can keep practicin' on me."

"Brave man." She chuckled when he playfully swelled up his chest. There was a lot more to Winston Neeley than she had ever realized, more personality and depth than most people figured. Most folks thought he was just a big blowhard. She had, too, until he showed her the kinder, gentler side of his nature.

He discovered that she was as blind as a bat but was afraid someone would make fun of her if she wore glasses. The next day he took her out to eat at Thomas and Sarchfield Restaurant in Grinnell. Afterward they walked over to the park, where they strolled leisurely down the walkways among the maples, elms, and cottonwoods, before Winston suggested they window-shop around the city block. That act alone amazed her.

When they were in front of the doctor's office, he stopped and quietly ordered her to go inside and get some glasses. When she refused, he gently cupped her face in his big, callused hand—right there on Main Street. "You're missin' too much of the world, Aggie. Don't let it pass you by. And if any man makes fun or even grins at your glasses, I'll bust his nose."

She had been nervous at first, but half an hour after she began wearing her spectacles she was too engrossed in looking at everything to care what anyone thought. And in her heart, she had blessed Winston Neeley more times than she could count. She awoke in the morning anxious for the day and the beautiful and interesting things it would bring. She had changed and it showed. She no longer twittered nervously when talking to people because now she could see their expressions clearly and gauge their reactions to her and the conversation. She was more confident and happier than she could ever remember being, and it showed in the subtle glow on her face.

She snuggled a little closer to Winston. "Rebecca Stephens was leaving Mr. Northcutt's when I arrived." She held her breath, waiting to see if it bothered Winston. Aggie knew that he had asked Rebecca to marry him dozens of times.

"Well, they are close neighbors. And, seems like he's been spending a lot of time at her place since he moved in."

"Does that bother you, Winston?" she asked quietly.

"Naw. I gave up on Rebecca a long time ago. I wasn't in love with her or anything. It just seemed like a good idea to get married since our farms run together. I hear she sent that Crowder feller packin', too."

"She seemed nervous today. Even a little flustered."

"That don't sound like Rebecca. You don't suppose Luke tried somethin', do you?" A second later he answered his own question. "Naw, he ain't the kind that would get rough with a woman."

"A man doesn't have to be rough to get a woman flustered, Winston. Something was going on because he seemed real edgy, too."

"Maybe they had an argument."

"Maybe. Another thing was odd. His hair was wet and there were several damp spots on his pants." Aggie blushed and caught her lower lip between her teeth. A lady wasn't supposed to notice such things, or at least not mention them to a man.

"Seems like you were lookin' awful close, Aggie Davis." Winston's arm tightened around her shoulders.

"It's your fault." She smiled up at him. The moon had risen, making it possible to see his irritated expression. "I wouldn't have noticed if I hadn't been wearing my glasses. I noticed a big damp spot on the side of Rebecca's skirt, too."

"What do you suppose they'd been up to?"

"I don't know, but he looked real uncomfortable. Something was sure eatin' on him."

"Speaking of eatin' . . ." Winston shifted a little, making the swing sway unevenly. He slid his free hand around her tiny waist, splaying his fingers across her rib cage. "You could stand to put on a little weight."

"I lost a lot after Robert died."

"Most people do when they're grieving."

"That was part of it. But mostly, I didn't like my own cooking."

He was quiet a moment. "You used to have a lot more curves."

She looked up at him in surprise. "You noticed?"

"I noticed."

"But Winston, I was a married woman when I met you."

"That's why I never let on that I noticed." He looked away, gazing out at the moonlit night. "You look pretty tonight in that bright blue dress."

"Winston, don't tease me. I'm not pretty. I never was, but especially since I got so skinny . . ." Her voice trailed off, and when she spoke again, her tone was scornful. "I didn't realize how terrible I looked until I got my glasses. With my hair pulled back in a tight bun—like my mama said all good widows should wear—and those dull black widow's weeds, good Lord, I looked like a crow. An old, ugly black crow."

"Aggie, don't talk like that!"

"I know what I am, Winston." Suddenly all her fears and inadequacies crashed down on her. "I'm a plain-faced, skinny, thirty-year-old widow who looks forty. And I'm the laughingstock of the county because I've thrown myself at every eligible man around." She jumped up from the swing and ran, but Winston caught her at the bottom of the porch steps.

"Aggie, stop it! You're not plain-faced, and you don't even look thirty—not now, not tonight." He caressed the side of her face. "You do look pretty in that dress; it brings out the blue in your eyes and puts color in your cheeks." He touched a soft curl at her temple. "I like your hair this way. You used to wear it like this."

Her tear-filled eyes grew wide as she looked up at him.

"I always thought those little curls around your face looked soft and inviting, just askin' a man to run his fingers through them." Winston's voice was rough with emotion. He'd heard somewhere that confession was good for the soul, but right at that moment he was more worried about what Aggie thought of him than about his soul.

"I wanted you, Aggie. You were married to Robert, and I still wanted you. That's why I didn't come courtin' after he died. I felt guilty because of what I'd felt for you. Then one night I got to thinkin' about the way you used to be, and I realized you were drying up from loneliness."

Aggie looked down, overwhelmed by his confession. Her first husband had been much older than either she or Winston. She had always been so thankful that Robert had married her and loved her in spite of her plainness.

"But I've made such a fool of myself this last year. I know people laugh at me."

"They laugh at me, too, Aggie. But I swear if anybody ever laughs or makes fun of you again, they'll answer to me. Whether you marry me or not."

"I'll marry you, Winston, if you really want me."

"Want you? Honey, I've wanted you ever since you walked into Lansing Dry Goods four years ago wearin' that bright red dress with all those black do-dads down the front."

"I'm not the same as I was then."

"We'll fatten you up." He sat down on the step and pulled her down on his lap. "Maybe I'l even plant a baby in that smooth, flat belly of yours." At her soft gasp, his expression grew serious. "I'm rough as a cob, Aggie. I'm loud, obnoxious, and my manners stink. But I'm a good farmer and a hard worker. You'll always have a roof over your head. You'll never grow hungry. I may embarrass you sometimes with my ways." He swallowed hard. "But I'll love you until my dyin' day."

"Oh, Winston. If you can teach me to cook, I can teach you manners." She whispered that she loved him, too, and touched his lips with hers.

Winston had made regular trips to Des Moines and even Chicago for nigh onto fifteen years, trips that had more to do with filling a man's needs than they had to do with business. He had been with plenty of women and fancied himself something of an expert at sex. So it came as a shock to realize he had never really been kissed before. Oh, some of the women he had been with had let him kiss them, although most were more interested in getting right down to business rather than playing around. But he had never been kissed by a woman who loved and desired him and only him. When he finally had the strength to pull back, they were both trembling.

"Aggie?" His voice was hoarse. "I can't handle a long engagement."

"We can get a license day after tomorrow."

"Maybe we could wake up the County Clerk tonight."

"I don't think he'd appreciate it."

"No, you're probably right. And people would talk." Winston settled back against the stair railing and snuggled her against him. "Guess I'd better see you home . . . or we could go inside . . ."

"You'd better take me home." Aggie sighed. "I don't want my reputation to be any more tarnished than it already is. But Winston, I promise, I'll make it worth the wait."

He closed his eyes, holding her tightly. "We'll be standin' on the courthouse steps when it opens Monday morning."

Chapter 10

LUKE INSISTED ON helping Rebecca with the dishes Sunday after dinner, using the excuse that the sooner they vacated the kitchen, the sooner they could catch the boy. That line kept Wylie from ribbing him and gave Luke a chance to talk to Rebecca alone.

He poured hot water from the tea kettle into a dishpan sitting in the dry sink, then pumped a little cold water in with it. He repeated his actions with the second dishpan, which he would use for rinsing. After adding some soap to the wash water, he picked up the glasses and dunked them in the water. Washing them with the efficient movements of a man used to taking care of his own house, he soon had all the glasses draining in the wooden dish rack at the back of the sink.

When Rebecca took a glass from the rack and dried it mechanically, Luke grimaced. She had not met his gaze all afternoon and had only talked to him enough to be polite. He knew she was embarrassed about what had happened between them the day before. Looking back, he was a little embarrassed about it, too. But he was honest enough to admit that he had enjoyed flirting with her. He liked the admiration he had seen in her eyes—and the traces of desire.

Her clear interest had kept him stirred up all night. When he had been awake, he wondered how it would feel to hold and kiss her. When he had finally slept, his dreams brought both pleasure and torment.

"Uh, Rebecca, about yesterday—"

"I don't want to talk about yesterday."

He kept on washing dishes and did not look up. "All right. We'll just forget about it." *Liar.* He started on the plates, determined to put aside those particular memories for the moment. Something else had been bothering him for a couple of days. "I'm not sure we should try to catch the boy."

Rebecca grew still, halting the twisting movement of her hand and the unbleached muslin dishtowel inside a crystal goblet. She looked up at him, her incredulous expression quickly turning defiant. "Why in the world not?"

"Because I'm not sure it's the right thing to do." He put another clean plate in the drain rack and sighed. It was the reaction he had expected, but it still made him uncomfortable. "He's afraid. I don't want to scare him even more."

Fear was a way of life for a boy on his own. Luke remembered it all too well. Besides the basic worries about food, shelter, and clothing, there were other things, things that made a young heart pound and a body shake—the blast of a shotgun and the peppering of buckshot inches behind him, the baying of dogs hot on his trail, a new bully to fight in every town. But the worst fear of all was the constant worry of getting caught, of being sent back to a life that was intolerable, to what had forced him to run away.

"Well, of course you don't want to scare him. Neither do I." She finished drying the glass and set it on the counter before picking up a wet plate. "But I'm afraid he's sick. Three of Wylie's handkerchiefs were taken from the clothesline on Tuesday. The boy needs to be in a home, not out trying to fend for himself."

"You mean in an orphanage?" Luke knew they were not all bad, but he doubted the boy would want to go to one.

"That's one possibility. Or maybe back to his family."

"And what if he doesn't want to go back?" Luke scrubbed a plate with more force than was necessary.

The brittle edge to his voice, which would have gone undetected by most people, caused her to look up. She glanced at the tenseness in his shoulders and the quick, almost fierce movement of his hand on the plate. "Then I would try to find out why."

He put the plate in the rack and quickly disposed of two more. "You'd take his word for it?"

"No, I don't think so." She frowned, pondering the question. "Not just his word. Since I don't know him, I would have his story investigated. Discreetly, of course."

"And if you decided it was a bad situation, even if he had family, would you send him back, or let him take care of himself?" He plunked the cast-iron skillet into the dishwater. It was something he couldn't break if he didn't like her answer.

"Neither. I'd try to get custody of him."

Startled, Luke jerked his head up to look at her. Water sloshed over the side of the dishpan into the zinc lining of the sink. "You'd adopt him?"

"Yes. Uncle Wylie and I have already talked it over. We could never send him back to a situation that would be harmful. We would let him live here for a while and then, if he agreed, I'd try to adopt him."

Luke experienced a little twinge of envy mixed in with his relief. As a boy, he would have given anything to have had a mother like Rebecca. A sudden lump clogged his throat. He ducked his head and scrubbed the pan for all he was worth. After a few minutes of awkward silence he cleared his throat and murmured in a still husky voice, "He's a lucky boy."

"No, I think I'll be the lucky one," said Rebecca, picking up the stack of plates. She carried them into the dining room and put them away in the sideboard, taking a little more time than was necessary. The longing and pain in Luke's face had been unmistakable, even though he had tried quickly to hide them. Her wish to offer him comfort pushed aside the shame caused by her actions of the day before. Only the suspicion that he would be embarrassed kept her from putting her arms around him and holding him close to her heart.

When she returned to the kitchen, he had dried the clean frying pan. He washed the last of the silverware and put it in the drainer. "Do I pour this water in the sink?" He looked at her expectantly, all traces of his earlier discomfort gone.

"Yes, it runs out into the backyard."

Luke poured out the water, pausing a moment to watch it go down the drain, then turned the dishpans upside down and leaned them against the side of the dry sink. "What are you going to put out for the boy?"

Rebecca grinned. "I have extra portions of everything we had for dinner and then some. There's fried chicken, yeast rolls, and cherry pie. I put the potato salad, lima beans, stewed tomatoes, and pears in jars." They set everything on the two kitchen windowsills, then stood back and admired the display of food. "Do you think he might finally get the idea that we want to be nice to him?"

"Maybe. More than likely, he'll figure it's a trap." Luke looked from the window by the back door to the other one on the adjacent wall. It would be impossible for the lad to carry everything at once. "It looks pretty obvious."

"Hopefully, he will be so hungry that it won't matter. If he tries to carry as much as he can, we'll be able to get down here in time to stop him."

"Don't count on it. All we can do is go upstairs, watch, and wait."

Rebecca led the way up the staircase to the guest bedroom, which was on the corner of the house above the kitchen. The windows of the second-floor room were directly over the windows in the kitchen.

Luke followed her into the bedroom, leaving the door open behind them. He glanced at the ornately carved walnut headboard of the double bed. The marble-topped dresser, commode washstand, and wardrobe matched the bed. A bow-tie pattern patchwork quilt in various shades and prints of red, green, and blue served as a coverlet. A crisp white eyelet ruffle fell from the mattress almost to the floor. He wondered how far down they would sink on the feather mattress if they were curled up together.

"Do you think we need to watch from both windows?" she asked in a hushed voice.

He walked briskly over to stand beside her, hoping she would not guess the direction his thoughts had taken. He inspected the view through the white crocheted lace curtain. The window overlooked the side yard, the garden, and the field beyond. "He won't come this way. It's too open. He'd be spotted too easily." Luke also spoke quietly, hardly more than a whisper.

He moved over to the other window and nodded. "This is the way he'll come." When Rebecca stepped up beside him, he bent down slightly, unconsciously bringing his head and body closer to hers. "He'll probably come up through the orchard and hide behind the barn. When he feels sure the coast is clear, he'll hightail it across to the wagon, then over behind Jackson's house." He followed the path with his finger.

"Why wouldn't he go by the chicken coop? That would be a more direct route."

"And set the chickens to squawkin'? I can tell you never tried to sneak up on anyone." He grinned at her and suddenly became conscious of her closeness.

"There are only a few old hens hanging around the coop right now."

"That's all it takes to make a fuss." He gazed out the window thoughtfully. "Of course, he's been around a while, so they may be used to him. They might not pay much attention to him. We'll have to keep an eye on it, too. Either way, he'll head for the back of Jackson's house." Luke straightened.

"I suppose he knows us pretty well by now."

"Yep. He knows Jackson spends quiet Sunday afternoons with Wylie down in the parlor playing checkers. He'll skirt around in back of the little house, then work his way up behind the shrubs and trees to the back door. There's lots of cover, but if we keep our eyes open, we'll see him."

He looked around for something to sit on. There was one straight-backed chair in the corner and a short, backless bench at the foot of the bed. He carried both pieces of furniture over near the window, setting them close enough to the wall so they could see out but far enough back to be sheltered by the lacy curtain. "You take the chair. I'll sit over here."

"Thank you." Rebecca perched on the bright blue velvet chair cushion as he straddled the matching cushion on the bench and leaned back against the side of the wardrobe. "Do you think he will come soon?" she asked.

"Probably not. In fact, he might not come at all. You don't always leave food out after meals, do you?"

"I did yesterday. A small pan of stew after dinner and some fried potatoes and salt pork last night." She squirmed under his dark frown. "Wylie was here after dinner. Both Jackson and Wylie were here last night."

"But Jackson wasn't here yesterday afternoon?"

"No. He went to town for a while." She looked away, staring out the window at the corner of the barn.

"You were taking chances again." Luke crossed his arms in front of him. He found it hard to watch the yard. He enjoyed looking at her a whole lot more. Studying her profile, he admired the creamy skin of her throat and neck. With her hair pinned up in a cluster of curls at the top of her head, the graceful arch of her neck and her delicate ears were beautifully displayed. Wispy little honey blond curls framed her face, kissing her cheeks, temples, and forehead.

She glanced at him and caught her breath. The frown had vanished, and he was looking at her with heart-stopping tenderness. "I thought he might not be so suspicious today if I put food out yesterday."

"You're probably right." He smiled, his gaze lingering on her face. With obvious reluctance Luke turned his attention to the window, and they sat in companionable silence for a while.

"Are you ready to plant the corn?" Rebecca slowly rotated her neck, trying to ease a deep ache in her shoulders.

"No, I still have to finish harrowing the back field and go over some places with the roller where there are some big clods. It looks like the last farmer started to work the field and changed his mind. Ought to take three or four more days." He frowned as she rolled her shoulders. "Got a sore neck?"

"Yes. I must have slept crooked." *What little I slept.* "I woke up with a kink in my shoulders and neck."

"Come here and I'll rub it for you."

Rebecca looked at the small space at the end of the bench. It would be impossible to sit there without touching him. Her heartbeat quickened. Earlier, when they had been standing together by the window, she had enjoyed being close to him. Perhaps she had even liked it too much. "There's no need."

"Come here, Rebecca," he said softly. "You'll get a headache if you don't let me rub out the soreness."

She searched his face and felt her cheeks grow warm. His expression held only concern, and although she thought she detected a flash of something in his eye, he did not appear to be having the same sensual thoughts as she was. "Well, I suppose it would help."

"Of course, it would." He sat up straight, watching the barn with pretended nonchalance while she moved over to him. When she sat down in front of him, his thighs cradled her hips. Luke closed his eyes, thankful that the draped overskirt on her dress was gathered into a big puffy bow at the small of her back.

"Luke?" Rebecca whispered uncertainly, keeping her body stiff and her gaze glued on the wall in front of her.

"Sorry. I thought I saw something move outside." He opened his eyes and brought his hands up to her shoulders, ordering her to relax. When she did, he began to knead the muscles gently.

"You can rub a little harder. I won't break." Rebecca smiled at his caution.

He increased the pressure of his fingers and thumbs as they dug into her knotted muscles. "Better?"

"Yes."

He massaged from the base of her neck across to her shoulders for a few minutes, then edged farther down her back, working on the tenseness between her shoulder blades.

"Mmm."

"Feel good?"

"Wonderful." She sighed as the pain slowly ebbed.

After several minutes, Luke brought one hand around and cupped her chin in his palm. "Rest your head in my hand. Come on, relax so I can work on your neck."

Rebecca did as she was told, picturing a loaf of soft bread dough in her mind. She tried to be as limp and pliable as the dough while his strong fingers kneaded and smoothed, molded and soothed. She enjoyed the massage for several minutes, until she began to feel guilty for taking advantage of his kindness. When she lifted her head from his palm, he lowered both hands to rest on his thighs. Rebecca looked back at him over her shoulder. "Thank you."

"You're welcome."

"That feels much better." She slowly bent her neck from side to side, then up and down, testing it.

When she leaned her head forward, Luke spotted three little red welts on the nape of her neck. He lifted his hand, resting it on her shoulder, and brushed the edge of his thumb near the bumps. "Looks like one of Drifter's fleas got you, too."

Rebecca chuckled, raised her head, and glanced back at him. "I think it had already adopted you when it came calling."

Her careless remark brought the events of the previous afternoon flooding back. Visions of his physical beauty and the memory of his arm beneath her hand and his leg pressed against her side taunted her. That same thigh, as well as the other one, caressed her even now, only this time there was no dampness to cool the heat.

"Sorry." His eyes darkened to the deep blue of a rain-filled cloud as he, too, remembered.

"Thanks for the neck rub." Rebecca looked nervously away and shifted her weight, preparing to stand. His hand was heavy on her shoulder, and the subtle scent of bay rum teased her nostrils.

"Stay," he whispered, stroking the nape of her neck with his thumb. "Sit here with me."

"I—I shouldn't." *But, oh, how I want to.*

"I know." He moved his hand from her shoulder, slowly skimming it down her arm until his fingers entwined with hers. The movement brought his chest up against her back. "You could lean against me and rest your neck. That would be more comfortable than sitting in the straight chair. You don't want to start hurting again, do you?"

"No. But it's not proper," she protested faintly.

"Are you always proper, Miz Stephens?" he teased. His warm breath brushed the top of her ear.

"Yes." She rested her head against his shoulder. "No, I guess I'm not," she said with a sigh. "I wasn't very proper yesterday."

"No, you weren't." He freed his fingers from hers and moved his hand around her waist to rest over her belly-button. He had figured she was wearing a corset, yet it disappointed him when he felt steel beneath his fingers instead of soft flesh. "You surprised me."

"I surprised myself. I was shameful." It felt wonderful to be so close to him.

"No. Just a little . . . mischievous."

"Like a schoolgirl."

"No," he said emphatically. There had been too much knowledge in her eyes for any schoolgirl. He chuckled and nuzzled her temple, brushing it with his lips when he spoke. "You realize we're not looking out the window at all, don't you?"

A sweet lethargy filled her. Rebecca knew she wasn't going to move. Surely, a simple embrace was not wrong. "Guess we'd better pay more attention."

"Guess so." Luke tightened his arm a fraction. This aching longing was new to him. He needed to be close to her, to feel her body next to his, to wrap his arms around her and absorb some of her gentle caring into his soul. He wanted it so badly that it scared him. "Will you stay here?"

"Yes."

Chapter 11

LUKE'S HEART POUNDED so hard he was afraid she would feel it. He carefully leaned back against the wardrobe, drawing her with him. She wiggled a little to get comfortable—and almost drove him out of his mind. He looked out the window, trying to keep his thoughts on their plan, but though his eyes watched the yard, the rest of his senses were finely tuned to her alone.

The wispy curls along her forehead grazed his jaw as she turned to watch out the window. With a tiny shift of her head the curls were brushed aside, allowing her silky skin to rest against the cleanly shaven smoothness of his. When he settled both arms around her middle, she rested her hands and arms on top of them. It was odd how that simple act filled him with contentment and a sense of belonging.

His thundering heart gradually slowed, allowing sounds other than his rushing blood to reach his ears. The song of a robin nearby, the bellow of a bull in the distance, and the whinny of a horse down by the barn were only the background music to her contented sigh.

The faint fragrance of wild roses mingled with the cool breeze blowing gently through the small opening in the window, and he knew that in all the spring days to come, he would remember this moment and cherish it in his heart.

For Rebecca it was a precious time. The steady beat of his heart and the quiet, gentle rhythm of his breathing reassured her. Any uneasiness she had felt at first vanished in the peace and happiness that filled her soul. Memories of other springs and of another man's arms threatened to infringe on her pleasure, but she forced them from her thoughts. These moments were for Luke, to give that gruff, cautious man the tenderness she sensed he craved, to show him she admired him and wanted to be near him.

And, yes, they were for her as well. She needed the tenderness he so often kept hidden; she needed his affection and to experience the pleasure of his arms around her. In her heart, she knew he could heal her brokenness, that dark corner of despair that could only be cleansed by a man's love.

"Luke?"

"Um?"

"Would you tell me about yourself?" When she felt him stiffen, she caressed the back of his hand, swirling the black, silky hair around her fingertip.

"What do you want to know?"

"Oh, everything." She shifted her head and smiled up at him. "Nosy, aren't I?"

"Yeah." He relaxed and returned her smile.

"Have you always been a farmer?"

"No. It's what I like best, but I've done a lot of other things, too."

"Such as?" She turned back to the window to keep their vigil, smiling as he toyed with her fingers.

"Well, I worked on a riverboat on the Mississippi, pounded steel in a factory in Chicago, operated a screw press at Cincinnati Screw Company, went to New York City and drove a freight wagon—"

"You've been to New York City?" She shifted her upper body so she could see him clearly.

"Yep."

"What was it like?"

"Interesting but too crowded. I only stayed about four months, just long enough to see the sights on my Sundays off. I needed wide-open spaces so I left."

"I've always thought it would be exciting to go to the theater in New York. I've read about the plays and how fancy everyone dresses. It would probably be as much fun to see all those elaborate gowns as it would be to see the play." She moved back around, snuggling her temple against the side of his neck.

Her words reminded him of the differences in their farms and levels of income. His happiness faded somewhat. "I went to a vaudeville show once, but I didn't have the money or the clothes to go to one of the high-class theaters." He wasn't about to mention the raunchy burlesque show he had seen.

"I probably wouldn't go, either. I might spend the money for the ticket, but I know I couldn't bring myself to throw away a small fortune on an elaborate gown. I like nice clothes, but I try to be careful with my expenses. That's one advantage of having a father who owns a dry goods store. He won't let me pay for any of the material I want and is always giving me special pieces. I make my everyday wrappers myself, but Mrs. Ellsworth makes the nicer dresses. She's an excellent seamstress and quite reasonable."

"Are you trying to impress me with your thriftiness?" He smiled lazily when she glanced up at him, his happiness restored.

"But of course." She smiled back, then looked down at their hands for a moment. His were large and strong, capable of hard work but also of infinite gentleness. She curled her fingers over his. "Where were you born?"

"Ohio."

She sensed by his short answer that he did not want to discuss his family, but she could not help heal his wounds unless she knew what caused the deep pain he tried to hide. She decided to push him a little. "Did you live on a farm?"

"Yes."

"Brothers and sisters?"

"Yes." Luke sighed heavily. "Have I ever told you that you're beautiful?"

She looked up at him in surprise. "No." He was frowning down at her. She frowned back.

"Beautiful but relentless. Let's drop it."

She pulled away slightly and turned, leaning back against the support of his arm, and searched the depths of his eyes. Stroking her thumb across the deep lines between his brows, she whispered, "I don't think I can. Earlier, when you were talking about the boy, you were speaking from experience. I need to know what your life was like, so I can understand. Both for you and him."

Luke studied her earnest face for a long moment. Compassion filled her eyes, yet she was vulnerable, too. She was asking him to trust her, and she would be wounded if he refused. But trusting was hard for Luke. Too many people had failed him too many times.

"Please."

Luke swore silently. How could he deny her request when she looked up at him with those beautiful eyes? He could detect each different color—the blue, gold, and brown flecks that hid in the gray green mist until a man was close enough to kiss her. That was what he wanted—to kiss her instead of shredding up his heart.

"You can't sit like that. You'll make your back hurt again." Luke moved swiftly, sliding an arm beneath her legs and lifting her to sit across his lap, her legs dangling over his thigh. With a challenge in his eyes, he removed his arm from beneath her knees and rested it across her lap, planting his hand firmly on the side of her hip.

Rebecca swallowed hard and tried to calm her heart. His sudden movement had startled her, but her excitement had nothing to do with fright. It had everything to do with how close his lips were to hers, the intimacy of sitting on his lap, and the flare of desire in his eyes. She sat very straight and still. If she leaned against him, she was afraid they would forget all about talking.

Luke took a deep breath and looked away. His gaze was turned toward the window, but he did not see the yard. Instead, places and people long forgotten marched before his mind's eye like the moving slides of a Magic Lantern. "There's not much to tell, really. The old man was too lazy to work. The only thing he was good at was making babies.

I think there were twelve of us in all. Ma didn't work either, not even around the house. I reckon she was too tired from always being pregnant. By the time I came along, my sister Flora did all the cooking and cleaning. She's eight years older than me.

"They kept me around until I was almost two, then I was packed off to first one relative, then another. My grandparents would keep me five or six months, then send me to one of my aunts. I'd stay there until her old man started bellyaching about how much I was eating, then she'd send me back to Grandpa or to another aunt."

"Did you ever see your parents?"

"Not until I was older. They just kept having babies and sending them off to live with relatives. By the time I was five my parents and the kinfolks decided I was old enough to work for my room and board. There were all kinds of shirttail relations on both sides of the family that would put me up for a few months as long as I worked hard."

Oh, Luke! Rebecca thought her heart would break. Tears burned her eyes, but she fought not to let them show. He would not want her pity.

"Right after I turned nine, the old man decided I could hire out to work for more than just my keep."

"You were just a child!"

His sad eyes focused on her briefly. "No, Rebecca. I was never a child."

For a few minutes, she thought he would not continue. She watched him battle the pain and wished she had never asked him to tell her about it.

"Actually, being farmed out wasn't too bad in a lot of ways. Most of the farmers treated me decent. I usually had good meals and a warm pallet by the fire. Some of the wives even taught me how to read and do figures. Oh, there were a couple of bullies that liked to beat up on me, but then some of my kinfolk had enjoyed that, too." At her gasp, he gave her a bitter smile. "It served a purpose. Made me tough." He broke away from her anguished eyes.

"I worked on various farms for the old man until I was eleven. All the money I earned went to him to help support the family. One day I dropped by there on my way to another job. I had my wages in my pocket, and as usual, he grabbed them the minute I walked in the door. Ma had just given birth to a stillborn baby, so I helped her bury it."

"The poor woman. It's good you were there to help ease her grief."

Luke wasn't sure he could go on. How could he tell the generous, loving woman in his arms that his mother had no love for her children? But if he didn't tell her, she would think he was terrible to have run away.

"She didn't grieve."

"What?"

"She didn't care enough about the child to grieve for her. I realized that day that Ma was as bad as the old man. She didn't care about any of us, or what happened to us."

"Oh, Luke. You can't mean it."

"She was glad the baby died! It would have been just another mouth to feed. She even said it was too bad all the other brats had lived."

"Oh, Luke!" The tears slipped from Rebecca's eyes and rolled down her cheeks. She cradled his jaw in her hand. "What did you do?"

"I left and never went back."

Rebecca leaned against him, burying her face against his shoulder, and curved an arm around his neck. "Luke, forgive me. I shouldn't have pushed you to talk about such painful things."

"Aw, honey, don't cry." As her tears formed a large wet spot on his shirt, Luke's heart twisted. No one had ever cried for him, for his pain. "I'm not worth it."

She raised up, frowning even as the tears cascaded down her cheeks. "Yes, you are!" she said, cupping his face in both hands. "You're a good, kind man. You're worthy of my tears . . . and so much more."

He caught one of her hands and turned his head, kissing the palm. "Please don't cry, Rebecca. I don't know how to handle it."

His helpless expression brought a weak, trembling smile to her face. She sniffed loudly. "Well, the best way is to share your handkerchief, since I don't seem to have one."

Luke shifted his weight to one hip and pulled a clean, but ragged handkerchief from his jean pocket. "It's not too fancy," he said apologetically.

"It'll do." Rebecca dried her eyes, then blew her nose. She tucked the handkerchief in her dress pocket. "I'll send it back after I launder it." She looked up to see him nod. The spark in his eye suddenly made her nervous. "I must look a fright with a red nose and my eyes all swollen."

He shifted slightly, drawing her closer until her softness pressed lightly against his hard chest. His face was inches from her own when he whispered, "You're beautiful."

"And relentless, I'm afraid." Anticipation raced through her. Her gaze traveled from his eyes to his lips and back again. The spark had flared into open desire.

"No, I was wrong. You aren't unyielding." In fact, he thought, at the moment she was far more yielding than he had ever expected. He closed the tiny distance between them and feathered a kiss against her cheek. "You're just determined . . . and your skin is like satin. Right now your nose is red." He dropped a tiny kiss on the end of it. "But soon it will be pretty again."

"Nobody's nose is pretty," she said with a chuckle.

He smiled. "And your eyes are like drops of ocean spray sparkling in the sunlight, catching a golden ray and shattering it into a prism of jewels. You have eyes that see into a man's soul."

Rebecca's smile was warm and tender. Her body sang at his touch, her heart at his words. "Pressed next to mine beats the heart of a poet," she murmured.

"A poor one. But I can borrow from the best." His eyes darkened and his gaze dropped to her mouth. " 'Here will I dwell, for Heaven is in these lips.' "

As he buried his fingers in her hair and curved his hand around the back of her head, Rebecca let her eyelids drift closed, giving herself up to the sweetness that was a heartbeat away. He drew her face to his, touching her lips with exquisite tenderness.

A sudden crash sounded outside the kitchen. They broke apart, startled and disoriented. Luke looked out the window, spotting the towheaded boy running for his life toward the orchard. "We forgot about the kid," he said with a groan.

"Can we catch him?" Rebecca hoped he would say no. She didn't want to go anywhere. Her legs were so weak, she didn't think she *could* go anywhere.

"No. But we'd better get down there before Wylie sends Jackson to see what in tarnation we're doing up here."

"Oh, dear. You're right." Her eyes widened in dismay, and hot color filled her face. She started to get up, a surge of adrenaline giving strength to her wobbly knees.

"Not yet." Luke's hold tightened minutely. He leaned forward and gave her a hard, quick kiss. "There will be another time, Rebecca. And then I'll kiss you like I want to."

Chapter 12

"WE SHOULD'VE STAYED down by the creek." Ten-year-old Saul Miller plucked a piece of hay from his pale blond hair and tossed it behind him as he peered over the edge of the hayloft. He looked nervously toward the barn door. "He ain't even said good night to his horses yet." He glared at his twin brother Paul in the twilight. "And he always makes one last check on Charlie and Old Joe."

"It's startin' to rain, and it's too cold for Sissy to stay out again. That snotty nose will turn into somethin' awful if we don't keep her warm," said Paul.

"Yeah, I know." Saul crawled back to the corner where his brother and sister were huddled together. He watched as Paul pulled the little girl's socks up higher beneath her pants legs and tied one shoelace. They had cut her hair and dressed her in some of their old clothes, figuring it was safer if she looked like a boy. "Guess I'm just jumpy. Droppin' that jar of pears scared the pea-waddle out of me."

"Me like pears."

"I know you do, punkin." Saul smiled at his sister and rumpled her short curls. Nearly three years old, Hester, known to all as Sissy, was a little doll with her strawberry-red hair and bright blue eyes. "Sorry I broke the jar. I just couldn't carry everything they had in my window."

"Me, either." Paul grinned. "I sacrificed some lima beans. Bet they're still tryin' to figure out how one kid took all the stuff they had out."

"They were trying to catch us, or at least one of us." Saul opened his pack and took out metal plates and spoons for each of them. He split the potato salad three ways, carefully dishing out equal portions for himself and Paul and a smaller portion for Sissy. "There's six pieces of chicken. We'll each eat one piece now and save the rest for tomorrow. We can have a slice of pie, but we'd better save the other stuff. No telling when she'll put anything else out." The others nodded in agreement as he dug in the pack once more.

He took out a round tin and pried off the lid. "This was one strange chicken. It had three legs! Da, da!" Saul pulled the chicken legs out of the container like a master magician and waved them in the air with a great swirl of his arm. Sissy giggled, and Paul shared a smile with his twin.

Sissy scooped up a bit of potato salad, using her fingers to push the food onto the spoon. She licked her fingers, then lifted the spoon to her mouth, polishing off the bite. "Hope her gots more pears," she said wistfully.

"Don't talk with your mouth full, Sis." Saul ate another bite. "And don't chew with your mouth open, either. Pa always said it wasn't polite to chew with your mouth open."

"I think her nose is too stuffed up to breathe." Paul reached in his shirt pocket and pulled out a handkerchief, one he had "borrowed" from Rebecca's clothesline, and held it to his sister's nose. "Blow."

She wrinkled up her face and blew with all her might.

"Good. Wait a minute. Let me wipe your nose. Better?"

Sissy nodded emphatically, bouncing her curls. "Me ready for pie."

"Oh no, you don't, squirt. Not until you finish all your chicken and potato salad. Pa never let us eat dessert until everything else was gone."

Tears welled up in Sissy's big eyes. She looked down at the half-eaten food on her plate.

Paul and Saul glanced at each other. The little girl had been a real trouper most of the time they had been on their own. She was a loving and agreeable child and had seldom given them any trouble. But now she was tired and sick. If she decided to let loose with a wail, they were in trouble.

"Now, Sissy, you know you gotta eat right to get well," Saul said in a rush.

"We'll give you a big piece of pie if you eat the other stuff," Paul added, putting his arm around her.

Sissy shook her head sadly. When she looked up, her lips trembled.

The twins braced themselves.

"Sissy miss Pa," she said as the tears rolled down her cheeks. "Sissy wanna go home." She burrowed her head against Paul's shoulder in a valiant attempt to cry quietly.

The twins looked at each other with pain-filled eyes, each boy swallowing the lump that clogged his throat. "We don't have a home anymore, Sissy," they said in unison.

"Me want Pa." The little girl sobbed brokenly.

"We miss him, too, but he's in heaven—"

"—with Ma," interrupted Saul, finishing his brother's sentence, as he often did.

"Shh. Mr. Northcutt's comin'."

The big door creaked as Luke and Drifter entered the barn. Luke hooked the lantern handle over a long piece of wire that hung down from a beam and quietly surveyed the stables. The horses nickered softly to him in greeting and the milch cow raised lazy eyes to watch him as she chewed her cud. Her little calf bounced to the side of their pen and poked her head between the board railing.

"Evenin', ladies, gents. Everything peaceful tonight?"

Old Joe nickered in answer and leaned his head over the top rail of the stall. Charlie added a soft comment and stepped up expectantly, his giant chest brushing the boards.

"You'd say anything for a treat." Luke dug in his pocket and produced a lump of sugar for each horse. He patted each one in turn, talking softly to them and praising them for their hard work on the farm. Then he moved over to

Matilda and her calf, Daisy. They did not care for sugar, but Daisy wiggled in delight when he patted the top of her head. Her mama watched serenely and accepted his compliments with a lazy blink of her eyes.

His quiet words and the animals' low responses kept Luke from hearing Sissy's faint sobs. Drifter's sharp ears picked up the noise, but the youngsters had made friends with him even before he moved to Luke's farm and the dog did not reveal their presence. He was loyal to Luke, but the children had earned his allegiance, too, by sharing their meager meals with him before he found a place and a man to claim as his own.

By the time Luke sat down on a stack of fifty-pound burlap sacks of seed corn, Sissy had quit crying. Silent shudders wracked her little body every few minutes, but with the exception of an occasional sniff, she was as quiet and still as a field mouse hiding from a hawk.

Luke pulled a pocket knife and block of wood from his coat pocket and shifted around on the sack of corn until he was comfortable. The yellow light from the coal oil lantern cast eerie shadows around the barn, projecting the image of a brooding giant on the wall behind him. Drifter lay down at his feet, his head resting on his paws.

"You know, dog, this is a good farm. If the weather cooperates, I should make enough to completely pay off the note at the bank." He whittled quietly for several minutes, transforming one corner of the piece of wood into a horse's head. Thinking out loud, he worked on the neck and body of a plow horse. "I don't owe much. There might even be enough left over to buy a stove for the parlor." He glanced at the dog.

"Now, I know I probably don't need a stove in the parlor, especially since there's no furniture in there. But maybe I can get a few chairs, too. Then Wylie can come over and visit sometimes if he wants to."

Rain splattered nearby on the sack, dotting it and his pants leg with drops. Luke leaned over to one side and picked up a bucket, setting it under the drip. He squinted up at the roof. "Guess I'll have to climb up there tomorrow and try to fix that hole. From the sound of the rain I won't be planting for the next few days anyway."

He whittled a while in silence, unaware of the three pair of eyes that peered down from the haymow, watching in fascination as he transformed a plain old chunk of wood into a thing of beauty. He worked quickly, with sure strokes as his artist's eye saw the animal's form in the wood.

"I've got everything right here that I ever wanted. A farm of my own. The finest land in the country. I'm my own boss, answerable to no man." Luke paused and looked down at Drifter. "The house and barn aren't much. They need a lot of work, but they'll be pretty decent once I get 'em fixed up."

He went back to work on the horse, carving first one muscular leg then another. "I should be happy, but I'm not. Oh, I'm glad about the farm and all, but just between you and me, dog, there's this real empty feeling inside that I had not expected to still be there. I thought the farm would take care of that. But it hasn't."

He leaned back against another sack of corn, remembering the afternoon. When he had held Rebecca, there had been more to his feelings than mere physical attraction. Her nearness had stirred his blood and he wanted her, more than he had ever wanted any woman, but holding her had also brought him contentment. It was not the same happiness that came from owning the farm or bringing in a good crop. It was unique and foreign to his experience.

Somewhere along the way, what he felt for Rebecca had gone beyond simple admiration and friendship and turned into a deep affection. And affection was dangerous. Caring too much for someone led to wanting things that would never be. He had learned that lesson long ago. There was no need to learn it again.

He resumed whittling, mumbling to himself. "She liked me holding her this afternoon. Wanted me to kiss her, too, but that doesn't mean she's got any deep feelings for me. And even if she does, they won't last long. She's just lonesome and needs a man, and I happen to be around." *But she cried for your pain.* "Rebecca would cry for anybody that hurt."

Engrossed in his craft, Luke continued to work, shaving away tiny little pieces until he had a perfectly carved workhorse that would fit in the palm of a boy's hand. He held the figure up to the lantern, examining it carefully. Satisfied that the workmanship was good, he stood, walked over to the ladder going up to the haymow, and set the small figure on one of the wide rungs. "He ought to find it here."

As Luke took the lantern from the hook and moved toward the door, he heard a noise that sounded suspiciously like a muffled sneeze. His first impulse was to snuff out the light, but he reasoned that if the boy, or his companion, wanted to do him harm, he would have already done it.

"If you're there, boy, listen up. We know you're with someone because we saw two sets of tracks at Mrs. Stephens's house today." It irked Luke that he had not been able to tell more from the footprints. Whoever was with the boy had been in an area where the ground was still slippery, and he had not left any clear impressions. Luke's expression and voice grew hard. "There won't be any more handouts over at the Stephens place or anywhere else around here until both you and your partner come out in the open.

"Everybody's totin' a gun now, and they'll keep them real handy until we know who we're dealing with. Take my warning, boy, if your friend does any harm to Rebecca Stephens—if he so much as touches a hair on her head—I'll break every bone in his body. And I'll make sure you go back to where you came from, even if it's hell on earth."

The frightened children cringed, silently shrinking further back into the hay. None of them made a move until they heard the barn door close. After his eyes had adjusted to the darkness, Saul crept over to the side of the barn and peered though a vent hole. He watched the swinging lantern and Luke's shadowy form grow ever smaller in the blackness of the night. When Luke went inside his house and closed the back door behind him, Saul scurried back to the others.

"Holy Moses! That was close!" Paul sat up and brushed the straw off his sleeve with shaking fingers.

"Him was mad!" Sissy looked from one brother to the other in wide-eyed fear. "Them gonna shoot us?"

"Not if we're careful. But we'd better get out of here." Saul dropped down on the hay, facing his brother and sister.

"Where are we gonna go?" asked Paul.

"I don't know. But it's goin' to be tough around here to find something to eat when our stash runs out."

Paul broke a sprig of hay into tiny pieces. "Maybe we should just come out in the open. Go see Mr. Northcutt or Mrs. Stephens and ask if we can stay."

"Just like that?"

Sissy reached for her plate and took a big bite of chicken. "Her good cook. Him not."

Saul picked up his own plate and groped around in the hay until he found his spoon. He brushed the remnants of potato salad and straw off it with his finger. "You think one of 'em would take us in?"

"Maybe." Paul bit into his half-eaten chicken leg. For the moment, he forgot about being a good example to Sissy and talked while he chewed. "You heard him tonight. He's lonesome."

"Just like us," piped up Sissy.

"Yeah, and I think he's got it bad for Mrs. Stephens. He was holdin' her real close down by the creek."

Paul shook his head. "We might as well come out in the open. You're gonna get caught. You take too many chances."

"I had me a good hidin' place. Wish I could have heard what they were sayin'."

"It ain't nice to eavesdrop," said Paul as he cut Sissy a piece of cherry pie. "Use your spoon, squirt."

"You should talk! I wasn't the one who listened at her window yesterday."

"She was crying, and I was worried about her." Paul sadly shook his head. "She sure was grievin' for her husband and boy."

"It's rough to lose your family."

The children were silent for a few minutes. They knew all too well how hard it was to lose the two people they loved most in the world.

"Them need new family. Like us!" Sissy grinned and downed another bite of pie.

"Wouldn't that be somethin'? Mrs. Stephens is a lot like Ma." Paul drew up his knees and leaned against them, wrapping his arms around his shins.

"Her is?" Sissy tipped her head to one side and squinted. It was hard to see her brother's face in the dark. "Her look like Ma?"

"No. Ma looked like you, punkin. You've got her red hair and blue eyes. She was tall, too. Almost as tall as Pa. But she was kind and gentle like Mrs. Stephens," he said wistfully. "And she loved to work outside—"

"—in the garden," interrupted Saul. "Remember how much fun she used to have figurin' out what she would plant and where it would go?"

"She liked to dig in the dirt, too. And remember the scarecrows?" Paul laughed. "She used to stuff Pal's old shirt and pants with straw and sew them together, then dance around the barnyard with her 'fancy man.' "

Sissy giggled and Saul laughed, too. "And then Pa would tap the scarecrow on the shoulder and ever-so-polite-like ask if he could have a dance."

"And Ma would make the scarecrow bow before he got tossed aside—"

"—so Pa could dance with her . . ." Saul's voice trailed off as a lump filled his throat.

His twin sniffed loudly and wiped his eyes. "They looked so grand."

"And so happy." Saul cleared his throat and blinked back his tears.

The boys were quiet, lost in their memories. Little Sissy had never known her mother, and, young as she was, the memories of her father were sometimes cloudy. After what seemed like a very long time to the little girl, she said softly, "Me want Mrs. Stephens for a ma."

"Nobody can take Ma's place," Saul said fiercely.

"Or Pa's." Paul put his arm around Sissy. "At least nobody can take their place for me and Saul. But it's different for you, punkin. You never had a ma to do nice things for you. And

Mrs. Stephens would be a good mother."

"Mr. Nor'cutt be good pa."

"Maybe. He's kinda grumpy sometimes."

"Gets mad easy, too," added Saul, tossing a handful of hay to one side.

"Him make pretty toys."

"Yeah, he does. And he left it for us, so guess he wouldn't be a grump or mad all the time." Saul shrugged. "If they took us in, we wouldn't have to treat 'em like they were our parents. We wouldn't have to forget about Ma and Pa. They could be like an aunt and uncle or something."

"We'd better go to sleep and think on it a spell tomorrow," said Paul. "We can't be sure either one of them would take us in."

"Paul get horsey?"

"Better wait until mornin', Sis. It's too dark to see now, and I might step on it."

The children settled down in the hay, with Sissy cuddled in between the boys. They pulled the straw over them like a blanket until just their faces showed and listened to the multitude of croaking frogs down by the creek. Seemed like a good rain always served as a stage for the frog chorus.

"It would be nice to have a bed that didn't itch."

"Or one that didn't get dripped on. Scoot over."

They all shifted to the right and went through the process of bedding down once again.

"Mr. Nor'cutt sing Sissy night-night." She yawned and snuggled next to Paul.

The twins yawned in unison. "He probably doesn't know a lullaby," said Saul. He knew Sissy needed parents and supposed it wouldn't hurt to have somebody looking out for him and Paul, but it was hard to accept. Nobody could even come close to filling his pa's shoes.

"All pas sing night-night," she said with innocent confidence.

"He ain't your pa yet," Saul said irritably. "So don't go countin' on it."

"Okay. Him be uncle. Uncle almost as good."

Saul hugged his sister and wondered for the hundredth time if God had made a mistake and sent an angel down to them instead of a little girl. "I suppose it would be all right if he was like an uncle."

Paul gently squeezed his brother's shoulder, letting him know he understood what he was feeling. "But will he want to be?"

Chapter 13

WITH HIS BACK toward the peak Luke shifted to a sitting position on the barn roof and gazed out across the gently rolling farmland to the Ferguson place. The view would have been more pleasing if his land looked like Ralph's. As the dirt dried out in the afternoon sun, every square foot of his neighbor's fields was ready for planting. The soft earth was smooth and free of clods and weeds with a generous layer of moisture below the surface waiting to nourish the seeds of corn. The leaves on the oak trees were the size of squirrels' ears, a traditional signal for the right time to plant corn.

A little over half of Luke's fields was ready. Although the rains of late would benefit the crops once they were in the ground, they had delayed the preparation time. He looked up at the cloudless sky, thankful the sun had shone brightly all day. He would be able to start again with the harrow at the crack of dawn. If the good weather held, he would be ready to plant by the end of the week.

He turned his attention to the roof and grimaced. The whole thing needed replacing, but the jury-rigged repair job would have to do for now. He had covered the leak over his sacks of seed corn and the one above the back corner of the haymow, as well as a dozen others.

He picked up half an armload of lumber, a can of nails, and a hammer and stood carefully. Walking slowly across the roof, he surveyed his work. Since he had used scrap lumber he found in the toolshed, the wide roof was dotted with various shades and colors of odd-sized and odd-shaped patches.

Bet Rebecca could make a quilt pattern out of this mess. The thought made him smile. He had done a lot of thinking and smiling since the previous afternoon. And a good bit of frowning, too. More times than he cared to count, he had caught himself remembering how it had felt to hold her and daydreaming about the kiss they had almost shared. Barely touching her lips before they had been jarred apart had been only the beginning. The hard, quick kiss—born of frustration and a need he did not want to examine too closely—had been a very unsatisfactory ending.

He spied another place that needed fixing up near the peak. "I'm going to kiss you, sweet lady," he murmured. "And it's going to be long and slow and deep and drive you a little crazy." He shook his head. "I'm driving myself crazy just thinkin' about it. One kiss. That's all it'll take. Then I'll see that my imagination is just working overtime. The real thing won't be nearly as good." *And what if it is?* "Then I'm in real trou—"

Luke heard the loud crack a second before he felt the boards underneath him give way. There was a sharp, intense pain in his leg as he crashed through the rotted wood, followed by a hard blow to his knee. The scrap lumber, nails, and hammer flew in all directions as he threw himself forward and made a frantic effort to grab hold of the roof. His fingers curled over the edge of the shakes, only to have the wood come off in his hands as the section broke away. Suddenly there was nothing beneath him but dust-filled air with sawdust, chunks of wood, and shingles flying all around him.

It seemed as if the floor of the haymow rose to meet him with incredible speed, yet somehow time seemed suspended. *Not yet! Please, God . . . the farm . . . Rebecca . . . sweet Rebecca . . .*

He turned his head to the side and tried to hold it back even as the force of falling pulled it forward. Bending his arms, he hoped to lessen the blow, but when he hit the plank floor, he knew it had done little good. From mid-chest down, the floor was covered with almost a foot of hay, but from that point upward, the layer was much thinner, exposing the bare wooden floor in spots.

The impact was like the kick of an angry horse, knocking the wind out of his lungs and jarring him from head to toe. He lay on his stomach, his hands resting flat on the floor beside his head.

His mind seemed oddly detached and clear, noting all sorts of little things as the seconds ticked by—the brittleness of the hay as he wiggled a shaky finger, the stinging scrape on his cheek, the burning in his lungs as he tried to draw a breath, and Drifter's excited barking on the barn floor below. He opened his eyes, blinking to focus, and watched fine particles of debris float around in a ray of sunshine— dust, straw, sawdust. Even a fly buzzed by.

He hurt everywhere, although worse in some places than others. His right knee throbbed, but he could move his leg. The left leg worked, too. He wiggled the fingers on both hands and moved his arms a little, relief filling him that nothing was broken. The right side of his face was raw, and he could feel warm trickles of blood flowing down his cheek and temple. The pant leg below his right knee was warm, wet, and sticky. He blinked again as his vision blurred, but this time he could not focus.

Then the pain began. At first it was a vague headache, but in a few seconds it crescendoed to blinding agony. As he raised up on his forearms, intent on turning over, his head began to spin, whirling the image of the loft around him faster and faster. He lowered his head back to the floor, but the spinning did not stop. He closed his eyes, but it was worse. Luke moaned from the pain and nausea. When he opened his eyes again, darkness had already claimed the fringes of his vision and quickly overcame his efforts to resist it. His body slumped as he gave in to the sweet oblivion of unconsciousness.

* * *

"CLANCY, DON'T BARK." Luke's soft words slurred around his dry tongue. Sunshine no longer warmed him, although it was still daylight. He wanted to go back to sleep, but the dog was making too much noise. *No, not Clancy. Dang dog's givin' me a headache.* "Shut up, mutt," he mumbled, trying to wake up. *Drifter. Why's he barkin'? Oh, yeah. I tried to fly.*

His head throbbed with an intensity that frightened him; he'd never known a man could stand such pain. He wished he could go back to sleep. "Quiet, Drifter." *Louder, gotta talk louder.* He took a deep breath and braced himself. "Drifter, be quiet." The dog instantly hushed, then whimpered softly. "I'm alive, boy." *Hurts too much to be dead.*

The dizziness was gone but quickly returned when he rolled over onto his side. Breathing hard, Luke lay still, trying not to think about the pain. In a few minutes, the barn quit spinning, and he could breathe easier. He was surprised to see how his hand trembled when he raised it. Gingerly touching his face, he found a knot the size of an egg between the side of his forehead and his temple. "Thank you, Lord," he whispered, knowing that if he had hit his head directly on the temple, he would be knocking on heaven's pearly gates.

He moved his right leg out in front of him. The pant leg was torn below the knee, exposing an ugly gash on the side of the calf. The blood had clotted, stemming the flow from all but the center of the cut where a small but steady stream dripped. A dark bruise was forming on his knee, and the joint was swollen, too stiff to bend.

Drifter whined, scratching on the bottom step of the ladder.

"Wish you could come up here, too. Don't know how I'm going to get down." He breathed raggedly. "But I've got to try." He rolled back to his stomach and crawled on his belly, inching his way across the six or seven feet to the ladder. He kept his head as low and level as possible, attempting to lessen the dizziness and pain.

When he reached the ladder, he was gasping for breath. Sweat poured down his face, stinging the scrapes and cuts.

Waves of heat, dizziness, and nausea rolled over him, and his head felt as if a giant were jumping up and down on it. Lying on his side, he closed his eyes. *So tired. Gotta rest a while.* He drifted off to sleep. When he woke up, the sun was low in the sky.

Luke eased over to the side of the loft and looked down. Drifter whined and jumped up, resting his front paws on the second rung of the ladder. His tail whipped back and forth so fast his whole hind end wiggled. "I'm glad to see you, too."

Reaching up, Luke grabbed hold of the side of the ladder where it rose above the floor of the haymow and pulled himself to a sitting position. He hooked his arm through the ladder as the light-headedness hit again and the throbbing in his head increased. He waited a few minutes until the worst of it had passed.

He stretched one leg over to the ladder. When his foot was touching it, he reached for the other side and pulled himself around and onto the ladder. Swallowing hard and panting, he moved his foot down to the next rung. His legs were wobbly; his right knee was so swollen it wouldn't bend. Step after step, he moved down the ladder, slowly, painfully, wondering each time he released his hand if he would have the strength to grip the next rung.

The waves of dizziness came quicker, and the pain heightened. His shirt was soaked with sweat; one minute he was chilled, the next hot. Three quarters of the way down, the darkness began to creep in on him, and he knew he wasn't going to make it. His fingers grew numb, and they slipped from the ladder. His last conscious thought was to try to turn so he wouldn't smash the egg on his head.

An instant after he landed on the ground, Drifter was at his side. The dog whimpered and licked his master's face, but the man did not awaken. The dog tried again, pawing at Luke's shoulder and licking his chin, but to no avail. He nudged his arm with his cold, wet nose, but Luke remained motionless. Drifter whined and cocked his head as a shiver shook Luke. A moment later, the dog raced out of the barn and across the farmyard. He wiggled under first one rail fence then the second as he raced across the fields toward Rebecca's farmhouse.

SAUL, PAUL, AND SISSY walked around the back of Luke's barn, excitement mingling with their fear.

"Well, if worse comes to worse, we can always run away again," muttered Saul. "I still think we'd be better off going to Mrs. Stephens."

"And have someone shoot first and ask questions later? No, Mr. Northcutt's the one we gotta talk to first. Everybody else may be totin' a gun, but he didn't have one last night." Paul took Sissy's hand.

"That was last night. No tellin' what he's carryin' now."

As they walked around the front of the barn, they spotted Drifter racing full out toward the Stephens place. "What's got into him?" They peeked inside the barn and saw Luke sprawled at the foot of the ladder. "Holy Moses!"

The children ran to Luke's side. As the boys knelt beside him, Sissy hung back. "Is him dead?"

Saul looked up at her wide, frightened eyes and white face. He had hoped she had forgotten. But how could she? So much was the same—the still body . . . colorless face . . . the big lump on the side of his head. "No, Sis. He's still breathin'." He glanced up at the yawning hole in the roof. "He's hurt pretty bad, though. I'm goin' for help."

As his brother ran out of the barn, Paul put his arm around Sissy. "We need to keep him warm, punkin. See how he's shaking? You sit down here beside him and hold his hand. I'm going to find some horse blankets."

"Him gonna die?"

"Not if we can help it. I'll be back in a minute."

Luke heard talking, but it was so far away he could not make out the words. He tried to open his eyes, but his eyelids were too heavy. He felt someone beside him and something touching his hand. His eyelids slowly fluttered open. It took a lot of effort to focus on the smiling little face peering down into his. Red curls. Bright blue eyes. Innocence.

"Hi."

"Hi." *So sleepy.* It hurt too much to keep his eyes open. He felt a small pressure on his hand and realized the little one was holding it. A tiny smile touched his face as he drifted back to sleep. *Sweet cherub.*

Rebecca hurried to the door, drawn by Drifter's sharp barks. Her own dogs stood around him, tails wagging, happy to see their friend. Drifter's long tongue lolled from his mouth; his sides heaved from exertion. When she walked through the doorway, the dog ran down the steps and stopped. He looked at her and barked, ran six more steps and stopped, looking back again. There was no mistaking his urgency.

"What's wrong, fellow? Has something happened to Luke?" She looked over at the Northcutt place. Nothing looked out of the ordinary—except for the boy turning into her drive at a dead run. A cold knot of fear congealed in her stomach. "Oh, dear God, let him be all right!"

She flew off the porch and down the drive with Drifter racing ahead of her. She met Saul halfway to the county road.

"Mr. Northcutt's . . . been . . . hurt." Saul fought his need for air as he tried to force the words out quickly. "Fell through . . . barn . . . roof . . . unconscious."

Rebecca's heart pounded, more from fear than from her short run. "Wylie and Jackson are down at the hog pen. Can you get them?" Saul nodded. She put her hand on the boy's shoulder. "They've got the shotgun handy, so call out before you get to them." Luke's warning about her running into trouble came to mind. "Did you leave Mr. Northcutt alone?"

"My brother's with him . . . won't hurt you. Just . . . a kid."

Rebecca flashed the boy a smile, gathered up her skirt, and ran to Luke's farm as fast as she could. She was so out of breath when she walked into the barn that she could only stare in astonishment at the young lad before her. *Twins!*

"He was shaking mighty hard, ma'am, so we covered him up." Paul stepped aside, revealing Luke and Sissy. "He's still shiverin' but not as bad. There's a cut on his leg. It was still bleedin' some, so I tied a handkerchief around it. I didn't tie it real tight."

Rebecca smiled and nodded her approval as she moved quietly to Luke's side, trying to catch her breath. When she sank to her knees beside him, she glanced at the child tenderly holding Luke's hand beneath the blanket. In spite of the short curls and little-boy clothes, she was certain the tyke was a girl.

"Has he come to at all?" She gently turned his face to the side and studied the wound near his temple. *Oh, Luke! What have you done to yourself?* That side of his face was a mass of scrapes, cuts, and bruises. She carefully pulled out a long sliver that was buried just under the skin of his cheek. His face was covered with dirt and sawdust.

"Him said hi."

Rebecca tucked the blanket tighter around his neck as another shiver wracked him. She smiled at the little girl. "Did he open his eyes?"

"Uh-huh. Then him go night-night."

Rebecca looked up at the hole in the roof and shuddered, breathing a silent prayer of thanksgiving. If he had fallen closer to the end of the barn, where there was no loft, he would have been killed.

She curled her legs beside her and carefully settled against his side, hoping to share some of her warmth. She lifted the blanket and cautiously picked up his free hand from where it lay beside him. "Luke, can you hear me? Can you open your eyes? Help is coming, Luke." She continued to talk softly, gently chafing the back of his hand, cupping the scratched and scabbed palm carefully. His fingers and palm were filled with slivers.

Through the open barn door, she saw Jackson and the other boy ride up bareback on one of the plow horses. Jackson swung the boy down from behind him and handed him the reins as he dismounted himself. Jackson jogged to Rebecca's side as the boy led the horse into the barn and tied the reins to the side of a stall.

The hired hand knelt down beside her and shook his head. "Don't look good."

"The children said he regained consciousness for a minute, but he's been out cold ever since I got here. Is Uncle Wylie going for the doctor?"

Jackson nodded. "Going to send Winston over to help. Anything broken?"

"I haven't looked yet. He's so chilled, I've been trying to keep him warm."

Jackson nodded as he pulled back the horse blanket. He felt along Luke's ribs, arms, and legs with a knowledge that came from tending animals all his life. "Nothing broke. Mighta cracked some ribs."

Rebecca helped him cover Luke with the blankets. At the sound of another horse riding up, her gaze was drawn to the doorway. Her mouth fell open as the animal came into view. Winston rode bareback with Aggie Davis perched sideways on his lap. Her hair was loose and windblown. She wore a plain blue duster and work shoes with no stockings. Winston's hair was rumpled, and he had not taken the time to tuck in his shirt. Rebecca knew Winston had been courting Aggie, but she had never expected to see them like this.

Winston grinned at Rebecca as he carefully lowered Aggie to the ground. "Close your mouth, Rebecca. We got hitched this morning. Wylie interrupted our honeymoon."

She couldn't hide her surprise. "Oh! Uh, congratulations."

"We'll fill you in on the details later," said Aggie, as a soft blush touched her cheeks. "How is Mr. Northcutt?"

"Unconscious. He has a big lump near the temple, and his right leg is cut. The right knee is badly swollen. Jackson said there might be some cracked ribs, but he doesn't think anything else is broken."

Winston stepped up beside Aggie and absently put his arm around her waist. "We'd better move him on a board, then," he said with a frown. He looked up as Jackson approached with an old door. One corner was missing, but the rest of the door looked sturdy. "Good. That'll work fine."

Rebecca scrambled to her feet and called Drifter over to stand with the children, who hovered out of the way beside

Charlie's stall. Things that needed to be done in the house ran through her mind. She knew she should go see to them, but she did not want to leave Luke. She wanted to be there when he came to. She had expected Winston to take charge in his blowhard, know-it-all-way, but she was surprised at his efficiency.

He helped Jackson lay the door down next to Luke, then straightened. "Aggie, honey, could you come hold Luke's head when Jackson and I lift him on the board? And Rebecca, why don't you—" He looked over at her and saw the children for the first time. "So these are our outlaws. You boys want to help?"

"Yes sir." The twins spoke as one.

"You run up to the house. Turn down the covers on the bed and stoke up the fire. Keep an eye out and hold the door open when you see us coming."

"Yes sir." The boys dashed off.

"What do you want me to do?" Rebecca placed a comforting hand on Sissy's shoulder. She scratched the top of Drifter's head with the other hand.

"What you do best." Winston gazed at her with friendly affection. "Walk alongside and hold his hand. I 'spect he'd rather see your face than mine or Jackson's if he wakes up."

"I'll bring the little one and keep the dog out of the way." Aggie smiled at Rebecca.

"All right." Rebecca was surprised to realize how much she had wanted, even needed, to be with Luke as they moved him. It would hurt him, and she wanted to be there to offer comfort.

Winston took off the blankets, and with Aggie helping, he and Jackson lifted Luke onto the door. Luke groaned and rolled his head to one side. "Don't come to, now, friend," said Winston as he covered him up again. "Wait until we get you tucked into bed."

The men lifted the board and waited for Rebecca to take Luke's hand before they started out of the barn. Aggie, Sissy, and Drifter followed along behind. Luke groaned a few times between the barn and the house, and his fingers tightened on Rebecca's, but he never fully regained consciousness. The boys had taken care of the bed and the stove. Saul held the back door open as the men carried Luke inside, and Paul made sure the other doorways between the small room off the porch and the bedroom were clear. Winston sent the women and children from the room before he and Jackson stripped Luke and got him into bed.

"He's all yours," said Winston as he stepped from the bedroom a short time later. He grinned at the surprised blush that filled Rebecca's face. "I figured you might want to wash up some of the cuts before the doc gets here. Aggie can help if she wants—as long as you mind which parts you're washin'."

"I've seen it all before." Aggie sent her husband a sassy smile.

"Not on him, you ain't." Winston pulled her into his arms. "And you'd better not be peekin'." He dropped a quick kiss on her lips. "Jackson and I are going down and tend to Luke's chores. I'll be back as soon as I can." He released her and stepped back. "You kids want to help?"

"Sure. Can Sissy come, too? She's real good at finding the eggs."

"Don't see why not." Winston held out his hand to the little girl. "Come on, quarter-pint."

Sissy giggled and curled her tiny hand around Winston's thumb.

"You're about as big as a minute," said Winston. They followed Jackson out the back door. "Sissy, what do you call them brothers of yours?"

"Paul and Saul."

"Which one's which?"

Sissy giggled, shook her head, and dutifully pointed out each twin as they moved out of hearing.

"I didn't know Winston was fond of children." Rebecca filled a washbasin with steaming water from the reservoir on the stove.

"I didn't either until a few days ago." Aggie carried one of the kitchen chairs into Luke's bedroom as Rebecca followed her. "He's full of surprises," she said with a smile.

Chapter 14

REBECCA SAT IN the dim golden lamplight beside Luke's bed and prayed for his recovery. Doctor Clark had confirmed everyone's suspicion—Luke had a concussion. The doctor did not think he had cracked any ribs but said he could tell better when Luke regained consciousness. He stitched up the gash in his leg and had Jackson bring over some of the ice they had buried in the ice house at Rebecca's farm.

As the doctor had instructed, she had kept ice packs on his knee and head until the ice melted. Then she was to continue with cold cloths on his forehead until he regained consciousness. Both injuries were to be iced again the next morning.

Taking another cloth from the basin of cold water, she wrung it out and replaced the one on Luke's forehead. The shivering had stopped once they got him out of his damp clothes and into a warm bed. He had vomited once while the physician was there, and Doctor Clark told her he might do it again, many times if the concussion was extremely severe.

Rebecca ran her fingers gently down his left cheek, frowning because he felt too warm. Unlike the other side of his face, it was not a mass of tiny cuts and scrapes. His right eye was black and swollen, but the left one was amazingly normal. The doctor had picked several large slivers from his hands and his right leg and a few from his face. He said the smaller ones could wait or work themselves out. The physician surmised that Luke had probably hurt his leg when it went through the roof, but said the injury to his head was definitely from hitting the rough floor of the haymow.

Wiping a tear from her eye, she glanced at the clock. It was nearly eleven. *He has to wake up soon! It's been too long!* She stretched her arms over her head and yawned, although she did not consider going to sleep. Winston and Aggie had gone home with the promise to return the next day to help out. Rebecca had sent Wylie and Jackson home, too, but the children had refused to leave. They were curled up asleep on the floor in the parlor, snug in some of Rebecca's quilts.

A smile touched her face as she thought of Saul and Paul. They were self-sufficient and responsible young men in children's bodies. They insisted on staying to help her care for Luke and solemnly reminded her that it would not look proper if she stayed the night at his house alone. She had not pointed out that in his condition, even the worst gossips would have trouble finding something to talk about.

The boys had fetched water, chipped ice, brought her corn bread and milk for supper, and made sure she had a quilt. They had kept her company until they began nodding off, and she sent them to bed. She had been touched by their concern and care for their sister. Not many boys would cheerfully wipe a little girl's runny nose. Her smile softened. Her brother Eben had always looked out for her, and she could remember more than once when he had wiped her nose.

And little Sissy—what could one say about that precious child? Hardly more than a baby, she showed an unusual capacity to pay attention and ability to comprehend what was going on. Love seemed to pour out of her to everyone around. She had not only wrapped Winston around her little finger, but quickly added Wylie, Jackson, and Doctor Clark to her list of conquests. All she had to do was smile and they were hers. Aggie was enchanted with her and softly told Rebecca that if she did not want to keep the children, she and Winston would be glad to take them.

Rebecca was powerfully drawn to the youngsters. She had been from the first time she had seen the boy running away from her window. But her heart had been captured when Sissy crawled up into her lap and asked "Aunt Becca" for a hug before she went to bed. Rebecca had fought back tears as the child curled her arms around her neck and gave her a sloppy kiss on the cheek. At that moment, she was wrapped in love, the innocent, unconditional love that only comes from a child.

"Sissy kiss Mr. Nor'cutt night-night?"

"Of course, sweetheart. Just be very careful of the sore places." Rebecca lifted Sissy up to the bed. She leaned over and kissed him very carefully on his uninjured cheek.

When Rebecca settled her back on her lap, Sissy snuggled close for a minute. "Aunt Becca sing Sissy night-night?"

Hot tears instantly stung Rebecca's eyes. Michael had liked for her to sing him to sleep, too. Her throat aching from holding back her tears, she swallowed hard and hugged Sissy tightly. "I don't think I can tonight, dear." She cleared her throat and blinked at the moisture in her eyes. "I'll sing to you when Mr. Northcutt is better." She gently set the little girl on the floor. "Now you run along and go to sleep. Do you need to go to the outhouse?"

Sissy shook her head. "Paul taked me."

"All right. Sleep well, sweetheart. Good night."

"Night." Sissy had yawned and stumbled slightly as she padded barefoot from the room.

Luke stirred, bringing Rebecca's mind back to the present. "Luke, can you hear me? Try to wake up. Can you open your eyes?" She leaned forward in the rocking chair and rubbed his undamaged cheek. The thick stubble of his beard chafed her fingers, reminding her of the first time she had seen him. "Come on, Luke. You can do it. Wake up."

He groaned and flexed the fingers of one hand, which rested on top of the blankets.

She blotted his face with a cold, wet cloth. Flinching, he turned his head away. He shifted his body, moaning when he tried to move his leg.

"Come on, Luke. Wake up. I know you hurt, but the doctor says you need to wake up." When he licked his lips, she dipped her finger in a glass of water and gently rubbed the drops across them. He licked them again, and she dribbled a tiny bit of water into his mouth.

He swallowed and frowned. "Hurts . . ."

"I know, dear man. I know. But you're alive. And you're going to get well." Her voice was filled with determination.

"Ma . . ." He looked confused and slowly rolled his head from side to side. "Gran . . ." When he opened his eyes, they were glazed and filled with fear. "Please . . . ma'am . . . it hurts."

Rebecca thought her heart would break at his plaintive cry. Had there been no one? Had no one ever cared for him when he was in pain or frightened? Had he hoped at each new farm for the wife to like him, to treat him as her son? Tears ran down her cheeks as she rose from the rocker and carefully sat down beside him on the bed. She curved one hand around his bare shoulder and gently caressed his jaw with the other.

"I'm here, Luke. See, it's me, Rebecca."

His eyes were wild and unfocused. He reached up, his hand groping at the air. "Help me . . ."

Rebecca caught his hand and held it tightly, bringing it to her lap. "I will. I promise. Luke, I'm here and I'm going to help you." He closed his eyes and some of the tension left him. She continued to talk and touch him, coaxing him to wake up and recognize her.

"Thirsty . . ."

She dipped one corner of a clean washcloth in the pitcher of water and placed the saturated cloth against his lips. He sucked at it greedily. She repeated the process several times until he seemed satisfied. When he loosened the grip on her fingers, she replaced the cloth on his head with a cold one.

"Luke, I'm going to put some ointment on your lips so they won't be so dry." She dipped her finger into a small jar of petroleum jelly and smeared it carefully on his lips as he remained still. The ointment was one of several things, including her kitchen rocking chair, she had brought over from her house before Winston and Aggie went home. After screwing the lid on the jar, she clasped his hand again.

Luke heard the soft voice calling him. It was a nice voice, sweet and caring. *Ma? Fool! Ma was never sweet. But who? Not Gran. Gran always yelled. Mrs. Farley? She taught me to read. Yeah, and turned me out in the snow when she thought I took five cents out of her sugar tin.*

Luke didn't want to think anymore. It took too much effort. Nor did he want to wake up. Then it would hurt too much. *This is one heck of a hangover. Sure hope I had fun.* Then he remembered he hadn't been drunk in years, not since that time in Dodge City.

She's persistent. The gentle voice went on and on. He wished she'd quit talking. He wanted to go back to sleep. But when she did quit, he missed the soothing sound and wanted her to talk again. He felt something cold on his forehead and something soft and smooth brush across his jaw. *Must be in a garden. Wild roses. Smells like Rebecca. Sweet Rebecca.*

The voice began again, calling to him, urging him to wake up and open his eyes. *Rebecca?* He felt a cool hand touch his bare shoulder. One of his hands was beneath the covers and when he wiggled his fingers, he touched his bare hip. *Buck naked! And in bed. With Rebecca?*

It was a struggle, but Luke forced his eyes to open. Focusing was hard, but finally he saw Rebecca's face, worry wrinkling her brow. "Got your . . . clothes on," he said with a feeble smile. "Too bad."

"Luke!" She smiled, though her eyes filled with tears. She swiped at them with the back of her hand. She wanted to kiss him so bad it hurt, to welcome him back to the land of the living with open arms. But, as he had just pointed out, he was naked as a jaybird. Just like a man to mention it, she thought fondly. "How do you feel?"

"With my fingers," he mumbled.

Rebecca grinned. Maybe the man needed to get cracked in the head more often. It loosened him up. "How's your head?"

"Hurts like the devil." He closed his eyes. "What are you doing here?"

"Being neighborly."

He opened his eyes and searched her face. "Why?"

Because I was terrified when I heard you had been hurt. "Because we're friends. And friends take care of each other." She smiled. "Besides, I'll probably never get another opportunity to talk as much as I have in the last half hour."

"Yappity woman." He slowly brought up her hand and touched it with his lips. "Thanks. How'd you know I'd been hurt?"

"Drifter came to get me."

"I'll be . . ." Luke smiled a little.

"And then Saul came running over to get help." She frowned. "Or was it Paul? I never thought to ask."

"Who?"

"Our visitor. The boy—or I should say boys—we've been trying to catch. They are identical twins. Saul and Paul Miller. They found you sprawled on the floor of the barn. One of them stayed with you and covered you up with horse blankets. The other one came to us for help."

"Thought I'd died. Saw an angel." Luke knew it sounded silly, but the memory sure seemed real.

"Did she have short curly red hair and bright blue eyes?"

"Yep. And the sweetest little face. You been seeing cherubs, too?"

Rebecca laughed. "In a way. But this one is earthbound. Saul and Paul have a little sister named Sissy. She said you woke, and she spoke to you."

"I thought she'd come to take me to heaven."

Maybe she's brought a little bit of heaven down to us. "Looks like your time's not up," she said briskly.

Luke saw the pain flicker across her face and squeezed her hand feebly. He did not have the strength to do more. All this heaven talk must remind her of her son and husband, he thought. "How'd you get me here?"

"Jackson and Winston put you on an old door they found behind the barn. Oh! I almost forgot—Aggie and Winston got married this morning!"

"You're kidding."

"No, sir. Oh, Luke, I wish you could have seen them when they rode up." She grinned. "Of course, they rushed right over when Wylie asked for help. Winston was riding bareback, and Aggie was sitting across his lap. Her hair was down and she didn't have any stockings on." She giggled, not considering that this was a story a lady would not tell a man who was simply a friend. "Winston's hair was all rumpled and sticking out all over, and he hadn't taken the time to tuck in his shirt."

"Must have been busy." Luke smiled. He liked hearing her laugh and seeing her eyes sparkle. Lord, there wasn't anything he didn't like about this woman. It was nice being alone with her in the soft lamplight. Warm, cozy, intimate. *It'd be better if my head didn't pound. Too sleepy.*

Rebecca watched Luke's eyes drift closed. "Luke, would you like a drink before you go back to sleep?"

His eyes opened slowly. "Yes."

"The doctor left some arnica for your headache. I've mixed it in some water, so it won't taste right, but it should help your pain."

She picked up a glass and stood beside the bed, bending down to slip her arm beneath his shoulders. "Come up just a little. It's going to hurt terribly, I'm afraid."

Luke gasped as he raised up a few inches off the bed and pain slashed through his head. He was appalled to feel his whole body tremble with the effort. She quickly brought the glass to his lips. The cold water felt wonderful going down his parched throat even if it didn't taste good. He wanted a lot more, but he was too weak and in too much pain to keep his head up. When Rebecca eased him back on the bed, he was panting as though he had been running.

"Lord a-mercy," he muttered after a few minutes.

"You'll get better. Doctor Clark said if you regained consciousness tonight, you should be up and about in a week or so. And back to work in two or three."

"Can't wait." He stirred restlessly. "The corn . . ."

"Don't you worry about the corn. It'll get planted."

"Not ready. Be too late."

"Don't worry about it. Wylie will see that the harrowing is finished. And if you're not up to planting, that will be taken care of, too."

"No. I can't ask . . ."

"You didn't ask."

"Don't want to be beholden."

"You'd do the same if the situation was reversed." She tucked the blankets around him, noting again how old and worn they were. "That's what neighbors are for. You don't worry about anything except getting well. I expect Saul and Paul will be able to take care of the daily chores, and if the neighbors all pitch in, the other things will get done quickly and without too much effort on anyone's part."

"Bossy woman." Without the strength to argue, Luke gave up. As she smoothed a lock of hair off his brow, he thought maybe it was good no woman had ever pampered him. He hadn't really known what he was missing. Life would be a little harder, a little lonelier when he got well. As he drifted toward sleep, another thought popped into his head. "Doctor bill. Gotta pay doctor." *But how? The pig money.*

"The doctor's been taken care of." She knew he would insist on repaying her. "You can pay me back in the fall when you get the crop in. It takes a lot of money to get started in farming. I don't have that kind of expense."

"Interest." Why couldn't he stay awake?

"There will be no interest charged between friends, Luke Northcutt. Now hush and go to sleep. I might even catch a few winks myself. I have to wake you up again in a couple of hours. Doctor's instructions."

"Wanted to use . . . my new planter."

"Shh. It will work out." When she heard his slow, even breathing, she smiled gently and smoothed a little more petroleum jelly on his lips. She couldn't help it if her fingertip rested there a moment longer than was necessary.

Chapter 15

LUKE COULD SEE the sunlight through his closed eyelids. He had never given much thought to the way a person could tell if it was day or night without even opening his eyes. A choir of birds sang up a storm in the big oak tree just outside the closed window. Funny how a man could wake up most days and take things like that for granted, but not this morning. He supposed in time he would fall back into his old ways, but for a while at least, he would greet each new day with a thankful heart. He took a breath, expecting to smell the subtle fragrance of roses, and was keenly disappointed when there was no trace of the scent in the air.

In just a matter of hours, he had come to associate waking up with roses and Rebecca's soft touch. *Dunce! She can't stay here all the time.* Besides, he didn't want her to. *Got no use for a wife.* He promptly thought of several uses for a wife and decided he had better open his eyes and get facing the sunlight over with. The giant was no longer jumping on his head; he had turned that chore over to junior, and the kid was having a great time stomping around.

At the moment, Luke had a more urgent problem than a headache. He desperately needed to go to the outhouse. Since that was an impossibility, he would have to use the chamber pot. He slowly opened his eyes, only to discover that the right one was almost swollen shut. The room was not as bright as he had anticipated; the frayed, heavy curtains had been opened only a few inches. Surprisingly, the light did not hurt his eye. He tested the swelling around it and decided he'd had worse. There had been a few times he had not been able to stand the light at all.

Luke glanced at the empty rocking chair and then at the open door. Soft conversation, punctuated by childish laughter, drifted to him from the kitchen, along with the smell and sizzle of bacon cooking. For a minute, he thought he might be sick, but the queasy feeling passed. He raised up, then dropped back to the pillow with a groan. *Thunderation!* Lifting a hand to his forehead, he felt the lump. He could barely stand the slightest touch against it. But pounding head or not, a man still had to take care of some things himself.

Gritting his teeth, he sat up, then grabbed the headboard to keep himself upright. The room swam and his vision blurred before slowly clearing again. Holding on to the headboard, he slowly and painfully eased his legs over the side of the bed, being careful to keep himself covered with the sheet.

He stared at the old, simple country lamp table beside the bed. The top held a coal oil lamp, pitcher, and a glass of water. He had vague memories of the washbasin sitting there during the night and of Rebecca putting cold cloths on his forehead. He wiped the sweat from the uninjured half of his forehead with trembling fingers. The room reeled and his skin felt cold and clammy. He would have given all the tea in China for one of those cold, wet washrags.

The item he needed was conveniently and discreetly tucked under the bed, but it might as well have been out in the barn. If he leaned over to get it, he would fall flat on his face. Besides, he wasn't about to use it with the door open, and he couldn't any more close the door than he could jump over the moon. He would have to ask for help. His lips twisted in a grimace. *How in tarnation do I do that? Excuse me, ma'am, but could you hand me the thunder-mug?* He didn't think he had ever felt so helpless in his life. To his surprise and shame, hot tears burned his eyes.

"Mr. Northcutt?"

Luke's quick glance at the doorway sent his head to spinning like a top. As he swayed, the two boys peeking in at him rushed to his aid.

"You'd better lay back down, sir," said the lad who had taken hold of his arm to steady him. The other boy stood in front of him, ready to try and catch him if necessary.

"Can't." Luke took several slow deep breaths, and the whirling room gradually came to a halt. "Got to tend to business." He made a feeble motion with his hand toward the chamber pot beneath the bed.

"I'll shut the door." The boy who was standing in front of him hurried across the room. As he started to close the door, Rebecca called to him.

"Paul, is Mr. Northcutt awake?" Rebecca wiped her hands on her apron and walked toward the bedroom. The panicked expression on Paul's face made her halt. "Is something wrong?"

"No, ma'am. He's awake." The boy's face turned bright red. "He, uh, just needs a little privacy."

"Oh. Well, when he's settled back into bed, let me know."

"Yes, ma'am." Paul ducked back into the room and closed the door.

It seemed so long before it opened again that Rebecca had begun to worry. When the boys stepped from the room, trying to discreetly carry out the chamber pot, she relaxed. "Is he resting?"

"Yes, ma'am."

"I think I'll peek in on him. Breakfast is on the stove. You can eat after you wash up. Sissy has already eaten, but she can have another biscuit if she wants." She smiled as Paul held open the back door for Saul, and they hurried off to finish their task. Still young and awkward but such good boys, she thought.

"Me peek, too?"

Rebecca looked down at Sissy, who had quietly come up beside her. "After we wash that jelly off your face, sweetheart. Then we'll see how he's feeling."

With his eyelids half closed Luke watched them tiptoe hand in hand into the room. It was a picture to make a lonely man's heart ache. The woman and little girl, both so beautiful, shared a smile as they tried to walk soundlessly across the floor. When Sissy stepped on a squeaky board, she covered her mouth with her hand to hold back a giggle and slanted a mischievous look up at Rebecca. She grinned at the child, her face aglow with pure, unrestrained love. And Luke knew he would move heaven and earth to help her keep the children. He opened his eyes, pretending to be just waking up.

"Mornin'." Luke caught his breath as Rebecca looked at him, the warm, loving glow still in her eyes. The swell of hope that rose in his chest took him by surprise. Her expression changed to a frown, although he thought he detected a lingering warmth in her eyes. He decided the fall must have knocked what little sense he had clear to kingdom come.

"Good morning." Rebecca shook her head slowly. "Oh, my. You look worse in the daylight. How do you feel?"

Like an idiot. "Like I've been hit by a freight train. Guess I look pretty bad, huh?"

"I'll have to bring over my hand mirror so you can have a look. That shade of black and blue goes nicely with your hair and eyes, but it would look better in a shirt." Her gaze drifted down to his shoulders and the wide expanse of his upper chest that was not covered by the blankets. There were several large scrapes there, too. She was suddenly glad he had not been awake when she and Aggie had cleaned up his cuts. "Do you want to sit up a little?"

"Maybe a little higher. I don't think I want to try sitting up all the way again just yet. Makes my head hurt too much."

Rebecca helped Sissy up into the rocker, then piled the extra pillow behind his head and shoulders when he raised himself up. She noted that his arms shook as he held up his weight, and he closed his eyes for a few seconds when he settled back against the pillows. "There is still some of the water and arnica. It will help your pain. Would you like some?"

"Yes." He dreaded raising up again, but when she slipped her arm beneath his shoulders to help him, he decided it wasn't so bad. Her nearness helped him avoid focusing on the pain. She held the glass to his lips until he had drunk all he wanted, then quickly set it on the lamp table and eased him back down on the bed.

She fussed with the covers, longing to rest her hand on his shoulder, to offer the comfort and reassurance that a human touch could give. "Your lips are dry again." He looked up at her in surprise. "You had a little fever, I think. Anyway, this should make them feel better." She opened the jar of petroleum jelly, dipping her finger in the clear, smooth ointment. "Open your mouth a little bit."

I'm getting tired and rummy, she thought. Spreading the salve on his lips when he was awake should not have been any different than doing it when he was asleep—but it was. Feeling his searching gaze made her actions seem more intimate than they had the night before.

Luke thought he was the only one affected by her tender touch, until he saw the soft pink slowly rise in her cheeks. Her uncertain gaze met his, and the movement of her finger slowed as she gently slid it across his bottom lip and back again. Quick heat raced through his veins, and he marveled at the way a man could still desire a woman when he was half dead. Though amazed, he accepted the caress for what it was and tried to ignore the yearning it stirred in his soul.

Embarrassment flooded her face with hot color, and vulnerability filled her eyes before she glanced away. When she straightened, screwing the lid back on the jar with intense concentration, Luke curved his hand around her waist. She went still, then slowly set the jar on the table.

"You're tired, Rebecca," he said softly. "And when people are tired, they sometimes do things they wouldn't normally do." She looked at him, and he told her with his eyes that he liked her caress and wanted it again. He squeezed her side gently, relishing the warm softness of her body beneath his fingers. "You'd better see to your little friend.

She's getting wiggly." Wishing he could hold her longer, he drew his hand back to the bed.

Rebecca turned away quickly, glad he had let her off the hook so easily. Yes, she was tired, and her lowered inhibitions might have been brought on by weariness. But the longings he evoked in her heart and body had been there for days, even weeks. Yesterday afternoon, she had been dreaming of ways to claim that kiss he had promised her. She still wanted it, hungered for it and more.

The depth of her need—both physical and emotional— frightened her. Luke's accident had reminded her of the unpredictability of life. She had anticipated growing old with Anthony, but he had been taken before she had shed the blossom of her youth. She did not know if she could bear to love and lose again.

She plucked Sissy from the chair and gave her a hug. Sitting back down with the little girl on her lap, she smiled at Luke. "Sissy, this is Mr. Northcutt. Luke, this is Sissy Miller."

"How do, Mr. Nor'cutt." Sissy grinned at him.

"How do, Sissy. I think we've already met."

She nodded and pointed to his face. "Got an ow-y."

Luke smiled. "Yep. Several in fact. Did I make a big hole in the roof?"

She nodded again and spread her hands as wide as she could. "Dis big."

Amusement touched Luke's face, at least the half that wasn't puffed up and black and blue. "No wonder I'm so messed up. I think I needed a bigger hole."

Rebecca chuckled. "It was big enough. Jackson plans to patch it today."

"I don't want him taking any chances." Luke frowned. "Maybe he'd better cover the hay up with a tarp and leave the repair until I'm well."

"Don't worry about him. He's a very cautious man."

Sissy scooted off Rebecca's lap and stood beside the bed. "Sissy sit bed?" At Luke's slight nod, Rebecca carefully lifted her up beside him. "Wanna biscuit?" She unfastened a button on her shirt, dug around inside the garment, and produced a slightly smashed biscuit.

Luke chuckled. "You're going to have to find a better place to hide your stash if Mrs. Stephens keeps giving you hugs."

The little girl smiled at him, then sent Rebecca an adoring look. "Biscuits good. Hugs gooder. Squished biscuit okay."

"Smart kid." Luke took the bread when Sissy held it out to him. "Keep it up, and you'll have all the biscuits you want." *And probably everything else.* He was already tired, but he felt a twinge of hunger when he brought the food to his mouth and smelled the delicate flavor.

"Luke, the doctor said you should only have clear liquids for a couple of days."

"He can keep his clear liquids. I'm having hugs and biscuits." He took a huge bite of the bread and settled one arm around Sissy, giving her a weak squeeze. "How about a cup of coffee?"

"Nope. Weak tea." Rebecca crossed her arms in front of her. "That's as good as it gets."

He made a face—or tried to. Nothing seemed to cooperate much. From Rebecca's amused expression, it must have looked pretty funny. "All right. A coffee mug of weak tea. But not too hot." He yawned. "Then I think I'll take a nap."

Rebecca left Sissy on the bed with a quiet admonition to sit still. The boys were finishing breakfast when she poured the tea she had brewing in the pot. She added a little water to weaken and cool it down. "Better save a couple of those biscuits. Mr. Northcutt isn't too keen on the idea of broth for lunch."

The boys followed her back to the bedroom and reported to Luke on all the chores that had been done. "Mr. Neeley said he'd be over this morning to help Mr. Jackson with the roof. Then they're gonna work in your field."

It still did not sit well with Luke for others to be doing his work, but he knew he had to accept the help and try to be grateful for it. "Well, if I'm asleep when they come by, tell them I appreciate all the help. I'll be back on my feet pretty quick." He scowled at Rebecca's raised eyebrow. "I will." He yawned again. "Thank you, boys, for everything you're doing. When I'm a little more alert, you'll have to explain why you're on your own." He looked at Rebecca. "Did they tell you?"

"No. I didn't ask. I thought we could talk to them together. Now, boys, why don't you take Charlie and Old Joe a couple of carrots. But come back in a little bit." She yawned, too. "I'm going to have to leave Mr. Northcutt in your care for a while. I need some sleep. Sissy, you can give Mr. Northcutt a kiss like you did last night. He looks like he's going to drift off to sleep any minute."

Sissy leaned over very carefully and gave Luke one of her sloppy kisses. "Night-night," she whispered in his ear and slipped her arm around his neck for a tiny squeeze.

Luke felt his heart twist. "See you later, Sissy." He blamed the huskiness of his voice on his tiredness.

The boys took Sissy with them to see the horses, and Rebecca helped Luke drink his tea. By the time he drained the cup, he was worn out. When Rebecca started to step away, he caught her hand, cursing his lack of strength. "Thank you for taking care of me."

He wanted to look away, afraid of what his eyes might tell her in his weakened state, but he forced himself to hold her gaze. "I didn't expect it. There's never been anybody . . ." He searched for the right word and found it revealed too much, so he latched on to the name she had given their relationship during the night. "I've never had a friend like you."

"Good friends are hard to find but easy to keep." She smiled and started to go, but he tugged weakly on her hand.

He slowly tapped his cheek. "Good-night kiss?"

She smiled ruefully. "Only because you're as weak as a kitten." She bent down and touched her lips to his cheek.

As she started to straighten, he held her hand tightly, keeping her close. He pointed to his lips. "Here, too."

"Luke, I don't think—"

"—just a little one. Give us sweet dreams."

"Well, I need a good rest and so do you. Heaven knows we're both too tired to think straight. If sweet dreams will do it . . ."

"Will."

"Very well." She spread her free hand on his shoulder and bent down again, this time feathering a kiss across his lips. She kissed him again, a tiny bit harder. Although she pulled away, she would have much rather crawled in bed with him and held him close. *This is crazy, I'm so tired I can barely stand up and my brain is scrambled.* She straightened and brushed a wisp of hair from his forehead.

He squeezed her hand faintly. When she pulled it from his, he whispered, "Still owe you one."

Her heart did a flip-flop. *So he's been thinking of that promised kiss, too.* She smoothed the cover one last time and listened to his slow, even breathing. "Sweet dreams, dear man."

She turned away from the bed to find Aggie Neeley standing in the doorway.

Chapter 16

AGGIE STEPPED BACK as Rebecca left the room, pulling the door partway closed. "Sorry to barge in. I didn't knock. I was afraid I might disturb him. The children let me in the back door."

"That's fine." Rebecca's face flamed. She could only imagine what Aggie thought. "Uh, about just now—"

"Don't you think a thing about it." Aggie slipped an arm around Rebecca's shoulders and guided her over to the kitchen table and pulled out a chair for her. "What's between you and Mr. Northcutt—if there is anything—is your business and nobody else's. How's he doing?"

"Better. He regained consciousness during the night. His head still aches, and I'm sure he hurts all over, but he drank some tea and ate a biscuit a little while ago. He's very weak and tires easily. But the arnica the doctor left seems to ease his pain. He's sleeping now."

"Thank goodness. Last night I was afraid he might not wake up for days." She did not add *or at all,* but it had been everyone's unspoken fear. "Winston will drive you home in a few minutes. He's down at the barn checking on things. Jackson is coming over in a little while, and they're going to fix the roof. I'll stay here today and take care of Mr. Northcutt and the children. We brought over a pot of soup and some corn bread for dinner. I want you to go home and get some sleep. You look all done in."

"I am. I think my mind quit working about an hour ago." Rebecca propped her elbow on the table and rested her chin in her hand. In this state, her lonely heart could easily overrule her head and that was dangerous. "Doctor Clark said he would drop by this morning. Oh, we're supposed to put ice on Luke's head and knee again. I'll have Jackson bring some over later."

"We'll take care of it."

Winston came through the back door, carrying Sissy on his shoulder. The large man ducked as he crossed the threshold so she would not bump her head, then swung her down to the floor. She giggled softly and ran over to Rebecca, who promptly picked her up. Sissy put her arms around her neck and hugged her tight.

Winston stepped up behind Aggie and rested his hand on her shoulder. Rebecca noticed that his thumb moved back and forth in a caress as he talked. "The boys tell me Luke came around. That's good to hear. Mighty good. I've talked to Ralph and Artie. They'll be over tomorrow, and we'll finish up his field."

"He wants to plant it himself." Rebecca smiled, unaware of the tenderness that shone in her eyes. "Wants to try out his new corn planter."

"The field will be ready for him. We'll wait until next week and see how he's feelin'. If it's goin' to be a while before he's up to it, we'll do the plantin' for him. There will be plenty for him to do afterward."

"He doesn't like to be obligated to anyone, but I'm sure he will appreciate everything you do."

"He don't have to appreciate it. Goin' to do it anyway. A man takes care of his neighbors. That's just the way of things. Now, come on, Rebecca, I'll take you home before you drop off to sleep and fall out of that chair." Winston kissed Aggie and hugged Sissy before he left. They met the boys on the back porch, and he tousled their hair as he walked by.

"I didn't know you had such a way with children,

Winston." Rebecca let him help her up into the buggy, noting that his face was freshly shaven. It didn't bother her to sit downwind of him. And it wasn't even Sunday.

He climbed up beside her and tapped the horse's back with the reins. "I've always liked kids. Used to spend a lot of time with Bob's younguns before they moved out to Dakota. Miss those boys."

"How is your brother?"

"I think he's got a rough row to hoe, but he tries not to let on. Where they live is startin' to get settled so that'll help. His wife has missed havin' close neighbors."

He dropped her off at the front door, carefully handing her down from the buggy. Rebecca watched as he drove on to the barn to talk with Wylie and Jackson. If someone had tried to tell her how Winston had changed in the last month, and she had not seen it herself, she probably would not have believed them. "Maybe I should have given him more of a chance," she murmured and went inside.

No, she thought as she trudged upstairs. *Aggie's the right woman for him.* She took off her shoes and stockings and climbed up on the bed, not bothering to remove the rest of her clothes before she lay down and pulled the quilt up.

When she closed her eyes, she saw Luke, one moment laughing, the next gazing at her with open desire. Then the image changed as he thanked her for helping him, his face battered and bruised, his eyes a window to his wounded and lonely soul. *Oh, Luke, how do we know if I'm the right one for you?*

OTHER THAN STIRRING briefly when the doctor dropped by to check on him, Luke slept most of the day. When he woke up in the late afternoon, he felt much better. He still ached in all sorts of odd spots, but the pain was not as severe as earlier.

Something simmering on the stove smelled mighty good. *Chicken and dumplings?* His stomach growled. He smiled ruefully and decided it was more likely chicken soup. He had heard somewhere that it was a cure-all, or maybe it was just good for a cold. It didn't matter what it cured as long as he got to eat some of it soon. He thought how nice it was of Rebecca to cook it for him.

He opened his eyes and glanced around. No one was sitting in the rocker, or anywhere else in the room, but he heard soft snoring. *Drifter*. With a bit of difficulty, Luke rolled over on his right side and looked over the edge of the bed. The dog lay curled up in his regular spot, but when he sensed Luke looking at him, he opened his eyes. Luke could have sworn that dog grinned.

Drifter stretched and sat up, resting his lower jaw on the mattress. It was a position he had assumed several times before, gazing at Luke with those big brown eyes and silently begging to be petted. Luke had always resisted the request and simply talked to him. But the bond between them had been cemented, and he could no longer deny how much he loved the scraggly mutt. The dog had been there when Luke needed him. The man could do no less for the dog.

"Well, old fellow, I hear you're something of a hero." Luke gently stroked Drifter's head, and the dog's tail began to wag. When he scratched him behind his ears, the dog smiled again. "Ain't you something." Luke chuckled as Drifter's tail went faster. "I think you could sweep the floor if I worked it right."

"He's been laying there all afternoon, keeping an eye on you."

Luke's gaze shot to the doorway. Aggie stood there smiling and wiping her hands on her apron. His first impulse was to look for his pants. Instead, he rolled to his back and pulled the cover up to his chin. In the back of his mind, he wondered why it bothered him to be without his clothes with Aggie in the room. He had not been embarrassed with Rebecca, at least not after he got over the initial shock of finding himself in the buff.

He tried to hide his discomfort, although he realized he probably looked silly clutching the blanket up to his neck. "Lazy dog couldn't see much with his eyes closed." He forced a smile. Then he remembered that Aggie and Winston were married, and he relaxed a little bit.

Aggie chuckled and walked over to sit in the rocker. "How are you feeling?"

"Better. My head still hurts some, and I'm sore all over." He wanted to stick his leg out from under the blanket and see why it hurt so bad, but he wasn't about to do it with her in the room. "What did I do to my leg?" He had a faint recollection of seeing a bloody mess.

"You cut it and banged your knee up pretty good. Doctor Clark said the knee was sprained. The cut took ten stitches." Aggie smiled sympathetically. "Go ahead and look at it. I won't faint at the sight of a man's leg. Besides, Rebecca and I helped Doctor Clark stitch you up." At Luke's shocked expression, she laughed softly. "Don't worry, you were decently covered. Winston and Jackson undressed you. We just cleaned up the cuts and assisted the doctor. In fact, I'm supposed to put ice on that knee and your head, too."

Aggie rose and lifted the blanket from the side of the bed, pulling it back over Luke's leg. She was careful to expose his limb only from the knee down.

Luke raised up on his elbows and stared at his abused knee. Something told him that it was liable to bother him a long time after his head healed. *Wonder if I'll be able to predict the weather like Jackson?* The cut was neatly closed with precise, even stitches. The area around it was bruised but not nearly as badly as his knee. The joint bulged oddly, with the taut skin painted a mottled purple and black. The extra money he had put into farm implements on which he could ride was going to pay off.

Aggie helped him scoot up to a sitting position and piled the pillows behind him. "Would you like an undershirt?"

"Yes, ma'am. They're in the top drawer of the dresser." He would have liked to put on his drawers, too, but wasn't quite sure how to ask for them.

Aggie crossed the room to the dresser and returned quickly with his undershirt. She helped him slip it over his head as he leaned forward. When he settled back against the pillows, he saw she was holding up a pair of underwear with one short leg.

"These were the ones you had on yesterday. I cut off the leg where it was torn, picked the slivers out, and washed them. Thought they might be good to wear while that knee is so swollen."

Luke felt his cheeks grow warm. He appreciated what she had done, but he wasn't used to a woman handling his drawers. "Thank you. They'll be just fine."

"Are you hungry?" Aggie laid the garment beside him on the bed.

"Yes, ma'am. Whatever's cooking sure smells good."

"I made you a pot of soup. Nothing tastes as good as chicken soup when you're feeling poorly."

Luke felt a stab of disappointment because Rebecca had not made it, then told himself he was being silly. She had been there all night. He couldn't expect her to spend all day cooking, too.

"Don't worry. Winston ate some at dinner and gave it his approval. He's been giving me cooking lessons. I'm actually starting to like my own cooking."

"Seems like Rebecca said you and Winston got married. Is that right or did I dream it?"

"We got married yesterday over at the courthouse in Montezuma. We were at the county clerk's bright and early. Bought the license and marched right over to the justice of the peace. It was all over in about half an hour, but that's the way we wanted it. No fuss or bother."

"Well, you have my best wishes. Winston's a good man." Luke smiled, surprised to realize he meant it. "And a lucky one." He was even more surprised to discover he meant that, too. The woman standing beside his bed blushing so prettily was a different person from the one who had brought him that awful vinegar pie. In fact, she was attractive, although she wore a simple house dress and had spectacles perched on her nose. *Amazing.* He couldn't wait to see if Winston had made as drastic a change.

"I'll send the boys in to help you get dressed. Then I'll bring you some soup and an ice pack for your knee." Aggie bustled from the room, humming off-key.

That's how Rebecca found him a short time later, eating his supper with a bundle of ice tied up in oilcloth balanced on his knee. Saul—or was it Paul—sat in the rocker holding

Sissy. The other twin sat on the bed. He held the soup bowl in his hand and carefully spooned bites up to Luke. Drifter sat on the floor nearby, his ears pricked up and alert, coveting every swallow Luke took. The boys were relating an adventuresome tale of some sort, both often talking at the same time—using exactly the same words—or finishing each other's sentences.

She stood back from the door for a moment, letting her gaze roam over him. His hair was mussed and sticking up on one side. The three buttons on his undershirt were undone and the sleeves were pushed up on his forearms. The swelling had gone down some in his eye, although a good shiner remained. He appeared weak but in good spirits. To Rebecca, he looked wonderful.

"May I join the party?" She strolled into the room, smiling at Luke and the children.

"Aunt Becca!" Sissy wiggled down from her brother's lap and raced across the room.

Rebecca scooped her up in a hug. "Hello, sweetheart." She had seen the surprise on Luke's face when Sissy called out to her. Looking at him, she gave a slight shrug. "That's what she has called me from the beginning."

Paul got up out of the rocker and stood near the chair so Rebecca could sit down. He glanced nervously at Luke and Rebecca, then at his brother. "We told her that if we got to stay around, maybe you'd be like an aunt or something." He swallowed hard. "I'm sorry if you don't like it. We can tell her to call you Mrs. Stephens, if you want."

"I don't mind." Rebecca gazed down at the little girl on her lap. "In fact, I like it very much." She smiled at Luke, greeting him with the warmth in her eyes. He gave her a lopsided smile in return. "Don't you have any family?" she asked, turning her attention back to the boys.

"No, ma'am." Saul set the empty bowl on the table beside the bed. "We lost Ma when Sissy was born, and Pa died about three months ago. We lived up north of here aways, up near Ames. Pa was a tenant farmer. We'd been at this new place since last fall."

"What happened to your father?" asked Luke.

"We had a new team. They were young and pretty frisky. Pa was tryin' to get them used to pulling, so he rigged them up to a log that was about the same weight as a plow. He was walking behind the log, guiding them around the edge of the field."

"They were doing pretty good, too," said Paul, taking over the story. "But then something spooked the horses—we never did figure out what—and they took off like a shot. Pa ran along behind, trying to stop them—"

"—but they made a sharp cut to one side and it pulled Pa right in between the log and the horses. He managed to jump over the log, but couldn't stay on his feet. When he fell, he hit his head." Saul's eyes filled with tears, and he swiped at them with the back of his hand.

"We couldn't tell if he hit the log or a rock. By then they were in a little stretch of woods down by the creek where it was rocky. The horses stopped when they got to the creek. Me and Saul had been tryin' to head 'em off, but they had too good a start." Paul swallowed hard, adding in a voice thick with pain, "Pa was dead when we got to him." He looked over at Luke, blinking back tears. "Maybe if he'd hit his head where you did instead of right on the temple, he would've lived, too."

Rebecca slid her arm around Paul and hugged him close. Luke hesitated, then reached out and gently squeezed Saul's knee in comfort. "It must have been hard on you boys to find me. I thank you again for all you did."

"It was kind of a shock." Paul glanced over at his sister. "It even reminded Sissy of how Pa looked. I was surprised she remembered."

Luke looked over at the child, who snuggled up a little tighter to Rebecca. Her angelic face was pale and solemn. He glanced at Rebecca, his heart constricting when he saw tears glistening on her cheeks.

"We were just glad you were still alive, and we could get help." Saul glanced at Luke and looked quickly away, both proud and embarrassed at being considered a hero. It was as hard for him to accept comfort as it had been for Luke to give it.

"You don't have any relatives?"

"None that we wanted to live with. Pa had an uncle somewhere in Illinois, but he hated that old man. Pa had to stay with him some when he was a boy, and he used to beat him somethin' awful. He never mentioned anybody else. Both his parents and Ma's folks were already gone. We heard the landlord and the folks from the county talking—"

"They were goin' to send us to an orphanage. They said Sis would get adopted right away. They figured we were too old to be adopted but that some farmers might take us in as extra hands. It didn't sound like there would be much of a chance for us all to go to the same place."

"So you ran," murmured Luke. Stark, painful emotions swept over him. Feelings that had been buried for a lifetime swiftly rose to the surface, almost suffocating him. Rejection. Loss. Fear. Desperation. *I'm not up to this,* he thought frantically. Pretending to gaze out the window, he looked away from the others, struggling to regain control. Fighting for air, he willed his pounding heart to calm and cursed the quaking that seemed to come from the depths of his soul.

"You have a chance here." Rebecca's voice shook slightly. "I have a big house with lots of room. Uncle Wylie and I have already talked about it. You're welcome to stay with us."

"Aunt Becca gonna 'dopt us?" Sissy leaned back in Rebecca's arms as she asked the question. Her bright blue eyes sparkled with excitement.

"If I can, honey. I have to talk to the authorities." She looked up at the boys, her face somber. "We have to make sure you don't have any relatives searching for you. But I promise you, I won't let anyone take you unless they will love you as much as I will and can give you a good home."

The boys gave a shout that hurt Luke's head and drew his gaze back to them. They jumped up in the air, then hugged Rebecca and Sissy and each other. Barking in excitement, Drifter leaped around from one side of the chair to the other, trying to get in on the fun.

Laughing, Rebecca asked, "Now, I have one pressing question. How do I tell who is who?"

"That's easy. I'm Paul and my cowlick's in the front. Kinda makes my hair stick up on this side, see? Saul's got a cowlick in the back—makes him look kinda like a rooster." He laughed and dodged his brother's playful punch.

"And me Sissy!"

"I can tell who you are, sweetheart," said Rebecca with a laugh. Love and joy radiated from her as she gathered the boys close to her chair and slipped her arms around them. Their faces wreathed with happy smiles, the four of them made quite a picture. "Welcome to the family."

As Luke watched them talk excitedly about what their new life would be like, he was hit by another emotion. Overshadowing the happiness he felt for Rebecca and the children, the deep pang of jealousy was unexpected and unwelcome.

Chapter 17

"YOU UP TO handling that knife?" Wylie lowered his newspaper, eyeing Luke as he leaned over the kitchen counter and swayed slightly.

"Yes." He peered out the window at the dust drifting up from his field. Winston and the other neighbors had arrived at one, and though it was barely three o'clock, the work was almost finished. In less than an hour his field would be ready for planting. "I'm okay as long as I don't lean over too far. You want a ham sandwich?"

"Nope. I'm full. Had some cheese and crackers and a bowl of canned peaches for dinner. Becky made a big breakfast—cornbeef hash, scrambled eggs, and biscuits—so I wasn't too hungry. You should have seen those boys eat. They won't stay skinny for long."

"Well, I'm going to stay skinny if the only thing people feed me is soup or mush. Tell her to teach the twins how to fry an egg. Better yet, tell her to teach them how to make biscuits." Thinking he could sure go for a piece of Rebecca's fried chicken, Luke cut off a thick slice of ham and slapped it between two pieces of bread. It would have been better with some butter on the bread, but he was feeling woozy. If he tried to spread the butter, he might have to eat it lying on the floor.

"You sure you're all right? I won't be much help if you fall down."

"I'll make it." Luke sounded like a bear with a fresh bee sting on his nose. "And if I don't, I'll crawl."

"Just toss the sandwich my way, so you don't squish it."

"Mangy mutt would catch it midair." Luke hobbled to his chair, resting his hand for balance on the table, then the back of Wylie's chair, and finally his own chair. Once he sat down, he leaned his head against the cushion and closed his eyes. "I'm tired of this."

"It's hard on a man to be under the weather. But you're mending quick. You'll be back to work in a couple of weeks."

"Sooner than that. I've got corn to plant."

"It don't pay to rush things. Might set you back." That morning Wylie had decided Luke needed some male company, saying too much female fussing was apt to put a man off his feed. Jackson had brought over Wylie's wheelchair and helped him get from the buggy to the chair and inside the house. He would need his help to get back into the buggy again. Sometimes it took a little extra effort to do something worthwhile.

"Well, you made the second page." Wylie peeked over the top of the newspaper as Luke took a bite of his sandwich.

"I did what?"

"Made the paper. Says here, 'Mr. Luke Northcutt is recovering from a fall from his barn roof. Although he sustained a concussion and sprained knee, Doctor Clark says he will recover.' You're right after Mabel Wheeler's broken hip."

"That why Mr. Mack sent out those oranges?" Luke glanced at the basket sitting on the table. He had already had two of the sweet, juicy fruit. He saw the top of Wylie's gray head move when the older man nodded behind the paper.

"A good grocer knows how to treat his customers. Besides, he thinks a lot of you. Told me so himself."

A surprised look passed over Luke's face.

Wylie peeked over the top of the paper again and grinned. "Most store owners like a man who pays cash and minds his own business."

"I may not be paying cash for long." Luke reached down and lifted his leg up onto the wooden crate the boys had brought from the barn.

Wylie put down the paper. "Money tight?"

"I'll make it, although I guess I'll wait until I sell the corn to pay Rebecca back for the doctor's fee. The only extra money I've got is what I saved to buy pigs, and it wouldn't be good business to put off that investment. She said I could wait to repay her, but I don't like to. I don't like owing her."

"Better her than the doctor. Too many folks have to make them wait." He turned to the ads.

"Any good sales going on?" Luke tossed Drifter the last quarter of his sandwich.

"Carhart and Son has Gilpin sulky plows on sale. I'll have to stop by there. One of our plows has seen better days. I like to have Jackson and Ted both running them in the fall."

"I've got a Gilpin. I bought it secondhand from a fellow over in Ohio, but it looks brand-new. He liked the idea of being a landowner more than he liked the work. Gave up after a year and went to Cincinnati to sell somebody else's produce." They talked farming for a while, discussing the merits of the popular plow made by Deere and Company.

Wylie glanced at the paper again. "You can get a free nasal injector with a bottle of Shiloh's Catarrh Remedy."

Luke grinned. "I've got a cracked head, not a cold."

"Never hurts to be prepared." Wylie grinned, too. "Bet Rebecca stops by Johnson and Gruwell's and picks up some stuff for the kids."

"They don't carry clothes, do they?"

"No, but just about everything else. They're advertising baseballs and bats. Even got crayons. Sissy might like those."

Luke wondered if the youngsters had liked the horse he left them. They hadn't mentioned it, but they had been busy taking care of the farm and him. He had refused Rebecca's offer to stay a second night. She had promptly asked the boys to stay with him and they had willingly agreed. They had rolled out their pallet on his bedroom floor and took turns sleeping on the quilts and dozing in the rocker. One of them had been at his side every time he grew restless or needed something. He liked having them around.

When a buggy pulled up out front, Wylie folded up the paper. "Sounds like Becky and the kids are back."

The words were barely out of his mouth before the front door burst open and the children rushed in. "Mr. Northcutt! Uncle Wylie! Look what we got!" One twin held up a baseball bat, and the other one tossed the baseball a few feet in the air and caught it with his bare hand.

Wylie grinned and winked at Luke. "Told you. And what about you, little miss? I see you got a new dress and all the other female trappings that goes with it." Wylie reached down and picked Sissy up, setting her on his lap. She clutched a new rubber baby doll. It was not as pretty as a doll with a wax or china head, but it was perfect to be handled and hugged by a small child.

"Me get dolly. See?" She held up the toy for him to inspect. "Her pretty."

"Yes, she is. Did you name her?"

"Uh-huh. Her Dolly."

"Sounds like a good name to me. What else did you get?"

"Ca-yons." She held out her feet to show off the shiny new black shoes and lovingly touched the lace trim around the bottom of her skirt. "And clothes."

"Lots of clothes," said Rebecca with a laugh, coming through the door. "Seems like everyone in town had a sale going on. And of course, I picked up an armload of material at Papa's store. I'm going to put my sewing machine to good use for the next few weeks."

"We got knickers and ate dinner in a real restaurant!" said Saul.

Rebecca smiled at Luke. "We ate at Mr. Mack's. He said to tell you hello and that he hoped you get well soon."

Luke nodded abruptly. He couldn't quit looking at her. *Thunderation, man, don't stare!* But he couldn't help it. He had never seen her looking lovelier. Her whole face seemed to sparkle, especially when she looked at the children. She'd had a wonderful time buying things for the youngsters. *Heck fire,* he thought, *she probably spent more money in one day than I'll clear this year.*

"And we got a haircut from a real barber!" Paul turned around slowly, grinning at Luke. "Now I can see where I'm going."

Luke didn't return his smile, and some of the excitement faded from the boy's eyes.

"And we went to Stevens Drug Store and had an ice cream soda." Saul's voice and expression held a note of awe. "I ain't never had an ice-cream soda before."

Wylie glanced at Luke, his gaze narrowing at the deep scowl on the younger man's brow. "What kind did you have?"

"Sissy and Paul had vanilla, but Aunt Rebecca and I had chocolate. The soda water's all bubbly and kinda tickles when you drink it. And chocolate ice cream"—he rolled his eyes dramatically—"there ain't nothin' in the world like it."

Luke felt left out. And irritated. He wanted a chocolate soda. And he wanted to share it with Rebecca. He wanted to watch her take bite after bite and kiss away the tiny film of chocolate that stayed on her lips. He would wait until their lips and mouths were ice cold, then warm them with kisses, heat them with passion. But he couldn't afford to waste his money on ice-cream sodas. "Sounds like you had quite a day. Now get on outside. All this racket is making my head worse."

Rebecca frowned and crossed over to Luke, pulling off her driving gloves as she went, and tossed them on the kitchen table. "Boys, why don't you run on down to the barn and see what chores need to be done. Sissy, you go, too, but leave Dolly here with Uncle Wylie. He'll take good care of her. Don't get dirty."

Disappointment written all over their faces, the boys slowly and silently left the room.

Wylie lifted Sissy down to the floor. She paused before giving him her precious new toy and scampering after her brothers. A few steps short of the back door, she turned around and ran back across the room to Luke. She curled her fingers over his and looked up at him in concern. "Mr. Nor'cutt ow-y hurt?"

"Yeah, it hurts." Why did she have to be so sweet? And why did he get the feeling this little elf knew it wasn't the pain in his head that bothered him the most but the one in his heart?

"Me kiss it. Make it better." She held up her arms. Luke hesitated, then lifted her up to his lap. She ever-so-carefully kissed the lump on his forehead. "Bump pretty colors. Like me ca-yons." She grinned at him. "Hug, too." When she slid her arms around his neck and squeezed, Luke could no longer sit passively. He hugged her back. "All better?" she asked, looking up at him.

"Not quite. But a lot better. Thanks, Sissy."

She grinned, let him lower her to the floor, and dashed out the door after her brothers.

Rebecca put her cool hand on Luke's warm brow. "I think you need to go back to bed."

"I'm tired of being in bed." He was just as tired of sitting up, but would not admit it. He wanted her to fuss over him a little bit, to show him some of the attention she had lavished on the children. And that made him fighting mad. He didn't want to need anything from anyone.

"You look worn out. And you're too warm. You need some rest, or you'll take a fever." She felt his cheek. Even though his beard was prickly beneath her fingers, it felt good to touch him.

Oh, Lord, why does it feel so good for her to touch me? He pushed her hand away. "Quit fussing over me, woman. I'm all right. Go on home and unload your buggy. That ought to take you an hour or two. All I need is some peace and quiet."

Rebecca stepped back, stung by his rejection. She knew he felt bad and hated being laid up, but having him take his irritation out on her still hurt. "Very well. I do have a lot to do. Tell the boys to come home after they've finished the chores, and I'll send some soup over to you. They can stay with you again tonight."

"They don't need to stay with me. It's time they got to sleep in a bed instead of on the floor. They've got lots of new things to look at and enjoy. They don't need to be bothering with me."

"Luke, I don't think you should stay alone yet. What if you need some medicine?"

"Then I'll take some."

"What if you need something from the other room? Who'll get it for you?"

"I'll get it myself."

Rebecca shook her head. "Don't be so stubborn. You might fall again in the dark, then what would you do?"

"Get up. Look, lady, I don't need a nursemaid. I've been taking care of myself for thirty years, and I don't need anyone to take over now." Luke knew he was being bullheaded and mean, but he couldn't seem to help himself. He was mad at the world and at Rebecca in particular. She had made him care—for her, for the children, even for Wylie—and he did not want to. "And I don't want any more soup. I'm sick of soup. Go home and take those blamed kids with you. I'm tired of having them underfoot."

"All right, I will!" Rebecca grabbed her gloves and jerked them on. She leaned down and shook her index finger under Luke's nose. "Listen here, Luke Northcutt, you can snap at me all you want, but don't you dare say anything derogatory about those children. They've waited on you hand and foot and done chores they aren't big enough to do. And they've done everything willingly. What's more, they probably saved your life, you ungrateful clod."

She straightened and spun on her heel, snatching the doll from Wylie's fingers as she stomped by him. "I'll take Sissy now. Send the boys home the instant they've finished the chores." She halted at the kitchen doorway, looked back and frowned at her uncle, totally ignoring Luke. "Don't be late for supper." A minute later, the front door slammed as she departed.

"Well, I'll be jiggered." Stunned, Wylie gazed toward the front room. "I haven't seen her that riled up in a long time."

A part of Luke told him he had been smart to make her mad. Maybe now she would stay away, and he could forget her. But he knew he had hurt her, and he hated himself for doing it. He had not meant what he said about the children, either. He liked them and appreciated everything they had done. He was especially grateful for their help the day of the accident. Rebecca had been right about everything.

"You were pretty hard on her, son."

"I know." Luke found it difficult to look at Wylie. "I'm not used to anybody doing things for me. Or having people around much."

"A man gets set in his ways when he lives alone. And sometimes that's not so good." He glanced out the window. "I see Jackson coming. Guess it's time I got out of your hair, too."

"I'm glad you came over, Wylie. I enjoyed your company. Maybe the next time I won't be so ornery." He sighed deeply. "Please apologize to Rebecca for me. I didn't mean to hurt her. I do appreciate everything the kids have done, and her, too. I don't want anybody thinking I'm not grateful to all of you, because I am. It's just . . . it's just that I haven't had folks show me any kindness before, and I don't quite know how to handle it."

"Just accept it, and the good will that's behind it." Wylie pushed his wheelchair over to Luke's side and held out his hand. "Good to see you doing better. You need to get back to bed soon. You look like you might keel over any second. Want me to have the boys come in and help you?"

"No, thanks." Luke took the offered hand and shook it. "I'll manage. I want to stay up and talk to Winston and the others a minute. Then I'll go to bed."

"I'll stop by in a day or two, and we'll have another visit."

"That would be good. Thanks, Wylie."

Wylie gazed at him thoughtfully. "You know, Luke, oftentimes a fellow loses out because he's not willing to take a chance."

"Sometimes a man knows better than to be foolhardy."

"And sometimes it's worth the risk of looking like a fool. Don't set your limits too low, son. It's what a man is that counts, not how much he has."

IT WAS TWILIGHT when Luke finally stretched out on the bed. Winston, Ralph, and Artie had dropped by after the work was done and chatted a bit. They teased him about falling through the roof just so he could get some work out of them and promised to take advantage of him when harvest time came. He took Wylie's advice and accepted their help and goodwill with more grace than he had thought possible.

"Reckon you can help me pull off these pants, Drifter?" Luke rested his hand on top of the dog's head and scratched him behind the ears. "I didn't think about how hard it would be without being able to bend my knee." Drifter's ears perked up and half a minute later, Luke heard steps on the back porch. "Rebecca?" He tried not to sound too hopeful, but knew he didn't succeed very well.

The back door slowly opened. "No, sir. It's me, Saul."

"Come on in, boy. I'm in the bedroom."

Saul came in and stopped beside the bed. "How are you?"

"My head's pounding like a bass drum in a Fourth of July parade, and to tell the truth, I'm done in. Guess I shouldn't have stayed up so long."

"You want me to light the lamp?"

"Yes, but keep it turned low." A couple of minutes later, the room was bathed in soft golden light. "How are you doing? Are you getting settled in over at Rebecca's?"

"Yes, sir." Saul started to sit down, then reached for a bundle he had set on the night table. "Mrs. Stephens . . . Aunt Rebecca sent you some biscuits. They're still warm. I split 'em and put butter on 'em for you."

Luke scooted up in bed and wedged a pillow behind his back and another behind his head. "I was lying here trying to get up the ambition to fix me something to eat. I don't like to admit it, but she was right." He paused and opened a wide round crock. The biscuits were so warm the butter dripped out the middle and ran down the sides. "I'm not up to doing much cooking tonight. And I guess you can tell her so." He took a bite of the biscuit and sighed. *What would it be like to eat cookin' like this every day?* Then he wondered where that thought came from and told himself to watch out.

Saul chuckled and handed him a wedge of cheese.

"What's so funny?"

"She said you were cantankerous this afternoon, and that the way to drive the orneriness out of a man was with some light, fluffy biscuits."

"It'll do." *For now.* He took another bite and looked over at Saul. "Could I trouble you for a glass of milk?"

"Sure." Saul left the room and returned several minutes later with two glasses of milk. "There's still a little in the crock. Do you want me to put it in the cellar?"

"No. It'll stay cold enough tonight here in the house. How's Rebecca?"

"Still swelled up, if that's what you mean." Saul sat down beside the bed in Rebecca's kitchen rocker. "She was nice enough to us, but she was bangin' pots and pans around in the kitchen like she wanted to break something."

"The other side of my head, probably. I wasn't too nice to her this afternoon." He leaned back against the pillow and sighed again, disgusted with himself. "I was downright nasty."

Saul grinned. "I did hear her mutterin' your name a couple of times. She didn't sound too complimentary."

Luke looked down at the partially eaten biscuit—his third. "Did you eat any of these?"

"Yep." Saul laughed at the wary look that had spread over Luke's face. "All came from the same batch. Don't think she added anything that'll send you runnin' to the outhouse."

Luke chuckled and relaxed, finishing the biscuit. He watched the boy as Saul slowly drank his milk and rocked quietly. His thoughts seemed far away. Luke gave him some time to think and finished the cheese and milk. When he set the crock on the table, Saul glanced at him. "I'll save those for breakfast. Did you boys get in a little baseball before it got dark?"

"Yes, sir. We aren't very good, 'cause we never had a real bat and ball before. You ever play?"

"No. I never got around to it. I think Wylie said something about Rebecca's brother Will being something of a ball player. He could probably give you some advice. He's graduating from college in a few months, so he's still young enough to chase balls."

"Guess we'll be meeting him pretty soon, huh?"

Luke detected a hint of worry in the boy's voice, although the lad kept his face down as he petted Drifter's shoulder. "I expect you'll be meeting the whole family soon. From what I hear, there's a bunch. Met any of them yet?"

Saul looked up and smiled. "We met Aunt Rebecca's parents today. They seem like real nice people. They told us to call them Grandpa and Grandma, but that seems a little strange. Guess we'll get used to it."

"I understand they've got several grandchildren, so it won't seem so odd once you're all together. I've met Mr. Lansing. He was friendly enough. What's bothering you?"

"Well, like you said, she's got a bunch of kinfolks. We ain't used to being around a lot of people. Didn't have no cousins or anything. Sure, we had friends, lots of them. But it's different with family. What if some of them don't like us?"

"I think they will, but even if they don't, you shouldn't have to worry. Rebecca's not going to turn you out just because she has snooty relatives. She needs a family like you, and I think she figures the good Lord sent you to her doorstep."

"You need a family, Mr. Northcutt?" asked Saul quietly. He instantly regretted the question when the smile vanished from Luke's face. "I'm sorry, sir. That's none of my business."

"You're right. It's not. Just so you'll know, boy—I've never had a family, and I'm not looking for one. I wouldn't know what to do with one if I had it. Now help me get out of these pants, and you can go on home. You need to get there before dark, or Rebecca will worry."

Saul was silent as he helped Luke remove his pants. He brought him a fresh pitcher of water and mixed up some of the arnica in a small glass of water. After he made sure Luke had everything he needed, he gave Drifter one last pat on the head.

Then he reached in his shirt pocket and pulled out the horse Luke had carved. "You know, we got lots of nice things today, and I 'spect Aunt Rebecca will be givin' us lots more." He smiled slightly. "I think she had as much fun buying stuff as we did. But nothin' we got means more to us than this horse. Me and Paul take turns keepin' it. Sissy thought it was real pretty, too, but we were afraid she'd lose it. And we sure don't want to lose it."

The boy told Luke good night and headed for the door. When he reached it, he looked down at the statue, then slipped it back in his pocket. He glanced over his shoulder at Luke, his face solemn. "Mr. Northcutt, you may not need a family, but I sure think you know what to do with one."

Chapter 18

SISSY RESTED HER hands on the edge of the sewing-machine stand and watched in fascination as Rebecca ran the thread past various hooks and slots and finally through the eye of the needle.

"Be sure to keep your fingers out of the way, dear." Rebecca drew the shuttle thread up through the throat hole.

"Yes, ma'am."

"When you get bigger, we'll get you a toy machine and you can make clothes for your dolls. Then when you're older, I'll teach you to sew with my machine and to make pretty things by hand, too. But for now, you must only watch."

Rebecca slid the faded blue muslin material into place on the machine and lowered the pressure foot. An expert spin on the balance-wheel sent the wheel revolving and the needle in motion. By rocking her foot back and forth on the treadle in a steady movement, she kept the wheel spinning and the needle and thread dipping up and down through the material at a constant pace, making smooth, even stitches. In practically no time she had taken in the side seams on a hand-me-down dress for Sissy, one of several Rebecca's sister Elizabeth had given her.

Her Light-Running New Home Sewing Machine was her pride and joy. When she had purchased the machine at the beginning of the year, she had promptly sent a three-cent stamp and a request to the company in New York for a card showing the style of work done by the attachments. She had been so intrigued by the different devices that she bought every one of them from the tucker, ruffler, and hemmers on up to the automatic buttonhole maker. Most of them had ranged in cost from twenty-five cents to one dollar and fifty cents. The buttonholer had been a shameful extravagance at twenty dollars, but she had used the machine and the buttonholer a great deal in the week since she had first taken the children shopping.

"Aunt Becca?"

"Yes, dear?" Rebecca pulled the dress from the machine and clipped the threads with her scissors.

"Can me go outside and play?"

"May I go outside."

Sissy frowned. "Aunt Becca want to go outside, too?"

Rebecca laughed. "Well, yes, I do, but what I meant was that when you are talking about yourself, you say 'I.' The proper way to say it is, may I go outside? And, yes, you may go out in the backyard as soon as you change into some play clothes."

"Play clothes?" Sissy looked perplexed.

"Everyday clothes. Something that it doesn't hurt to get dirty."

"Oh, me . . . uh, I pants?"

"No, not your pants. Not I, either. When something belongs to you, you say my. My pants." Rebecca laughed and hugged the little girl. "Don't worry, honey, I don't expect you to learn everything in one day. Let's take one thing at a time. Little girls are supposed to wear dresses not trousers."

"Pants warm. Dresses not."

"I suppose." Rebecca smiled ruefully. "That's why I bought you the merino pantalettes and long stockings. We'll save the white stockings for church and going to town. The dark ones will be fine for around the house and playing." She turned the dress right side out and held it up for Sissy to see. "Now, this dress is from Maggie and Molly. It's worn so it isn't good enough to wear to town, but it's just right for every day. Let's get you out of your nightgown and dressed. Then you may go out and play while I work in the garden."

"Me like—" Sissy halted when Rebecca gently shook her head. "My like?" Again, Rebecca said no. Sissy sighed dramatically. "I like?" When Rebecca nodded, the little girl grinned. "I like Molly and Maggie."

"I do, too. You had fun with them last Sunday at Grandpa Lansing's, didn't you?"

Sissy nodded. "Aunt Becca gots big family."

"Yes, I do, dear. And they all like you very much." While Rebecca helped Sissy change clothes, she thought about her family and their loving response to the children. She had expected no less, but it still warmed her heart. Elizabeth's three girls had fallen all over themselves trying to be nice to Sissy.

Eben's three boys were a little more cautious, but she thought that was probably because Paul and Saul had been reserved at first. Within half an hour of their arrival at her parents' house, all the boys had become fast friends, with Paul and Saul captivating the younger boys with tales of their adventures on the road.

Just as she had grown worried that their rousing stories might prompt her nephews to seek their own adventures, the twins had told of a few of their more frightening experiences—the time they got caught in a snowstorm and almost froze to death, and the time Paul was attacked by a dog and was bitten on the leg. Saul had ended the story session by solemnly admitting that living with a caring adult was a whole lot better than trying to make it on their own in the world.

After Rebecca and Sissy went outside, Rebecca planted her pumpkins and a row of muskmelons while the little girl happily built a town out of piles of dirt. Rebecca was careful to plant the muskmelons well away from the pickling cucumbers. She had made the mistake of planting them next to each other one year and the vines intermingled, giving her bitter muskmelons.

She had not realized having three children to take care of would keep a woman so busy. The boys pretty much looked out for themselves, in fact, more so than she liked. But she still had to feed and clothe them, see that they did their chores and got enough sleep, and tried—it seemed vainly—to keep them from doing things that might cause them harm.

She had anticipated any number of problems, but the children tried hard to please her. And she was so happy having them with her that even the most mundane chores seemed lighter. Saul and Paul had made friends with the neighbor boys, John Ferguson, who was eleven and Andrew Jones, who was nine.

Since only a short time of the school year was left, she had not enrolled the twins. She and Wylie decided they needed to adjust to being with them and did not need to be thrust into another new situation immediately. After school was dismissed each day and on Saturdays, it had become commonplace to see the four companions strike off together across the fields or pasture.

Their new friendship had led to the first real confrontation between Rebecca and the twins. The day before the four boys had been sitting on her back porch devouring a batch of sugar cookies and a pitcher of milk. When she overheard their discussion of the nearby swimming hole, and their plans to try it out as soon as the weather was warm enough, she had told Paul and Saul that they were not allowed to go swimming. When they tried to convince her that they were good swimmers, she got angry and forbade them to even go near the swimming hole.

The youngsters were quiet and withdrawn all evening. She felt guilty for yelling at them and causing them disappointment. She was also terrified that one of them might drown. It was natural for farm boys to spend much of their free time in the nearest swimming hole; her brothers had spent hours down at the creek in the summer. But she could not bring herself to give in to the boys' wishes.

At Sissy's giggle, she looked up from her planting and smiled as the little girl chased a butterfly across the edge of the garden and then ran to meet her brothers. Rebecca shifted off her knees and sat down on the cool earth as the boys walked up.

"All done with your chores?"

"Yes, ma'am. And we've already been over to Mr. Northcutt's. He let us help him this morning, but said he wouldn't be needing us anymore."

"He's well, then?" As she had done every day for the past week, she waited anxiously to hear how he was. She had not seen him since he had gotten angry and had ordered her to go home. He had sent an apology through Wylie and another roundabout one through Saul, but she had not gone to see him, even though he lingered in her thoughts. She had sent over food and made sure the boys checked on him every day and helped with his chores, but she stayed away. Her actions in the days before and right after his accident had been much too forward and bordered on being shameful. As much as she wanted to see him—and oh, how she did—Rebecca knew she had to let him make the next move.

"No, ma'am, I wouldn't say he's well. He's still limping a lot on that knee. I think his head still hurts, too, 'cause he sure was grouchy." Saul plopped down on the ground beside her. Sissy crawled up in his lap, and he put his arm around her. "He's getting ready to plant the corn, though. I think he's only workin' part of the day, but he's bound and determined to get it done."

Paul dropped down beside his brother. "He said it won't be too hard, since he can ride on the corn planter."

"But stringing the trip wire and loading the seed in the hopper isn't easy." A deep frown settled between Rebecca's brows. "I wish he would let Jackson or Ted help him."

"He said they've got enough to do with your plantin' and all. He doesn't like needin' help."

"No, he doesn't. Do you think he's pushing himself too much?"

"Maybe, but I don't think it will do any good to say anything. We tried. So did Uncle Wylie. But it didn't seem like Mr. Northcutt wanted any of us around."

Rebecca sifted the garden dirt through her fingers, trying to decide if she should go see Luke. *I'll make him a peach pie and take it over myself. That should cheer him up.*

"Uh . . . he said you didn't need to send over any more food. Said he's up to doin' his own cookin'."

"Oh." That took the wind out of her sails.

"That's okay, Aunt Becca." Sissy deserted Paul's lap and crawled up onto Rebecca's. "Him get tired of beans quick."

Rebecca raised an eyebrow as she looked at the boys. They looked sheepish.

"We kind of checked out his cookin' before we moved in with you. He cooks eggs, beans, or makes a ham sandwich most days. A couple of times he made some stew, but it didn't smell too good."

"So that's why you came over here so willingly." Rebecca grinned and the boys grinned back. "What are you up to now?"

They glanced at each other. Paul made a slight motion of his head, encouraging Saul to speak. "John asked us to go to town with him. They have the day off from school."

"Who's going?"

"Us and his brother Tom."

"Is he taking the wagon?"

Saul crossed his legs, sitting Indian fashion. "No, ma'am. We're going to ride horses."

"Do you know how to ride?"

"Uh . . . yes, ma'am." Neither of the boys met her gaze.

"How well?" Rebecca watched them closely. Being raised on a farm, they must have ridden some, but neither one looked as if they wanted to answer her.

"A little bit," said Saul. "But he said the horses were real tame. I think they're old or something."

"Ralph Ferguson doesn't have an old, tame horse on his farm. You may not go." Rebecca knew they would not give up easily, but it still rankled when Paul spoke up.

"But his older brother's goin' with us."

"I don't care. You aren't riding to town—or anywhere else for that matter." She frowned, waiting for Saul to voice his objection.

"Not even in his pasture? Tom said he would teach us how to ride real good." Saul's expression was incredulous.

"No. Absolutely not. Tom's apt to be daydreaming over Ann Marie, and you'd have a runaway and get your neck broken."

"But Aunt Becca—"

"I don't want to hear another word about it. You are not to go riding with the Fergusons or anyone else. When Jackson gets time, he can teach you to ride."

"But the plow horses are too big, and Rusty is so cantankerous, Jackson won't let us go near him."

"Then you won't learn to ride," she snapped.

The boys jumped to their feet and walked away, muttering under their breath. Sissy looked after her brothers, then up at Rebecca's irritated expression. "Me go, too?"

"Yes, you may go with them." She helped the little girl up. "But be careful," she called as Sissy ran after them. The boys looked back and stopped. As they turned away, Rebecca thought she saw Paul roll his eyes.

Rebecca was out of sorts for the rest of the day, and the children were not any better. She knew she was being hard on the twins, but she had to protect them, even from themselves. After supper, she heard the boys talking quietly to Wylie. When they went out back to play ball, he rolled his wheelchair into the kitchen where she was finishing up the dishes.

"The boys tell me you won't let them go riding."

"They don't know how to ride."

"Tom said he'd teach them."

"He was going to take them to town on horseback. How can he teach them on the road and in the busy streets? How irresponsible can he get? He just wanted to go to town because Ann Marie takes their extra eggs and butter in to the baker on Wednesday afternoons. Once Tom saw her, he'd forget all about the boys."

"Becky, you need to give them some growing room."

"I'll get them a horse, and Jackson can teach them to ride."

"When?"

"I don't know. Later. *When I'm not so afraid.*"

"Don't scare them off, honey. They aren't yours yet."

"They are my responsibility. And I'm going to take care of them. I don't care if they don't like it."

"Give them some slack, gal. Boys need to be able to do the things their friends do."

"They have a lot of things to do. They just don't need to do anything silly and dangerous. That's all." She untied her apron and hung it on a peg on the wall. "Now if you'll excuse me, I'm going to finish Sissy's dress so she can wear it on Sunday."

Rebecca fled the room, leaving her uncle shaking his head. She worried that she might be driving the boys away from her, but she did not know what else to do. She did not know how to swim, so she was unable to make certain they could take care of themselves in the water. When she had grown up, it had been unthinkable for women or girls to swim. It had been improper to even consider it. There had never been any call for her to ride horseback, either. Her brothers had always taken care of the stock, and she had done women's work. If she wanted to go somewhere, she either walked or took a buggy.

Oh, Luke. I wish we could have a talk. She sat down in front of her sewing machine but did not pick up Sissy's new dress. She had no enthusiasm for sewing at the moment. When she absently fingered her locket, Rebecca realized she had not wished for Anthony's counsel as she had always done in the past. It had not been Anthony she had been longing to see, talk to, or touch. Hot tears stung her eyes. She knew there was no need for guilt; she could not grieve forever. But she could not remember a time in the last week and a half that she had thought of Anthony. She had not even looked at his picture before going to bed as had been her habit every night for five years. *I won't forget you, Anthony! I swear I won't!*

When the boys and Sissy came into the small sewing room about an hour later, Rebecca was still sitting in front of the machine. Nary a stitch had been taken.

"Aunt Becca, is it all right if Sissy goes out with us to dig night crawlers?"

"What do you want with worms?"

"We thought we'd take Sis fishin' in the mornin'. She likes it a lot. After we finish the chores, of course," Paul added quickly.

"No. You can't take her fishing. I don't want her to go near the creek. I don't want you boys going down there, either."

"Not go fishin'!" Saul's face turned bright red. "Holy Moses! Can't we do anything?" He spun on his heel and bolted from the room. Sissy ran after him. Seconds later, the back door slammed once, then again.

"Gee whiz, Aunt Rebecca. We've been fishin' since we were knee-high to a grasshopper. We ate more fish while we were on the road than anything else." Instead of being angry, Paul looked sad. "Pa taught us, so we know how to be careful. We always watch Sissy real good."

Rebecca stood and walked over to the unhappy boy. When she slid her arm around his shoulders, she said quietly, "I'm sorry, Paul. I don't mean to be harsh. I'm just so afraid something will happen to one of you. I couldn't bear it if you were hurt or perhaps killed. The thought simply terrifies me." She guided him into the kitchen where they sat down at the kitchen table.

"It's all right if you go fishing. And Sissy can help you dig night crawlers, but please don't take her down to the creek tomorrow. I'd be having the vapors by the time you got back. I'll think of something fun that she can help me with, so maybe she won't be too disappointed. Jackson has some cane poles tucked away somewhere. Why don't you ask him if you can borrow them?"

Paul smiled and reached over and squeezed Rebecca's hand. "Thanks. In a way, I guess I'm glad you worry about us. And I promise, we'll be real careful." Paul went out back to find his brother and sister.

Rebecca wandered into the parlor where Jackson and Wylie were playing checkers. When her uncle looked up at her, she frowned. "Don't say a word." She sat down in her rocker and picked up her quilting. There were only two more sections left to piece. She stitched in silence, rocking back and forth, listening for the children's return. When

Paul and Sissy came into the room a short time later, she looked up from her needlework.

"Well, we got a can of night crawlers. Boy, are they fat ones! And some of them are six inches long." He grinned at Rebecca. "You'd better plan on having catfish for dinner tomorrow."

"Only if you clean them." She smiled back.

"Yes, ma'am. We're good at that. Saul can fillet them so you can eat 'em without findin' a bone."

Rebecca opened her mouth to tell him she wasn't about to let Saul use a knife, but caught herself just in time. "Where is your brother?"

"He's out on the back porch. Lookin' at the stars or somethin'."

Avoiding me is more like it. "I think I'll go out and look at the stars myself." As she left the room, she heard Paul ask Jackson about the fishing poles. *I know you don't mind if they use your poles, Anthony. I just wish you could have taken Michael fishing at least once.* Blinking back a tear that threatened to fall, she opened the back door and walked out on the porch. Saul sat on the top step.

She sat down beside him. "How many did you count?"

"About six zillion. Saw a shootin' star a little bit ago."

They sat in uneasy silence for a few minutes, listening to the crickets chirp and the distant hoot of an owl. Finally, Rebecca cleared her throat. "Have you ever been so afraid of something that you just couldn't bring yourself to do it? Even when you knew that nothing bad was likely to happen?"

Paul thought a minute. "Chickens. I'm scared to death of tryin' to get an egg out from under an old hen."

"Have you ever been able to make yourself do it?"

He squirmed. "No. Paul goes after those. But he doesn't like to milk, so I do that."

"I don't like trying to get eggs away from a hen, either. I'm always afraid she'll peck my hand, although only a couple of them ever have. I feel the same way about some of the things you boys want to do. I know you ought to be able to go swimming and horseback riding, but I can't bring myself to let you do it. I'm too afraid."

"That we'll get hurt?"

"Yes." She held out her hand and was thankful when he closed his fingers around hers. "You've been placed in my care, and I'm responsible for you. I love you children very much, and I want to protect you. I know I shouldn't keep harping at you, that I should let you do more of the things you want to do, but the chance that you might get hurt terrifies me. And I just can't bring myself to tell you to go ahead."

"So you treat us like babies." He stared off into the darkness.

"Is that the way it feels?"

"Heck fire, yes."

Rebecca smiled. "I can tell you've been hanging around Luke."

"I've heard worse, but not from him. Or from Pa." He let go of her hand and slid down a step, drawing up his knees and hugging them. "We got kinda used to doin' what we wanted to."

"I know. And I realize I'm being hard on you."

"You ever gonna let us go swimmin' and ridin' and stuff?"

"Maybe. In time."

"I don't want to wait until I'm full growed." He paused a moment, then said with quiet conviction, "I'd rather be on my own if that's the way it's going to be."

Rebecca fought a surge of panic. "Give me some time. Please, Saul. Give me time to get used to being a mother again."

"I reckon I can wait a while. But Aunt Rebecca, it's real embarrassin' when you won't let us do stuff that Andrew does. He's barely nine, for Pete's sake."

ON THURSDAY MORNING Luke decided he might live after all; he woke up without a headache. After milking the cow, he turned her and the calf out into the pasture, then fed the horses and did all the other morning chores—and wished he had waited longer to tell the twins he did not need their help. He tried to hurry but that only made his knee throb. By the time he hitched the team to the check-row corn planter and headed for the field, he had spent over an hour longer than usual on the chores. Somewhere between tossing out cornmeal to the chickens and mucking out the stalls, a dull ache had begun in his head.

Luke drew the horses to a halt at the fence and stepped down from the metal seat, being careful with his knee. He slid the top loop of smooth wire off the gate post and lifted the post from the bottom loop, dragging the four-stranded barbed wire gate around to the side. After a quiet command from their master, Old Joe and Charlie walked through the opening and stopped far enough from the gate to give him room to close it.

Luke drove the team halfway across the field and stopped. Once again he eased down from the machine, this time to check the two strands of wire that he had strung across the field the previous afternoon.

Satisfied that the wires were tight and straight enough, he lined the horses and planter up on the two rows and hooked the wires through the planter. He climbed back up to his seat and gently urged his team forward. The horses walked in a straight line, pulling Luke and the machinery down the rows. The wire contained knots at regular intervals which tripped a mechanism on the planter boxes to release the corn seed. This resulted in rows of corn that were straight and even in both directions, giving the fields the appearance of a checkerboard. This pattern enabled the farmer to cultivate the young corn plants thoroughly, going north and south as well as east and west to rid his field of weeds.

Luke worked steadily all morning, stopping now and then to refill the planter boxes from the bags of seed he had stationed along the fence row. Driving the planter was not hard, but moving the check-wires and pounding the stakes into the ground would have gone much smoother and faster if he had been able to get around better. By noon he was worn out and thankful that the horses required a rest. Because he fell asleep, he was later getting back to the field than he had intended. He had made a couple of rounds when he spotted the twins waiting for him at the edge of the field.

He pulled the team to a halt when he drew up beside them. "Afternoon, boys. What are you two so down in the mouth about?"

"Aunt Rebecca won't let us do nothin'," they said in unison.

"Like what?"

"She won't let us ride horses with the Fergusons, and we can't go swimmin' when it gets warmer. We finally persuaded her to let us go fishin', but she said we couldn't take Sissy like we used to," said Paul.

"And that made Sissy cry. Aunt Rebecca's always tellin' us not to do this or that and to *be careful*," said Saul in disgust.

"She about had a fit when she saw me climbing a tree."

"Uncle Wylie talked to her, but it didn't do no good. She told us she was afraid we'd get hurt or killed."

"What do you want me to do about it?" Luke shifted on the seat, stretched his right leg out straight, and rubbed the knee.

"Could you talk to her?" the twins said at the same time.

"She might listen to you," added Saul. "Uncle Wylie can't talk any sense into her."

"And you think I can? Sorry, boys, I doubt if I'd be much help." *Not after the way I talked to her the last time.*

"Please, Mr. Northcutt. She's not mad at you, honest."

"No?" Luke raised a brow, slightly amused. "Well, she should be."

"Aw, you know her, she's the forgivin' type. She knew you were just feelin' lousy. I think she's wishin' you'd come over," said Paul with a grin.

"I'm too busy."

"Truth is, sir, we ain't very good at ridin' anyway—"

"—and we kinda thought you might teach us. Aunt Rebecca said she would get us a horse sometime and let Jackson teach us, but we think she might do it sooner if she knew you were the one givin' the lessons. Would you do it, sir?"

Luke studied their earnest faces for a long moment. He didn't want to get in tight with the boys. The best thing for him would be to stay away from them, their little sister, and especially Rebecca Stephens. But he owed them. He owed them all.

"I'll teach you to ride if she gets you a horse. I'll talk to her the next time I see her. Now you two run along. I've got work to do."

"Will you talk to her soon, Mr. Northcutt?"

"I said I'd talk to her when I see her." Luke turned the team around and watched the boys walk dejectedly down the road. They knew as well as he did that he wouldn't be seeing her any time soon unless he called on her—and he wasn't about to do that.

Wylie stopped by late in the afternoon while Luke was currying the horses. The older man only stayed a few minutes, simply long enough to invite Luke to supper the next evening. He said he had checked with Rebecca, and she had assured him it would be fine.

Self-preservation told Luke to decline, but, instead, he accepted the invitation. He had a debt to pay.

Chapter 19

REBECCA GREETED LUKE warmly when he arrived, and in those few moments that they were alone, the cross words they had spoken the week before were forgiven and forgotten.

But as soon as they all sat down at the kitchen table and joined hands to ask the blessing, the old feeling of not belonging settled over him. The year he had turned ten years old he had worked for a family who held hands when they said grace. Because the farmer had eight children there had not been room at the table for the plowboys. Day after day, Luke and another youngster had sat off in the corner by themselves, envying the other children.

Although he was included in tonight's circle of thanksgiving, he did not feel a part of it. The children held hands and bowed their heads without being prompted. In the short time they had been with Rebecca—and possibly even before, when they had been with their parents—thanking God for their meals had become a tradition.

It was hard to have traditions when a man was alone.

"We made a quick trip to town this morning." Paul took the tureen of chicken and cornmeal dumplings from his brother and grinned at Rebecca.

Luke expected Saul to pick up the story as he usually did, but the boy had a mouthful of green beans. Luke cut through a dumpling, revealing the flecks of yellow cornmeal and kernels of corn sprinkled in the dough, and scooped up a bit of chicken and thickened broth to go with it. When he took the first bite, he almost groaned with pleasure. He had missed Rebecca's cooking almost as much as he had missed her.

"Us buyed a chicken."

"You bought a chicken? You've got a whole barnyard full of them."

"Aunt Rebecca has a problem killin' chickens." Saul and his brother shared a grin.

Luke figured Rebecca had a problem killing anything, even flies, but he didn't say so. He just watched and listened as they bantered back and forth, sharing teasing and laughter without offense. Love passed around the table as easily as the bowl of canned peaches. It was not official yet, but Wylie, Rebecca, and the children were a family. Even Jackson seemed a silent extension of the family group.

"I just have a problem killing a chicken I know on a first-name basis," said Rebecca with a smile.

Wylie chuckled. "And they all have names. This is probably the only farm in the state where the chickens all die of old age."

"Well, picking feathers is a messy job. That's why I bought the icebox anyway, so I could keep fresh meat for a day or so if I wanted to. It comes in handy now and then."

Rebecca worried about Luke during the meal. He obviously enjoyed the food and spoke occasionally, but he was almost as reserved and uncomfortable as the first time he had come to dinner. She decided his leg probably hurt more than he let on. When the meal was finished and he offered to help her with the dishes, she promptly refused.

"No, thank you. The boys are pretty good with a dish towel." She looped her arm through his and escorted him down the hall to the parlor, walking slowly to accommodate his sore leg. "You sit here in my rocker and put your leg up."

"I don't need to take your chair."

"Nonsense. I can sit in any of the others just as easily, but I can tell you're tired. You probably should be home in bed."

As he accidently brushed against her bosom, Luke wondered if she realized how closely she was holding his arm. "You want me to leave?"

"Of course not," she said, squeezing his arm in emphasis.

Luke thought he might go up in smoke.

"Now, you sit and relax." She released him and fussed over him until he sat down. She immediately pulled a footrest over for his feet.

"Rebecca, you don't have to wait on me." Luke sat down, grateful for the comfortable seat and place to put up his aching leg.

"I'm not. Now, sit and relax." She bustled off, but returned in a few minutes carrying a kettle. "I warmed a cloth to go on that knee." She set the pan on the floor and took out a thick bath towel. "It's not wet so we can put it over your jeans." Kneeling beside him, she wrapped the hot towel around his leg. When she stood, he caught her hand.

"Thanks. That's easing the ache already."

Rebecca smiled down at him and tried to hide the longing from her eyes. She made up her mind then and there to invite him to sit in the porch swing before the evening was over. When he caressed the back of her hand with his thumb, her whole body came to attention. It was definitely a night for a little time alone.

He was holding her hand too long. He knew it, and for the life of him, he couldn't seem to do anything about it. Out of the corner of his eye, he saw Wylie lever himself from the wheelchair over into his big armchair. After a pause, the older man cleared his throat, but Luke barely heard him.

He watched his callused thumb slide over the back of her hand and wondered how she kept her skin so smooth with all the work she did around the farm. He thought, too, of how incredibly soft the rest of her would feel beneath his hands. Sliding a fingertip up her wrist, he captured her racing pulse. *Do you know what you do to me, sweet Rebecca? Do you feel the same?*

Wylie cleared his throat again, louder.

Luke released her hand, afraid he had embarrassed her. He glanced up at her and almost wished he hadn't. Her face glowed with soft color, partially from embarrassment if the nervous way she smoothed her apron was any indication. But the light burning in her eyes had nothing to do with chagrin.

"I'd better get back to the kitchen and make sure Sissy doesn't try to help too much. She has a tendency to splash water everywhere." Rebecca turned and hurried from the room, barely keeping her feet from running.

When she and the children joined the men in the parlor fifteen minutes later, Luke and Wylie were discussing boxing. To her amazement, both men seemed highly informed about what she considered a barbaric sport. She waved Luke back to his seat when he started to stand. Sitting down in one of the side chairs, she listened as they continued the conversation.

"I saw them both fight," he said as he settled back down in the chair.

"Who, Mr. Northcutt?"

"Paddy Ryan and John L. Sullivan."

"Holy Moses!" shouted Saul. "You saw Sullivan beat Ryan for the championship?"

"Saul, keep your voice down, please." Rebecca wondered at the fascination fighting held for the male of the species. She found it appalling that boys as young as the twins would know so much about it.

"No, I didn't see that fight." Luke glanced at Rebecca's frown of disapproval. "Sit down, boy, and relax. I saw Ryan in a bout a couple of years ago and Sullivan last summer. I figured then Sullivan would beat the champ. John L. was real fast with his hands and feet. He could get in a punch before his opponent saw it coming."

"Aw, speed ain't what won him the title." Saul plopped down on the floor beside Luke. "It was the mighty Sullivan punch."

"You're right. His strength had a lot to do with it, too."

"Boxing is not a fit topic for children. Where did you learn about such a disgusting thing as bare-knuckle fighting?" Rebecca shook her head in consternation. She was thoroughly annoyed with Luke for persisting in the discussion.

"From our pa," said Paul quietly.

"He did some boxing when he was younger. Won a bunch of fights, too." Saul glared at Rebecca. "There wasn't nothin' wrong with it, either."

"Oh," said Rebecca softly. She was at a complete loss. Although she heartily disapproved of fighting in any form, she had not intended to cast aspersions on the boys' father.

"Take it easy on Rebecca, boys. Women don't understand about men and boxing. If you look at it from their point of view, it seems pretty awful. All that pain and blood doesn't make much sense. Especially if they have to clean up their man," said Wylie.

"It proves a man is tough," said Saul.

"That's ridiculous!"

The boy ignored Rebecca. "Nobody messes with a man who can take care of himself."

"The best way to keep someone from bothering you is to avoid trouble." Luke caught Rebecca's eye and lifted one finger from the arm of the chair, silently asking her not to speak. Steam practically came out of her ears, but she yielded to his request.

"Have you always been able to avoid trouble, Mr. Northcutt?" asked Saul.

Luke glanced at Paul and Sissy sitting on the floor beside Rebecca's chair. The boy kept the little girl occupied by poking at the palm of her hand with his finger while she tried to catch it. He had let his brother do all the talking, but Luke could see he was keenly interested in what was being said.

"No, not always. I've done my share of fighting. Probably more than my share, come to think of it." He shifted in the chair, uncomfortable beneath Rebecca's irritated gaze. "Seems like everywhere I went when I was younger, there was a bully that wanted to prove he was boss. Sometimes I won; sometimes I lost. Somewhere along the way, I figured out it made more sense to try and talk my way out of a fight or avoid the situation altogether. It was a lot less painful. And it didn't make me any less of a man.

"I've known some mighty fine men who've never been in a fight in their lives. Some just look tough, and trouble passes them by. Then there are others who are so upstanding and well liked that even the bullies respect them. You said your father did some boxing when he was younger and that's all right. But I suspect that after he had a family he decided it wasn't the thing to do. It's hard to see good enough to bring home the bacon if you've got a black eye or two."

"Pa quit fightin' when he and Ma got married. She didn't like it, either." Paul sent his brother a pleading look, asking him not to stir up any trouble.

"Your father sounds like a very wise man," said Rebecca. "A man of both moral and physical strength. Saul, I apologize for unintentionally slighting him. I don't approve of fighting, but then as Uncle Wylie said, I'm looking at it with a woman's feelings."

"Sorry I got mad," mumbled Saul.

Sissy clambered off Paul's lap and walked over to Luke, holding up her arms. He picked her up, setting her on his lap. "You look sleepy."

The little girl yawned and snuggled next to him. "Uncle Luke sing Sissy night-night?"

Uncle Luke? The seed that had been sown in Luke's heart sprang to life, reaching for the light of a child's love like a new plant greedily stretches toward the sunshine. He tightened his arms around her. "Honey, I'm not much of a singer."

He was, but the songs he knew had been learned on river barges and herding cattle. At the moment, he could not think of any tune a man could sing to children. If Rebecca had disapproved of the boxing discussion, she would really fly off the handle when she heard his lullabies. He sent her a helpless look.

"Maybe Uncle Luke could tell you a story. Would you like that, dear?" Rebecca smiled at the child. When she glanced at Luke, she caught a flash of pain in his eyes.

"I don't know any bedtime stories."

Because no one ever told you any. Her heart ached for him. "But you've traveled a great deal. Tell a story about something you've seen or done."

"I could probably do that. Let me think a minute."

Before he had time to gather his thoughts, Sissy pulled on his shirtfront. When he looked down at her, she grinned. "Me gonna be this Sunday." She held up three fingers.

"You're going to be three? And Sunday is your birthday?" When she nodded Luke looked at Rebecca.

"Actually, it's a week from Sunday. May twenty-first. We're having the whole family out for a party."

"That's great, Sissy. You're getting to be a big girl. Now, let's see if I can think of a story." He paused a minute, then grinned. "I've got one. When I was down in Texas working as a cowboy—"

"You were a cowboy?" exclaimed Saul.

"In Texas?" Paul's voice held a note of awe.

"Yep." Luke's eyes twinkled. "I rode on a trail drive all the way from South Texas to Dodge City, Kansas. I hired on at the Sweet River Ranch a couple of months before they were to head up the trail. I was a farm boy from Illinois who didn't know the first thing about cowboyin'. But an old-timer took a liking to me and showed me the ropes, so to speak. The first time I tried to lasso a steer I fell clean off the horse." Luke chuckled along with the rest of them. "Guess that's when he figured he'd better teach me a few things."

Luke continued with his story, which turned out to be such a rousing yarn that Sissy barely blinked her eyes. By the time he was done with his tale, the boys were rolling on the floor with laughter and the older folks were holding their sides from laughing so hard.

"What was Dodge City like, Uncle Luke?"

Paul's unconscious use of Luke's new title caused another flurry of affection in Luke's heart.

"Pretty wild." His gaze met Rebecca's for a moment. Dodge had been wild all right. He had shot up his quota of store signs and gotten falling-down drunk for the only time in his life. He won more money at poker than he made on the drive, and then promptly lost it on the next hand of cards.

And he had his first woman. Lucille or Lulu or something. She wasn't pretty, but she was experienced and didn't mind that he was awkward, shy, and scared. She was reasonably clean, but Luke felt dirty. In the years afterward, he wasn't always a saint, but he never went to a prostitute again.

"Yeah, it was pretty wild. Lots of shooting at store signs and drinking. Not the kind of place a man wants to visit more than once." He grinned at the boys' disappointed expressions. "Maybe I'll tell you more about it someday, say when you reach twenty-five or so."

"Do you have another story? Something a little tamer." Rebecca smiled. "You're a great yarn-spinner, Luke Northcutt, but that was not a bedtime story."

"True. Well, there was the time over in Ohio that we picked half a field of corn by the light of the moon." He proceeded with his tale, talking quietly and letting his voice rumble low in his chest. Sissy cuddled against him, and though she made every effort to listen, she was asleep long before he finished the story.

"Much better," whispered Rebecca. "Do you want me to carry her upstairs?"

Luke shook his head and carefully stood. Rebecca picked up a small lamp near the door and led the way up to the child's bedroom. Luke climbed more slowly than normal because of his stiff knee, but he would not have traded the moment for anything in the world. This is how it must be for a real family, he thought. The wife lighting the way for the father to carry their child, a child conceived in love and joy.

He held Sissy for a few seconds longer, storing away the feeling of her little body against his chest, laying up the treasure of her trust and unconditional love in his heart. When he was old and sat on his front porch whittling plow horses for no one in particular, he would remember this night and think about the life that might have been.

Rebecca pulled down the covers and stepped aside. Her heart swelled with tenderness as Luke laid the little girl down on the bed with the gentleness of a loving father.

He eased off her shoes and drew the sheet and quilt up over her. Brushing her red curls with a kiss, Luke whispered, "Good night, punkin. Sweet dreams."

Sissy stirred and opened sleepy eyes. "Kiss?" She pulled her arms from beneath the covers and wrapped them around Luke's neck when he bent down. After kissing his cheek, she murmured, "Me like stories, Uncle Luke."

"I'm glad, sweetheart." Luke patted her shoulder as she lowered her hands to the bed. "I'll tell you more sometime."

"Night-night."

Luke told her good night once more and stepped out of the way so Rebecca could help her change into a nightgown. After tucking the covers around Sissy's shoulders and giving her a kiss, she picked up the lamp. Turning to leave the room, she caught a glimpse of quickly hidden sadness on Luke's face.

At the bottom of the stairs, she turned to him. "It's a lovely night. Would you like to go sit on the back porch for a while?"

Her invitation took him by surprise, but he did not have to think about his answer. "Yes."

"I'll put this lamp back in the parlor and get my shawl. I'll just be a minute."

Luke walked into the kitchen to wait for her. The twins were seated at the kitchen table playing a game of dominoes. Saul impatiently turned his lone piece around in his hand, waiting for his brother to lay down something he could match with the four-five. Paul played his next piece, placing a double three down on one end of the long row. Saul groaned in frustration and drew a domino from the boneyard and then another when he did not get a match.

Rebecca strolled into the room, draping her shawl around her shoulders. She took a plate of oatmeal raisin cookies out of the pie safe and set them on the table for the boys, taking a couple for Luke and one for herself.

As they walked out the door, she handed the cookies to Luke. He smiled and leaned down close to her ear. "Are you trying to sweeten me up?"

She sent him a saucy smile. "Do you need it?"

"Most folks think so."

"That's because they don't know the real Luke Northcutt," she said as she sat down in the porch swing.

"Oh?" He sat down beside her, making the swing sway a bit. He steadied it, then began to push it slowly back and forth. "And which one is that?"

"The man with the soft heart."

"There's nothing soft about me, Rebecca." He bit off half a cookie and chewed it vigorously.

"You're not as hard as you let on. Not in here"—she poked him in the chest with her finger, over his heart—"or here." Taking him off guard, she jabbed him in the stomach, a couple of inches above the waistband of his jeans. True, her finger did not go in very far, but being in a sitting position had left the muscles more pliable than normal. She laughed when he jumped. "You're ticklish!"

"Rebecca, keep your hands to yourself." Luke laughed as she waved her fingers in front of him, wiggling them like a spider's legs. "We'll tip over the swing."

Laughing, she reluctantly placed her hands on her lap. "I'll stop for now. But you'd better watch out. One day I'll attack when you least expect it. And then you can't use the swing as an escape."

"Watch who you're threatening, lady."

"It's not a threat." She grinned impishly. "Just a warning."

"I see." He nodded minutely and looked up at the rising moon.

Rebecca followed his gaze, sighing softly at the loveliness of the night. The steady creak of the swing blended with the crickets' serenade as the large three-quarter moon bathed the yard and orchard in soft light. Her shoulder and arm touched Luke's arm, and the side of his thigh rested against hers. Each time he pushed the swing, she felt the muscles in his leg tighten. His nearness warmed her heart as well as her body.

"Well, I guess there's only one thing I can do."

Rebecca glanced at him. "What?"

"Attack you first."

Chapter 20

LUKE'S GAZE WARMED her through and through. "I'm not ticklish," she said softly, knowing full well tickling her was not what he had in mind.

"Good. I don't think I'd like a woman to giggle every time I touched her." Luke let the rocking of the swing slowly cease and slipped his arm across the back of the seat. When she didn't protest, he moved his hand down to caress her shoulder. He looked into her eyes, eyes that were filled with wanting.

"Domino!"

"Aw, rats! I only had one left."

The twins' laughter reminded them they were not alone. Luke jerked his arm back down to his side and kicked the swing into motion. Seconds later, the kitchen clock struck nine and the twins popped out the back door.

"Who won?" Rebecca was grateful that the porch was shadowed, lit only by the light shining through the window nearby. Her face was red, and she suspected Luke's was, too.

"Paul. But I'll get him next time." Saul surveyed the grown-ups' cozy seating arrangement and yawned elaborately. "Well, it's time for bed. Guess we'd better mosey on upstairs."

Paul leaned over and hugged Rebecca. "Good night, Aunt Rebecca. Those cookies sure were good." He straightened. " 'Night, Uncle Luke."

Saul quickly followed his brother, giving Rebecca a hug. But when he moved around to the other end of the swing and bent down to Luke, he caught him by surprise. "Don't forget to talk to her," Saul whispered, hugging his neck.

Luke awkwardly patted Saul on the back. "I won't," he answered quietly. When the youngster straightened, Luke added, "Good night, boys."

The twins hustled through the back door, closing it behind them with a loud click. The lamp in the kitchen went out, leaving Rebecca and Luke in the dark. It took a few moments for their eyes to adjust to the moonlight.

"Looks like you've made a friend."

Luke chuckled. "I think so, but mostly, he was reminding me of my mission."

"Your mission?"

"I've been assigned to convince you to let the boys go swimming and horseback riding."

"Absolutely not. They're just children."

"Rebecca, the boys are ten, going on eleven. They've been taking care of themselves for over two months. They assumed a man's responsibilities the minute they ran away from home, especially since they took Sissy with them. Being told they can't do something, especially if it's something they have done before, isn't going to sit well.

"I was only a few months older than they are when I struck out on my own. The day I walked away from my folks' house, I made myself a promise—that nobody would ever run my life again."

"And did that happen?"

"No, not until now. There was always a boss or a sheriff or somebody telling me what to do. I figured a boss had a right to order me around on the job and a sheriff could tell me what to do as long as it pertained to the law. But nobody else had any claims on me. What I did on my own time was my business."

"Saul says he'll leave if I don't let them do the things their friends do." Rebecca fidgeted with the belt of her lavender wrapper-style dress.

"And he probably will. Now, I'm not saying you should approve of just any old thing but going swimming in the creek or riding a horse is as much a part of being a farm boy as feeding the chickens or milking cows." He slipped his arm across the back of the swing, keeping his hand on the wooden slat.

"There's no need for them to put themselves in danger."

He cupped his hand around her shoulder. "They've been in a lot more danger these past months than they would ever be down at the creek."

"Have they told you about how they got along? How they managed to survive? They haven't said much about it to me." She continued to pleat the belt between her fingers and leaned against him a little more. She felt chilled, but the cold did not come from the night air. It came from the depths of her soul.

"No, they haven't talked about it much. But I can tell you how it was. I've been there, and I've seen enough over the years to know it hasn't changed much." When she looked at him, he didn't meet her gaze but stared out into the night. "A lot of folks wouldn't be kind like you. Oh, they might be if they knew about Sissy, but then the well-meaning adults would try to take her away from the twins. I'm sure the boys kept her out of sight most of the time to protect her.

"Occasionally, a boy finds someone like you who gives out food for nothing, but most of the folks that share their food want something in return, usually a lot of work. Then there are those who don't want anything to do with him, who treat him like something less than human. Those are the ones who go after a boy with a shotgun or sic the dogs on him."

"Oh, Luke, how could anyone be that cruel?"

"It doesn't take much to make a person mean. It's easier to be bad than good. Running into that type a few times makes a boy get real careful about who he asks for work. I suspect that's why the twins took to stealing from your windowsill and helping themselves to the milk and eggs, then doing work secretly as repayment. Of course, they didn't want to risk having Sissy taken away, so there is always the possibility they didn't run into anybody real low-down. But that's not likely."

"I don't want to be hard on them. I know I'm being unfair." When she looked up at him, worry filled her eyes. "But Luke, they're like my own children. I couldn't bear it if anything happened to them." Her voice trembled. "I think I'd die if I lost another child."

Luke gathered her close, holding her gently. His heart ached for her fear and her pain. "Why don't you let Wylie get them a couple of horses? You know he'll pick out gentle ones. And I'll teach the boys to ride. I'm an old cowhand, remember? I'll make sure they can handle themselves. When it gets warmer, I'll take them swimming in the creek and see how well they do. I won't lie to you, honey. If they can't take care of themselves in the water, I'll tell you."

Rebecca's head rested against his shoulder, and his jaw brushed against her forehead as he spoke. She slid her hand around his waist, drawing peace and strength from him. "All right." She moved her head back, looking up at him. "I trust you, Luke. I know you would never let them do anything they aren't ready to do."

"I promise I'll teach them everything I know about horses and swimming." He smiled. "And come to think of it, that's quite a bit."

Rebecca felt the fear and worry ebb away. She had not known him long, but in many ways, she knew him well. He was a good man, trustworthy and solid. In spite of what he thought of himself, he had a gentle soul. His smile slowly faded, and the moonlight illuminated his face, revealing the deep yearning in his eyes. The chill she had felt earlier disappeared in a rush of heat, and her heartbeat quickened. She slowly moved her hand up his chest, pausing for the space of a shallow breath over his pounding heart. She raised her hand, caressing his jaw. "Do you always keep your promises?"

His eyes grew dark, and he lowered his head toward hers. "Always," he murmured against her lips. His touch was cautious and tender at first, but when she tangled her fingers in his hair, he deepened the kiss.

His arms tightened around her, surrounding her with caring and desire. Happiness filled her, a sweetness unlike any she had ever known. She had expected kissing him would be good, but it was more wonderful than anything she could have imagined.

"Sweet, beautiful woman." He brushed a kiss across her cheek, then moved back to her lips, taking, giving, sharing the feelings hidden deep in his heart, feelings for which he knew no name.

Rebecca heard a tiny whimper, barely realizing that it came from her own throat. He teased her with his lips until she sought more. Then he kissed her long and deep and drove her a little crazy. Yet, as a new love blossomed in her heart, and a new life lay ahead of her, bittersweet pain tinged her joy. It was time to say farewell to her first love.

Luke knew he was in trouble. One kiss wasn't nearly enough. Heaven help him, a thousand kisses wouldn't be enough. And from the way she pressed against him, from the way her lips clung greedily to his, one kiss wouldn't be enough for her, either. A sense of triumph surged through him—she wanted him, hungered for him. The jealousy he had felt for Ben Crowder disappeared like cool morning mist evaporating in the heat of the sun.

He ran his fingers along her jaw and down her throat, pausing at the throbbing pulse. At the instant his fingers brushed across the chain of her locket, he whispered a kiss against her cheek—and tasted the salty moisture of her tears. Shocked, he pulled back. "Rebecca?"

Tears shimmered on her blushed, heated skin, and the silver locket—that ever-present memorial to her dead husband and son—glistened in a beam of moonlight. She wiped her cheeks with trembling fingers. "It's all right."

He shifted, bringing the arm that was around her shoulders up to rest on the back of the swing. His other hand curved loosely around her waist. "I made you think of Anthony, didn't I?"

"Luke, it's nothing. I'm just a bit emotional."

Unconsciously, he tightened his fingers against her side. "Were you thinking of your husband?" His voice was strained, angry, hurt. "Answer me!" he whispered fiercely.

"Yes, for a moment."

He released her and lurched to his feet, rushing down the steps.

"Luke, wait. Don't go." She jumped up and ran after him.

At the bottom of the steps, he swerved around, glaring at her. "Don't go? Why should I stay when I kiss you, and you think of another man?"

She reached for his arm, but he jerked it away and took a step backward. "Luke, it wasn't like that."

"Go inside, Rebecca. Go in that fine, expensive house Anthony gave you and dream of the man you love. I can't give you fine things or make you happy like he did. I can't compete with him."

"You don't have to, Luke. Just love me."

"While you still love him? What kind of fool do you think I am?"

She stepped toward him, holding out her hand. "Please—"

"Stay where you are." He couldn't stand to see her beg. If she touched him, he would give in and lock himself in a lifetime of pain. "Don't you understand? I *can't* love you. I don't know what love is, and I'm not going to find it with you. Every time I kissed you or made love to you, I'd wonder if you were thinking of him. I won't spend my life like that, knowing I'm just filling in for another man and waiting for you to get tired of my services." He ignored her gasp. "I'd rather live alone."

Biting back words of love, Rebecca watched him walk away. Drifter fell into step beside him, glancing up at him as if to gauge his mood. She knew Luke would not believe her if she tried to explain her feelings, at least not at that moment. He was too hurt and too angry. He needed time to cool down.

She went inside, bidding her uncle and Jackson good night and peeking in at the children on her way to bed. Sissy was asleep and the boys pretended to be. She let

them go on pretending; morning would be a better time
to discuss horses and riding lessons.

Moonlight shone through the window in her bedroom,
giving her sufficient light to undress. When she removed
her locket, she did not lay it on top of the dresser as she
always did, but placed it in a small box that also held her
wedding band and put it in the dresser drawer. She looked
at the small portrait of Anthony, a face she knew so well
that she could see it clearly in the soft light.

"You'll always have a place in my heart, Anthony," she
said, trailing her fingers across the ornate silver frame. "But
the time for mourning is over. He's so different from you,
but I know you would like and respect him, and I think
you would approve. I'll have to tread carefully and not rush
him. It takes time to build trust, especially in someone like
Luke." She held the picture against her heart. "I hope you
won't mind if I still talk to you now and then to help me
think things out. It's kind of a habit, you know."

Rebecca placed the picture beside the box in the drawer.
Both rested on top of a silk scarf Anthony had given her
on her first anniversary. The scarf had blown out of her
hand once on the way home from town and had caught
on a barbed wire fence at the side of the road, ripping
the delicate material. Although the tear was irreparable,
she could never bring herself to throw the gift away.

With a sense of finality, she closed the drawer and walked
to the window, gazing out across her land toward Luke's
farm. "I love you, Luke Northcutt. And you're falling in
love with me, even if you don't realize it."

ON SUNDAY MORNING, Luke decided he needed to show
some respect for the Lord's day and not work in the field. He
had never been much of a church-going man and wouldn't
know which of the three churches in Grinnell to attend
even if he had been so inclined, but he was grateful to
still be alive.

After the necessary morning chores and breakfast, he
went to the toolshed and opened up a large wooden chest.
Ever appreciative of fine equipment, he carefully removed

the woodworking saws, planes, and chisels from the chest. He intended to set up a regular shop in that corner of the building, the first one he had been privileged to have, but assigning everything a special place would have to wait. He needed to spend his time on something more important.

He pried the nailed-down lid off a second box, which was even bigger than the tool chest. It contained selections of wood he had collected over the years, some fairly large, others smaller odds and ends. He had several nice pieces of walnut, although that kind of wood was beginning to get hard to find. Oak and pine made up the rest of his supply. Mahogany had to be imported and had always been too expensive for his pocketbook.

He carefully sorted through the walnut until he found the pieces he needed—the ones to make a doll cradle for a very special little girl.

Luke worked on the cradle all Sunday afternoon, carefully cutting the wood to match the sketch he had drawn that morning at breakfast. He planed the wood, working it first with one tool then another until it was the right thickness and smooth as glass.

On Monday evening, he took the wood and a set of chisels and gouges to the house and began to carve the design. An oak branch, complete with leaves and acorns, would adorn the sides and one end. On the other end, he pictured a little animal that would bring a smile of delight to Sissy's face.

Luke worked on the cradle every day, staying up late at night and carving by lamplight. Often his eyes burned from the strain and his neck ached from looking down at his craft, but the memory of a precious child curled up in his lap and kissing him at bedtime kept him at the task.

The twins came over Tuesday morning to thank him for speaking to Rebecca on their behalf and to tell him Wylie was looking for a couple of horses for them. When they hesitantly asked if he still intended to teach them to ride, he assured them that he would.

He finished planting the corn at dusk on Wednesday and fell asleep in his chair after supper. The hope of making Sissy happy had not been the only reason he had worked himself practically to exhaustion. He had been trying to keep his mind off Rebecca. Unfortunately, planting and carving left a man a good deal of time to think.

After avoiding her all week, he missed her terribly. He called himself a fool and several other unflattering names, but he still wanted—needed—to see her. By late Friday afternoon, the only thing left on the cradle was for the varnish to finish drying. He sat on his front porch, watching long fingers of brilliant orange stretch across the deep blue sky, and tried to decide on the best way to deliver Sissy's present. Drifter plodded up the steps and curled up beside him, plopping his head on Luke's lap.

"What've you been up to, you lazy mutt?" Luke stroked the fur on Drifter's head and scratched behind his ears. Drifter's hind leg twitched and wiggled as if he were the one doing the scratching. "Guess I'll just have to swallow my pride and drop in on them Sunday evening. The folks should all be gone by then, so I wouldn't interrupt the party."

Sometime earlier in the week, he had gotten over being angry at Rebecca's reaction to his kiss. Some of the hurt still lingered; however, sweeter memories gradually eased the pain. Her smile. Her laughter. The warmth in her eyes sometimes when he caught her watching him. The yearning in her face seconds before he kissed her. The way her lips parted beneath his in invitation.

"And I made her cry." He sighed and glanced down at Drifter when the dog shifted his eyes to look up at him. "I kissed the woman and it reminded her of her husband." *Yes, for a moment.* Luke's breath caught. He had been so angry he had barely heard her whispered words, but they had hidden in his memory. He thought carefully, trying to remember everything that had been said that night. . . . *it wasn't like that.*

Luke sagged against the porch post, his mind racing. "Of course, the first time another man kissed her it would make her think of Anthony." He frowned. Ben Crowder had kissed her first. "She said she didn't feel anything with Ben," he whispered. "But she did when I kissed her, that's for sure."

Just love me. A new ache spread through Luke's heart. "I wish I knew how, sweetheart. I wish I knew how."

Drifter raised his head and looked down the lane. Luke followed his gaze and almost jumped out of his skin. Walking down the drive toward him—thankfully beyond hearing distance—was Rebecca. Behind her, soft peach flowed across the sky as if left there by the broad stroke of an artist's brush. In an instant, the white puffy clouds above her were painted a darker peach outlined in gold. Awed by the beauty of the scene, Luke slowly stood, never taking his gaze away from Rebecca and the grandeur in back of her.

"Hi." She stopped in front of him, her smile warm but somewhat uncertain.

"Hello." Without thinking he reached out and took her elbow, guiding her over to the porch. "You're missing quite a show." He tipped his head toward the sunset.

She sat down on the porch, resting her feet on the second step, and feasted her eyes on the slowly changing panorama before her. They sat in silence for a few minutes, watching, waiting, and wondering what the other would say.

"Did you finish planting?"

"Yes. Did you find some horses for the boys?"

"I think so. Uncle Wylie heard about two near Montezuma for sale, but the man is out of town until next week. The boys are trying to be patient, but I know it's hard." She glanced at him, thankful that he was at least being polite. "They said you still wanted to teach them to ride."

Luke stretched his leg out in front of him and massaged his knee. "I do. I shouldn't be too busy next week, so if Wylie can buy the horses, it would be a good time."

"Thank you, Luke. I appreciate it." She frowned slightly as he continued to rub the muscles above his injured knee. "But will it hurt your leg?"

"No, it shouldn't bother it. Gets a little stiff by the end of the day no matter what I've been doing."

"Should you go inside where you can put it up?"

"I'll just shift around here. I like being outside this time of evening." He moved around so he could lean against the post and rest his leg on the porch. "Besides, if we went inside, I might be tempted to kiss you again, and maybe that's not something I should do." His heart pounding, he slowly brought his gaze around to meet hers. He had to know if he had been wrong the week before, if he had read more into her reaction than was really there.

She looked away, out across the prairie. "We'd better stay here."

Disappointment left a bitter taste in Luke's mouth and a keen ache in his heart.

"Otherwise, I might be tempted to let you."

When she turned her face toward him, he drew in a sharp, audible breath. He was not certain what mixture of emotions her expression revealed, but anger and revulsion were not among them.

"I liked it when you kissed me, Luke," she said quietly. "I didn't want it to end."

Luke's gaze dropped to her bodice as she reached for her locket—something she often did when she was nervous—but it wasn't there. He had never seen her without the silver necklace. His gaze shot to her face as she quickly lowered her hand to her lap.

Rebecca read the question in his eyes and swallowed hard. She had sought all week for the best way to word the changes taking place in her heart and still did not know how to explain. She turned away from his penetrating gaze, wishing she could take the advice Wylie had once given her and simply tell Luke the truth. Fearing he was not ready to accept her love and would reject her, she skirted around it.

"I've put the locket away. I'll always love Anthony and Michael, and I don't need the locket to remind me of them. Now that the twins and Sissy have come into my life, I've realized that the heart has a much larger capacity than I once thought. It is amazingly easy to love again."

It didn't surprise Luke to hear she loved the children. What caught him off guard was the pain her words caused. *Why should I care if she doesn't include me? I don't want her to love me. I don't—can't—love her.* Luke knew he was lying to himself. He did want her love. Selfishly, he craved it, ached for it. But he was what life had made him—an empty shell with a hard heart, a heart too wounded to give anything in return.

Looking back at the sunset, he forced himself to take a breath. "They're easy kids to get attached to." He cleared his throat. "I've got a little something for Sissy's birthday. Could I bring it over Sunday evening?"

"No." She smiled at him when he quickly looked at her. "But you could bring it when you come for Sunday dinner. That's why I walked over—to ask you to dinner."

"Are you still having all the family out?"

"Yes. I'd like for you to meet them."

The warm glow in her eyes sent Luke's pulse into double time. Panic rose in his gut. If he had felt like a storefront window display the first time he met the neighbors, how would it be to meet her family over dinner? He was bound to use the wrong fork or make some worse social blunder. And if she looked at him with the same open admiration, what would those brothers of hers think? They'd be lining up to take him down a peg or two.

"I'd rather come over later." *Coward.*

"Sissy will be disappointed if you miss her party. She particularly wants you to be there." Rebecca remembered how hard it was for him to meet new people and how uncomfortable he had been with the silver and china. She wanted him to feel welcome, not ill at ease. "Come after dinner for the party." She smiled. "We can always use another strong arm to crank the ice-cream freezers."

That made him feel a little better. It would not be so hard if he could do something besides sit around and try to sound halfway intelligent.

"And I'm baking a chocolate cake." Rebecca grinned. "If you'll come, I'll make an extra one for you to take home." When he licked his lips, she knew she had him.

"Talked me into it." He grinned and relaxed. "What time?"

"Come around two-thirty. I'll let Sissy have her presents shortly after that. We'll eat the ice cream and cake later in the afternoon." She stood and he followed suit. "I'd better get home. It will be dark before long."

"Thanks for the invitation. I'm glad Sissy wanted me to be there."

Rebecca glanced up and down the county road to make sure no one was driving by. With her heart pounding, she stepped closer to Luke. She could not leave without giving him some small indication of what he meant to her. "It will make Sissy happy." Lifting her fingers to his rough, whiskered jaw, she smiled. "Growing a beard?"

"No, just lazy." Luke's breathing became quick and shallow and almost stopped completely when she took a tiny step closer. There was barely room for the light breeze to blow between them. He clenched his fists to keep from pulling her hard against him.

She gripped his arm with the other hand and stood on tiptoe, bringing her lips within a few inches of his. "It will make me happy, too." She stroked underneath his jaw with her thumb. "I especially want you to be there."

Luke trembled beneath her touch and at her words. It took every ounce of willpower he possessed not to sweep her into his arms and carry her inside the house. But some small thread of reason kept him from acting. Out here, where someone might drive by at any moment, was much safer, if no wiser. He lifted his hands to her waist and lowered his head until their lips touched, allowing her to be in control. Beneath his fingers, a shiver raced over her, but she kept the kiss light and sweet.

As her heels returned to the ground and Luke straightened, Rebecca took a deep, unsteady breath, bringing her hand down to her side. "I'll see you Sunday, then."

Luke nodded. "Do you want me to walk you home?"

"No. I'll be fine. I can make it before it gets dark." Her eyes lingered on his face for a moment before she released his arm. He lifted his hands from her waist and stepped back.

"Be careful of the ruts."

She smiled. "I will. You go prop that leg up on the stool."

"Yes, ma'am." Luke smiled and gave her a mock salute before she walked down the lane. He glanced at his front door, wondering how hard it would be to walk through a seven-foot doorway when he felt ten feet tall.

Chapter 21

"AUNT REBECCA, UNCLE Luke is here." Saul ran to the front door and opened it when Luke walked up the porch steps on Sunday afternoon. The boy grinned at Luke as loud laughter came from the parlor. "Two of Aunt Rebecca's brothers are arm-wrestling. Uncle Eben isn't as strong as Uncle Tobias, but he keeps crackin' jokes and makin' Tobias laugh so he can beat him."

Luke smiled faintly. *Maybe this isn't going to be so bad after all.* "Sounds like they're having a good time. How are you, boy?"

"I'm okay. I think I've finally got everybody's name down, except for Aunt Elizabeth's girls. I get them mixed up sometimes." He rolled his eyes and leaned closer, lowering his voice. "There's Maggie, Molly, and Mary, and the next one's going to pop out at any time. Aunt Elizabeth is as big as a house!"

"Watch what you say, son. Rebecca is liable to tan your hide if she hears you." Luke's eyes twinkled with amusement.

"Aw, I don't talk like that around the womenfolk." He winked at Luke. "That's just between us men." Luke chuckled, then bent down when Saul beckoned him closer with his finger. The boy's expression grew serious. "They're all real nice to us. If anybody's bad-mouthed us, we haven't heard about it. But I heard Tobias talkin' to Eben about you. He's worried that you're courtin' Aunt Rebecca just to get her money."

"Heck fire," Luke muttered as he straightened.

"Eben told him to behave himself today. Cousin Robert said Tobias has a quick temper, so watch your step, Uncle Luke."

Luke felt like shoving Sissy's present into Saul's hands and hightailing it out the front door. *I'm not courting Rebecca,* he thought irritably. A trill of soft laughter drew his gaze to the staircase. Rebecca and Sissy walked down the stairs hand in hand. *Or am I?* He suddenly wished he had a bouquet of hothouse roses to give her. *Her brothers would love that.*

He had wrapped the doll cradle up in a towel so Sissy would not see what it was. He handed it to Saul. "This is for Sissy."

"I'll take it in the kitchen. We've got stuff hidden all over the house."

When Sissy spotted Luke, she let out a squeal and raced down the stairs. "Uncle Luke! It me bir'day!"

He caught her up in a big hug. "I know it is, princess. Happy birthday." He shifted her to one arm. "Let me see, did you say you were this many?" He held up five fingers.

"No." She grinned and pulled down his thumb and little finger. "This many."

"And how many is that?"

"Three!"

"Good girl." Luke made a show of examining her new light royal blue dress. The color was perfect for her red hair and ivory skin and made her blue eyes shine like sapphires. "Where did you get such a pretty dress?"

"Aunt Becca buyed it for me."

Rebecca stepped up in front of him, and he turned his attention to her. She wore a long-sleeved, orchid silk dress with a small stand-up ruffle around the throat. The pink and orchid print gauze overskirt was draped across the front and gathered into a fashionable pouf at the back. With her hair done up in a soft chignon at the nape of her neck, she looked delicate and utterly feminine. "Your aunt Becca sure knows how to pick clothes, doesn't she?"

"Uh-huh." When Sissy squirmed, he set her down on the floor, and she scampered off to find the other girls.

"Good afternoon." Rebecca smiled into his eyes. She had paused on the stairs long enough to feast her gaze on him without being too obvious. His hair had been cut, and he wore a new light gray flannel shirt, slightly faded denim Levi's, and a pair of freshly blacked cowboy boots.

"Good afternoon. Sissy's as pretty as a picture today. And so are you," he murmured.

"Thank you. You look nice, too."

Luke shifted uncomfortably. The other men were probably dressed up. He was going to stick out like a sore thumb. "I'm not much for dressing up."

She stepped beside him and slipped her hand around his arm. "You look fine to me. Are you ready to run the gauntlet?"

Luke glanced down at her in surprise. "Is it going to be that bad?"

Rebecca laughed. "I hope not. My brothers are very protective of me, but they are civilized most of the time." Tobias had cornered her the minute he found out Luke had been invited and gave her a stern I'm-your-big-brother-I-know-best lecture. "Just don't let Toby get your goat."

He took a deep breath and prayed he could practice what he had preached to the boys. On today of all days, he would much rather avoid trouble than get into an argument, or worse, a brawl. She squeezed his arm as they neared the parlor and gave him an encouraging smile. Through the open doorway, he saw a whole room full of people. Every man in the room, including Jackson, wore a white shirt and dress pants. Rebecca's father and Wylie also wore suit coats. "This is all family?"

"Every last one."

It occurred to Luke that if all his brothers and sisters with their respective spouses and children ever got together, they would fill the whole house and not just the parlor. A sharp twinge of regret stabbed him. He didn't know if they were all still alive, much less if they were married and had families. In fact, he had siblings he had never met.

The laughter died as they walked into the parlor. He quickly scanned the room. Wylie nodded in silent greeting and smiled in encouragement. The women's polite smiles did not hide their curiosity. Although Rebecca's brothers obviously sized him up, only one openly frowned. *So that's Tobias.* His gaze paused on the large man. He was a couple of inches taller than Luke and outweighed him by twenty pounds. Their entrance had broken up the arm-wrestling, and as Tobias slowly rolled down his shirt sleeve, he gave Luke plenty of time to note the powerful muscles in his arm. *Tarnation, the man's itchin' for a fight.*

An older, but still beautiful woman stood and glided across the room to them. Her eyes were blue, but she had the same honey-blond hair as Rebecca, though it was now tinted with gray. There was no mistaking the resemblance between mother and daughter.

"You must be Mr. Northcutt. I'm Rebecca's mother, Clara Lansing." She smiled warmly and held out her hand. "I'm so glad to finally meet you."

Luke shook her hand carefully. "It's nice to meet you, too, ma'am."

Clara asked if his injuries were healing, and when told they were, she related a story about her boys and the time they tested their theories of flight. "Of course, Will was the youngest and smallest, so his brothers tied him to the kite and pushed him off the barn roof. Thankfully, the kite did slow his descent somewhat, but unfortunately, not enough. He wound up with a broken leg, and his brothers got a session behind the woodshed."

Luke smiled politely, although he thoroughly enjoyed seeing the older brothers squirm. The youngest caught his eye and grinned.

"Eben kept yelling at me to flap my arms," said Will. "But I was too scared to pry my fingers from the braces on the kite. It was almost worth a broken leg to have these big galoots doing all my chores and waiting on me hand and foot for a couple of months." He glanced at his nephews and the twins. "Almost, but not quite. That leg hurt terribly and slowed me down for nigh onto a year."

Declaring she was anxious to give Sissy her presents, Clara went off in search of the girls while Rebecca introduced Luke to the others. Everyone except Tobias was friendly, and even he was polite.

After the introductions, Howard engaged Luke in conversation while the women and twins gathered up the presents. When Saul brought him the cradle, still wrapped up in the towel, the boy took up a position beside his chair. There was something almost protective in the way he casually draped his arm over one side of the chair back, letting his hand rest on Luke's shoulder. Luke glanced up at him and smiled, touched by the lad's concern and friendship.

Soon all available seats were taken, with the children sitting on the floor. Sissy was given the place of honor in the center of the Turkish rug as one by one her gifts were revealed and given to her. The child was delighted with everything. With a wisdom and gratitude beyond her years, she thanked each person, and with more patience than some grownups possessed, she took the time to examine each item carefully.

Luke was so proud of her he was afraid the buttons were going to pop off his shirt. When Rebecca caught his eye, he knew she felt the same. Their shared moment, tender and intensely intimate, filled him with a sense of wonder.

He watched in amazement as the pile of gifts grew around Sissy. Besides a number of dresses, there appeared to be enough toys to fill the toy section of the Montgomery Ward Catalog. There were alphabet blocks as well as building-block acrobats. A set of wooden Russian dolls, in graduated sizes and with various faces and costumes of peasant women painted on them, nested one inside the other. Will gave her a wooden Mary and her lamb, which rolled around on wheels. Rebecca's sister Elizabeth and her husband Moss gave Sissy a toy garden set, complete with a child-sized wheelbarrow. Eben and Amanda gave her a monkey on a tricycle, and

Tobias and Charlotte gave her a doll that walked when wound up.

There were other mechanical toys—a duck that flapped his wings, a frog that hopped, and a mouse that ran. Wylie gave her a spring horse-riding toy, and Howard and Clara gave her a cane-seated rocking chair that matched Rebecca's kitchen rocker. When Rebecca rolled out a folding baby-doll carriage with an umbrella canopy, and Sissy squealed in delight, Luke's heart sank.

He knew the cradle was beautiful; it was the finest thing he had ever made. But it was not nearly as practical as the doll carriage. And it wasn't store bought. He had waited to give it to her, figuring it was more polite to let the family members go first. Now, he wished he had slipped it in sometime in the middle.

"Here you go, Uncle Luke." Saul handed him the cradle. "I peeked and it's really something," he said softly. "Sissy, come here. Uncle Luke has something for you, too."

Sissy reluctantly stopped her perusal of the baby carriage and came over to Luke, standing beside his knee. When she smiled at him, his heart melted. "I didn't know Rebecca was getting you the carriage, but maybe you can use this anyway." He unwrapped the towel from around the cradle. "Dolly might not want to sleep in the carriage all the time." *Please let her like it. Let her want it.*

He heard Rebecca gasp as the cradle was revealed, and Sissy's eyes grew wide.

"Ooh," Sissy breathed, touching it reverently. "It boo-ti-ful, Uncle Luke."

A lump the size of Gibraltar instantly formed in his throat. Unable to speak, he turned the cradle around, resting it on his knee.

"A squirrel! Look, Aunt Becca. A squirrel's got a—what that called?"

Rebecca knelt beside the little girl. "It's an acorn, honey. Looks like he followed the branch all around the cradle until he found just the acorn he wanted." She looked up at Luke. "It's exquisite, but where did you find it? I've never seen anything like it, even in Des Moines."

"Him whittled it." Sissy beamed him a smile.

"He what?" Rebecca was clearly confused.

"He made it," Saul said proudly. "Just for Sissy." He reached in his shirt pocket and pulled out the wooden plow horse. "He made this, too."

Focused on Rebecca's shocked expression, Luke barely heard the murmurs of the others in the room. Was she pleased, or did she think he was showing off? When she raised her hand and ran her fingers along the intricate carving, Luke's stomach did a somersault. She might as well have caressed his skin.

"Luke Northcutt, you've been holding out on us!" She smiled up at him, her face and eyes glowing with adoration. His heart stumbled all over itself. "Now, I know I'm going to let you replace that little lamp table." She held out her hand, and he clasped it, helping her to her feet. He squeezed her fingers before he released them.

"Uncle Luke . . ." Sissy held up her arms, waiting expectantly. He quickly set the cradle on the floor beside the chair and picked her up. She curled her arms around his neck and hugged as hard as she could, then leaned back to look him in the eye. "Thank you. Dolly sleep good in new bed. Me love it." Her radiant smile slowly faded, and her expression became unusually serious. "Uncle Luke, me—" She paused, obviously considering her words very carefully. "I . . . love you."

He had waited for thirty-three years.

Luke pulled her against his chest in a giant hug and gave a name to the powerful emotion sweeping through his soul. "I love you, too, Sissy." He cleared his throat and closed his burning eyes. "I love you, too."

A long moment passed before he opened his eyes and blinked back the mist, meeting Rebecca's tender gaze. Moisture clung to her eyelashes, and her gentle smile was almost his undoing. Everyone in the room was touched by the scene, but she alone understood.

An hour later, Luke turned the crank on one ice-cream freezer while Eben and Howard operated two more. Jackson, Moss, and Tobias took their turns when needed, and once in a while, Will or one of the twins dropped out of the baseball game to help.

"Need a break?"

"I'd welcome it." Luke slid over on the porch and shook a kink out of his arm as Tobias took his place. "Will looks like a pretty good ball player."

"They have a team at the college. This is the first year he hasn't played. Since he got the job at the *Herald,* he doesn't have the time." Tobias rotated the crank at a steady pace. "I used to hit the ball pretty good myself, but I'm rusty now. I'll have to practice up before the July Fourth picnic. You play?"

Luke shook his head. "No. Never learned. I like to watch a good game, though. I lived in Cincinnati for a while and went to a few Red Stockings games."

"I've never been to a professional game, but I hear the Red Stockings are quite a team. You seen a lot of the country?"

"I've done some traveling." When Saul caught a fly ball and turned to see if he was watching, Luke smiled and waved. "Done all I'm interested in."

"Ready to settle down, huh?"

Luke glanced at Rebecca's brother, but Tobias kept his gaze fixed on the ball players. "I've got my farm. That keeps a man from wanderin' too far."

"Ain't that the truth. I've been working the family farm since I was old enough to plow. I bought it from Pa five years ago." Tobias looked over at the women sitting in the shade of the house. His wife, Charlotte, was only eighteen, eleven years younger than he was. "A man gets mighty lonesome living alone."

"I'm used to it."

"I was too for a while, but that all changed last year when I met Charlotte. All of a sudden that old house was awful empty. A wife makes it a whole lot nicer to go home come evening time."

"I've never figured myself for a marryin' man."

"If you mess around with my sister, you'd better be a marryin' man." Tobias didn't miss a turn on the ice-cream freezer as he drilled Luke with a piercing gaze.

"I respect Rebecca more than any woman I've ever met. I won't take advantage of her."

Tobias fell silent, but Luke sensed he had more to say. He waited, listening to the quiet conversations going on around them, the tuneless squeaks of the ice-cream freezers, and the laughter and shouts of the ball players.

"When you got here today, I was ready to clean your plow." Tobias switched hands on the crank. "Sight unseen, I pegged you for a man out to better his situation by marrying a rich widow."

"You change your mind?" Although Luke kept his eyes on the twins, it was unsettling to realize how much he wanted Tobias and the rest of Rebecca's family to think well of him.

"I'm reserving judgment." Tobias rested his hand on the ice-creamer freezer and looked at Luke. "Rebecca is happier now than she has been in a long time."

"The children are the cause of that."

"Partly. But you've put the light back in her eyes, Luke. I hope you can keep it there."

Chapter 22

"JUST RELAX, SON. Move with the horse. That's it. Good."

Listening to Luke's calm instructions and words of encouragement to the twins, Rebecca continued with her gardening and daydreamed a little. She could easily grow accustomed to having him around all the time. Cutting a tender red and green stalk of pieplant, she added it to the rest of the rhubarb in her basket. They would have a nice pie for supper tonight with lots of sweetened whipped cream. She glanced over to see if Sissy was still sitting with Wylie in his buggy and smiled. Those two seemed to be having as much fun watching the lessons as the twins were riding.

This was the second morning in a row Luke had come over to teach the boys to ride their new horses. Slow and Poke, as the mares were called, were perfect for the twins. The animals were five years old and extremely gentle and patient with the youngsters. Although Luke had taken each horse for a good hard gallop, they were not inclined to take off on their own.

The grown-ups had gotten a kick out of the way the boys settled on which horse would belong to which youngster. They decided that since the animal's names started with the same letters as their names, they would keep it simple. Saul took Slow. Paul took Poke.

Rebecca decided she had a big enough batch of the rhubarb and tucked her knife into the basket. Straightening, she
hooked the basket over her arm and watched the proceedings
down by the barn. Paul was walking Poke around in a wide
circle. Luke had a long lead line attached to the bridle and
stood in the center of the circle giving instructions.

"Do you feel comfortable?"

"Yes, sir."

"Okay. Now, nudge her a little with your heels and get
her up to a trot."

Paul did as ordered, and the horse responded accordingly,
happily trotting around the circle. "Do I—I ha-ve to do th-is
for lo-ng?" Paul clung precariously to the saddle horn.

Rebecca bit her lip. The poor boy was bouncing so hard
he was going to snap his neck.

Luke chuckled. "Nope. Kick her again, just a little bit."

Paul obeyed and Poke moved into an easy gallop around
the circle.

"Oh, wow! This is great, Uncle Luke!"

"Don't get too excited. You don't want to spook her.
That's it, just relax. Let go of the saddle horn."

No, hang on! Rebecca pressed her lips tightly together to
keep from calling out. Paul was doing well. Unfortunately,
she was still terrified. *He's so far off the ground.* If he fell,
Poke might step on him. She gave herself a stern reprimand.
Her brothers had survived far more dangerous pursuits, and
Luke was an excellent teacher. Although she knew he had
worked on a ranch in Texas, she had been surprised at the
proficiency and ease with which he handled the horses.
Wylie had commented that the man should be raising horses
instead of corn.

Paul released the pommel and bent his arms, holding them
steady but relaxed. When Luke told him to do so, he slowly
pulled on the reins and brought Poke to a stop. "How was
that? How did I do?" The boy carefully dismounted and led
his horse over to Luke.

"You did just fine. Saul is doing well, too. You boys are
quick learners. Tomorrow, I'll saddle up Rusty, and we'll
go for a little ride down in the pasture."

Rebecca walked toward them, stopping to help Sissy down from Wylie's buggy. "Hold my hand, honey. Stay clear of the horses' feet."

Saul led Slow over beside Paul and Poke. "We can't go riding tomorrow morning," he said.

"Why not? Got something else going on?"

"Yes, sir." Paul smiled lovingly at Rebecca. "Aunt Rebecca is going to adopt us tomorrow."

Luke looked at her in surprise. "You heard from their kinfolks?"

"Yes. Since I didn't get out here before you started, I was going to tell you after the lesson. I had written the children's great-aunt in Illinois. We got a letter from her yesterday. They have some distant cousins, but everyone thought it would be just as well if I claimed the children as my own. I'm delighted."

"Well, I'm real happy for you." Luke looked at the four beaming faces and cleared his throat—twice. "For all of you. You'll make a good family."

"Will you come with us tomorrow? We have to go to the Circuit Court Clerk in Montezuma. Wylie will be one witness, but I need another one."

"Sorry, I don't have time. Boys, why don't you go give the horses some water. They look thirsty. Sissy, you can help them." Luke was kind, but his orders were clear. He wanted to speak to Rebecca alone, and they knew it. Paul grabbed Sissy's hand and kept her away from the horses as they led them away.

"We would all be pleased if you could be there."

"Thanks for the invitation, but it's a time for family. You should have your parents go with you."

"They will if you can't go." She hesitated, not certain of how hard to push. "You're like family to the children. They want to share it with you."

"Sorry, can't make it." *It would be too hard to see them become yours and not mine, too.*

Because she was looking for it, Rebecca caught the glint of pain in his eyes. "All right, but you'll be missed. Can you come over the next day and take the boys riding?"

"Sure." Disappointing her made him feel bad. "Maybe we could go on a picnic after the ride. You and Sissy, too. We could take them fishing."

"That would be lovely! I'll fry up a chicken."

"Don't go to too much trouble. We'll be feasting on catfish for supper."

As they strolled toward the house, she slanted him a flirtatious look. "You're sure about that?"

"Yes, ma'am. Those fish will jump right up in the basket just to see that pretty smile of yours." *The one that's got me saying stupid things and turning me inside out.*

"Oh, my. Then I'd better bring a big basket if it's that easy. I have a feeling I'm going to be grinning for at least a month."

THE NEXT MORNING, Rebecca waited anxiously as the Circuit Court Clerk read over the legal document prepared by her attorney stating her intention of adopting all three children. She had read it so many times, she knew it by heart. The clerk set the sheet of paper to one side and carefully perused the death certificates of their parents and the letter from their great-aunt.

The clerk cleared his throat and lowered his chin, looking at Rebecca over his spectacles. "Mrs. Stephens, I need to go through this with you as a matter of formality, just to make certain you understand these proceedings." At Rebecca's nod, he continued. "You are Rebecca Stephens?"

"Yes, sir."

"And it is your intention to adopt Saul Kenneth Miller, Paul Keith Miller, and Hester Eugenia Miller as your own lawful children?"

"Yes, sir. It is." Rebecca smiled lovingly at the three children sitting beside her. Like the boys, Sissy's expression was somber.

"Will you be the sole parent?"

"Yes, sir. I am a widow. But I own a large farm, which my uncle manages for me. I can provide for them adequately."

The clerk nodded and made a note on a piece of paper. "I see here that they intend to go by their current names.

You don't want them to take your last name?"

"We have discussed it. They would like to keep their own name in honor of their parents. The twins are almost eleven years old. I think it would be difficult for them to change, now."

"Very well. They can always have their names changed later if they so desire. You reside in the Grinnell Township of Poweshiek County?"

"Yes."

The clerk laid aside his pen and set the papers on the desk. "You understand, Mrs. Stephens, that the children become your rightful and legal heirs, and upon your death, will receive the same rights of inheritance as any of your natural-born children?"

"Yes, sir. I do."

"Then, it is my pleasure to consent to your adoption of these children." He stood and placed the document on the front of his desk, facing Rebecca. "If you will sign here, ma'am." When he pointed to the correct line, Rebecca signed so quickly that it made him chuckle. "Mr. Montrose, you may sign here. Mr. Lansing, your signature goes underneath his."

The clerk added his signature and his seal, making the adoption official. He turned and leaned against the front of the desk, looking at the children. "Saul, Paul, and Hester, you now belong to Mrs. Stephens. She is your new mother. It is her duty to care for you and provide for you. It is your duty to obey and respect her. I think you will be a fine family. Congratulations to you all." He shook each child's hand as well as Rebecca's, then stepped to one side and smiled. "It would not be improper if you wished to hug your children, ma'am."

Gathering them to her, she did just that. Then they hugged Wylie and their new grandparents. All the while the clerk looked on, his face beaming. As the new family turned to go, Rebecca thanked him.

"You had everything you needed to make it legal, ma'am. And, it is I who should thank you. This is the nicest part of my job."

*   *   *

THAT NIGHT AFTER she tucked the children into bed, Rebecca returned to the kitchen. Wylie and Jackson had both retired early, but she was still too keyed up to sleep.

After leaving the clerk's office, they had gone back to Grinnell to celebrate. The first thing they did was stop by the photography studio and have a family portrait taken. Wylie bought them dinner at Mr. Mack's, and Howard took them all over to Stevens Drug for a soda. After arriving home, the boys barely had time to change into their everyday clothes before their friends John and Andrew arrived, and the four took off on an adventure of some sort. Sissy took a short nap and then spent the rest of the afternoon playing with the dogs outside.

Not bothering to light a lamp, Rebecca sat down in her rocker. My, this has been quite a day, she thought. She leaned her head against the cane back and rocked slowly, letting the gentle motion soothe her mind as well as her body. *I wish it had been the two of us adopting those children, Luke. They need you. Just as I do.*

She rocked slowly, letting her mind wander. It no longer troubled her that she did not often think of Anthony. She had made peace with her past and looked toward the future, one she hoped and prayed would include Luke. When a board creaked near the hall doorway, she looked in that direction. One of the twins stood in the darkness.

"Aunt Becca? It's me, Paul."

"Come in, dear. I'm still too excited to sleep. Is anything wrong?"

"No." The boy's bare feet made no sound on the wooden floor. He quietly moved a chair over beside her. "Guess I'm still excited, too. My mind's racin' all over the place."

"Do you want some warm milk?"

"No, ma'am. I just needed a little company to get my mind off . . . things."

Rebecca took his hand. "Are you thinking about your parents?"

"Some. A lot, actually. I'm afraid I'll forget them, and I don't want to."

"You won't. You'll always have them in your heart, and it won't let your mind forget. It would also be good if you talk about them, to each other and to me. It is especially important for you to tell Sissy things about them. She is young enough that she might forget."

"She never even knew Ma. We brought a picture of Ma and Pa with us. It was taken the first year they were married. It was the only one they ever had." He hesitated and slipped his hand from hers. "Could Saul and I set it on our dresser?"

"Of course! Or you may set it on the mantel in the parlor with the other pictures if you wish. We can set our new one right next to it."

"I like that idea. I'll see what Saul says." They fell into a comfortable silence, disturbed only by the hushed movement of her rocker and the various pops and cracks as the house settled for the night.

"Aunt Becca, do you think you and Uncle Luke will get married?"

The question caught her by surprise. She hesitated, then decided that if she wanted honesty from them, she would have to give them the same consideration. "I don't know, but I hope so. I love him and think he would be a fine husband and father."

"We do, too. Have you told him?"

She smiled. "No. It's not the woman's place to declare her love first."

"That's kinda dumb."

Rebecca chuckled. "Sometimes I agree, but there are good reasons. If a man knows a woman loves him, or thinks she loves him, he might feel obligated to marry her, even though he does not want to. Those kind of marriages seldom are happy ones. On the other hand, if a woman proclaims her love and the gentleman does not return her affection and says so, it could prove very embarrassing to both of them."

"Seems to me it would be just as embarrassin' if a man was the one talkin' of love and the lady didn't feel the same."

"Yes, I think it probably is," she said quietly, remembering Ben's hurt expression when she told him she would not be his wife. "But women are considered more fragile than men."

"Uncle Luke is in love with you."

"How do you know?"

"He looks at you the same way Pa used to look at Ma when she wasn't watchin' him. It's kind of a softness in his eyes, like he cares about you and is feelin' it real deep. If you can't say somethin' to him, maybe me and Saul could."

"Oh, no you don't. I appreciate that you want to help, but I think we'd better let Luke work this out on his own. He's had a hard life, Paul. We just need to be patient and show him lots of love. That will win him over." *It has to.*

Chapter 23

"I GOT ANOTHER one!" Saul pulled on his cane fishing pole as the line jerked.

"I'll get the net!" Paul waited until his brother hoisted the fishing pole upright, bringing the line and his fourth catfish out of the water. Paul scampered across the grassy bank and nabbed the fish with the net. Saul dropped the pole and ran to his brother's side to help free the hook from the fish's mouth.

"This is a big one, Uncle Luke. Boy, are we gonna have a good supper."

Luke chuckled and leaned back against the trunk of a large oak tree, stretching his legs out in front of him on an old quilt. "I'm glad you boys are catching plenty because I sure haven't had any luck."

Saul grinned at him and drew up a bucket which was submerged in the water at the creek's edge. He lifted the wire mesh lid, and Paul dumped the catfish from the net into the container. Saul fastened down the lid and lowered the bucket back into the water, using the rope which connected the handle to a nearby tree. "That's because you haven't been payin' attention to your fishin' line."

"Guilty as charged." Luke crossed his arms and turned his gaze back to Rebecca with a lazy smile. "I'd much rather watch your aunt Rebecca than go to sleep staring at a fishing line. Keep up the good work, boys."

Rebecca sat at the edge of the tablecloth that they had spread for their earlier picnic. She glanced at Luke and smiled, enjoying the teasing gleam in his eyes, then turned back to watch Sissy rummage through the picnic basket. "What are you looking for, honey?" she asked, although she knew very well the child was after another raisin cookie.

"Me hungry. Want a cookie."

"Don't you think you've had enough?"

Sissy shrugged. "Me . . . I don't know." She shot Luke a mischievous grin. "Me can't count."

"Well, I can," Rebecca said with a laugh. "And you've had three already."

"Want more. This many." She held up two fingers.

"No, you can't have two more."

"This many?" Sissy held up one finger and smiled. Only a troll could have refused her.

"All right. Just one. But no more, you imp." Rebecca leaned forward and searched for the cookie tin in the basket. Drifter quickly took up residence beside Sissy.

"Don't feed that mangy mutt any cookies. He's already spoiled rotten." Luke patted the side of his leg, calling the dog. Drifter glanced at him, then turned his attention to the cookie passing from Rebecca's hand to Sissy's. "Drifter. Mind your manners. You don't take a kid's cookie." With a hearty sigh, the dog lay down and enviously watched Sissy chew every morsel.

"I don't think you're ever going to fill him up. He's so much fatter now than when you first got him, but you'd think he was still starving."

Luke laughed and gazed affectionately at the dog. "I didn't get him. He got me. He's had to grab what he could whenever he could for so long that he'll probably never be quite civilized. I'm just happy he doesn't actually steal food out of people's hands." Rebecca offered Luke a cookie, but he shook his head. "No thanks. I'm stuffed. I ate enough fried chicken to last me a week."

"Until suppertime, more likely." Rebecca smiled and settled back to her original spot. "I've never seen a man eat fried chicken the way you do."

"You're just too good a cook, darlin'." Luke's eyes twinkled as he spread the Texas drawl on real thick. "I've tasted some mighty fine chicken down in Dallas, but it didn't even begin to compare with yours."

Rebecca playfully batted her eyelashes. "Why, Mr. Northcutt, such flattery."

Luke laid a hand over his heart and looked heavenward. " 'Tis the truth, ma'am, or I'll give up . . . asparagus forever."

She faked a frown. "Why do I have the feeling you don't like asparagus?"

"Have you ever seen me actually turn away from any kind of food?" he asked with a look of purest innocence.

"No, but I can think of one thing you couldn't have liked." She grinned.

He smiled ruefully and nodded. "Aggie's vinegar pie. I thought I was going to choke to death." An involuntary shudder shook him. "It was awful."

"I figured it would make your lips pucker."

"Make my lips pucker? Why, ma'am, it drew my throat up so tight a squeak couldn't get out. One bite turned me halfway into a dill pickle." When Rebecca laughed gleefully, he continued. "I thought sure I'd wake up the next morning with green, knobby skin. My voice was wheezy and my eyes were crossed for the rest of the day. All of a sudden, I had four horses instead of two. Do you have any idea how much four draft horses eat?"

Caught up in laughter, Rebecca swayed backward, bumping the calf of his leg with her elbow. "Oops. Sorry," she said with a giggle.

"No problem. Why don't you scoot over this way, and I'll bend my knee. You can use my leg for a back rest."

"I don't mind if I do. I'm tired of playing Miss Prim. Heaven forbid, I might even slump a little bit."

He bent his knee and sighed softly when she leaned against his leg. She sent him a questioning look. "I think I'm going to like being a back rest. I'm glad Miss Prim decided to go home. Did she take Miss Proper with her?"

"Perhaps." She glanced at the children, then looked back at Luke, her smile knowing. "But it's hard to be improper with three little people underfoot."

Luke nodded. "Ready-made chaperones. We could send them over to my place to pick blackberries."

"You know it's too early for blackberries."

"Yep. But they would be gone for a while, especially if they waited until they were ready to pick."

Grinning, she shook her head. "You're incorrigible."

"I'm not sure, but I think I've just been insulted."

"Only in jest."

He unfolded his arms, stretched them out to each side, and glanced toward the creek. "Sissy, don't get too close."

"Me want to catch fish."

"You can catch them easier if you don't go near the edge. Bring your pole this way." When the little girl immediately backed up, Luke smiled. "That's my girl."

Yes, she is. She loves you as much as she does me. Rebecca longed to say the words out loud, but caution held her tongue. He would only claim that Sissy loved everyone, which was true to some extent. But it was Uncle Luke the child constantly prattled about to Dolly. Every time Sissy put the doll to bed, she mentioned to her silent friend how Uncle Luke had made the cradle because he loved her.

Rebecca kept her eye on Sissy, waiting for her to tire of holding the fishing pole. It was simply a long, skinny branch that had been trimmed of all twigs, but Sissy didn't care. Her worms attracted fish as well as the boys', and she had a fish in the bucket to prove it. After a few minutes, the child carefully laid the pole down on the ground and wandered over to talk to her brothers.

Luke caught Rebecca's hand in his, resting them on the grass beside his leg. "The boys are doing well with riding. I don't think they're ready to venture off to town yet, but it won't be too long."

"Thank you for teaching them. It does a lot to ease my mind. I don't want to be such a scaredy-cat, but it's hard not to worry." She relished the gentle caress of his thumb on the back of her hand, and briefly reconsidered his idea of sending the children off on a wild-goose chase.

He shrugged. "You worry because you care. And you've got enough sense not to let it get out of hand."

"I didn't until you stepped in. I needed your help." She met his gaze, allowing a tiny bit of the love she felt for him show in her eyes. His fingers tightened on hers. "And I'm grateful for it."

He held her gaze for a long moment, searching her face. *Don't be afraid, dearest man,* she thought. *My love is real. It won't fade.*

"They want to go swimming today in the worst way." He looked over at the twins. "But the water is still too cold. We'll try it in a couple of weeks. I did promise I'd go inspect the swimming hole with them." He turned back to her. "I understand the Ferguson boys have used it for years."

"Yes, it's down the creek. Less than a hundred yards, I suppose. They could almost swim here. Unlike most of the stream, the stretch between here and the swimming hole is seven or eight feet deep."

"But it's not wide enough. Saul says the river bends downstream, and it's easily twice as wide as here." He shifted. "I think I'll see if they want to go down there now. My backside is getting numb." A soft pink touched her cheeks, bringing a chuckle from him. "Sorry, ma'am. I forgot my manners."

I wish you'd forget them completely. Heat rushed to her cheeks at the wayward thought.

When he leaned forward, the movement brought their clasped hands up against the side of her thigh. "Why, Rebecca, whatever were you thinking?" he asked softly.

"Nothing." She couldn't meet his gaze. She thought she must be blushing all the way to her toes; his nearness certainly made her warm enough.

"Sounds like some kind of nothing. The kind we might enjoy. A lot." He eased back, putting a bit more distance between them. "Guess I'd better take the boys down the stream. Do you want to come along?"

"No, thank you. I'll stay here." *And gather my composure.* Still avoiding his gaze, she looked for Sissy. The little girl was bent over, intently watching something on the ground. "I think Sissy has found a trail of ants. That should keep her busy for a few minutes."

"We won't be gone long." He released her hand, and after she leaned away from his leg, he pushed himself to his feet. "You need to move into more shade. Looks like you're getting a sunburn." With a grin and a teasing gleam in his eye, he sauntered over to the twins.

Rebecca got up, also, and joined Sissy. "My goodness, that's a whole army of ants. They are fun to watch, aren't they?"

"Uh-huh." Sissy looked up as her brothers and Luke started downstream. "Where they go?"

"They're going to look at the swimming hole."

"Us go?"

"No, let's stay here and watch the ants. See, that one has a big load. Do you think he'll be able to carry it all the way to his home?"

"Maybe. Where he live?" Sissy looked around. "No see house."

"Ants live under the ground. Let's follow along beside them and see if we can find their entry hole." She took Sissy's hand and they carefully followed the stream of ants. "There it is. See all the ants scurrying about? We don't want to get too close. They might not like it."

"Ants hurt Sissy?"

"They might sting a little. Let's sit on this log. We should be able to watch them from here." Rebecca sat down and lifted Sissy up onto her lap. They quietly observed the ants for several minutes.

"Sissy go swimmin'?"

"Perhaps when you are older, Uncle Luke could teach you."

Sissy frowned. "You swim?"

"No, I don't know how. When I was a little girl, we weren't taught such things. But it is becoming more acceptable nowadays. They even have bathing suits for women and girls in the catalogs."

"Wear clothes to take bath?" Perplexed, Sissy looked up at Rebecca. "No can swim in bathtub. It too little."

"Well, they are called bathing suits, but they are made for swimming in something bigger than a bathtub, like a creek or lake."

"Twins no wear bathing suits. Them go—" She paused, obviously trying to remember the right words.

"Without anything?" Rebecca said quickly.

Sissy nodded, then her face lit up. "Me know. Them wear bir'day suit. They told me."

"Well, I suppose that as long as it is just the boys, and they are here at the swimming hole, it doesn't hurt." She knew her brothers had never worn any clothes when they went swimming. But then, a visit to the swimming hole by a female had been unthinkable. "But if girls or women are around, they will have to wear suits."

"Why?"

"Because that's the way it's done." Rebecca crossed her fingers, hoping the answer would be sufficient for her precocious child.

Sissy nodded as if that explained everything. "Maybe Uncle Luke teach you, too."

Oh, my, that might be very nice. Especially if we were married. And alone. "Good heavens, Rebecca, get hold of yourself," she muttered.

"Huh?"

"Oh, nothing, dear. Yes, maybe someday he can teach me, too. Are you tired of watching the ants?"

"Yep." The little girl grinned at Rebecca's chuckle. "Me fish, now."

"All right. We'll go check on the poles." She put Sissy down on the ground, and they strolled back to their picnic spot. "Oh, dear! It looks like there is a fish on Paul's line. Quick, get the net." Rebecca grabbed the pole and backed up the slope. Once the fish was near the bank, she took the net from Sissy and handed the pole to the child. "Stay here until I tell you."

Rebecca scurried down to the edge of the water and caught hold of the heavy string they were using for line. Pulling the fish toward her until it was within arm's reach, she scooped it up in the net. "There!"

Sissy dropped the pole and ran over to her side. "Me open bucket."

"Wait! Let me haul it out of the water. Then you can open it." Rebecca struggled with the net. The fish was a good twelve inches long and wasn't the least bit interested in being someone's dinner. "Quit wiggling!" She kneeled down and, with a burst of adrenaline, pulled the bucket up out of the water with one hand. "Now, honey, lift the lid. Good girl." She dumped the fish into the water with its cousins.

Sissy ran over to check on the other lines while Rebecca closed the lid. "Me gots one!"

In the middle of lowering the bucket back into the creek, Rebecca paused and looked over her shoulder. To her horror, she saw Sissy skidding down the gradual slope toward the creek, hanging on to her makeshift fishing pole with all her might. Rebecca dropped the bucket, unmindful of the water that splashed on her skirt. "Sissy, let go!"

"Me catch." Determination filled Sissy's face. She dug her heels into the soft dirt, but to avail.

"Let go of the pole!" Rebecca jumped up, only to trip over her skirt. As she threw out one hand and caught herself, a frenzied motion in the water drew her gaze. At the end of Sissy's line a huge carp fought for freedom. There was no question of who would win the battle. The tiny, fragile girl didn't have a chance. "Sissy, turn loose of the pole!"

Her heart breaking, Rebecca scrambled to her feet and ran toward her precious child. Sissy was at the edge of the creek, her white-knuckled fingers frozen around the flexible branch, her eyes wide with terror. "Sissy, let go!" Rebecca's frantic cry melded with the little girl's terrified shriek as she flew through the air and into the water.

"Noooooo! Sissy! Luke!" Rebecca searched the creek, desperately trying to find her daughter. "Luke!"

Sissy's head bobbed to the surface out in the middle, some five feet downstream from where she had fallen in. She thrashed her arms but could not keep her head above the water.

"Sissy! Oh, dear God! Luke, help me!" Rebecca ran a little way downstream, and still screaming his name, jumped into the icy water.

Chapter 24

As THE WATER enveloped her, Rebecca fought against the mounting panic that meant death. Holding her breath, she forced her eyes open and searched the clear depths. Sissy was in the exact middle of the stream, facedown, unmoving. *Oh, God, no! Please, don't let her die.*

Kicking and clawing the water, Rebecca broke to the surface, gasping a quick breath, filling her lungs with air before her heavy cotton skirt pulled her down again. She pushed against the water, trying to get to Sissy, but made little progress until her feet touched the creek bottom. Walking along the pebbly ground, she reached the little girl.

She turned Sissy over so that she faced upward. Wrapping the material around her fingers, she grabbed the child's dress with one hand and shoved her arm up straight, pushing Sissy's face up to the air. Kicking and struggling against the water with her other hand, Rebecca broke the surface. She was able to keep her face out of the water for a few seconds, before the current pulled her under again.

The frigid water took away the feeling in her fingers, and she had to look to make sure she still clung to Sissy. Her feet and legs quickly grew numb, and behind her tightly closed lips, her teeth chattered. *Luke, please come. Come for Sissy . . . for me. Air . . . need air. Legs won't move.*

Must kick. Legs, move! Her lungs burned and sparkles of colored lights filled the blackness behind her closed lids.

Suddenly, a strong arm wrapped around her, and she shot to the surface. Coughing, she drew in a gasping breath. Saul pulled Sissy from her locked fingers and, treading water with one hand, passed his sister to Paul who was closer to the bank. Swimming on his back, Paul kept Sissy's face above the water until he reached the side of the creek. Saul swam past him and, grabbing a tree root, hoisted himself out of the water. Turning, he took Sissy from his brother.

Luke swam in the same manner as Paul, one arm tightly around Rebecca, keeping her face up out of the water. In three giant strokes, he reached a point where he could stand. He pushed her toward the bank, where Paul waited on the ground to help her out.

"S-sissy. H-help h-her." Rebecca's eyes pleaded with Luke to save the child.

"I will, honey." Luke shoved Rebecca upward as Paul pulled, then he levered himself out of the water and dropped to Saul's side.

"She's not breathing, Uncle Luke." Saul's voice and body shook from fear and cold. With eyes filled with worry and tears, he handed her to Luke. "C-can you save her?"

"We're going to try. You go get the quilt. Paul, fetch the tablecloth for Rebecca. It might help warm her up." Luke's calm instructions hid his fear. As he talked, he gently opened Sissy's mouth and uncurled her tongue. Then he laid her on her stomach, turning her head to one side. Kneeling, he straddled her legs and pressed on her lower back with one hand, very carefully shifting his weight forward. A small amount of water gurgled out of her mouth. He rocked back, moving the pressure to her lower back again, then shifted forward. Another tiny stream of water poured from her mouth.

"Come on, princess. Breathe!" Luke pressed on her back again, his terror mounting. Her lips and cheeks were blue, and her body was ice-cold.

"P-please, S-sissy, breathe." Rebecca crawled over to Luke's side. "P-please, God, d-don't take her," she whispered. Paul came up behind her and draped the tablecloth around her. It was saturated in seconds. He knelt beside her and put his arm around her shoulders, tears pouring down his face.

Luke shifted Sissy to her back. "Sissy, you've got to breathe!" he ordered sternly. Using both hands, he pushed her elbows against her chest, firmly compressing it. Then he swept her arms out and upward, alongside her head, until her hands touched. He firmly pulled upward for a few seconds, hoping to elevate the chest, then brought her elbows back down and pushed on her chest. The third time he raised her arms over her head, Sissy's body gave a tiny jerk. With a faint, wheezing sound, she filled her lungs with air.

"Oh, thank God!" Rebecca and Paul clung to each other as their weeping became tears of joy instead of despair.

Luke continued the motion a few more times until he was certain Sissy could breathe on her own. "We've got to get her warm. You boys rub her legs." He rubbed her arms briskly for a few minutes, then ripped her dress and petticoat off her. Wrapping her in the quilt, he reached beneath it and stripped off her shoes, stockings, and drawers. He held her tight for a minute, then held her so Rebecca could see her face.

Sissy's eyelids slowly opened. She looked at Luke, then Rebecca. "Aunt Becca?" she asked in a hoarse whisper. "Fish?"

"He g-got away, h-honey." Rebecca tried to smile, not sure whether to laugh or cry. "He was t-too big f-for you." Rebecca's voice was raspy, and her teeth chattered so hard, it made talking difficult.

"Swim?" Sissy's eyelids were heavy. Even wrapped in the heavy quilt, her body had begun to shiver violently.

"Not t-too well t-this time. B-but we'll m-make sure y-you learn."

"We've got to get you two home and warm. Boys, you take Sissy. Get her to the house and into a warm bed as quickly as you can. One of you carry her, and the other rub her legs or arms to help her circulation. Try to keep her head down a little bit. If she stops breathing, yell. I'm going to help Rebecca, and we'll be right behind you." Luke handed Sissy to Paul, and the boys took off at a run.

Rebecca put a trembling hand on his arm. "Y-you take her. Q-quicker."

"No, honey. The boys would never be able to get you home. You almost drowned, too. I don't expect you can even stand up." He put his arm around her and lifted her to a standing position, but her legs instantly buckled. "Do you have any feeling in your legs?"

Too cold to talk and feeling drowsy, she shook her head.

Luke swept her up in his arms and headed for the house as fast as he could. He wanted to run, but he knew his knee would never hold up to it. The joint protested even at the brisk walk. He wished he could get her warm, but because he was also soaked to the skin, there was little he could do. His worry increased when she tucked her forehead against his neck and murmured something about his heat. *Lord a-mercy, if she's getting any heat from me, she must be almost frozen.*

When they reached the house, Wylie already had foot warmers and flannel cloths on the kitchen stove. "Jackson's in my room with Sissy. Figured we could keep an eye on her better in there for now. We were down at the barn when the boys got here. I sent them up to change into dry clothes."

"How's Sissy?" Luke tossed the question over his shoulder as he hurried through the kitchen.

"Sleepy, but breathing all right. How's Becky?"

"Freezing. She hasn't lost consciousness, but she may yet if we don't get her warm."

"You'll have to help her, Luke. I can't get up there."

Luke paused, meeting Wylie's gaze. "I'll try to respect her modesty."

"Right now I'm a whole lot more worried about her freezing to death than I am with modesty. You just get her warm. We'll take care of Sissy. Jackson will go for the doctor as soon as the boys get back down here to help me."

Luke carried her upstairs to her bedroom and eased her down on a chair. She slumped against the back, shivering.

Her wet clothes soaked the cushion, but he figured she would not be too upset about it. He knelt in front of her and slipped off her shoes, thankful that the high-topped gaiters had elastic inserts in each side instead of being fastened with buttons or laces. The stockings came off next.

"Rebecca, I'm going to help you take off your clothes." He pulled the tablecloth back, draping it over the chair. When he lifted his fingers to the front of her shirtwaist, he hesitated a second, then fumbled the first button free. He kept the material as close together as possible and focused his attention on each succeeding button instead of allowing himself a glance at her beauty.

When he reached the waistband of her skirt, he searched until he found the buttons at the middle of her back. "Lean forward a little, honey, so I can unfasten your skirt."

She obeyed, resting her cheek against his shoulder. All she wanted was to get warm and go to sleep. "You're wet," she mumbled.

"That's what happens when you jump in the water with your clothes on." He gently shoved her back against the chair. "Sit still. I'll be right back."

"N-not goin' anywhere," she said, her teeth chattering and her voice slurred.

Seconds later, he returned, draping a heavy quilt around her. "This will be a little tricky, but I'll try to take your clothes off and keep you covered."

"Nice man." She poked her arm out from beneath the folds of the quilt so he could hold the cuff of her sleeve. After a few minutes of trying to shove the sleeve off her shoulder, Rebecca gave up. "Can't. You." Another shiver shook her, but she was thankful her teeth had quit chattering so hard.

He released the cuff of her sleeve and held the quilt in front of her with one hand while reaching up beneath it with the other. Shoving the shirt off her shoulders, he then held the cuffs while she shrugged her arms free. He jerked the shirt tail from her skirt and pulled the shirtwaist out from beneath the quilt.

"Does your petticoat tie?"

She nodded. "Right side."

He loosened the waistband of the skirt and ran his fingers around to the side of the petticoat until he felt the ties. "No knot," he murmured in relief. Tugging on the strings, he unfastened the petticoat. "All right, pretty lady, let's stand you up." Standing to one side, he slid his arm around her and helped her to rise. Rebecca managed to clutch the quilt in one hand, holding it in front of her. Seconds later, the skirt and petticoat lay in a puddle on the floor. "The drawers are next."

Keeping his arm around her, he supported her waist as he felt for the tie on her drawers. When he found the string, he pulled it loose. Rebecca shivered and the drawers shimmied down to her knees. Being very careful to cover her with the quilt, Luke guided her back down to the chair. "I should get a medal for this," he muttered.

She planted a kiss on his cheek. When he looked at her in surprise, she smiled faintly. "Mouth's getting warm."

He dropped down to one knee beside her. "If you didn't feel like an icicle, I might try warming you up with kisses. Blankets and hot flannels will have to do this time." He slid the drawers the rest of the way down her legs and off her feet, pulling the skirt and petticoat out of the way at the same time. "Can you get your arms out of your chemise?"

She nodded. "Think so."

"Where do you keep your flannel nightgowns?"

"Second drawer."

He crossed the room and took one of her nightgowns out of the drawer. Spying some thick wool stockings, he brought a pair of those, too. On his way back, he grabbed a thick towel from the rod on the washstand. Rebecca had one arm free of the quilt and was trying to pull the chemise off over her head. "Here, I'll do that."

He dropped the nightgown and stockings in her lap and carefully pulled the delicate, lace-trimmed chemise over her head, laying it on top of the pile of clothes on the floor. The graceful line of her shoulder was appealing, even when covered with goose bumps. He knelt in front of her. "Give me your feet." He pulled the stockings over her feet and up to her knees. "I'll put the nightgown over your head, but you'd better do the rest. Can you?"

"Yes. I'm getting warmer. I know because my feet and hands are being pricked by a thousand needles, and my teeth aren't bouncing together anymore. Where is Sissy? Have you checked on her?"

He shook his head. "Wylie and Jackson are taking care of her. They put her in Wylie's bed. He was heating up foot warmers and hot flannels when we got here." He smiled tenderly. "I'm glad to see you feeling better. You had me scared." He slipped the nightgown over her head and wrapped her hair in the towel before he stood. Keeping his back to her, he walked over to the bed and drew down the covers. "He sent the boys to change clothes. Jackson was going for the doctor as soon as they got back down to help Wylie."

Rebecca slipped her arms in the sleeves of the nightgown. Holding the quilt in front of her, she stood, letting the nightgown fall over her body. Luke still stood with his back to her, briskly rubbing his arms. She did not see how it was possible to love him any more than she did at that moment.

"I'm decent now." Gathering the quilt around her, she started toward him on wobbly legs. He rushed over to her side and put his arm around her for support. "You need dry clothes, too." When they reached the bed, she handed him the quilt and crawled beneath the covers. "Put that one around you. It's a little wet, but it helps."

He tucked the bedding up around her neck, then draped the other quilt around his shoulders. "I'll go check on Sissy. I'll be right back."

Rebecca nodded. She could not remember a time in her life when a warm bed felt so good. Fighting the strong urge to sleep, she clung to wakefulness. The shivering had stopped completely by the time Luke returned.

"She's sleeping. The color is returning to her face. She sounds a little wheezy, but I think it is coming more from her throat than her chest." He lifted the side of the quilt and slid a hot metal warming pan next to her feet. "Wylie and the boys are with her. Jackson went for the doctor." He held up a rolled-up piece of flannel. "This is hot. Can I pull the quilts down?"

"Yes."

He pulled down the quilts, quickly spread the warm piece of cloth over her, and drew the covers back up again.

"Oh, that's heavenly." She yawned, then frowned up at him. "You're going to catch your death. Get out of those wet clothes."

"I'll go on home if you think you'll be all right."

"I need to be with Sissy, but I'm so tired. Can't think too good." She pushed one hand from beneath the bedding and reached for his. "Thank you for Sissy's life. For mine."

"I'm thankful we reached you in time. The boys were a big help. They are good swimmers." He clutched her hand in a firm grasp. "When you get your strength back, you'll have to tell me how you both wound up in the middle of the creek. Now, get some sleep. Wylie and the boys will take care of Sissy."

"Hurry back?" She yawned again.

"Yes."

"Need you here." She gave his hand a faint squeeze and drifted off to sleep.

When she woke up, she was stifling. Luke, wearing clean, dry clothes, sat beside the bed in a ray of sunshine. Throwing back the covers, she met his tender gaze. "What day is it?"

"It's still Friday. You slept about an hour and a half. The doctor checked Sissy over and said she will be fine."

"Thank God," she said fervently.

"Amen. Her lungs are clear. She has a sore throat and a little headache, but the doctor said that wasn't anything to worry about. She is supposed to take it easy for a few days and sleep a lot. Jackson is cooking up a pot of broth for her. She had a little of it earlier, then went back to sleep."

Rebecca inhaled deeply. "That's not broth I smell."

"No. He's also frying up the catfish for supper."

"He never told me he could cook." She smiled and shook her head. Luke's gaze dropped to the front of her gown, and she realized how immodest she must appear. When she discreetly pulled the sheet up higher, a dull red spread across his face.

"Sorry," he muttered, glancing away.

"Don't be." *I wish I could tell you how much it pleases me that you want to look at me.* "I feel like getting up now."

"Do you need some help?"

"Luke Northcutt, you've already undressed me. You think I'm going to let you dress me, too?"

He blinked, then smiled when he saw she was teasing. "You'd probably get dressed quicker if I let you do it alone."

This time her face turned pink. "Scat, you scoundrel. I'll be down in a few minutes." As soon as he left the room, she threw back the bedclothes and sat up. Other than being stiff, sore, and a bit weak, she felt pretty good. She dressed quickly in an everyday calico shirtwaist and matching skirt. The comfortable shirtwaist was made to wear on the outside of the skirt. When she pulled the pins from her hair, it was a damp mess, but she only took the time to run her fingers through the worst tangles.

Carrying her hairbrush, she hurried downstairs and made straight for Wylie's bedroom. She found her uncle sitting beside the bed, reading. "How is she?" she whispered.

"Sleeping soundly. How do you feel?"

"Not bad. A little wobbly, but that should go away after I eat." She carefully sat down on the side of the bed, studying her daughter's peaceful face. The trace of color in her cheeks was only a shadow of the rosy glow normally there, but her breathing and sleep were natural. Curled up on her side, her dolly snug in her arms, Sissy looked more like an angel than ever. Rebecca felt the child's hand, reassuring herself that she was warm enough, then rose from the bed and sat down in a chair nearby. "I'll stay with her a while if you want to go eat."

"You should go first."

"No, I need to sit here a while."

Wylie patted her hand. "I understand, Becky gal. I'll leave you alone with your little girl."

Rebecca watched him roll the wheelchair from the room

and down the hall, once again grateful for his strength of character and love.

She sat there for half an hour, brushing her hair and watching Sissy's every move, loving all the tiny wiggles and childish noises she made. In a way, it seemed no different than the first few nights after she had taken Sissy in. The little girl had been uneasy sleeping alone in a strange place, and Rebecca had sat beside the bed until long after she fell asleep. On those nights, she had prayed desperately to be allowed to keep the children. This time her prayers were filled with thanksgiving that Sissy was still alive.

Sissy stretched and yawned, then frowned as she opened her eyes.

Rebecca was at her side instantly. "What's wrong, honey? Do you hurt?"

Sissy nodded and pointed to her throat. "Ow-y," she said in a raspy voice.

"That's probably because you swallowed half the creek and did a lot of coughing. I'll go get you a bowl of soup, and I bet it will help it to feel better. Do you hurt anywhere else?"

Sissy shook her head.

"I'll be right back. Dolly can keep you company." When Sissy smiled and nodded, Rebecca felt a hundred-pound weight lift from her shoulders. She had not realized how much she had needed to see a glimmer of Sissy's usual enthusiasm and life.

When the boys heard their sister was awake, they rushed in to see her, promising to follow Rebecca's admonition not to excite her. Rebecca returned a few minutes later with a bowl of soup to find Sissy sitting up in bed with the twins hovering beside it.

"Can I feed her, Aunt Becca?" Paul looked up at her anxiously. "I won't spill."

"Of course you can." Rebecca experienced a faint twinge of disappointment since she had looked forward to sitting beside the little girl and spooning the soup up to her mouth. But she knew that no matter how much she loved Sissy, the love the children shared was special. They were close in a way that she never could be, bonded not only by blood but by loss and hardship. "I'll just sit here and keep you company."

Sissy devoured the soup. The soothing broth quickly eased the ache in her throat and seemed to loosen her tongue as well. After the meal, she tried to tell the boys about her adventure. "Me catched a fish this big." She spread her arms as wide as she could.

The twins laughed. "Sissy, you're too young to be tellin' stories about 'the one that got away,' " said Saul.

"But him was that big." She looked to Rebecca for confirmation.

"Bigger, I think. It was one of the biggest carp I've ever seen in the creek. Sissy could never have brought him in. I'm not sure I could have, either. But she wouldn't give up." Rebecca took a deep breath. She wanted to tell Sissy she could never fish again but knew it probably would be the wrong thing to do. "If you catch a fish that pulls you harder than you're pulling him, let go of the pole. Just let him go."

For the first time, fear darkened Sissy's countenance. "Me no like to fish. Not go to creek ever."

"You don't have to, honey. We'll let the boys catch the fish from now on. Someday, when you're bigger, you might want to try it again, but we can wait until you're ready."

"Me no like water." Tears welled up in her eyes. "It scary."

Rebecca tapped Paul on the shoulder and he eased off the bed, giving her room to sit. She gathered Sissy onto her lap, snuggling her close. "It scared me, too. I was afraid when it covered my head."

Sissy looked up at her and touched her wet hair. "Fish pull Aunt Becca in?"

"She jumped in after you, squirt," said Saul, his voice thick with emotion. When Rebecca glanced at him, his misty eyes were filled with a new respect as well as love.

"But Aunt Becca no swim."

"No, I can't." Rebecca wished her voice hadn't suddenly grown shaky. "And it probably was a dumb thing to do, since I came real close to drowning. But I didn't think; I just jumped in."

"Sounds like a proverb in there somewhere." Luke walked through the doorway.

"Like, look before you leap?" asked Saul.

"More like fools rush in where angels fear to tread," murmured Rebecca.

"Maybe." Luke came around the bed and stopped beside Rebecca and Sissy. "But this time, foolishness may very well have saved the angel." He rested his hand on Rebecca's shoulder, giving it a gentle squeeze. "How are you, princess?" he asked, looking down at Sissy.

"Me okay. Throat hurts."

"Didn't the soup help?" Rebecca frowned slightly and felt Sissy's cool brow.

"Uh-huh. Hurts when me talk."

"Then you probably shouldn't be talking so much." Luke smiled at the little girl and fluffed her curls. "Are you sleepy?"

Sissy shook her head.

"Would you like me to tell you a story?"

She nodded emphatically.

"All right. But why don't you let Aunt Becca hold you. I think she'd like to snuggle for a while."

"Okay."

Rebecca looked up at Luke, smiling her thanks. She moved over to the chair and cuddled Sissy close. He sat down on the foot of the bed, relating a humorous tale about the mischievous horse that pulled the freight wagon he drove in New York. Before the story ended, Sissy was fast asleep in Rebecca's arms.

She laid the child on the bed and covered her up, tucking Dolly into the crook of one arm. When she turned back toward the chair, Luke caught her elbow.

"You need to eat supper. Let the boys stay for a while."

When Rebecca's stomach growled as if on cue, she smiled and nodded her agreement. They left the boys to play a game of checkers and keep an eye on Sissy. Her stomach growled again when she reached the kitchen. Jackson had fried hush puppies along with the catfish. Although everyone else had already eaten, more than one serving of each remained. She filled her plate and was almost ashamed at how quickly the food disappeared.

"Oh, my. I was ravenous." She touched her mouth with the napkin, then wiped the cornmeal crumbs from her fingers. "Are you sure you don't want another hush puppy?"

"Nope. I'm full up. I think I'll go on home."

He had grown quiet while she ate, answering her questions with two words only if one would not suffice. She sensed his effort to distance himself from her and the children. *Love hurts, sometimes, Luke. It's a risk to care.* Intuitively, she knew that if he left in his dark mood, he would hide from his feelings and from them. "Don't leave just yet. Why don't you take a walk with me?"

He roused from his musings to look at her in surprise. "It's dark out."

"I don't mind. It's still fairly warm. I'm a little stiff and sore. A walk will do me good, but I don't want to go by myself." She reached across the corner of the table and curled her fingers around his. "Please come with me. I don't want to be alone just now."

Luke hesitated, then nodded, his expression grim.

Chapter 25

THE MOONLIGHT PLAYED hide-and-seek behind a wispy cloud, teasing them with its soft light. Arm in arm, Luke and Rebecca wandered across the farmyard and into the orchard. They talked of unimportant things—the different kinds of trees in the orchard, whether crops really did better when planted by the signs of the moon, and if the two frogs croaking down by the creek were serenading the same fair damsel.

In the back of his mind, he told himself it was stupid to be alone with her. He should be running as fast and as far as he could go—sell the farm and find another one a thousand miles away. Getting close to her and the kids was a big mistake. He decided he had been better off not caring about anyone. In the past, if someone he knew had come close to dying, he had experienced concern, even worry, but not agony.

They strolled down a gentle slope until the lights of the house were only a distant twinkle. "Let's sit for a spell." When Rebecca sat down, Luke hesitated.

"Are you chilly?"

"No, I'm fine." She looked up at him and held out her hand. He took it and sat down beside her, facing her. She held his hand with both of hers, caressing the back of it. "You can't keep us away, you know."

"What?" The moon skirted behind another feathery cloud, hampering his view of her downcast face.

"The children would be lost without you."

And what about you? "They have plenty of folks around now that care about them."

"Yes, they do. But you're special to them." She looked up at him. "And to me. Don't run from what you feel. Give us a chance."

"Rebecca . . ." He looked down at her face, so beautiful in the pale light, so filled with tenderness. Her hair hung loose, his to touch. He ran his fingertips down the soft strands then lifted a handful, letting it sift through his fingers. Catching a moonbeam, it shimmered and sparkled, dancing across his lap. He curved his hand around the nape of her neck and lowered his head toward hers.

She met him halfway, wrapping her arms around his neck, burying her fingers in his thick hair. He brushed her lips gently, but in a heartbeat, a mere touch was not enough. Deepening the kiss, he slid his hand around to her back, drawing her tightly against him. He kissed her until they were breathless, then pressed his cheek to hers as they gasped for air. "I thought I'd die when I saw you under the water." His voice was strained, filled with heartache. "And Sissy . . ."

Crushing her to him, he brought his mouth down hard on hers, desperately wanting her love and yet terrified that she might give it. He kissed her again and again, and if he paused, she sought his lips impatiently. One minute her hands caressed his chest and shoulders, the next they were tangled in his hair, her fingertips making tiny circles against his sensitive scalp.

He did not consciously undo the buttons on her shirtwaist, but suddenly only a thin cotton chemise lay between his hand and her supple, heated skin. Knowing he shouldn't but unable to stop, he skimmed his fingertips up her ribs and gently stroked the underside of her breast with his thumb. She made a tiny sound in her throat and arched against his hand, begging for a closer intimacy. A shudder wracked him as he caressed her softness and tasted the sweetness of her mouth.

As she unfastened the buttons running down the front of his shirt and tugged it from his jeans with trembling, hasty fingers, his heart soared. And when her hands first touched his chest, his pounding heart skipped a beat. For so many days and nights he had dreamed of her caress, but the dream had been nothing compared to the utter joy of the reality. "Rebecca . . . my sweet Rebecca," he whispered.

Lowering her lips to his chest, she heard his words, the cry of his heart. *Yes! Yours alone my love*, she silently cried in answer. She spread kisses across his chest and made him tremble; that he should hunger so for her touch filled her with awe and humility.

He cupped her face in his hands and guided her up to his lips. His deep, urgent kiss fueled her desire, and when he kissed her neck and began a slow descent, she trembled in anticipation. Lost in love and the torrent of passion evoked by only this man, she cried out softly when he feathered kisses across the upper curves of her bosom, and then dropped lower still.

Having been so long without a man's love, Rebecca lost all sense of reason beneath his gentle caresses and fervent kisses—until he lifted her over his legs and lay her down beside him. The shifting movement hiked up her shirtwaist, and the cool grass hit the small of her back like a splash of cold water. Instantly, the convictions of her faith, deeply held and respectfully honored, flashed through her mind. Her body clamored for satisfaction, but her mind forbade such a trespass.

To her surprise, her heart also decreed she must go no farther. Luke was an honorable man, and if she gave him her body tonight, tomorrow he would ask for her hand. He would come to her nobly but without a choice, trapped by desire but uncertain of love, haunted by the rejections of a lifetime.

Capturing her mouth again with a hungry kiss, he drew back when she did not respond as she had seconds before. He gazed down at her with worry and confusion in his face. "Rebecca?"

"I'm sorry, Luke. We have to stop."

He kissed her quickly and deeply, with a hint of desperation.

His need was almost her undoing, but when he took a breath, she tried again, her voice ragged and unsteady. "Luke, please stop."

"Not now, honey." He nuzzled her lips with half a dozen tiny kisses and pulled her body tighter to his. "Please, not now."

"Luke, we can't do this. It . . . it isn't right."

With a groan, he buried his face against her neck, crushing her to him. "I didn't mean to get so out of control." He clung to her, breathing hard. "Forgive me, Rebecca, please," he whispered in a voice heavy with shame.

She put her arms around him and held him close, gently caressing his back. "Luke, there is nothing to forgive." Taking several slow, deep breaths, she tried to calm her pounding heart and tame the desire that begged to be fulfilled. "We probably did more than we should have, but what we just shared was not sordid. It was beautiful. I want you, Luke." She smiled ruefully. "I guess that was pretty obvious. I didn't have any more control than you did."

He raised his head, and she looked up into his eyes, rubbing her fingers lightly along his jaw. "How would you feel if we made love?"

"A lot more relaxed," he said with a faint smile.

"For now." She smiled and traced the other side of his jaw. He turned his head and nipped a fingertip. "But how would you feel tomorrow?"

He thought a moment. "Guilty."

"And what would you do about it?" Rebecca lifted her torso slightly off the ground and pulled down her shirtwaist.

"I . . ." He rolled over onto his back, staring up at the stars. She thought she heard him gulp. When he spoke, his voice sounded as if it had rubbed over sandpaper. "I'd ask you to marry me."

"Because you felt guilty." She kept her voice calm and gentle as she buttoned up her shirtwaist. Staring up at the heavens, she wondered if God was frowning down at them or listening to their discussion with patient interest.

"Partly." The word was almost a croak.

Rebecca turned over on her side, facing him. "Then you do care about me?"

"Of course I care about you. I wouldn't be here if I didn't."

She smiled. The grumpy bear was back. "And that scares you."

"It scares the life out of me," he muttered.

She raised her head, resting it in her hand and leaning on her elbow. "I'll tell you a secret." When he looked at her, she moved her gaze from his uncovered chest to his face. "I love you deeply and that scares me, too." He frowned and started to speak, but she quickly touched his lips with her finger. "Wait, please. I know it's improper for me to say anything, but it was bound to slip out anyway. I love you so much I'm practically bursting with it. I want you in every way a woman wants a man, as friend, lover, provider, a father to my children, and probably a dozen more ways I haven't even thought about."

Wearing a deep frown, Luke sat up abruptly. He jerked the front placket of his shirt together, jabbing the buttons through the buttonholes. "Is this a proposal, Rebecca?"

"No, I'm not quite that forward." She sat up too, and finger-combed her hair. "Luke, I know you are uncertain of your feelings, and I understand why. I also know it's hard for you to believe that I love you, or to trust in my love. But I do have one request."

"What?"

"Let me court you."

"What?" Staring at her, he dropped his hands to his lap.

She reached up and fastened the button below his collar, then gave him a peck on the lips. "Let me show you what it's like to be loved by someone—with one major limitation, of course."

"No lovemaking." He stood and turned away from her. Seconds later the waist of his pants loosened, and he stuffed his shirt back where it belonged.

Contemplating the movement of his arms as he buttoned his jeans, Rebecca's mouth went dry. *Dear Lord, I'm going to need a lot of help to be good. Having been married before has its disadvantages.* She looked away quickly, so he wouldn't see her watching him, and scrambled to her feet.

"Right?" He turned around to face her, resting his hands on his hips.

"Um, right. No lovemaking. It would be too difficult if we did, and then you decided you didn't want me as a wife."

"And if I do decide that I don't want to get married, you won't throw a fit?"

"I'll be deeply disappointed, but I promise I'll accept your decision as long as you give me enough time."

He lifted his chin at a slight angle and crossed his arms in front of his chest. "How long is enough time?"

"I don't know." She frowned and crossed her arms, too, unconsciously mimicking his stance. "How long do you think you'll need?"

He rubbed his chin thoughtfully. "Six months."

So long? "All right. You have to wait six months before you can tell me that you are not interested in marriage." She grinned. "Of course, if you decide you're in favor of it, you may ask me to marry you at any time."

"Nice to have an option." He stepped up close and trailed a fingertip down the side of her neck. "Is kissing still allowed?"

"By all means."

"How about touching?" He moved his finger back up her neck and toyed with her ear.

"I believe some touching should be allowed." *Legs, don't you dare turn to jelly.*

He nodded. "With certain limitations, of course."

"Of course."

"How about walks in the moonlight?" He slid his arm around her back and combed the fingers of his other hand through her hair.

"We might have to be careful of those."

"Too much temptation." He leaned down and kissed her

softly. "But we might venture out once or twice."

"Maybe even three times."

"Gettin' brave, lady." He kissed her again.

She curled her arms around his neck. "This is where we started a while ago, remember?"

"One difference. We're a little wiser than we were a while ago." His kiss was long and tender.

When he raised his head, she had to stop and think what it was they were talking about. "Luke, did you ever agree to let me court you?"

"No." He kissed her again.

"Will you?"

"Yes, ma'am, Miz Stephens, I do believe I will." Then he tapped his lips and told her just exactly how she could favor him with her attentions.

DETERMINED TO WIN her man, Rebecca enlisted the aid of her allies. The next morning, she asked the children to help her, but was very careful not to reveal that she had all but proposed to Luke. As one, they agreed she and Luke should marry. The boys offered to help him with his chores whenever they could and to spend more time with him "doing man stuff." When Sissy asked what she could do to help, the decision was unanimous—just be herself and love him like she always did. Wylie watched the proceedings with an amused, happy twinkle in his eye and suggested inviting Aggie, Winston, and Luke over that evening for pie and dominoes.

Rebecca agreed with the idea and launched her campaign with the strategy of a general, sending the twins over early to invite the Neeleys and Luke for the evening. Sissy had bounced back from her brush with death with amazing resilience, hitting the floor at full speed the moment she woke up. A trace of huskiness lingered in her voice, and she tired a bit quicker than normal, but after a long afternoon nap, she was ready for company.

Luke had grown more at ease with Winston and Aggie, and during the evening, even went so far as to tease Winston a few times. The twins, Wylie, and Jackson set up a second game of dominoes nearby on the game table, but half the time they enjoyed themselves by joining in the friendly banter and watching the others play. Most of the time, Sissy sat in Luke's lap and "helped" him. He would decide which domino to play, and she would lay it down if the spot was within reach. Every time he won a round, she rewarded him with a hug and kiss.

Winston and Aggie departed around nine-thirty. Because they had company, the children had been allowed to stay up late. The boys took Sissy upstairs to change for bed while Luke helped Rebecca clean up the dessert dishes. When the children came back down for their good-night hugs, Sissy asked Luke to carry her up to bed.

As they had done once before, he followed Rebecca up to Sissy's room and tucked the little one into bed. She was so sleepy there was no need of a story or song. He kissed her cheek and pulled the covers up under her chin. "Good night, Sissy.

"Night-night, Uncle Luke. I love you." She smiled sleepily up at him.

"I love you, too, princess. Sleep well."

After Rebecca kissed Sissy, Luke put his arm around her shoulders and they walked down the stairs. "It's been a nice evening, but I'd better get home. Drifter gets grouchy if I keep him up too late."

"I'll walk to the porch with you."

Wylie and Jackson were still in the kitchen, with Wylie carrying on their normal one-sided conversation. Jackson would nod or grunt now and then. On rare occasions he offered a one- or two-word comment. Luke bid his friends good-bye, then he and Rebecca went out the back door.

The instant he pulled the door closed behind him, he settled his hands on her waist. Lifting her off her feet, he swiftly stepped over to the darkest corner of the porch and wrapped his arms around her, pressing her back against his chest. "I've been wanting to kiss you since I got here," he murmured, gently nipping her earlobe.

She turned in his arms and slid her hands up his chest and around his neck. "Wait not, want not."

He chuckled. "Do you often misquote proverbs?"

"Only when it suits my purpose, and I think of it." She leaned against him. "Time's a-wasting, Farmer Northcutt. You'd better see to your chores."

He nibbled on her lips. "Ma'am, this is not a chore," he whispered, coming back for more. Several delightful minutes later, he stepped back and slowly lowered his hands to his sides.

"Will you come over for dinner tomorrow? It will just be family."

"How much family?" he asked with a grin.

"Just the ones that live in this house. I've got a pot roast."

Luke decided this wooing business had some distinct advantages when the woman was the one pressing her suit. "Well, I've never been one to turn down a pot roast, especially the way you fix them."

"Luke Northcutt, you're going to make me wonder whether you're interested in me or just my cooking."

He turned toward the steps, catching her hand so she would walk with him. "Oh, you're the one I'm interested in." Then he grinned mischievously. "But it doesn't hurt that you're a great cook."

LUKE WENT TO dinner on Sunday and spent a lazy afternoon at Rebecca's house. Since Jackson was in town with Ted and Ellen for the day, Wylie challenged Luke to a game of checkers and soundly beat him. Afterward, they chatted some, then Luke browsed through a farm magazine while the older man dozed in his chair. Later, he and Rebecca tried to sneak off for a walk, but once the kids spotted them, they wanted to tag along. Drifter and all the dogs went, too.

He lingered at her place, postponing his leave until he absolutely had to. There was no chance for him to say good-bye to Rebecca the way he wanted because the boys went home with him to help with the chores.

Even so, when he stretched out in bed that night, cherishing the memories of the day, he realized it had been the nicest Sunday of his life. He closed his eyes, and as always, his thoughts were of her—this woman who said she loved him. His mind wandered back to when they met, then traveled over all the moments they had shared since.

She had penetrated his defenses, forging through a minute crack with dogged determination until she learned his deepest secrets and hidden fears. Having discovered his vulnerability, she set about building him a new sanctuary, one made strong by layers of give-and-take, of love and healing, of trust and commitment. The fortress was not finished; fear and uncertainty still slipped through.

But he had caught a glimpse of heaven in those gray green eyes, in her arms he had found shelter for his wounded soul. No, the fortress was not finished. Although the layers of trust and commitment were in place, they lacked the mortar to seal them securely. Yet, he had a vision of what could be, and for the first time in his life, the road before him beckoned with promise and was paved in hope.

Chapter 26

"ME SEE THEM! Me see them!" shouted Sissy from her perch on Luke's shoulder. "It's an ef-a-lant!"

"Elephant, squirt," laughed Saul. "I see them, too! Oh, wow! Look at all those white horses!"

Luke, Rebecca, Wylie, and the children, along with practically everyone from Grinnell and the surrounding countryside, stretched and ducked, wiggled and giggled, peering down the main street for their first glimpse of the circus parade.

Soon, the mama elephant and her baby, decked out in red and gold plumes, braid, and tassels, came into view. A pretty black-haired woman, wearing a gown made of yards and yards of red silk, rode on the pachyderm's back. With a haughty glance, she skimmed the crowd, catching Luke's eye. Her black-eyed gaze ran over him and, with a knowing smile, she inclined her head regally, catching the sunlight in her cut-glass tiara.

Beside him, Eben chuckled. "Better watch out, or she'll have you cornered. Might be hard to get away from a woman who has an elephant at her command."

Luke felt Rebecca slip her hand around his arm and hold it possessively. When he glanced down, she seemed thoroughly engrossed in the parade, but she kept a good grip on him long after the lady and her pet lumbered by. Not wanting to tip Sissy off his shoulder, he bent his knees, sinking down until his face was level with Rebecca's. "No need to worry. I'm more interested in a woman who can cook than one who can herd an elephant," he said with a grin, then straightened.

She slanted him an irritated glance.

He ducked back down again, this time to whisper against her ear. "Besides, I much prefer lusty green-eyed women over lusty dark-eyed women."

She slapped his arm, then mumbled, "You'd better," and dropped her hands to her sides.

Behind the sultry wench and her elephant came a wagon painted bright red, yellow, and blue, drawn by four prancing white horses. The noble steeds seemed to take no notice of the music pouring from a small organ mounted on the wagon. The musician played with great enthusiasm and proficiency while a monkey, dressed like his master in a black top hat and a red coat with long tails, scampered from one side of the vehicle to the other, waving at the crowd.

Sissy laughed so hard she almost fell off Luke's shoulder when a clown waddled up to them in his long, long shoes. He tweaked his big red nose and a bouquet of silk violets popped out of the top of his hat. He knelt down on one knee, pretending to propose to Rebecca, and when she laughingly declined, he pushed the flowers back down in his hat, fastened the lid closed, and did a cartwheel back to the center of the street. Half a block down, another lady caught his eye, and he repeated his performance.

Another clown, dressed as an exceedingly voluptuous woman with purple hair, chased a tiny little man up and down the street. The "lady," whose profuse bosom and equally gigantic hips brought roars of laughter from the men and blushing titters from the ladies, carried a makeshift harness in the form of a horse collar with some short reins attached. The clown kept waving a large sheet of paper that said "license to commit marriage."

Additional clowns cavorted along the other side of the street, entertaining the spectators on that side. Behind the clowns came another brightly painted wagon carrying the stars of the show, as proclaimed in the colorful handbills that had magically appeared around the county—the daring young man on the flying trapeze, the acrobats, and the strong-lady, who sat demurely beside the driver.

Six white horses with red bridles and red plumes in their manes, along with riders dressed in gold satin, followed the second wagon. The riders consisted of three men, a young woman, and two boys somewhat older than the twins. Instead of sitting in saddles, they stood on the horses' bare backs. Saul and Paul gaped, their eyes wide as saucers.

"You boys are not to try that," Luke said sternly. "At least not until you're older and excellent horsemen. Those youngsters probably learned to ride before they could walk."

Trailing the horses were three more elephants. The trainers walked beside the animals' shackled legs, guiding them with small sticks with hooks on one end. Although these animals, too, were dressed for the occasion, wearing blue and gold braid and plumes, Luke sensed their dislike of the crowd and the chains. He slid his arm around Rebecca, ready to carry her to safety should the need arise.

She glanced up at him, her expression questioning.

"Those elephants don't look too happy," he mumbled, slightly embarrassed. *She probably thinks I'm crazy or a coward.*

Her warm, pleased smile told him otherwise.

Three caged wagons, containing a lion, a leopard, and a tiger, brought up the rear of the parade. The animals paced angrily back and forth in their tiny domains, and Luke was thankful that iron bars separated him and those he cared about from the ferocious beasts.

If he had been alone, the animals would not have worried him nearly so much. He felt responsible for Rebecca and the children, even for Wylie. Caring did that to a man. But the most sobering realization of all was that if he married Rebecca, responsibility would not simply be a feeling—it would be a fact.

AN HOUR LATER at the city park, the mayor of Grinnell turned toward the fifteen-member cornet band in the pagoda.

The esteemed gentleman had finally finished his welcoming speech, to the relief of the hundreds of picnickers scattered through the park. With a flourish of his arm, he proclaimed, "Strike up the band!"

The band launched into a lively version of "Oh, Susanna," and Luke turned to Rebecca. "Is His Honor always such a windbag?"

"That was a short speech. You should hear him on the Fourth of July."

"I'd rather avoid it."

"Impossible, unless you don't come to the celebration, and no one stays home on the Fourth."

Luke glanced around the lushly shaded park, past the tall liberty pole and white pagoda with the band members in their bright blue uniforms. The twins, followed by Eben's boys, raced a hoop along one of the walkways, guiding it with the special stick. Rebecca's mother was showing Sissy off to some of her friends, and Howard and Wylie were in a lively political discussion with two of their cronies. Everywhere he looked, families and friends were talking and laughing. Here and there, sweethearts strolled along the sunlight-dappled pathways hand in hand, oblivious to the throngs around them.

"This is quite a celebration in itself." He reached over and caught her hand, resting their clasped fingers unobtrusively on the quilt between them.

Rebecca smiled and tickled his palm with her thumb. He shifted his hand, trapping her thumb, and tried to look threatening. She just laughed. "We use any excuse for a party, but this is one of the best of all. The circus doesn't come through here every year."

"I'm glad Wylie twisted my arm. I don't like him paying my way, but to be honest, I probably would have stayed home otherwise."

"We need your help to corral the children. And if Uncle Wylie's wheelchair gets stuck, you'll have to help Jackson get it out. Besides, it was something he wanted to do. He likes you and wanted you along—almost as much as I did."

"Well, just between you and me, I think I'm almost as excited as the kids. I've never been to a circus before."

She looked at him in amazement. "You haven't? Even with all your travels?"

"Nope. Never was in the right spot at the right time."

"Well, don't get your hopes up too high. White's Circus Extraordinaire isn't anything like P. T. Barnum's Greatest Show on Earth."

"It has a big top, and that's good enough for me." He leaned forward, resting one arm on his bent knee. "You know what I want to see the most?"

"What?" She studied the excitement on his face, the hint of wistfulness in his eyes.

"The acrobats. A troupe was supposed to perform at one of the vaudeville shows I went to in New York, but about half of them got sick so they didn't go on. I was so disappointed I never went back."

"You'll see them today." She pulled a handbill from the picnic basket. "As well as a lady who can lift an elephant." She chuckled at Luke's snort. "And a young man who flies through the air on a trapeze."

"I might close my eyes on that one. I remember all too well what it's like to fly through the air." When she squeezed his hand, he smiled. "Maybe I'll take that time to wander around and see what kind of mischief I can get into."

"No, sir. I'm not letting you out of my sight, not while Pachyderm Jezabel is in the county. If you're in the mood to wander, why don't you track down the children, and I'll spread out our dinner."

Spotting Ben Crowder and an exquisitely beautiful young lady heading their way, Luke acted on impulse and leaned close to Rebecca. "Givin' orders already, Becca, honey?"

"Oh, I didn't mean for it to sound like an order." She turned her head and froze. His face was inches from her own. Lightly applied Bay Rum mingled with the fresh scent of the sprig of mint he had nibbled a few minutes before. The teasing light in his eyes faded, replaced by another glow far more seductive. The haunting strains of "Shenandoah" and unrequited love drifted around them.

"I suppose it would embarrass you if I kissed you right now."

"Yes, I suppose it would."

"But you almost want me to, don't you?"

"Almost. It's been so long."

"Six days, thirteen hours—"

"—and about twenty-seven minutes." She smiled tenderly. "But who's counting."

"Sounds like we are." He grinned and drew back, releasing her hand. "I have a confession to make."

"You don't look very contrite," she said dryly.

"Ben Crowder's about twenty feet from us and headed this way."

"Why, Luke Northcutt, were you trying to make him jealous?"

A dull flush stained his cheeks as he shrugged. "It didn't take him long to find a new lady."

"Mother said she's seen him with two different women in the past two weeks." She glanced over her shoulder. "Make that three women. Now, behave yourself. I'm hoping Ben will remain my friend."

Luke glanced at the banker, who had stopped to chat with another couple. "You think that's possible?"

"I hope so."

Luke raised a brow but said nothing, nodding minutely in Crowder's direction.

Rebecca turned, greeting him and his companion with a smile. "Hello, Mary Jane, Ben. How nice to see you."

Ben and Mary Jane returned the pleasantry, and Ben introduced the young woman to Luke. The two couples talked about the sunny weather, the picnic, and the music, until Mary Jane spied an old school chum.

"Oh, Ben, darling, I simply must speak to dear Ginny. Will you excuse me for a minute?"

"Go right ahead. I'll wait for you here." Ben watched her glide gracefully away, then dropped down beside Rebecca on the quilt.

"My stars, Ben Crowder, you can do better than her!"

Both Luke and Ben were startled by Rebecca's soft but harsh words.

"Jealous?" asked Ben with a tiny, sad smile.

Luke was wondering the same thing.

"Of course not. But for goodness' sake, Ben, she's fifteen years younger than you and doesn't have a brain in her head."

"But she's beautiful and has been trained to be the consummate hostess—according to her mother." Ben glanced at the younger woman before turning his attention back to Rebecca. "She would look lovely in my new house."

"Ben! A wife should be more than just a pretty ornament."

"You're right, of course. Even I know that." He sighed deeply. "And you're right about Mary Jane, too. She couldn't come up with an original thought if her life depended on it. I had hoped she might be different from the rest." He glanced at Luke and smiled ruefully. "I've never spent a more boring day in my life."

To Luke's surprise, he felt a touch of sympathy for the man. "And it's only half over." He smiled back at him. "Think you'll survive the rest of it?"

"I'll have to." Ben grimaced. "Not good form to dump a lady in the middle of a crowded park. Even worse to leave her stranded at the circus." He was silent for a minute, his gaze slowly scanning the scenery. "I miss you, Rebecca."

Luke's gut twisted.

"Oh, I know I couldn't make you happy. Seeing you with Luke makes me certain of that." He flicked an ant off the quilt. "I wasn't very nice the last time I saw you, and I sincerely apologize."

"Apology accepted. You were a bit upset."

"I was furious. Wounded pride, I suppose." He looked toward the pagoda and said quietly, "I miss our talks."

"We can still have our chats. Why don't you come out to dinner Sunday?"

He glanced at Luke. "I can't make it this week, but perhaps another time." He put one hand down on the quilt and pushed himself up to a standing position. "If you come across any intelligent ladies, send them my way. That big old house is a lot lonelier than I had expected." He looked across the park, a hint of sadness in his expression for a moment, then he collected himself and his face brightened. "Well, I'm off to play the gallant. Have a good time at the circus."

Luke contemplated Rebecca's pensive countenance and felt a prick of fear. "Having second thoughts, Rebecca?"

"About marrying Ben?" She turned toward him and laid her hand over his where it rested on his knee. Shaking her head, she said, "I know clearly where my love lies. Ben is a good man. I would like to see him happy, that's all. And he won't find happiness going around with flighty women like her. The two others he has taken to dinner are just as bad."

"I think you hurt him more than you realize."

"You may be right. I didn't want to hurt him at all, but our marriage would not have been a happy one, not when I was falling in love with you." She took a deep breath, setting aside the problem for the moment. "Let's see, I think I asked you to go find the children."

Luke chuckled. "Asked? I don't think so."

"Oh, bother. Please dear sir, love of my life, will you go find the children so we can eat and wash up their dirty faces and get Sissy to rest a few minutes"—she took a huge breath—"and then go to the circus and eat all sorts of sweets and nuts and gasp at the acrobats and laugh at the clowns and cheer for the horses—"

"I'll go, I'll go." Laughing, Luke jumped to his feet and took off before she could get started again.

After they ate and rested, they packed their belongings, gathered up the kids, and piled in the surrey. A lot of folks walked out to the circus, but it would have been impossible to push Wylie such a distance over the dirt roads. They parked the surrey near the gate and embarked on the big adventure.

"You kids stay right with us. Don't go wandering off on your own. This is a big crowd, and it will be real easy to get lost or hurt." Luke abruptly stopped speaking. His words echoed around him as other men, fathers all, gave the same instructions to their bouncy, excited children. Uncomfortable, he looked over at Rebecca. Her warm, loving smile encouraged him to continue. "Uh, if you want to see something, tell us and we'll give you time to look at it. Sissy, you hold on to Rebecca's hand until we get through the gate." He glanced at Rebecca. "Then I'll carry her if you want."

"That would be fine. Boys, stay right with us, now. Uncle Wylie, are you ready?"

"You'd better ask Jackson. He's the one doing the pushing."

Jackson nodded and they started off, joining the stream of people flowing up to the ticket wagon. Rebecca's brother Will trotted back to meet them. "Hello, folks. Thought I might tag along with you. I've already got my ticket."

"Why aren't you squiring a pretty girl on your arm, boy?" Wylie shook his nephew's hand.

"Been too busy with my new job to chase any of them." Will grinned and fell in step beside the twins.

Luke purchased everyone's ticket with the money Wylie had given him. He wished he was the one paying for the day, but at fifty cents a head that was impossible. He hoped to be able to do it the next time.

The next time. Would he be included in the next family outing to the circus? He paused by the ticket wagon, putting the change into his wallet, and gazed across the crowd at Rebecca and her family. A swell of affection and tenderness rushed through him. What other woman would take in three orphans without batting an eye, especially a woman who had no husband to help her?

She had dressed simply for the outing in a sky blue gingham dress. It had the draped front that she favored and a high collar with a ruffle. The brim on her straw poke bonnet, decorated with blue and white satin bows and ribbon, slightly shaded her face. The boys were dressed to beat the band in new checked coats with solid-colored knickers. Their caps matched their pants. The outfits were identical except for color; one was blue, the other light brown. Sissy's frilly

little dress was the color of a ripe apricot. They made a
fine-looking family, one that any man would have been
proud of.

He wasn't exactly being dragged kicking and screaming
toward marriage, but he was being roped into it none too
slowly. The thought of life without her and the children was
looking more dismal day by day.

Luke rejoined the others, helping Will and Jackson lift
Wylie's wheelchair a few times when it became stuck in
the soft dirt. They walked through the entrance and down
the stretch of smaller tents containing the sideshows. Here,
the ground had already been trampled down enough for the
wheelchair to move freely. The billowing canvas screens
held rudely painted scenes of what awaited them—a bearded
lady, the tallest man in the world, the tattooed man, and
other never-seen-before wonders.

The barkers sat by each doorway, young, brazen-faced,
and alert, intent upon separating the Iowa farmers from their
hard-earned money. "Step right up, folks. See Madam Zelda
charm the serpents of the Amazon. Ten cents, folks. That's
right, one thin dime. Step right up—"

"—See Meredith the Magnificent, England's greatest
magician, on a special tour of these United States. See
him change a rabbit into a dove, which all the ladies love.
Step right up, sir, and bring the pretty lady. Ten cents each
and the little angel gets in free."

They stopped to see the magician and left grinning. Luke
had seen many a sleight-of-hand artist in his time, but
Meredith the Magnificent turned out to be one of the
best. He pulled coins from behind his ears, eggs from
his mouth, and a rabbit from a hat. Playing cards seemed
to appear in thin air. And he did, indeed, put the rabbit
into the hat, smash it flat, fluff it back up, and pull out
a dove.

Promising the boys that they would see the other wonders
later, they walked through the menagerie on their way to
the big top. The snarling leopard frightened Sissy, causing
her to bury her face against Luke's shoulder. He left the
boys to watch the big cats with Wylie and Rebecca and

carried her over to see the parakeets. When the others joined them a few minutes later, Sissy had recovered from her fright and was busy pointing out her favorites among the multicolored birds.

Rebecca slipped her arm through his, her smile making him go weak in the knees. "You're a good man, Luke, and you would make a wonderful father," she said quietly. No one heard her comment but Luke, and he made no reply. He couldn't. Her praise touched him deeply, causing him to wish for things he wasn't sure he had a right to have.

The monkeys were next, amusing the viewers with somersaults and funny expressions. They scurried up and down a fake tree, swinging from the branches and chattering in monkey-talk at the gawking humans.

At the python's cage, Rebecca shuddered and shifted closer to Luke. He slipped his arm around her, shamelessly glad the giant snake was so big and frightening.

They moved on into the main tent, taking seats in the front row so Wylie could sit beside them in his chair. Moments after they were seated, the show began with a marvelous display of trick riding. One horseman rode two horses around the ring, balancing one foot on one beautiful steed and the other foot on the second. Another rode around the ring at a steady gallop, jumping through giant rings held up by his partners. The young woman rode out doing a handstand, and the two lads guided their animals through the intricate steps of a dance routine.

"Peanuts, get your peanuts right here! Fresh roasted peanuts."

Saul tugged on Luke's sleeve as the peanut vendor moved their way. "Can we have some peanuts, Uncle Luke? I'm starving."

Luke grinned. "Yep. You're better off eating peanuts than candy."

"Aw, shucks. I was gonna ask for that next." Saul gave him half a grin.

"We'll get you some when we're ready to leave. Otherwise, you'll make yourselves sick."

Luke bought peanuts for everyone but Will, and he

declined his offer, saying he would wait a while. A fan vendor came by next, and Rebecca bought one to fan herself and Sissy. Although the canvas overhead lifted and billowed in the breeze, the air inside the tent was hot and smelly from so many bodies and animals. Every now and then, when the poles creaked and groaned, Luke glanced up to make sure they were secure.

A crew quickly cleaned up after the horses and were comically chased out of the ring by the clowns. The "lady" clown finally caught her man after many attempts and hooked the harness over his neck and shoulders. Dragging him before a clown Justice of Disorder, they were dutifully "hitched."

The strong-lady performed next. Dressed in a gown quite suitable for an evening party, she balanced a man on her shoulders and lifted two others off the floor with her outstretched arms. She lifted barbells of varying weights and even balanced a wooden chair by the back legs on her upper chest—made all the more interesting because a man was sitting in it at the time. But everyone agreed her crowning achievement was lifting the baby elephant. Wylie pointed out that the special platform was probably levered in some way to make it easier, but it was still an impressive performance.

The elephants did a dance, led by the black-eyed woman who had picked Luke out of the parade crowd. Rebecca had to endure Eben's teasing when she refused to admit the woman had a way with animals. She grew downright huffy when her brother suggested that Luke was the one who could find out if she had a way with men, too.

"Keep your bright ideas to yourself, Eben Lansing. Amanda, can't you keep that brother of mine in line?"

Without thinking about the hundred or so people sitting behind them, Luke slipped his arm around her waist and squeezed gently. "Enjoy the show, honey," he said quietly. "I'm right where I want to be." Rebecca looked up at him, her gaze searching his, asking questions he was afraid to answer. "For now, at least," he added gruffly, not wanting her to read more into his statement than he had intended, not even sure himself what he had meant.

Thoughts churning, he almost missed the acrobats. Used to being in control of his emotions and his well-ordered life, he shoved aside his uncertainties and worries—he couldn't do anything about them at the moment anyway—and let himself take his own advice. He enjoyed the acrobats immensely, watching in amazement as they tumbled and twisted and threw each other in the air, turning somersaults before hitting the ground. They did handstands on ladders, on tipped chairs, and on each other's shoulders, and formed a pyramid three people high. To him it was worth the whole price of the ticket just to see them.

The trapeze act was the grand finale. He had removed his arm from around Rebecca sometime during the acrobats' part of the show. As the high-flying star climbed up to his tiny platform above their heads and the crowd hushed, Rebecca slipped her delicate hand around his. While the others "oohed" and "aahed," Luke looked everywhere but up. He didn't see the man hang by his ankle or do a flip from one trapeze to the other, but he did not have to see it to know what was going on. The twins' exclamations kept him well informed. Long after the daring young man had somersaulted from the trapeze to the net below, Rebecca's fingers remained curled around his.

They stopped at the sideshows on the way out, but they were merely interesting after the excitement of the big top. Curled against his chest and resting her head on his shoulder, Sissy was asleep before they reached the surrey. Wylie drove and Luke was content to hold the little girl all the way to his house.

On the way home, with Sissy in his arms and Rebecca tiredly leaning her head against his other shoulder, he finally accepted what his heart had known for so long—he loved her. He loved them all. A phrase from William Wordsworth came to mind—

> She gave me eyes, she gave me ears;
> And humble cares, and delicate fears;
> A heart, the fountain of sweet tears;
> And love, and thought, and joy.

*   *   *

THE POEM DIDN'T quite fit. His cares were not humble nor were his fears delicate, but she had opened the door to his heart. Since meeting her, he looked at the world in a new way and listened with new understanding. She had indeed given him love, thought, and joy.

He dreamed of how it would be if they were already married. Instead of going to his house, with only Drifter for company, he would be carrying Sissy up to tuck into bed. After a light supper, the boys would drag themselves upstairs and fall asleep the instant their heads touched the pillow. He and Rebecca would chat a while with Wylie, probably laughing just like the kids over the things they had seen during the day. Then he would take his wife—his only love—up to bed, slowly undress her, and show her how much she meant to him.

The daydream ended when they reached his house. He shifted the child gently into Rebecca's arms. "Go for a walk later?" she asked softly.

He shook his head. "No, I'd better stay around here and get caught up on a few things." He saw the disappointment in her eyes, but he couldn't explain. Even if they had been alone, he doubted if he could tell her what he felt at that moment. Being loved—and loving—was so new to him that he could not quite grasp it all at once.

He wanted her in more ways than he had ever thought a man could ache for a woman, not only as a lover but as a friend, a helpmate, a mother to his children. Until the twins and Sissy had come along, he had always been uneasy around children, never quite sure of what to do with them. Now, he loved these three as his own, but he wanted more. He wanted at least one child, born of his flesh and hers, conceived in love, joy, and ecstasy.

If they were alone tonight, there would be no holding back. He would make her his, body and soul. He had once made God a promise never to shame her again. And because she was the kind of woman she was, if he made love to her without benefit of marriage vows, there would be moments of regret, moments of shame. He was determined to keep his promise, though it would be torture.

Climbing down from the surrey, he turned and curled his fingers around her upper arm. He didn't want her to be hurt, or even have a moment of disappointment. "Would those city folks throw a rag-tag farmer out if he didn't have a proper suit for Sunday morning?"

"Of course not! Goodness, Luke, with the size of our congregation, people wear all sorts of things. Do you want to go with us tomorrow?"

No! He couldn't remember when he had last set foot in a church building. Just the thought of it made him jittery. "Yes." His voice sounded strange.

"Oh, Luke, I'm so glad. We'll pick you up. See you in the morning."

Drifter came up and sat down beside him as he watched the surrey go down his lane, up hers, and disappear behind her big house. Her place was so much better than his. He felt a sharp pang of uncertainty. He had so little to offer her—nothing but his heart and a strong back. Then he reminded himself that he had one hundred and twenty acres of prime Iowa farmland. Joined with hers, it would make their farm one of the biggest in the county.

In the fall. When the crops are harvested and I've proven to her and her family that I'm a good farmer, when they know I can provide for her and tend well what is hers, then I'll marry her, Lord, if you're willing.

He walked through the doorway and slowly scanned the empty front room. It would be hard to live in the fine house Anthony had built, always being reminded of how much Rebecca's first husband had given her. But maybe in time, he could give her things, build things that pleased her, and make the house more his own.

And what if you can't measure up? What if she grows tired of you and your stubborn, selfish ways? What if she tells you to leave? The thought terrified him, bringing back the bitter anguish of his childhood.

"I'm not a child anymore." He spoke forcefully to vanquish his demons. "And Rebecca is not like anyone in my family. She's not like anyone I've ever known. She'll keep on loving me."

He returned to the porch and called Drifter to go with him to the barn. The dog happily trotted along beside him, looking up at him quizzically when his tone became dejected. "And if she stops loving me, then I'll go. It will hurt, and I'll add more painful memories to the storehouse. But for once in my life, for a little while at least, I'll have known what it's like to love and be loved. And that, my friend, has to count for something."

Chapter 27

"ELIZABETH, WILL YOU please sit down? You're making me tired just watching you." Rebecca took her sister by the arm and steered her away from the stove to a comfortable sitting area nearby. "We came to help out a little bit, not make more work for you. There, now put your feet up."

"You don't have to pamper me." Elizabeth eased down in her favorite chair and sighed heavily. "On second thought, go ahead. This feels so good I may not get up until bedtime." She rested her hand on her very round stomach and patted it gently. "This baby has tired me out more than the others did."

"Probably because you've got three little ones underfoot already." Rebecca stirred a pot of soup on the stove, then resumed kneading the bread dough. She had brought out her Universal Mixer just for that purpose. "I miss seeing you at church."

"It will be a while before I go back. I'm too huge now to go out in public. And once the baby comes, it will be some time before I'll want to take her out in a crowd. Moss said Luke went with you last Sunday."

"Yes, he did. And I didn't even ask him. I was so happy to have him with us. He was a bit uncomfortable, especially at first. But he relaxed after some other men came in who didn't have on suits. He seemed to really enjoy the music and listened attentively to the minister's sermon." She smiled. "Thankfully, it wasn't a fire-and-brimstone one. That might have scared him off. Afterward several men he had met in town came over to welcome him. And, of course, Ralph and Artie were there and made a point to say hello. He said he would go again next week."

Rebecca worked away, slanting her sister a glance every few minutes as they chatted. She noticed Elizabeth flinch several times. The baby was not expected for a few weeks, but she had a suspicion the little one had other plans. "Are you having pains, or is the baby kicking extra hard?"

"It's not kicks, but I've been having the pains for several days now. The doctor said it was probably false labor." Her face contorted for an instant. "Ouch! That one was stronger than the others."

Rebecca put down her mixer and went to Elizabeth's side. "Is this baby on her way, little sister?" she asked, taking her hand.

"I'm not sure yet." She grinned. "You'd think I'd know after having three. I'll shift the chair so I can see the clock. I think I'd better see how often these little twinges are coming."

Rebecca helped her to her feet, and they turned the chair at an angle. When she sat back down, Rebecca pushed the footstool under her feet. "I'd better get these loaves of bread in the pan to rise. Things may get busy after a while."

"I wish Moss hadn't gone out to your place. I don't think he intended to come home until late this afternoon. But poor man, he can't hang around here all the time." Elizabeth gasped softly as another contraction hit her. Suddenly, she paled. "Becky, my water just broke!"

Rebecca grabbed a couple of towels from the cabinet and rushed to her sister's side.

Elizabeth grimaced. "I don't think the towels will do much good. My skirt is soaked." She looked at her older sister with a worried frown. "There's no one here but us. Our hired man went to town a little while ago." She gasped and grabbed the chair arm. "This baby's not going to take five or six hours like the others," she said when she could catch her breath.

"Don't move." Rebecca ran to the kitchen door. The twins were out in the yard, keeping an eye on Sissy and Elizabeth's little girls. "Paul, Saul. Come here, please."

At her urgent tone, the boys ran to the house. "What is it, Aunt Becca?"

"Elizabeth is having her baby. You've got to go for help."

"Us?" The twins spoke at the same time, then looked at each other warily.

"Luke says you're good riders, now. You're the only ones here that can go."

"But we don't have our horses."

"You'll have to take two from the stable. I know Moss has some gentle ones. We'll find out from Elizabeth which ones you should use. Paul, I need you to go to town and get the doctor. Saul, you can ride out to our place and get Moss. He's out there with Uncle Wylie today. Do you think you can do it?"

"Yes, ma'am. I think so," said Saul. Paul agreed with a solemn nod.

"I think you can, too." Rebecca was afraid to send them off on their own, but she refused to speak of her fear. "Come inside with me for a minute, and we'll ask Elizabeth about the horses."

Elizabeth quickly told the boys which animals to use and where to find the bridles and saddles. "We don't have any small saddles, so you may have to help each other carry the regular ones." She closed her eyes and held her breath during another contraction. After a few minutes, she said quietly, "I appreciate your help, and I know you'll do just fine. Before you leave, bring the girls in so I can talk to them, please."

The twins did as she requested, while Rebecca threw the bread dough into the pans. The loaves would be misshapen, but she did not care. Still, the family would need food, and it filled in the moment while Elizabeth explained the situation to her daughters. She knew, too, that she needed to keep up an appearance of normality for the girls so they wouldn't become afraid.

"Maggie, you're the oldest, so you have to keep an eye on your sisters. Aunt Rebecca and I are going to be busy for the next several hours, and you girls are going to have to behave the best you ever have. The twins are going for Papa and the doctor. They will be here soon. I want you to get out your dollies or a game and play here in the sitting room. You stay away from the stove and don't go outside without asking me or Aunt Rebecca. Is that clear?"

"Yes, ma'am. We'll be real good, Mama."

The twins ran out to the stable to saddle up, while Rebecca helped Elizabeth into her room. Their home was large, but only one story, so she could keep an eye on the girls and tend to Elizabeth. She quickly stripped the sheets off the bed and spread down a covering of oilcloth over the mattress, adding several layers of old sheets over it and a top sheet and blanket tucked in at the foot. Then she helped Elizabeth change into a nightgown and get into bed.

They set a clock near the bed so they could time the contractions. "They're coming every five minutes." Elizabeth smiled at Rebecca. "I'm so glad you're here. Even though I'm an old hand at this, it's good to have female company. Moss tends to fall apart. About all he's good at is rushing off to get the doctor."

Maggie knocked timidly on the bedroom door. "Aunt Rebecca, Paul and Saul are at the back gate."

"Thank you, dear. I'll be right there." She hurried from the room and out the back door.

"We're ready to go. Where is Doctor Clark's office?"

"It's in the Bank Block. Do you know where that is?"

"Yes, ma'am."

"Tell the doctor that Elizabeth Heartfield is having her baby. And tell him it's coming fast. If you forget her last name, just tell him Moss and Elizabeth, and he'll know who it is. After you see the doctor, go to the store and tell Grandpa. He will take over from there."

"What if the doctor isn't in his office?"

"Then go right to the store and tell Grandpa what is happening. He'll find the doctor or get another one. Saul, do you remember where the cutoff road is?"

"Yes, ma'am. It's by that house that has the rickety old barn. I turn right there and it takes me to the road that runs in front of our place."

"Very good. Now, go quickly but not recklessly. You won't do yourselves or us any good if you get hurt or hurt one of the horses. Be careful." She smiled at them, her eyes a bit misty. "I'm proud of you."

The boys took off at a gallop, riding together until they reached the cutoff, where Saul turned off with a wave to his brother. Paul did not slow down until he reached the edge of town. Although he was in a desperate hurry, he knew better than to ride too fast through the busy streets. He found the doctor's office easily, and almost burst into tears of relief to find the good gentleman in.

"Doctor Clark, Aunt Elizabeth is having her baby!"

The doctor calmly stood up from behind his desk and retrieved his coat from a hook on the wall nearby. He looked at Paul over the spectacles sitting low on his nose. "That wouldn't be Elizabeth Heartfield, would it?"

"Yes, sir. Aunt Rebecca's with her, but she said to tell you the baby is coming fast."

"Well, I'd best get a move on then, hadn't I?" The doctor smiled kindly. "Are you going back with me?"

"No, sir. I'm supposed to go over to Grandpa Lansing's store."

The doctor picked up his medical bag and opened the door to his office, letting Paul go out first. "I hear Rebecca Stephens adopted you and your brother and sister."

"Yes, sir. We're a real family now."

"How's Mr. Northcutt?" he asked casually, double-checking the contents of his bag. "See him very often?"

"Oh, we see him most every day. He's feeling fine now, except his knee gets stiff sometimes."

"It probably will for a long while. Well, I'll go welcome your new cousin into the world. See you in a while, lad. I'm

certain your grandparents will be heading out to Elizabeth's
place right away."

Paul climbed back on the horse and rode over to Lansing
Dry Goods, where he broke the news to Eben and Howard.
Howard immediately sent Paul over to tell Clara and he
followed, being somewhat slower because he walked to
work every day. By the time he reached his house, Clara
had gathered up everything she might possibly need and had
it loaded in the buggy. Howard quickly hitched the horse
to the buggy, and within half an hour of Paul's arrival in
town, they were on the road to see about Elizabeth.

Luke was working in the field, running his cultivator
beside the rows of tiny corn plants, when Saul rode past at
top speed. He raised the shovels clear off the ground, then
riding on the cultivator, drove his team over to Rebecca's.
He arrived in time to see Moss hastily saddling his horse.
When Saul spotted Luke, he ran to meet him.

"What's going on, son? Is everything all right?" *Has
something happened to Rebecca?*

"Aunt Elizabeth is having her baby. Aunt Becca is with
her." The boy beamed. "She trusted us to ride for help,
Uncle Luke. All because you taught us how. Paul went for
the doctor, and I came out here for Uncle Moss."

Moss rode up, his face pale and worried. "Looks like this
baby is coming a bit early. Thanks, Saul, for coming to get
me. I'll see you later." He took off down the road at full
speed.

"Hope he doesn't break his neck on the way," Luke muttered. A twinge of fear nudged him. He might go through
the same thing someday if he and Rebecca had a baby.
He wanted children with her, but did he want her to go
through the pain? Did he want to risk losing her? *She's
already had one baby, so maybe she would be all right.*
He thought of the fear in Moss's eyes. *It's always a risk.*
And one he knew Rebecca would want to take. "Is Wylie
here?"

"Yes, sir. He's down at the hog pens. He told Uncle Moss
we'd follow along later and get Sissy and Paul. Didn't figure
they needed too many people underfoot."

"Is Rebecca going to stay with Elizabeth?"

"She didn't say, but Uncle Wylie figures she will. He said usually Grandma takes the other kids home with her and Aunt Becca stays and helps out. Guess she's done it with all of Aunt Elizabeth's babies."

Luke climbed down off the cultivator and tied the reins to a hitching post. He and Saul walked down to the hog pens where they found Wylie looking over a new litter of piglets.

"Afternoon, Luke. Looks like we're having babies born all over the place today. You might want some of these when they get big enough. They're the best in the county."

Luke remembered the first day he had met Rebecca. She had promised him the best meal in the county, and she had been right. He wondered if Wylie's opinion of the pigs was as accurate.

"You going to need some help around the house for a few days?"

Wylie grinned. "You volunteering to do housework?"

"I could help out with the children and maybe cook a little." Luke smiled. "Very little. I fry a pretty good egg and make decent corn bread."

"Well, that's more than either Jackson or I can do. It's a funny thing. That man can fry up the best catfish and hush puppies this side of Texas, but that's the only dad-blamed thing he knows how to cook. We tried doin' for ourselves a few times when Becky was gone, and he burned the eggs to cinders every time." Wylie grew solemn. "I'd be grateful for the help, Luke. Jackson and I are just two old bachelors who don't know too much about taking care of children."

"And you think three old bachelors would do better?" Luke laughed. "Don't tell me you don't know how to take care of children, Wylie. I've seen you in action. But I'd be pleased to stay and help out."

"THIS BABY'S NOT going to wait for the doctor." Elizabeth gasped. "I have to push."

"Then push. I've got everything ready." Rebecca grinned uncertainly at her sister. "My hands are shaking so, the poor child will think she's being born in the middle of an earthquake."

"You've . . . been through . . . this before, . . . with Doc Clark." Elizabeth screamed as a hard contraction hit.

"Push, Lizzie. Let's have this baby." Rebecca gently squeezed her sister's leg. "We can do it."

Elizabeth groaned and pushed. The contractions were coming less than two minutes apart.

"Here it comes! The head's through! Push, Lizzie, push! Oh, my! You have a boy! Lizzie, you have a boy!"

"Would you like me to take over, Rebecca?" Doctor Clark stepped up beside her, drying his hands on a clean towel. He looked over at Elizabeth and winked. "Looks like I missed all the fun."

"Is that what you call this?" Elizabeth's faint smile widened into a delighted grin when her son let out a hearty yell. "I guess it is fun, after all."

The doctor cut the cord and tied it off, then handed the little one to Rebecca to wrap in the clean linens awaiting him. "Show this fat little rascal to his mama."

The doctor continued with his work while Rebecca and Elizabeth laughed and cried over the newborn. "He's perfect. Plump and pink, and has all his fingers and toes. Welcome, son. Oh, your father is going to be so happy!"

"What are you going to name this one? Not Matthew, Mark, or Madison, I hope," said the doctor with a grin.

"No, since it's a boy, he's going to be called Ethan. Ethan Richard. Richard is Moss's middle name."

"And the Ethan? Is that for anyone in particular?"

"No. We just liked it." Elizabeth looked down at her son, cuddled in the crook of her arm. "Welcome, darling boy. You're going to be spoiled rotten."

Howard, Clara, and Paul arrived a few minutes before Moss. Rebecca's mother stayed with Elizabeth while Rebecca took a break and told the girls they had a baby brother. When Moss arrived, everyone, including the doctor, gave them a few minutes alone with each other and their long-awaited son. Then the doctor finished up, declaring Elizabeth and the baby both fine and healthy and went on his way.

When Wylie and Paul arrived an hour later, Rebecca was surprised to see Luke with them.

"Wylie wanted me to help take the kids home." He shifted uncomfortably and stuffed his fingertips into his jean pockets. "I wanted to see how you were, see if everything went all right."

Rebecca smiled and reached up, brushing a lock of hair back off his forehead. "Well, I'm fine for having just delivered a baby."

"You delivered it?" Luke's eyes widened, then his brow furrowed with a deep frown. "You mean the doctor wasn't here?"

"He arrived seconds after the baby. Actually, all I did was catch the little fellow. Doc Clark did the rest. I'll go bring him out for you and Wylie to see. I don't think Lizzie will mind."

When she returned a few minutes later with the baby, Luke had stepped into the kitchen for a drink of water. She followed him, carrying the blessed bundle in her arms. As he turned and saw her, her heart jumped to her throat at the tenderness and love in his face.

"You look mighty pretty holding a babe in your arms, Becca." He smoothed his fingers gently along her cheek. "Like a natural mother."

"He's a lovely little boy." Rebecca carefully held him so Luke could see his face. "Makes me wish I had a tiny babe of my own." She met Luke's gaze, letting all the love in her heart shine in her eyes. "One with black hair and sky blue eyes like his father."

"Or a little girl with honey blond hair and eyes kissed by the sea, like her mother," he said softly, curling his fingers alongside her neck.

"We would make beautiful children, Luke," she whispered.

"Yeah, I guess we would," he murmured in a husky voice. He brushed his thumb across her lips.

The baby wiggled, then woke up with a cry of protest. Luke lowered his hand to his side.

"I'd better get him back to his mother. She'll be upset if he starts to cry. Thanks for coming over."

"I'm going to stay over at your place until you get back. Thought I might be a help with the kids."

"Oh, Luke, thank you." Rebecca soothed little Ethan, rocking him gently until he quickly went back to sleep. "It will make it so much easier on Wylie and Jackson. I'll probably only stay two or three days. I think Moss's mother wants to come and help, too." She looked up at him, loving the sight of him, loving his thoughtfulness, loving the man who had been hidden behind a gruff facade. "You don't have to leave once I get home," she whispered.

He looked down at the floor. "Yes I do. It's too soon, Becca. I'm not ready. There are things I have to do. Things I have to work through."

"All right." She hesitated, not wanting to be pushy, yet needing to be held after the worries and exhilaration of the day. "Luke?"

At her faintly plaintive tone, his gaze shot to her face. "What is it, honey?"

"Could I have a hug?"

His expression softened, filling with tenderness. "Feeling a little wrung out?" She nodded. "I'm all for a hug, but won't that be a little difficult with you holding the baby?"

She wrinkled her face, appraising the situation. "I guess I'll have to settle for one arm."

"Or maybe one from behind?" He stepped behind her and slipped both arms around her middle, resting his jaw against the top of her head. "How's that?"

"Wonderful," she said with a sigh. After a long minute, she turned her head and tipped her face up toward his. "Now a kiss, please, to see me through the next few days."

"Demanding woman," he said with a smile, his lips touching hers in the sweetest kiss they had ever shared.

Chapter 28

REBECCA STAYED WITH Elizabeth for four days, returning home Sunday evening. The children were delighted to have her home but were disappointed when Luke came downstairs carrying his old carpetbag, ready to leave.

"Sure wish you could stay, Uncle Luke," said Saul, with a determined glint in his eye. "We got used to havin' you around all the time. Kinda like it."

"Well, I liked being with you kids, too." Luke draped an arm around Saul's shoulder. "But you know, people might talk if I stayed here now that your aunt Rebecca is home."

"They wouldn't if you two got married." Saul didn't look at him but tilted his chin up in a small show of defiance.

"Well, that's true." Luke met Rebecca's gaze across the room. "And maybe we will one of these days. But I'm not quite ready to take a wife just yet."

"Why not?"

"Saul, don't be impertinent," Rebecca scolded softly. "Luke's reasons are his business. Marriage is something a person must be certain of before making the commitment. I respect that, and I respect Luke for weighing the decision carefully. You should, too."

"Sorry if I was out of line, Uncle Luke." Saul looked down at the floor.

"No offense taken, son." Luke gave the boy a hug. "I know you've got good intentions. Tell you what, if that pretty lady over there and I ever do decide to get hitched, you youngsters will be the first to know."

Sissy looked from Luke to Rebecca and frowned. "You not get hitched."

"Why not, honey?" Rebecca asked in surprise.

"No gots big collar." Sissy sighed at everyone's perplexed expressions. "No gots harness. Like lady clown."

Rebecca looked at Luke, and they both burst out laughing. "Oh, she's got one, all right, princess. But it's invisible."

"What that?"

" 'Invisible' means something that can't be seen." Luke set his bag on the floor and picked Sissy up. "You'll understand when you get older." He hugged the little girl, then set her down on the floor. After a tender glance at Rebecca, he left.

During the following week, life fell into a pattern, although a different one than before. Luke became a regular guest at the noontime meal, leaving Charlie and Old Joe at his place for food and a rest while he walked over to Rebecca's. Sometimes in the afternoon she walked out to the field where he was working, taking him freshly baked cookies or a cold jug of water. Sissy always accompanied her and occasionally the boys did, too, depending on their activity at the moment.

They grew closer in subtle but important ways, often spending more time talking than either of them should have taken from their chores. The corn had come up nicely, and Luke put in long hours running the cultivator in a checkerboard pattern between the rows to dig up the weeds. The goal was to go over every row three or four times by the Fourth of July, which was less than three weeks away. By then the corn should be knee-high and large enough to battle the weeds on its own. The timothy and clover thrived in the spring rains and warm sunshine. All his crops were doing well, even better than his expectations.

Rebecca's garden also flourished under the perfect weather conditions and constant care. The twins were diligent, both at keeping down the weeds and sampling the produce. The trees in the orchard were loaded with small fruit which would grow plump and juicy by fall.

Late Saturday afternoon, about half an hour before sunset, the twins came into the kitchen. Rebecca removed an apple pie from the oven and turned to set it on the windowsill.

"I don't think you ought to put it up there, Aunt Becca. Looks like we've got a storm coming."

She glanced at Paul's worried expression and set the pie on a warming shelf above the stove. "Does it look like a bad one?" She took a wire rack from the cupboard and set it on the counter, moving the pie to it.

"Yes, ma'am. You'd better come look. The sky looks real funny."

Rebecca hurried out the back door with the boys. Her steps slowed as she walked to the edge of the porch. Conical, downward-pointing clouds filled the northern sky. "Oh, my. I've never seen anything like that."

She rubbed her arms as goose bumps marched over her skin, suddenly cold in spite of what had been a warm day. Wylie had mentioned that the thermometer at the hardware store had read seventy-eight degrees when he was there in the afternoon. A light wind blew from the southeast, but the ominous sight before them filled her with an ill-defined dread. "Go get Uncle Wylie," she said quietly.

Paul ran inside, returning with Wylie in a few minutes. The older man released a low whistle. "Looks like we may be in for a rough night. Boys, why don't you gather up the dogs and put them in the barn. Then make sure all the chickens are in the coop and the door is closed tight."

"Do you know what it is, Uncle Wylie?" Rebecca turned to her uncle as the twins and Sissy ran off to collect the dogs.

"No, Becky gal. I've never seen anything like it. But it's not going to be good. We may be in for a cyclone."

Rebecca went inside, going through the house and closing all the windows and the front door with shaking hands. She had seen pictures of the destruction and death left by tornadoes. It was something she hoped never to see firsthand.

When she returned to the porch, the rest of the family was observing the rapidly building cloud formation, which had expanded from the north to fill the western sky as well. The setting sun lit the sky and clouds with an eerie light.

"Children, I want you to go inside and gather up your coats and slickers. I expect we'll be going to the cellar."

"But Aunt Becca, why do we need slickers and coats? Won't we use the root cellar?"

"Not if we can get to the one in the yard. Anthony lost some kinfolk in the cyclone that hit Iowa in 1860. They were in their root cellar but were killed when the house fell in on top of them." She pointed to the dome of dirt some twenty or thirty feet from the back porch. "He dug that cellar before he built the house. We always used it when he was alive."

"But we have only used it once since I moved in," said Wylie quietly. They had built a wooden ramp off the porch and a wooden walkway to the cellar so he could travel to it in his chair. But they had not been able to come up with an adequate way to get him down the steps. The one time a storm seemed severe enough to warrant going outside, Jackson had been there to carry Wylie. This time, he was spending the weekend in Des Moines.

"Go on, children, and gather up your things. Uncle Wylie, I'll bring our coats into the kitchen. Maybe we'll be all right in the house." She leaned down and hugged him. "We'll get you down there if we have to. I promise."

He caught her hand when she straightened. "Becky, you take care of yourself and those children. I'll take my chances in the root cellar if need be."

Rebecca nodded because she knew it was useless to argue and silently vowed to do everything she could to get him to safety. She thought of sending one of the boys after Luke, but she did not want to chance his being caught in the storm, especially if Luke was not at home. Darkness was gathering, but lightning, continuous like the beating of a pulse, lit the whole western sky in a brilliant and unearthly light.

"Well, there's been lots of storms before, and we've done

just fine in the house," she said with more conviction than she felt. She went inside to fetch their coats just in case.

LUKE CAREFULLY SKIMMED the plane across the top of the walnut lamp stand he was building for Rebecca. Thunder had rolled across the heavens several times in the distance, but he had been engrossed in his work and had paid it little mind. This time, however, the rumble was much closer. There was barely a pause before another peal of thunder sounded, and the tools on Luke's workbench rattled with the reverberation.

Drifter whined and ran to Luke's side, trying to hide under the workbench. "Afraid of thunder, huh? Well, the noise isn't going to hurt you." He put down the plane and rubbed the dog's head. "But what's causing it might. Let's go take a look."

He walked to the barn door with Drifter pressed against his leg. "Come on, dog, ease up. You're going to trip me." Luke peered out the door and took a slow, deep breath. The lightning illuminated the sky, exposing a band of conical clouds at the front of the churning, boiling thunderclouds. He had seen that kind of sky once before down in Texas. "Lord have mercy," he whispered.

He ran back to the barn and grabbed the lantern. "Come on, Drifter." When the dog hesitated, he commanded, "Drifter, come," and the dog instantly obeyed. Luke closed the barn doors and ran to the house as heavy, scattered drops of rain began to fall.

Moments after they reached the back porch, a hard gusty wind hit, snapping limbs off the trees like a man breaking a matchstick. He slammed the back door behind them and set the lantern on the kitchen table. A loud groan sent him running to the window. He curved his hands against his face, blocking the lantern light from his eyes, and peered out into the blackness. Another screeching groan sounded as one of the maple trees toppled to the ground with an earthshaking crash.

Luke ran across the room and opened the door leading down to the root cellar. He called Drifter to his side. "Boy, I'm going to see about Rebecca and the kids. I'll leave this open, and you go down there if you're scared. Understand?"

Drifter looked up at Luke and then down the dark steps.

"Go on down there, boy. You'll be safe there." With one last look at his master, the dog whined and slithered down the steps. Luke left the cellar door open and grabbed his coat. He jerked it on and added a yellow slicker over it. He yanked his old hat from the peg and smashed it down as far as it would go on his head. After blowing out the lantern, he opened the door.

When he stepped out onto the porch, the wind almost knocked him down. He stumbled toward the barn, fighting the gusts that tried to blow him off course. Once inside, he slowed his frantic pace, stopping to lift down a bridle from where it hung on the wall, and walked calmly over to Charlie's stall. The horses were nervous and frightened; he didn't want to make them worse.

"I have to take you out in the storm, boy. There's no way I can make it to Rebecca's without you." Luke eased the bridle over the giant horse's head and the bit into his mouth. He had ridden Charlie often enough to know he would let him, but he had never ridden him without a saddle. There was not enough time to put one on him now.

When he led the obedient animal outside, Charlie shied at the lightning. Luke kept him under control and patted his neck. Slamming the barn door shut, he jammed the crossbar into place. Then he clutched the horse's mane in his hands and with a jump and strenuous heave, pulled himself onto the horse's back. Bending low against Charlie's neck, Luke nudged him in the sides, sending him down the lane at a gallop.

The wind had slackened off a bit, but the rain still pelted down. They covered the distance to Rebecca's in a few minutes. Luke rode the horse right up to the barn, dismounted, and took him inside. He looped the reins around the top board of a stall and ran back outside, closing the door behind him.

As he raced toward the house, the rain eased up to a light shower. The lightning danced over his head, accompanied by a barrage of thunder. Suddenly, the wind died. The dead calm sent a chill down his spine.

"Rebecca! Where are you?" Luke yelled at the top of his lungs, but he doubted if anyone could hear him above the cannons going off overhead. He spotted one of the boys carrying a lamp across the porch and running for the outside cellar. In the circle of light from the lamp, he could see the other boy carrying Sissy. Luke cut across the yard, meeting them.

"Uncle Luke!" Paul yelled in relief as Luke caught him by the arm.

"Where is Rebecca?"

"On the porch. Trying to help Uncle Wylie."

Luke jerked open the cellar door and ordered the children down the stairs. Then he ran up the board walk, meeting Rebecca and Wylie at the edge of the porch. "Go to the cellar! I'll get Wylie!"

Rebecca waited a split second, holding the wheelchair steady as Luke lifted the older man from it. Hiking up her skirt and petticoats, she ran on ahead with Luke right at her heels. She took the steps two at a time in her haste to stay out of his way. Luke moved down the steps more carefully, so he would not trip with Wylie in his arms. He quickly deposited him on a wooden bench that ran along one dirt wall and raced back up the stairs, pulling the door closed. He fastened it tight by wrapping a chain from the door around two hooks securely driven into a wooden brace of the wall.

Removing his slicker, he walked down the steps and looked around the small cellar at the wide-eyed, frightened faces of those he loved. Rebecca scooted over on the bench to make a place for him.

When he sat down beside her, she leaned against him and laid her arm across his chest, curving her fingers over his shoulder. "I'm so glad you're here. Thank you."

Luke started to reply, but stopped, listening intently to a new sound that had joined the thunder.

"Train?" asked Sissy in a tiny voice. She buried her head against Paul's shoulder as the noise grew louder and louder.

"Tornado," breathed Wylie, slipping his arms around the boys who sat on either side of him, holding them close.

Luke wrapped Rebecca in his arms as the roar grew deafening, like the mighty rumble of a dozen heavy freight trains. It passed right overhead. Something slammed into the cellar door, making them all jump and gasp. A loud thud hit the mound of dirt above them, followed by a dozen more thumps and bumps.

Please, God, let the animals be safe, prayed Rebecca. *And the neighbors. Oh, please keep them all safe!*

As quickly as it came, the terrible rumbling moved on. Rain poured down in torrents, slashing against the wooden cellar door. In spite of the door's tight fit, water trickled down the dirt and wooden walls of the stairwell. The wind lashed around the vent pipe, blowing drops of rain into the cellar. For a short time, hail beat against the door like a line of drummers tapping out a rapid cadence.

"At least we're all safe," murmured Luke.

"Where's Drifter?" asked Saul.

"In my cellar, I hope. That's where I left him."

Rebecca straightened and held out her arms to Sissy. The little girl climbed down from Paul's lap and crawled up onto hers. Luke kept his arm around Rebecca's shoulder, and Sissy reached up behind her, curling her hand around his finger.

"Do you think the cyclone took our house?" asked Paul, watching Rebecca with sorrowful eyes.

"It might have. It certainly destroyed something." Strangely, she felt very calm, although her voice held a tremor. *The house is probably gone. Maybe the barn, too.* "But we're safe. That's all that matters."

She silently kept repeating the words, especially as thoughts of things irreplaceable drifted through her mind. Portraits of Anthony and Michael, and of the children's parents. Her locket. Her gold wedding band. The china her parents had given her on her wedding day. Michael's little silver spoon. On and on, her list of treasures grew. Things she had not thought of in months now seemed impossible to live without.

The furious wind and rain kept up for nearly half an hour, forcing them to remain in the cellar. Finally, the bulk of the storm moved on and Luke silently stood. He trudged up the cellar steps and unwound the chain that held it fast. Putting his shoulder against the angled door, he pushed, straining with the effort.

"Is something on top of it?"

He paused. "Yes, but I think I can get it. Whatever it was slid over some." He pushed again, and this time the door slowly moved upward. With a heave, Luke shoved it all the way open, resting it at an angle against an upright post put there for that purpose. Lightning flashed behind him, and in that second he saw the ruins of Rebecca's fine, big house strewn everywhere. Not a wall remained standing. Stunned, he turned in the direction of the barn. Another lightning flash revealed the structure, in one piece and possibly unscathed.

Rebecca knew before she saw his face that her home was damaged. His dejected stance told her as much. When he walked back down the steps, his drawn, ashen face told her the rest.

"Is the house gone?" she asked, handing Sissy to Paul and standing.

Luke nodded and his eyes filled with tears. "The barn is still standing, but the house is completely destroyed." He opened his arms and she stepped into his embrace. "I'm so sorry, honey."

She clung to him, numb with shock, unable to even cry. *All my treasures taken by the wind.* She felt the children huddle around them, holding her, too. *No, my treasures are here, alive and safe. Thank you, God. Thank you.*

She tried to think, to reason, and stayed in Luke's arms for several minutes before pulling away. "There are some extra lanterns on a shelf over there in the corner. Boys, will you get them, please?" She looked up, meeting Luke's gaze. "We need to get the children and Wylie to a warm place. We can take them to your house . . . if it's still there."

"I'll go check out the barn. If it's safe, we can go there for now." Luke studied her face.

"I'm numb, which is probably good."

Luke lit the other two lanterns, taking one with him as he walked up the steps. "The yard is full of rubble so watch your step," he called down from the top of the stairs. "I'll be back in a minute."

Rebecca set Sissy beside Wylie. "Honey, the boys and I are going outside for a minute. I need you to stay here and keep Uncle Wylie company. Can you do that for me?" When Sissy nodded and hugged Wylie's arm, Rebecca smiled. "Thank you, angel. We'll be back soon," she said to her uncle.

He nodded and wiped a tear from his eye. "Be careful. We'll have to wait until daylight to go through everything. Too easy to get hurt when things are piled up."

Rebecca nodded her agreement, picked up a lantern, and walked to the top of the steps. The boys followed with another lamp. Knowing her home was destroyed was one thing; seeing it was another. Picking her way slowly, she walked about ten feet from the cellar door. Her home lay in a million tiny pieces, scattered across the yard and farm yard. The walls were mere splinters, the furniture bits of wood and shredded cloth.

She held the lantern out at arm's length and suddenly began to laugh. Laughter quickly turned to tears. The counter from the kitchen cabinet lay on the ground in one piece. Sitting on top of it, still on the wire rack, was the apple pie she had baked earlier. A piece of wood had fallen over it at a slant, protecting it from the rain, but the boys' closer inspection revealed that the pie was full of splinters.

Luke worked his way over to her and put his arm around her shoulders as she swiped at her tears. Saul held his lantern down to the pie so Luke could see it. "Well, honey, if that pie made it all in one piece, there's bound to be other things. But we can't look for them tonight. The barn appears safe. Why don't we move in there while I hitch up the surrey. I can't tell for sure, but I thought I got a glimpse of my place in the lightning. Looked like the house was still there."

They returned to the cellar for Sissy and Wylie, carrying them to the barn. The boys led the way, holding the lanterns so they could see. Rebecca's dogs were waiting for them, although their greeting was much more subdued than normal. The farm animals were nervous and some still trembling with fright. The children went around to the different stalls in an effort to reassure them while Luke hitched up the team.

He lifted Wylie into the surrey and tied Charlie's reins to the back of it. Rebecca and the children climbed up to their seats and Wylie drove the surrey from the storage shed attached to the barn. Luke fastened the doors and blew out two of the lanterns, setting them in the back of the carriage. He kept the other one lit and stepped up to talk to Wylie.

"I'd better walk in front with the light. There's no telling what might be in the road." They had to stop several times between the house and the county road so Luke could move debris out of the way—a small section of roof, a large tree limb, part of the dining room table. When they came to a kitchen stove, he motioned Wylie around it. "There's no way I can move that thing by myself."

"Luke, wait. Hold the light next to it." When he did as she asked, Rebecca gasped. "That's not my stove!"

Although he walked the rest of the way to his house, nothing else blocked the way. They were relieved to find his place relatively untouched. Tree branches were broken and scattered around the yard, but from all appearances, the tornado had skipped his place completely. Drifter came up out of the cellar when Luke opened the front door, greeting him with a happy bark.

"I can see lights over at the Neeley place," called Paul from the front porch. "Looks like the house is still·there because there are lights upstairs, too."

Saul ran through the house to the back porch. "Looks like lights over at the Ferguson place, too. Hard to tell for sure for the trees."

"Maybe the tornado just went down that side of the road," said Paul as the boys met the others in the kitchen. "That would be good 'cause there aren't many houses on that side between here and town."

"Oh, merciful heaven! I'm so rattled, I didn't think about town." Rebecca turned to Luke as he lowered Wylie into his big chair. "We have to go to town! My parents!" She grabbed his arm when he straightened. "We have to see about my family!"

"We'll go, honey, as soon as I can hitch up the wagon." His expression was grim. "There might be a need for strong horses."

"Can we come, too, Uncle Luke?"

"No, boys. You need to stay here and help Wylie take care of Sissy."

"But couldn't they come, too?" asked Saul.

"No, son," said Wylie. "There's no telling what has happened at town. Sissy and I would only be in the way, and I doubt if you boys could help much at the moment. I'm afraid Luke's right. Without my chair, I'm stuck, so I'll have to depend on you two for now."

Luke hugged Rebecca's shoulders. "I'll be back in a few minutes."

"Hurry, please." She made Wylie a pot of coffee while she waited. "If anyone in the family is hurt, we'll get word to you as soon as possible. If they are all fine but others are hurt, we'll probably stay and try to help."

"I'll worry until you get back regardless, but if you're needed in town, Becky, you stay. Getting word to me is not as important as helping if there's a need." Wylie caught her hand. "I'm awful sorry about the house."

"I am, too. I ache inside every time I think about it, but we're all safe. And if the rest of the folks fared as well, I'll count my blessings instead of grieving over what I've lost."

Winston and Aggie drove up as Luke helped Rebecca into the wagon seat. "Thank goodness you're alive!" cried Aggie. "When we didn't see any lights at your place, we were worried sick."

"We lost the house. But we were in the cellar so none of us was hurt. How about you? Did the storm hit your place?"

"Lost the barn and all the outbuildings. Some of the stock, too. Didn't touch the house. You headed for town?" At Luke's nod, Winston grimaced. "Let's go. I'm mighty afraid it's goin' to be bad."

Chapter 29

THEY MET EBEN half a mile from town and learned that her family was safe, with the exception of Will. "We haven't located him yet. We think he was at the college, and it was hit hard. The brick building is completely destroyed and the stone building lost the roof, top floor, and part of the second floor. Ma and Pa, Tobias, and Moss are over there trying to help clear the wreckage. Quite a few of the students went to Tama today for a baseball game, so they were not at the college."

"What about the rest of town?"

"North of Fourth Street, it's pretty bad. There are a lot of houses completely leveled in that part of town, as well as many that are damaged." Eben looked at Winston and Luke. "We can use all the help we can get. I'm afraid the number of wounded is going to be high."

Although they knew what to expect, they were still dumbfounded when they drove into town. The devastation was unbelievable. Block after block was in total ruin. In other places, one side of the street was swept clean of buildings while the other side of the street was relatively untouched. Many houses that remained standing sat at odd angles to their foundations or had portions of the roof and chimneys blown away. Stunned and bruised, people wandered around, unsure of what to do or where to go. The more severely wounded lay on the sidewalks or in the middle of the street while being cared for by those who had not been injured. Winston and Aggie stopped to help when a man stumbled out of pile of rubble beside their wagon, blood streaming from a deep gash on his head.

Luke and Rebecca followed Eben to the college. Rebecca spotted her mother, jumped down from the wagon, and ran to her side. "Mother, have they found Will?"

"Yes. He's under that pile of debris," Clara said shakily, pointing to a mass of bricks and wood. Howard, Tobias, and Moss were working furiously to move the wreckage. "He told Howard that he isn't hurt badly, just bruised. He is wedged in a tiny space under a beam and can't get out. Your father said there is probably six feet of bricks on top of him."

Luke had stepped up while she was talking, slipping his arm around Rebecca. When his love looked up at him, her eyes wide and beseeching, he kissed her temple. "We'll get him out, honey. You stay here with your mother. I think you both need each other's company right now."

Rebecca put her arm around her mother as Luke walked over to Howard. "He's a good man, Rebecca. And he loves you."

"I know. And I think he is finally realizing that, too."

After a brief discussion with her father, Luke went back to the wagon and unhitched the team. He took a long, heavy chain from the wagon and hooked it to the traces. Guiding the team, he backed them up as close to the mound of debris as he could. Tobias and Moss carried the chain up the pile of bricks and hooked it over the top section. Luke stood to one side, urging his horses forward with a voice command. They obeyed, moving slowly and pulling down a thick layer of the bricks.

Howard called down to Will, and once assured that he was still safe, they repeated the procedure. After using the chain four times, they decided to remove the rest of the bricks by hand. In fifteen minutes, they were easing Will from the ruins. He hugged his rescuers, including Luke, then slowly walked over to his mother and Rebecca and embraced them, too.

"Have they found any of the others? I think there were about eight of us in the building."

"You're the last one, dear. Although one young man is still trapped. They are working to get him out, but I fear he is badly injured."

"We were all on the third floor. I was visiting a couple of the fellows in their room, when suddenly the whole building started shaking. Then we were falling." He shuddered and hugged his mother, resting his cheek against her hair. "It was terrible."

"Are you sure you aren't hurt?"

"Bruised and a little wobbly. Otherwise I'm fine. I'm going to sit down for a few minutes, then I'd better get down to the office and see what the boss wants me to do."

"Will Lansing, you can't go to work!"

"Mother, I have to. People need to know what happened and who is hurt. The best way to do that is with the paper. I'll rest a while." He smiled faintly. "And wait until my hands quit shaking. I couldn't write now anyway."

"You can go to work in the morning. After you rest, I want you to go out to Luke's place. We need to get word to Wylie that none of us is injured. He may need help getting into bed. He doesn't have his wheelchair, and I'm not sure the twins will be able to move him on their own." Clara put her arm around her youngest child's shoulders and guided him over to her waiting buggy. "You get a good rest tonight, and you'll do a much better job tomorrow. Please, Will, do this for me. We will make sure your editor knows why you aren't there. I'm sure he wouldn't expect you to work under the circumstances."

Will climbed into the buggy and leaned back against the padded cushion. "Talked me into it. You know, I'm sure glad I was sitting on the bed. I went down right on top of the mattress." He shifted, rolling his shoulders. "Still hard to have a soft landing when you fall three stories."

Clara and Rebecca stayed with him until his nerves settled down. He was stiff and sore when he left for Luke's place, but he was fully capable of making the trip on his own.

When word reached them that a hospital had been set up in the Central School House and that ladies were needed to nurse the wounded, Rebecca and Clara went there immediately. The sight was appalling. Many were seriously injured, some beyond saving. Some had been picked up with their houses and dashed back down to earth with terrible force. Others had sought shelter in the cellars under their homes, only to have those homes fall in on top of them.

Doctor Clark was there, although bruised himself, for his house had been swept away by the storm. Several of the other doctors had suffered the same fate, yet they, too, worked diligently to save lives.

Those who were not so seriously hurt refused treatment until those worse off were cared for. And some people whose injuries warranted immediate attention tried to endure, thinking others must be more in need of the doctors' care. Clara joined a group of ladies helping the new arrivals. Under Doctor Clark's direction, Rebecca fell to work cleaning wounds and helping him set broken limbs.

The wounded kept coming, hour after hour.

City Hall became a morgue.

While Rebecca and the others worked to save the injured who had been found, Luke and the other men fought to rescue those trapped in the ruins of some seventy-three houses.

BEN CROWDER CAREFULLY raised up on his knees, extending his hand cautiously above his head in the darkness and touched cold, wet wood. To his left, he could feel a pile of wood and stone. The spaces to his right and in front of him were vacant, for at least an arm's length. His head pounded and he could feel a cut on his back, but the blood had clotted, sticking to his shirt. A soft groan sounded in front of him, slightly to the right.

It took him a minute to remember what had happened. He had been in Des Moines all week and had arrived home during the first assault of wind and rain. He had just driven the buggy into his barn when he heard the distant rumbling of the tornado. Fearing for his elderly neighbor's safety, he had raced across the street, bursting into her home a minute before the tornado hit.

He did not know if Mrs. Peters was even home. All he remembered was a woman, unknown to him, ordering him to run for the cellar door. The memory evoked a bemused smile. He had only glimpsed her face in the lightning flashes, but her image was clearly stamped in his mind—late twenties, plain of face, prim hairstyle, and an expression and tone that commanded instant obedience. He expected she usually received it.

"Mrs. Peters?"

"She's not here." The woman made a tiny sound of pain. "My aunt is visiting with some friends on the other side of town."

"I'm going to try to get to you, ma'am. Keep talking so I'll know where you are. How badly are you hurt?"

"My arm is broken. Otherwise I seem to be all in one piece. Don't raise up. I don't believe there is enough room to stand. Are you hurt, sir?"

"I've got a goose egg on my head and a few scrapes, but like you, I think I'm all in one piece." Ben crawled carefully, exclaiming once or twice when his hand connected with a sharp stone. His fingers scraped across a board, and he stopped to examine it by touch. Thinking it might prove useful as a splint, he slid it ahead of him. "I'm Ben Crowder."

"I'm Olivia Sayers. Aunt Augusta is my mother's sister. Oh! Careful, Mr. Crowder, I'm not used to a gentleman running his hand up my leg."

"I beg your pardon, ma'am. I was only trying to determine your direction." Ben paused, wishing he could see her face. She almost sounded amused.

"I'm attached in a straight line with my legs, sir. Continue on course for a foot or two. Any further and you'll soundly smash your head against the wall."

Ben crept forward, then raised up on his knees, but his head spun unexpectedly. He threw out his hand toward what he thought was the wall, but, instead, his fingers curved around a soft, nicely rounded part of her anatomy.

Her fingers clamped around his wrist, and she lifted his hand to her shoulder with a muffled sound of pain. "Are you listing, sir?"

"Yes, Miss Sayers. It would seem I am leaning a bit to the right."

"Good."

"Good?"

"I may be an old maid, but I assure you I am not desperate. From what my aunt has told me, neither are you. You will find the wall approximately an inch from your fingertips, so slide your hand on up."

Ben did as he was told, found the wall, and eased himself around in the narrow space to sit against it. His shoulder rubbed against hers, as did his leg when he straightened it out in front of him. There was no help for it. The space was too small for decorum.

"Are you a schoolteacher, by chance, Miss Sayers?" He began loosening his necktie.

She chuckled, then gasped softly.

"Your arm?"

"Yes. I wish I could say it only hurts when I laugh. Unfortunately, that is not the case."

"I have a board here that we could use as a splint. My necktie should serve to hold it in place."

"There is another one here beside me." He felt her move and heard her bite back a cry of pain. "Here," she said, breathing heavily.

He pulled his tie from around his neck and leaned forward. He had regained his equilibrium, so he did not fall into her lap. "Is the break below the elbow?"

"Yes. About halfway down my forearm."

He carefully placed one board beneath her arm and the other on top of it, tying them securely in place. "May I be so bold, ma'am, as to shred your petticoat?"

"Only if it's for a sling," she said, obviously in pain.

"Considering our tight confinement, it can be for nothing else. Besides, I don't usually shred a lady's underclothing." He lifted her coat and skirt out of the way and grabbed her petticoat in both hands, ripping a long, wide strip from it. "I just take them off," he muttered.

"Do you, now?" Amusement colored her voice.

Ben groaned and quickly flipped her skirt and coat into place. "It must be the bump on the head. Yes, that's it. I'm not responsible for anything I've said or done since the tornado hit." He hesitated, disappointed when she had no comeback. "It has been several years since I removed a woman's clothing."

"That is good to know. My aunt would be keenly disillusioned to learn you are a bounder."

He noted a sudden weariness in her voice. "What is wrong, Miss Sayers?"

"I'm cold. Glad I wore my coat." She stumbled slightly on the words.

"I suspect that you don't go anywhere unprepared." Ben shrugged out of his slicker and spread it over her, worried that she was going into shock.

"Sensible me. Always."

Ben carefully placed his arm around her shoulders and held her firmly against his side. He readjusted his slicker so that he, too, was covered, wrapping them in a warm cocoon. "I know you want to sleep, but you must talk to me." He rubbed her uninjured arm briskly. "We need to lie down."

"I think not."

"Come on, scoot down. We need to get your head lower." He helped her move, then pulled her close, resting her head on his shoulder, and covered them back up again. He kept her talking and in the process learned she was indeed a teacher and owned a small private school for young ladies in an equally small town in East Texas.

They lay curled up together for several hours until they heard people moving around above them. Ben sat up and called out, notifying the rescuers of their plight. Less than an hour later, Luke reached down to help them out of the wreckage.

"Careful of her arm. It's broken."

Luke stepped over part of the chimney and gently lifted the woman out of the cellar. He handed her to Tobias, who waited behind him, then turned to give Ben a hand. "Is there anyone else down there?"

"No. I came over to check on her aunt, but she is visiting in another part of town." Ben stumbled through the rubble and looked over at his place with trepidation. To his utter amazement, his house was still standing.

Seeing the expression on the banker's face, Luke said, "It only took the houses on this side of the street. I don't think there is a one on your side damaged."

"How bad is it?"

"It cut a two-block-wide path clear through this part of town. It didn't go straight, made some loops. Wiped out the West College building and damaged Center College, but most of the students were gone. There were some injuries, but I don't know how many. Center College caught fire a couple of hours ago and burned to the ground."

"Will Lansing?"

"He was buried for a while, like you two, but we got him out. He's gone out to spend the night with Wylie and the kids."

"Were many folks killed?"

Luke nodded, his tired face filled with sorrow. "Last count I heard was eighty hurt and twenty dead. But there are still folks missing and cellars that haven't been uncovered. We'd better get you two over to the doctor. They've set up a hospital at the high school."

"I'll drive Miss Sayers over. My horse should still be hitched to the buggy in the barn. How did you fare?"

"My place is fine." Luke looked down at the ground. Strangely, he felt guilty that Rebecca's home had been destroyed instead of his. Because he had not wanted to live there, he couldn't help but feel that somehow it was his fault. "Rebecca lost her house."

"Oh, no! Was anyone hurt?"

"No, we were all in the cellar, the one out in the backyard. Wylie and the kids are over at my place. You'll probably see Rebecca at the hospital."

"I'll make it a point to speak to her. Does she need a place to stay?"

"No. Her parents' place is intact."

"Good. Well, I'd better get going." He shook hands with Luke. "My thanks to you and everyone who worked to get us out. I'll be back to help after I take Miss Sayers to the doctor."

Teams of men worked throughout the night until every destroyed home had been thoroughly checked. Amazingly, over three hundred people had been in those homes. Most who survived had been in the cellars. By the next day they counted the wounded, almost one hundred and fifty people. The death toll reached thirty and was expected to go higher. There were no church services on Sunday morning as most of those able to attend were caring for the injured or homeless. In spite of the tragedy, there was much rejoicing. The loss of life and limb could have been far greater.

Chapter 30

ON SUNDAY MORNING, Clara persuaded Luke and Rebecca to stay at her house for a while and sleep. They drove out to the farm in the early afternoon.

The children came running from Luke's house when they drove up. To Luke and Rebecca's astonishment, Wylie came out on the porch behind them in his wheelchair.

"Where did you find it?" Luke asked as he helped Rebecca down from the wagon.

"In the top of an apple tree. The boys spotted it early this morning," said Wylie with a grin. "Beats me how it stayed in one piece, but it's as sound as ever. I'll have to write a letter to the company and brag on it."

The children engulfed them in hugs. "We found some other stuff, too. Some pots and pans and even a few clothes. Aunt Becca, your dresser is layin' where the back porch used to be. It's tipped over on the front, so we couldn't see if the drawers are in it. There's a big beam on top of it. We tried to move it, but couldn't," said Paul.

"We were real careful and didn't climb on stuff that looked dangerous. Oh, we found your quilt trunk! The trunk's split open, but the quilts were still inside. They were wet so we got a wheelbarrow out of the toolshed and hauled them over here and spread 'em out on the maple tree." Saul looked up at Luke. "Sorry it fell down, but it makes a good clothesline."

"Sounds like you've been busy. Did you find anything to eat?" Luke picked Sissy up and followed Rebecca and Wylie inside. The boys walked in behind him.

"Sure. We had boiled eggs and toast for breakfast. And cheese and crackers at noon." Paul smiled up at Rebecca. "Sure glad you're back. I was afraid I'd have to open a can of beans for supper."

"We may still have to." Luke gave Rebecca an apologetic look. "There's not much else in the larder."

Rebecca took a deep breath. "Well, why don't we go over to the house and see what we can find. Maybe there are still some things in the root cellar."

Luke put his arm around her. "Are you up to it, honey?"

"I'd like to get it over with."

Luke helped Wylie into the wagon seat and put his wheelchair in the back. Rebecca and the children climbed up in the wagon bed, and Luke drove the team. As they pulled up to what remained of her house, the site was even more disheartening in daylight than it had been in the dark. The foundation was bare. Piles of rubble filled most of the cellar. Debris was strewn across the yard, farmyard, and out into the orchard and the field.

Rebecca scanned the farmyard. "The chicken coop's gone."

"We found a few chickens wanderin' around behind the barn. There's not a feather on them."

"Oh, those poor things. Are the rest of the animals all right?"

"Appear to be. Neither one of the cows had any milk this mornin', but Uncle Wylie said that's understandable."

Luke helped the rest of them down from the wagon, except for Wylie. He couldn't maneuver his chair in the rubble, so he decided to sit where he was. He asked Sissy to stay in the wagon with him and "supervise."

The boys led them to Rebecca's dresser, and Luke pushed the beam aside. With the boys' help, he turned it over and lifted it upright. It had several long scratches on the side, but otherwise appeared to be unharmed. Her fingers trembling, she pulled open the top drawer and began to weep. There, tangled in the scarf Anthony had given her for their anniversary, was the box containing her locket and wedding band. Lying up against it was Anthony's picture.

Luke took the box from her shaking hands and carefully opened it. "Knowing these weren't lost helps." When she nodded, he closed the lid and put the treasures into her hand. She clung to the box for a few minutes, then placed it carefully back beside Anthony's picture and shut the drawer.

"Let's see what else we can find. I'll put the dresser in the wagon later."

She wiped her eyes with her fingertips and buttoned her light jacket. Although the sky was clear and the sun warm, a strong cool wind blew from the west. "Let's look for other pictures." *Please God, let me find Michael's portrait.*

"We pretty much went over the surface this morning," said Saul. "But there could be a lot of stuff buried."

They began the tedious job of sifting through the rubble, and the hope of finding many things in one piece faded quickly. Paul came up with Sissy's cradle. One end was broken off, but Luke reassured the little girl he could replace it. Under another pile of wood and bits of furniture, Saul found her doll without a mark on it. Sissy was happy with the world once again.

"Hallelujah!" shouted Paul. "Ma and Pa's picture!" He held the portrait up, waving it in the air. The frame and glass were nowhere to be found, but the picture itself had been buried under the loose door of the icebox. Saul clamored to his side, and they hugged each other, tears streaming down their cheeks.

Luke climbed down into the cellar and poked around. "I'll be jiggered! Here's a whole cabinet of canned goods. Not a single jar is broken." He smiled up at her. "Looks like we'll have some fruit tonight, even if we don't have much else." Further search revealed a ham and her Universal Mixer.

The handle was broken, but Luke thought he could fix it. He found the milk safe intact and several more pots and pans, dented but still usable.

Rebecca poked here and there, discouraged and broken-hearted. *All I have left is a lock of Michael's hair.* She was thankful for that, but wanted more. She shoved aside some small pieces of the china cabinet and gasped. Dropping to her knees, she wrapped her hands in her apron and dug frantically through the mound of wood and broken china. *Oh, thank you! Thank you!*

Luke came up and knelt down beside her as she carefully withdrew Michael's picture from underneath the rubble. The glass was cracked, but the picture did not appear to be damaged at all. Turning into Luke's arms, she leaned against his wonderful shoulder and wept tears of joy.

"Now I can go on," she said as he helped her to her feet. "I'll miss the house and all my things, but they can be replaced. This couldn't."

They took the drawers out of the dresser and put them in the wagon. Then the twins helped Luke carry the dresser over to the wagon and lift it in. They gathered up the other odds and ends they had found and took them back to Luke's house. He set everything in his front room.

Jackson rode up a few minutes later. "Couldn't get on the first train. Sure sorry about your house, Miss Rebecca."

"We'll build another. But I'm afraid your place and things are gone. We couldn't find anything of yours."

Jackson shrugged. "Didn't have much. I'll sleep in the barn." With that, he was off to tend to the chores.

Rebecca fried up some salt pork and made biscuits for supper. After they had eaten and done the dishes, she and Luke walked out into the backyard. The maple tree had smashed in half the blackberry vines when it fell. "Can you use the wood for your furniture?"

"Probably. I'll have to cut into it before I know for sure."

"I like maple furniture. And oak. The new, cleaner lines are nice, although I love the type of carving you do, especially in walnut." She slipped her arm through his. "Will you make some of the furniture for our new house?"

Luke stopped, looking down at her. To save her life, she couldn't read his expression. "Our new house?" he asked.

"Yes, the one we're going to start building right away. The one we're going to fill with love and children." She pulled her arm from his and turned to face him. "We have a pretty good start on the children, what with three already. But I wouldn't mind a couple more. A boy with black hair and blue eyes . . ."

"Rebecca, my six months aren't up yet."

"True. But since my circumstances have changed drastically, I think we should shorten the time, say to . . . tomorrow."

"I thought you were going to let me propose."

"I'm not proposing." When she smiled, a spark of mischief twinkled in her eyes. "I'm just giving you a golden opportunity."

"I wanted to wait until I raised a good crop." He looked away. "I needed to prove to myself and to your family that I could take care of you."

"Luke, you proved that last night. You were there when we needed you. Not just me, the children, and Wylie, but Will, too. And the folks in town. You did more than anyone to take care of all of us." She cupped his face in both hands. "I love you with all my heart, Luke Northcutt. I don't want to live my life without you. I can build a new home, and I can fill it with a mother's love for those three children in there. But they need a father's love, too." She moved her hands down to his shoulders.

"Don't say another word," he said sternly. He leaned down and kissed her with exquisite tenderness. "Will you always love me, Rebecca?"

"Always. I'll probably get angry with you, and I might even yell at you sometimes, but I will never stop loving you. I'll never send you away."

He curved his hands around her face, his eyes gentle and loving. "You've taught me what life is all about, sweet lady. You've shown me what it's like to be loved. I was angry and you gave me laughter. I was hurt and you gave me comfort. I was afraid and you gave me courage. I was alone and you gave me a family. I was empty and you filled my heart. Because of you, I laugh. I hurt. I cry. *I feel.* Because of you, I love."

He brushed her lips with his—once, twice, three times. "I love you, Rebecca, with every beat of my heart and every breath I take. I will love and cherish you forever. I'll build that new house with you, and I'll work your farm and mine, and we'll have a good life. Will you marry me?"

"Yes, my heart, my love." She wrapped her arms around his neck and raised her lips to his, as they sealed their pledge with a long, lingering kiss. "Can we be like Winston and Aggie, waiting on the courthouse steps in the morning?"

"Don't see why not. Do you think the minister will have time to marry us tomorrow? I expect he'll be busy."

"We can ask him, but I see nothing wrong with being married by the justice of the peace in Montezuma. I just want to be your wife. I don't care who performs the ceremony."

"We'd better tell the kids and Wylie."

"I think they already know." She motioned her head toward the back window.

Luke followed her gaze. Wylie and all three children peered out the window, watching them with keen interest. He looked back at her with a bemused smile. "Is it always going to be like this?"

"Oh, I expect we'll manage some time alone." She smiled up at him, her eyes full of promise.

"Wish you didn't have to spend tonight at your folks'."

"Me, too. But it wouldn't be a very good example for the children if I stayed here." She smiled. "They were worried about what people might think when I stayed the night after your accident."

"Very prim and proper, those two."

"I bet we could send them scampering away from the window."

"How?"

"Give me a kiss that will make my toes curl."

"Sure they'll run?"

"No, but I'm sure Wylie will send them away."

"Wise woman."

*   *   *

THEY WERE MARRIED in the minister's study of the Congregational Church the next day, Monday, June 19, 1882, at five in the afternoon with only Rebecca's family and Jackson in attendance. It was an unfashionable day and time for a wedding, but no one in the family or the town was concerned with fashion at the moment.

Rebecca wore one of Elizabeth's gowns, quickly taken in and shortened that morning by Clara while Luke and Rebecca drove to Montezuma for the marriage license. While they were in the county seat, they had picked up new clothes for the children because the stores in Grinnell were already running low on supplies.

The ceremony was short and simple and filled with love. The family returned to Howard and Clara's for a potluck meal afterward. Nothing was fancy, but no one cared. Their hearts grieved for their neighbors and friends who had lost loved ones in the storm. They rejoiced because their loved ones had been spared, and that Luke and Rebecca and the children were beginning a new life.

The newlyweds left the children with Howard and Clara, who promised to watch over them for a few days and not spoil them too much in the meantime. Wylie had moved in with Rebecca's parents, agreeing to return to the farm when the new house was built. Neither Luke nor Rebecca could imagine life at the farm without him.

Luke borrowed Howard's buggy to take his wife home. When they arrived, he carried her over the threshold and deposited her in his big, slightly lopsided chair. "You sit right here and relax while I put the horse and buggy away." He kissed her quickly before he straightened. "I cleaned up the place as well as I could. There are no dirty dishes for you to wash, no dirty floors to sweep, no dirty clothes to pick up."

"None to wash, either?"

He grinned and dropped down on one knee beside the chair. "There wasn't time to do laundry. But that doesn't matter. We aren't going to need too many clothes for the next day or two anyway."

She looped her arms around his neck and kissed the corner of his mouth. "Shall I get undressed while you're gone?"

"No, ma'am, Mrs. Northcutt. I want the pleasure of taking every pin from your hair and removing every stitch of clothing from my beautiful wife. And you can do the same for me."

"I didn't know you pinned up your hair." She smiled seductively and glanced down at his cowboy boots. "I don't think I want to be a bootjack."

He looked at her high-buttoned shoes. "I'll make one concession. I'll take off my boots, if you take off your shoes."

"Agreed." She kissed him again, lingering this time. "Now, hurry. I'm a lusty green-eyed wench, remember?"

"I remember." He curled his fingers around the nape of her neck and kissed her hard. "I'll be back soon."

When he returned, Rebecca was waiting in the bedroom. She had turned down the freshly made bed and fluffed up the pillows. Her shoes were sitting by the wall, near the bootjack. He had moved her dresser into the bedroom that morning, and he watched from the doorway as she set a brush, comb, and hand mirror on the dresser. The set was a present from her mother to replace the ones that had blown away.

He crossed the room and took off his boots, lining them up beside her shoes. Seeing them side by side made him feel loved. When he turned, she was watching him, her face glowing with the rich and abundant love in her heart. He walked to her slowly, not wanting her to see his impatience. "I love you, Becca."

"I love you, too." She reached up and began unbuttoning his shirt.

He did the same for her.

They undressed each other slowly, stopping often for kisses and caresses. And when she stood before him, unclothed and beautiful, comfortable with him because she knew she pleased him, he eased the pins from her hair. He combed the long tresses with his fingers, then smoothed them with his hand, following the gentle waves as they draped the curves of her body.

"Have I ever told you that you are magnificent?" she whispered, kissing his upper arm and across his shoulder, remembering the day she caught him outside in his drawers.

He chuckled. "I believe you mentioned the word once."

"I wanted you that day," she confessed.

"I know. I saw it in your eyes. And it only made me want you more."

"I want you now, Luke. I can't wait anymore."

"Neither can I, sweetheart. Neither can I." He lifted her in his arms and placed her on the bed, then lay down beside her. "I want to leave the lamp lit, so I can see your face when I make you mine."

She nodded. "I'm already yours, heart and soul."

With urgent kisses and caresses now bold, she welcomed him. No thoughts of her past love invaded her happiness, her delight. This man was her husband, her love, her life. She had been chosen for him, and he for her. And his touch— tender, passionate, loving—gave her the greatest pleasure she had ever known.

As they became one, Luke gazed down at the woman he loved, and in her face, he saw love and joy shining for him alone. In that moment, he became whole.

HE AWOKE IN the middle of the night and turned on his side, enjoying the simple pleasure of watching her sleep in the moonlight.

She had healed the hurts of his past and given him hope for the future. The fortress was finished; trust and commitment were firmly sealed in place.

His sanctuary was secure.

Luke was home.

Epilogue

TWO WEEKS AFTER their first anniversary, Rebecca and Luke rocked slowly in the swing on the back porch of their new home and watched the fireflies dart across the yard. The twins and Sissy had gone to bed a few moments before, and three-month-old Rosie slept peacefully in her mother's arms. She was a beautiful child with black hair and blue eyes that held hints of green. To Luke's relief, the pregnancy and birth had been an easy one.

The twins were almost twelve now and growing like weeds, adding some weight to their lanky frames. They had done well in school but were now enjoying the freedom summer brought, swimming, fishing, and horseback riding after the chores were done. They were a big help to Luke on the farm; he often told them it was their hard work that made it such a success.

Sissy continued to be a joy to all and kept a watchful eye over her little sister. The four-year-old grew prettier every day, and her loving, gentle ways made life a better place for all who knew her. She was especially fond of Wylie, who had moved back in with them after the house was finished.

After the baby came, the children had decided that it was no longer appropriate to call Luke and Rebecca their uncle and aunt. Paul said they were concerned that it might confuse their new sister, so they decided to call them Papa and Mama. That way, they reasoned, they were not replacing their pa and ma, but were getting a second set of parents.

The house was bigger than the first one. Although not ornate, it held all the modern conveniences the family might need. Luke had made much of the furniture himself, sticking mostly to the clean, smooth lines popular at the moment. He added his own special carvings here and there to Rebecca's delight.

Grinnell had recovered surprisingly well after the tornado. Part of the college was already rebuilt and more work was being done. Many houses had been replaced, but not all. There were still empty lots, now cleared, but conspicuously vacant; a sad reminder of the thirty-nine lives that were lost. But the people had rallied, helping their neighbors as they could and receiving an outpouring of help from around the country.

Ben Crowder had surprised Rebecca and Luke with the gift of a new buggy and team for their wedding present. He told Luke it was a small way of thanking him for saving his life, and a way of showing them that he wished them well. She had been surprised again when she learned he had opened his home to Mrs. Peters and several other neighbors who had lost theirs. He had confided to her later that it had not been too bad, especially after Miss Sayers pointed out in her sensible way that he should store any valuable breakables in the attic until the families with the children, almost a dozen of them, found other places to live.

Miss Sayers had stayed in Grinnell a month, then went back to Texas after settling her aunt in a new place. As far as Rebecca knew, the spinster and Ben did not correspond. He mentioned her occasionally, keeping up with her through her aunt.

Ben visited Luke and Rebecca often, and she noted a change in him. He was restless, often a bit sad, and threw himself into his work with increasing tenacity. He continued to escort various beautiful ladies to the local functions but did not favor anyone in particular. Rebecca had no wisdom to share with him, for she could only guess at what troubled him.

Winston and Aggie were expecting their first child any day. They had rebuilt the barn and other buildings and restocked the farm. Aggie had actually won a blue ribbon at the county fair that fall for her apple pie, and Winston's manners had improved drastically.

Luke curled his arm around his wife's shoulders and held her close. "Do you think the mayor would be offended if I slept through his Fourth of July speech tomorrow?"

"As long as you don't snore, I doubt if he would notice."

"I don't snore."

"You do sometimes. I just tickle your side and you turn over."

"Are you happy, Becca?"

"Yes, and very much in love. Are you happy?"

"Yes, ma'am. I have everything I ever wanted and a whole lot more." He tenderly brushed a kiss on her temple. "I could lose this farm and everything we own, and I'd still be a happy man as long as I had you."

852